R0200790996

12/2019

PRAISE FOR KYLIE BRANT

DISCARD

"Kylie Brant is destined to become a star!"
—Cindy Gerard, *New York Times* and *USA TODAY* bestselling author

"A complex, page-turning mystery plus a heartfelt romance blend into a fast-paced story that kept me reading until the wee hours."
—Allison Brennan, *New York Times* bestselling author of *Make Them Pay* on *Deadly Dreams*

"Dark and compelling suspense."
—Anne Frasier, author of *The Body Reader*

"*Pretty Girls Dancing* is a complex and character-driven mystery that will keep you turning pages until late at night."
—Kendra Elliot, Daphne du Maurier Award–winning author of *A Merciful Truth*

"*Pretty Girls Dancing* is Kylie Brant at her chilling best as she delivers a compelling thriller with a shocking twist."
—Loreth Anne White, author of *A Dark Lure*

D1417065

PA.
LIBRARY SYSTEM
3650 Summit Boulevard
West Palm Beach, FL 33406-4198

DOWN THE DARKEST ROAD

ALSO BY KYLIE BRANT

The Cady Maddix Mysteries

Cold Dark Places

The Circle of Evil Trilogy

Chasing Evil
Touching Evil
Facing Evil

Other Works

Pretty Girls Dancing
Deep as the Dead
What the Dead Know
Secrets of the Dead
11
Waking Nightmare
Waking Evil
Waking the Dead
Deadly Intent
Deadly Dreams
Deadly Sins
Terms of Attraction
Terms of Engagement
Terms of Surrender
The Last Warrior

The Business of Strangers

Close to the Edge

In Sight of the Enemy

Dangerous Deception

Truth or Lies

Entrapment

Alias Smith and Jones

Hard to Tame

Hard to Resist

Hard to Handle

Born in Secret

Undercover Bride

Falling Hard and Fast

Heartbreak Ranch

Undercover Lover

Friday's Child

Bringing Benjy Home

Guarding Raine

An Irresistible Man

McLain's Law

Rancher's Choice

DOWN THE DARKEST ROAD

A CADY MADDIX MYSTERY

KYLIE BRANT

This is a work of fiction. Names, characters, organizations, places, events, and incidents are either products of the author's imagination or are used fictitiously. Any resemblance to actual persons, living or dead, or actual events is purely coincidental.

Text copyright © 2019 by Kim Bahnsen
All rights reserved.

No part of this book may be reproduced, or stored in a retrieval system, or transmitted in any form or by any means, electronic, mechanical, photocopying, recording, or otherwise, without express written permission of the publisher.

Published by Thomas & Mercer, Seattle

www.apub.com

Amazon, the Amazon logo, and Thomas & Mercer are trademarks of Amazon.com, Inc., or its affiliates.

ISBN-13: 9781542006026
ISBN-10: 1542006023

Cover design by Rex Bonomelli

Printed in the United States of America

For the simply irresistible Sloane

Chapter 1

The task force rolled up quietly, seven team members spilling from dark vehicles to unload the necessary equipment for the fugitive apprehension operation. Beneath the watery glow of the remaining unbroken streetlamps, they moved efficiently around the house, setting up the lights and perimeter guards, while one member attached a radar device to the peeling gray siding.

Deputy US Marshal Cady Maddix directed the activity in near silence. They'd planned for this, down to the last detail. But she'd been on enough ops to know even with the most flawless preparation, something could go awry.

The entry unit headed toward the house, splitting up to take spots on either side of the front entrance. According to their intel, Michael Simmons, prolific carjacker and chop shop owner, was in the Weaverville home.

"Three people inside." The low voice came through her headset. "One in front, within six feet of the door. Two in the southwest corner of the home." The speaker was Buncombe County deputy sheriff investigator Andy Garrett. He was operating the Range-R device that detected human presences inside a structure. His words verified their earlier surveillance.

She did a quick perimeter inspection. "Positions set?"

"Position two confirmed." Another low voice sounded in her headset.

"Position three confirmed."

One by one, each of the team members checked in. Because she knew where to look, Cady could see the dark figures crouched in the patchy snow as she circled the house. She took up a station near the back door. If things went south, the bandit would try to escape through this exit or a window.

When she'd heard from each of the team members, Cady spoke into her whisper mic. "Light 'em up." The spotlights they'd placed on the patchy lawn lit the home like a tacky Christmas display. She brought up the megaphone she held in one hand. "Michael Simmons. You are surrounded. Walk out the front door with your hands behind your head." She waited a minute before repeating herself, this time adding, "We don't want anything to happen to the woman or child inside. Walk out that door, Michael, so no one gets hurt."

Cady lowered the megaphone, impervious to the biting February breeze. She'd feel the cold later, but right now adrenaline was running high.

"Someone's at the front window," a voice murmured through the mic. "Looking around the shade."

Her muscles bunched. Whoever was there would be unable to see anything but the blinding glare of spotlights, regardless of the direction he looked. She brought up the megaphone and repeated her message, ending with, "You can do the right thing now, Michael. Come out peacefully."

Another minute ticked by. She was about to reengage when the back door cracked open. A moment later, a figure bolted through it, sailing over the three pitted concrete steps to land on all fours in the yard. "Stay down! Stay down! Hands behind your head!" Cady dropped the megaphone and drew her weapon, approaching the figure cautiously. The newest member on the Violent Offender Task Force, Watauga County deputy Lee Tompkins did the same. Her gaze was fixed on the figure already scrambling to his feet. Simmons. His hands seemed empty. "Arms up . . ." He darted to the side, heading for the shadows. She reholstered her weapon as she gave chase.

The snow crunched beneath her feet, her boots giving her traction. Simmons was in shoes, slipping a bit as he ran but staying upright. She saw then where he was headed. An old pickup at the back of the neighboring lot, next to the alley. Cady put on a burst of speed. Launched herself.

Simmons outweighed her by at least eighty pounds, but she caught him low in the back. Her tackle, coupled with the slick ground beneath his feet, took him down. She regained her balance first, and when he rolled, started to get up, she had her weapon trained on him. "Be best if you just stayed put," she advised as Tompkins ran up to them. "On your belly. Arms behind your back."

"Fucking bitch. You got no right sneaking up on a guy's family like that."

"Keep him covered," she said to Tompkins as she reholstered her weapon and reached for her cuffs. When she had Simmons restrained, she and the deputy pulled him to his feet. "Suspect's in custody," she said into her mic. The other deputy marshal on the team, Miguel Rodriguez, would join her to take Simmons back to the federal courthouse for booking.

"I got him if you want to deal with the team," Deputy Tompkins said.

"Wait for Rodriguez."

Tompkins grasped Simmons's shoulder and began to guide him toward the front of the house. The man jerked away from him and whirled. Cady stepped forward to assist and took a headbutt to the side of her face before she swept his legs from beneath him. He went down, and this time he'd stay there.

Tompkins shot her a shamed look. "Sorry, Cady."

The left side of her eye stung, right beneath the temple. She leveled a stare at the man. "Wait for Rodriguez."

"I'm here." The spotlight caressed Deputy US Marshal Rodriguez's too-handsome face like a lover as he strode across the yard to them. "He giving you problems?"

"He's got itchy feet. Help the deputy get him contained, will you?"

Together, they hauled the man up and led him away. She went to retrieve the megaphone. "Mindy Gallup. Come out through the front door, hands in view." The woman was known to them. Cady had spoken to her in the course of tracking down Simmons. Given her earlier cooperation, Cady didn't expect trouble. But caution dictated that they ensure no one was able to fire on them as they departed.

A moment later, one of the entry team members was heard over the mic. "Occupant is in custody. Claims no one else is inside except the child." That matched their surveillance intel.

"Search the house." Cady waited for the entry team to complete the task. Once the house was clear, she said, "Allow Mindy back inside. Let's pull out."

Cady went to help load up the equipment. She'd take a pain reliever for the dull throb that was beginning in her temple and oversee the withdrawal of her team. Maybe she'd get lucky enough to ward off a black eye and make it home before the sun came up.

Chapter 2

Cady was off on both of her earlier estimates. The red welt near her eye was showing no signs of dissipating, and it was nearly 8:00 a.m. before the paperwork was filed and Buncombe County had taken Simmons off their hands. Wearily, she headed for the office of Supervisory Deputy Marshal Allen Gant. He'd grant her and Miguel leave so they could grab some sleep before returning to the office.

She rapped at his door and stepped inside at his greeting. Then wished she hadn't when he glanced up and stared.

"What happened to you?"

Seeing no reason to reveal the deputy's screwup, she said merely, "We had a runner. I chased him."

"With your face?"

She dropped down in the chair he waved her to. "Doughnuts make you hilarious." Remnants of his breakfast were still visible on his desktop. He swept the telltale crumbs into one hand and discarded them in the wastebasket.

"Other than your injury, how'd it go this morning? Was Simmons able to offer any useful information on Forrester?"

Stretching out her legs, she crossed her booted feet. "He wasn't feeling especially cooperative." She'd started looking into Michael Simmons because he'd been a cellmate to Bruce Forrester, who was wanted for the abduction of Cassie Zook from a Bryson City parking lot. It was just Simmons's bad luck there had also been an outstanding warrant in his name. She'd tried questioning him before the Buncombe County deputies came for him but had gotten very little.

"Maybe the lab will pull something from his phone or computer. In the meantime, I have more on those older charges against Bruce Forrester." Allen got up and crossed the room to shut the door before returning to his desk.

Her earlier exhaustion evaporating, she straightened. She'd gotten the Forrester kidnapping warrant only days ago. Cady knew she had a lot of catching up to do.

He stood in front of his computer and tapped a few keys. Then he swiveled it so the monitor faced her. "It's Cumberland County's interview footage from five years ago."

Intrigued, she scooted her chair forward until her knees touched the front of the desk.

"Press 'Play.'"

She obeyed, opening a black-and-white video clip that she immediately identified as CCTV footage from a witness interview, with accompanying sound. A small boy, nine or ten, was seated on one side of the table. A uniformed deputy on the other. "State your name for the record."

"Dylan."

"You'll have to speak up, son. And give your full name."

"Dylan . . . Castle." The boy reached for a can of Mountain Dew sitting on the table in front of him and gulped from it.

"I know you're tired, son. But I want you to tell me one more time everything that happened Tuesday night."

A voice was heard off camera. "He done told you a dozen times already. You oughta have it memorized by now. God knows I do."

"Ms. Bandy, I'm going to ask you to be patient a little longer." The unseen woman made a rude noise. The deputy faced the boy again. "Go ahead, Dylan." Cady leaned forward.

"I snuck out two nights ago and went to Trev's house."

"Trev being Trevor Boster."

"Yeah. He had this remote-controlled boat, and we'd been talking about taking it down to the creek to try it out."

"Which you oughta get your butt whipped for," the woman inserted. "You know it ain't safe after these heavy rains we been getting."

"Ms. Bandy." The deputy's voice held an edge. "Enough."

The boy ducked his head, his chin nearly touching the top of the can he still clutched. "I waited until Colton—my brother—was asleep. Musta been around midnight. Then I snuck out to the living room. The front door squeaks, so I opened a window. Climbed out." His shrug spoke of long ease with the act. "It was dark outside. And real sticky. It'd been raining all week. I was sweating by the time I got to Trev's. I tapped at his window. Twice, I think. 'Cuz he didn't come right away, so I did it louder, and then I thought, shi—" He glanced guiltily over the deputy's shoulder. "I mean, shoot, maybe I got the wrong room. Bosters switch around bedrooms some. Once I accidentally woke up Miz Boster, and she cussed me out something fierce."

"Did you have the right bedroom?"

"I guess. I mean, yeah, because a couple of minutes later, someone grabbed my shoulder."

"And it was Trevor."

Dylan nodded, then remembered to add, "Yeah. I jumped a mile."

"What happened then?"

"I gave him a shove. Said he sure took his time. He said it took a while to find the boat. His little brother had used it in the bathtub or something. Then we headed to the road. Well," he corrected himself, one thumb rubbing the side of the can, "we walked on the rocky area next to it. On account of the storms turning the road into muddy goop."

"The one leading toward the creek?"

"Yeah." Dylan's head bobbed. "I mean, the road leads to Hanson Woods. It just sort of stops where the trees get thick." His voice wobbled a bit on the last words.

"It's all right. Take your time." The deputy's tone was sympathetic.

A full minute passed before the boy started again. "So it was even darker at the end of the road. Trevor started saying how maybe we should turn around because he was afraid we wouldn't be able to see the boat in the creek, and then he'd lose it. But I had a flashlight I took from Amos Stedder's shed. I was gonna bring it back," he hastened to add, lifting his gaze. "But I lost it somewhere . . . I don't know where."

"I'm sure Mr. Stedder will understand, under the circumstances. You got to the end of the road," the deputy prompted him.

"Yeah. The trees and bushes are thick all along there. Trevor was going on about losing his boat, and I said something like, 'That's what the light is for, dumb-ass,' and then we started kind of horsing around, you know. Pushing each other and laughing. That's when I heard something."

"What did you hear, Dylan?"

"Voices. Real faded like. But when I turned to look into the woods next to me, I saw a light. Someone was there."

"Which side of the woods are you talking about? As you faced the creek, were they to your left or to your right?"

The boy thought for a minute. "On my left. And then Trevor said maybe it was Colton again . . ." His words trailed off as he looked toward someone not in view.

"Why did Trevor think it was your brother?"

"One time we saw him in the woods making out with some girl from school. Trevor said, 'Let's go sneak up on 'em and scare 'em,' but I didn't want to. If I didn't go along, though, Trevor would call me a pussy forever, because he never shuts up about stuff like that . . ." He stopped, his expression stricken.

"It's all right." The deputy's words were soft. "You're doing fine."

"So we crept into the woods. It was farther than I thought at first. But I figured we could watch 'em while we hid in the bushes. We stopped when we saw this clearing. There were four guys there. Grown-ups."

"What else did you see?"

Dylan moistened his lips. "Two big spotlights. There was a bunch of trash around. Propane tanks. Coolers. Some plastic buckets, rubber tubing, and empty soda bottles—the big ones. There was a rope tied over a tree limb. I never saw it there before, and Trev said someone musta made a rope swing and how we should go try it out. There was a tent, too, sort of tan, I think. It was way past the people. It'd been hard to see without the lights. I grabbed Trevor's shirt and pulled him down, made him be quiet. We had to get out of there before we were seen."

"Why did you need to get out of there, Dylan?"

There was something in the deputy's tone that Cady could only guess at. But Allen wouldn't have pulled her in for a refresher course on conducting interviews. Dylan's revelation was going to be bad. And she couldn't help a stab of empathy for the unknown boy.

"I recognized one of the men. Bruce Forrester. People say he's a drug dealer. That he's been in jail. I wanted to get out of there. But Trevor was real excited about the rope swing and kept saying maybe we could swing over the creek. Then a guy said, 'There's someone out there.' Forrester turned around and started coming toward us."

"He wasn't facing you?"

"The men were sort of standing in a circle. I could see the side of his face. Enough to recognize him." A shudder was working through the boy's body, tremors racking his frame. "I heard one of them men say, 'Fuck, get rid of 'em!' and I grabbed Trevor's arm and dragged him with me as fast as I could."

9

"Where were you going?"

"Somewhere else, man. Anywhere else. That dude—Forrester—was chasing us. I could hear him crashing through the woods behind us. We got to the road and ran right across it to the trees on the other side."

"You didn't run home?"

"Too far." The shudders were stronger now, and Dylan let go of the can to wrap his arms around his middle. "And he'd a seen us. I thought we could hide. Maybe climb a tree. There's this hollow log we discovered a while back. If we could just get to it . . ."

"Did you hear anything else as you ran?"

Dylan swiped the back of his hand across his mouth. "Forrester was yelling stuff. Said if he caught us, he'd drown us both. I just kept running. Trevor was right behind me. I went to this spot where him and me have climbed trees before. I climbed to the top, but . . ." His voice dropped off. "Trevor wasn't there. I thought . . . I hoped he'd found another hiding place." Tears were running down the boy's face. He mopped at them with the hem of his T-shirt.

A woman moved into view. "Remember what the doctor said. You're not s'posed to push him."

"Just another few minutes, Ms. Bandy. Almost done."

She grabbed the pop can from the table and handed it to the boy. "Go on, now, drink. Calm yourself down so we can get out of here and go home."

Cady squelched a flicker of irritation at the unknown woman. It had to be Dylan's mother. The relationship was apparent despite the different last names. The same pointed chin and slight frame as her son, although hers was clad in tight jeans and a skimpy top tied below her breasts, leaving her midriff bare. Her hair might have once been the same blond as Dylan's, although it looked now as if it owed its color to a too-distant dye job.

"What else can you tell us, Dylan?"

The boy heaved a sigh. "Nothing. I could hear people moving around. I thought maybe Forrester got his friends to come and look for us. I climbed as high as I could, and I just sat in the tree all night. And most of the next day, I guess. I didn't come down until I heard you guys calling for me."

There was more, but Allen Gant spoke then. "You've heard the gist of it." He turned the computer back toward him and stabbed a finger at the button to turn off the video. His gaze rose to meet hers. "That was five years ago. Dylan Castle was ten. Trevor Boster nine. When Mrs. Boster found Trevor missing in the morning, she started checking with friends in the area. Once Tina Bandy discovered Dylan gone, too, they called the sheriff. Later on, Trevor's mom searched the house for the boat and it was nowhere to be found. That's when a couple of deputies went down to the creek. They found Trevor's body in the water, three hundred feet downstream from where the road ends. He'd suffered a head trauma. The deputies hunted for Dylan and discovered him hiding half a mile away in a tree, unaware of what had happened to his friend."

Something in Cady's chest went tight. "And Forrester?"

"Well, that's where things get interesting." Allen's chair creaked as he adjusted his position. "He disappeared. They eventually rounded up two men Dylan ID'd as having been there that night. One verified that Forrester went after the boys but claimed he wasn't gone more than a few minutes."

"Homicide doesn't necessarily take much longer than that," Cady observed.

Allen nodded. "A meth lab was discovered right where Dylan described it. It took months for the state lab results to come back, but Forrester's prints were found on some of the containers."

"Places him in the area. But what does this have to do with Forrester kidnapping a woman from a motel parking lot in Bryson City six weeks ago?"

He held up a hand. "No idea. But there's a lot more to the backstory, and I don't have all the details. I do know the State Bureau of Investigation is involved in Dylan's case. When word reached the staties about Forrester's new kidnapping warrant, the SBI director reached out to our agency. Marshal Redding recommended you be assigned to it."

Stunned, Cady could only stare at her supervisor. She'd figured she'd been called in for a reason, but it would never have occurred to her that the marshal for the Western District of North Carolina had gotten involved. She'd never met Redding. Had only heard him speak once at a training she'd attended.

"Why?" She'd been assigned to the Asheville office for less than a year, having transferred from Saint Louis. "He doesn't know me."

Allen rubbed his stomach, as if his breakfast hadn't agreed with him. Or maybe it'd been the coffee he'd washed it down with. "Your reputation precedes you. The Aldeen case a few months ago vaulted you into the agency limelight."

Inwardly squirming, Cady said nothing. Last November, Samuel Aldeen had escaped a Haywood County facility for the criminally insane. She'd been part of a team tracking him. By the time she'd figured out who his next victim was, she'd almost been too late.

Almost.

"Forrester's been on the loose for years, and Redding is counting on you to bring him in. That means even if the family moves again, you stay on the case."

Cady nodded. She was assigned to the Asheville office, and their territory ran to the western side of the state. But for continuity purposes, deputy marshals followed the fugitives, regardless of district or, in some cases, state lines. "Am I working solo, or will Miguel join me?" There were five other deputy marshals in the Asheville office, and only she and Rodriguez worked warrants full-time, while the others also had federal court duties.

"You'll have a better idea of the manpower needed once you attend the background briefing."

"Which is when?"

The expression on Allen's face confirmed her worst suspicions. "It'll be held in the Mecklenburg SBI office at noon. They tried to split the distance for all agencies involved. Sorry, Cady. I realize you've been up all night. Garrett already knows about it. Maybe you can ride with him and any other members of the task force you think need to be there. After the meeting, of course, you can take the rest of the day off."

Considering it'd be midafternoon before she got home—if she was fortunate—the offer lacked generosity. "You have a heart of gold, Allen," she said, rising from her chair. "Don't let anyone tell you different."

"Just passing along orders. Blame yourself. Your rep's drawing notice."

The words had a thread of unease working through her as she walked out of his office, shutting the door behind her. It didn't hurt to get work-related recognition, she supposed. It was preferable to scrutiny of her personal history.

Cady went back to her desk to make some quick calls. She could update most of the team later. But she did reach out to a couple of feds she thought would be able to help. A half hour later, she grabbed her coat and purse before heading out.

Nodding to the security officers stationed in front of the courthouse doors, she exited, jogging down the steps. While she waited for her ride at the curb, she took the time to text Haywood County sheriff Ryder Talbot, who'd volunteered for dog duty while she'd worked last night. **Meeting in Mecklenburg. Not sure when I'll get back.**

She'd no more shoved her cell in her pocket when it pinged with a reply. He must have had his phone in his hand when she'd messaged him.

Fed Hero and let him out this morning. Let me know when you're heading home.

She stared at the answer for a long moment. They'd gotten close when working the Aldeen case and had drawn closer since. Their friends-with-benefits relationship had been extended to swapping dog-sitting duties as needed. That had necessitated them exchanging keys, a step she'd never before taken with a man. The thought still had her gut clenching, but it'd been done for Hero's sake. Her job occasionally had her working nights, and that schedule didn't always jibe with her pet's needs.

She put the phone away and spied a sheriff's vehicle turning the corner to approach the federal courthouse. Casting a quick glance in either direction, she strode across the street and continued down the walk toward it until it pulled to a stop along the opposite curb. Yanking open the back door of the vehicle, she slipped inside. The outdoor temperatures had warmed only slightly since Simmons's arrest last night.

Buncombe County deputy sheriff investigator Andy Garrett was behind the wheel. Two others were already inside the vehicle. "Jaywalking. I could write you a ticket for that." His words were interrupted by a huge yawn.

"You could." She fastened her seat belt. "If you weren't too tired to wield a pen."

He grunted in agreement. "But you trust me to drive you more than two hours?"

"Trust. Desperation. It's all semantics." She addressed the man beside her. "Hi, Curtis." Curtis Weddig was a DEA agent stationed at the federal building next to the courthouse.

The other man in the front seat half turned. Offered her a smile. "Cady. Been a while."

"Gabe."

She thrust aside a sliver of discomfort. A few months ago—before she'd known Ryder well—she and ATF agent Gabe Pearson had had a brief casual relationship. Casual, because that's how she kept all her relationships. Brief, because his suggestion they exchange keys had sent her well-developed guardedness into overdrive.

The irony of having done so with Ryder wasn't lost on her. But letting him help out with the dog just made sense. And if the thought didn't completely silence the tiny inner alarm shrilling inside her, it at least quieted it.

Gabe was still studying her. "Seems like every time I see you, you're banged up."

Her hand rose to the eye that still throbbed. "Ran my face into a guy's head," she said lightly.

"That's an improvement." For the others' benefit, he added, "Few months back she got a bit too close to a car bomb."

She settled back in her seat as the other two men made the inevitable demand for details. Retelling the story gave her no pleasure, but it was infinitely preferable to dwelling on her sex life.

Chapter 3

There were seven of them around the table, including the Asheville contingent. SBI special agents Kyle Davis and Sue Rebedeau were joined by Cumberland County deputy investigator Blake Patten.

After introductions, Davis shoved folders across the conference table to each of them. "These are file summaries to update the members of the fugitive task force. They'll bring you up to speed. But the complete case file is digital. You'll find log-in information inside the folders." His tone was neutral. Cady wondered when he'd learned of the case's change of status. And what his reaction had been. "First, though, I'll have Deputy Patten recap the beginning of this case."

Cady had spoken to Patten on the phone when she'd first started delving into Bruce Forrester's criminal history. The deputy was at least ten years older than the SBI agent but had a similarly broad build and sported the same buzz cut as the other man, although his was gray. In the distinctive dialect pegging him as a transplant from the Pamlico Sound region, he quickly condensed the events Dylan Castle had recounted on the video she'd seen in Allen's office, adding, "Castle was in bad shape when we found him, at least emotionally. He was under a doctor's care for a couple of days before we could question him. He identified two of the other men with Forrester the night in question—Charles Weber and Stephen Tillis. Both were arrested. One of them finally admitted to having been there and also gave us information about Forrester's drug operation. Tillis denied his involvement all the way to Craggy Correctional."

A few scattered laughs were heard around the table. "We issued an arrest warrant for Bruce Forrester," the man continued, "and he's also wanted for questioning in the death of Trevor Boster. A separate warrant was filed for Eric Loomer, the fourth man at the scene. Weber, the cooperating witness, named Loomer as a longtime accomplice in Forrester's drug operation. We were unable to apprehend either man."

Davis took up where the deputy had left off. "Tina Bandy felt unsafe with Forrester on the loose and moved to Greensboro, where she has a sister. They were there just over a year before Tina called the police to report that Dylan had seen Bruce Forrester driving by in an old dark-green pickup." The agent picked up a remote sitting on the table in front of him.

Patten put in, "Forrester had two vehicles registered to him, a 1960 green Ford pickup and a 2010 Chevy Suburban. When we went looking for him, both vehicles were gone, along with most of his personal belongings. We were never able to trace either of his vehicles or the one registered to Loomer. We assumed they got rid of them. Neither man has shown up in the state's DMV database in the years since. We checked surrounding states, as well, with no success."

Because they'd left the region? Or had new identities? *Maybe both,* Cady thought. If Dylan hadn't been interviewed for a couple of days, they'd had time to clear out before the law had arrived.

"Bandy's report was followed up on, but the Greensboro police department never did find the vehicle." The SBI agent spoke again. "Two days later, a friend of Dylan's, Ethan Matthis, was killed in a drive-by shooting. A witness saw an older-model dark pickup speeding away from the scene."

"Was Dylan with the victim?"

Davis shook his head at Cady's question. "No, but Matthis was wearing an article of clothing that belonged to Dylan. Apparently the boys had switched hoodies. For reasons I've never determined, teenagers do that." He sounded as if he had personal experience in the area. He fiddled with his laptop before pointing the remote to a big-screen TV on the wall. When it flickered to life, the screen filled with a school photo of a preteen boy. "Ethan Matthis." He flipped to an image from the crime scene. Cady winced. It would be difficult to compare the picture to the school photo. Part of the head was blown away.

"Son of a bitch," someone muttered. She could appreciate the sentiment.

"That's when we were called in," Davis continued. "Tina Bandy was convinced Forrester had found the family. No proof of that, of course, but the vehicle description was persuasive. The state doesn't have a witness protection program, but Bandy wanted to relocate again, and we did what we could to help. We've stayed in touch with the family ever since and keep their address shielded from public records. Even gave them a cell phone with our number programmed in it for emergencies. The boy carries it every day."

"Why do I think this isn't the end of the story?" Curtis wondered aloud.

Davis gave a grim smile. "The family relocated to Ayden. They were there a year and a half before Dylan sighted Forrester in the truck again." Cady's chest went tight in anticipation of the man's next words. "Later that week, another teenage boy was murdered in a drive-by shooting as he was riding his bike. One witness ID'd an old green pickup in the area."

"Relationship to Dylan?" she asked.

"None." The agent raised the remote and flipped to another school picture. "Chad Bahlman went to the same school, but they weren't in the same grade. Dylan knew him only by sight."

She studied the photo. With his light hair and slim build, the boy bore a slight resemblance to Dylan.

When Davis flipped to the next photo, she steeled herself against the grisly crime scene image. "He was riding a bike that used to belong to Dylan Castle. He'd bought it from Tina Bandy on Craigslist a few days before. His body was found in a drainage ditch a mile from his rural home."

So no direct relationship to Dylan, Cady mused, *but a superficial connection nonetheless.*

"Could both homicides be the result of mistaken identity? Was Forrester shooting at boys he mistook for Dylan Castle?" she questioned.

SBI special agent Sue Rebedeau spoke for the first time. "We have only circumstantial evidence that Forrester was involved. Dylan thought he saw the man in his truck shortly before the killings. Witnesses saw a similar vehicle in the vicinity of each of the crime scenes. Our office assisted with the investigation. But no one got a license plate off the truck, and leads quickly dried up."

"Tina Bandy was adamant the family relocate again," Davis put in. "We briefly discussed their moving out of state, but she was unwilling to do so. They went to Raleigh, where they remained until last October, when Dylan contacted our office saying he thought he'd seen Forrester driving by the school. We reached out to the local law enforcement and assisted with a search for the vehicle. No verification could be found, but the Bandys moved again, landing in the Asheville vicinity last October." He looked at Cady. "Since you're handling Forrester's abduction warrant, SBI administration determined it was best for USMS to take over his entire case. I understand that you'll be handling the Loomer warrant too."

That was news to her. "Good to know," she said wryly. North Carolina had no statute of limitations on felonies. Even the older outstanding warrants on Forrester and Loomer remained active, and her agency chased fugitives.

She looked at DEA agent Curtis Weddig. "With your resources, maybe you can discover whether Forrester is still involved in the state drug trade. At this point, we can't be sure he's still living in the state, but he has to be getting money somehow." The man nodded.

He'd snatched Cassie Zook from Bryson City, Cady recalled. So even if Forrester wasn't hiding out in North Carolina, he may not have gone too far.

"Any recovered spent brass from the Matthis or Bahlman homicides?" Gabe asked.

Rebedeau nodded. "They were a match."

"If and when the weapon is recovered," Cady told Gabe, "I'm hoping you can personally oversee the ownership investigation."

The ATF agent replied, "I'll be interested to see the ballistics reports. How far away was the shooter from Matthis and Bahlman when they were killed?"

Davis clicked off the TV. "The lab did scene reconstructions. Their analysis suggests the driver slowed or stopped alongside the victims and shot through an open window. Distance between the shooter and victims was estimated to be eight to twelve feet."

It's one thing to shoot at a target from a distance, Cady thought grimly. That could allow the shooter to depersonalize his victim. Being close enough to see the emotions . . . witness the carnage . . . that was cold.

"Who besides Forrester would want to harm Castle?" She looked at the faces around the table.

"No one we can determine," responded Agent Rebedeau. She wore her dark hair short and sported a pair of trendy large-framed glasses. She sent Cady a quick smile. "We've spent a lot of time trying to figure out how Forrester keeps finding the family, if indeed he is the shooter. We've combed through Tina's and her kids' friends and acquaintances and failed to find a link to the man."

"Special Agents Davis and Rebedeau updated us when they moved Dylan's family into the area," Andy put in. "Other than keeping an eye out for the man and the vehicle, we haven't had much involvement." Cady nodded. He'd said as much on the way over here.

"SBI will remain involved with the family. Special Agent Rebedeau will liaise with your Violent Offender Task Force, as needed." Davis's tone went expressionless. "As you can imagine, Tina Bandy has become increasingly agitated by what she sees as a lack of progress in the case."

Recalling the woman who had appeared briefly in the clip she'd watched earlier, Cady could appreciate his understatement. But who wouldn't feel the same way, under the circumstances? The woman's family's life had been upended continuously in recent years. Her son could be in danger.

"I'll want to speak to the family."

"We'll reach out to them after this briefing to update them about your role," Rebedeau promised. "I should warn you, Tina Bandy is volatile, and the older boy, Colton, isn't particularly cooperative, either."

"Marshal Maddix, do you want to update us with what you've learned since being assigned the kidnapping warrant on Bruce Forrester?" Davis asked.

"Six weeks ago, Tennessee resident Cassie Zook was reported missing when she didn't arrive home after a conference in Wilmington," she began. "She'd stopped in Bryson City to visit a friend but never showed up to their planned meeting. Footage from a security camera in the parking lot shows a man forcing her into the trunk of a car and driving away. Facial recognition software identified the abductor as Forrester. The angle wasn't helpful when it came to identifying the vehicle. I reached out to Deputy Patten, and he summarized the events that elicited the arrest warrant in Cumberland County. I managed to track down Michael Simmons, who was Forrester's prison cellie several years ago. We brought him in today on his own outstanding warrant." She noted the exchanged glance between the two SBI agents and stopped.

"We've been trying to find and question Simmons for some time now," Agent Rebedeau murmured.

"I got lucky," Cady said diplomatically. "He was uninterested in answering questions about his former cellmate after the arrest. I'll be talking to him again. And the Buncombe County sheriff's office has his electronics, so we'll discover whether he's used them to communicate with Forrester."

"We've been using the Greensboro crime lab," Davis told Andy Garrett. The other man nodded. "They've been expediting the evidence analysis on this case."

"What would be Forrester's motivation for tracking Tina Bandy's family from town to town?" It was the one question that had been nagging at Cady since the briefing began. "From what's been said here, it doesn't appear that Dylan was an eyewitness to Boster's death, so he's no threat to the man."

Deputy Patten scratched his head. "Thing is, Marshal, we were never actually sure what the boy saw at the end. I spoke to his doctor at the time, and he said the trauma could be causing an emotional block. Course, Forrester wouldn't know that. If he did kill Boster, that could give him cause to want Dylan Castle silenced."

Cady's nape prickled. There were lots of unknowns in the case from five years ago. But if Forrester was the shooter, he'd found the family two or three times already. Which meant the man was more successful at hunting the family than law enforcement had been at trailing him. The sooner she changed that, the better.

Before a fourth boy wound up dead.

Chapter 4

Although it was tempting, Cady didn't nap on the return trip from Mecklenburg. It seemed unfair to Andy, who'd been up as long as she had with last night's arrest. And there was no way she could sleep in a car full of men. Not because she didn't trust these individuals. But because she didn't trust, period.

It was midafternoon by the time they got back to Asheville. She bypassed the office and went directly to her vehicle. As if it possessed a divine GPS, she ended up at a drive-through coffee shop in an effort to stave off sleep a few more hours. Picking a corner of the lot to park in, she sipped from the steaming to-go cup while flipping through the pages in the report. Thirty minutes later, she was less than a third of the way through the file but had come to a couple of conclusions: Davis's team had been thorough. And she still wanted to speak to Dylan Castle's family.

"Bang, bang! You're dead, Mama!"

She jerked her head toward the window. A young woman was pushing an empty stroller on the nearby sidewalk while a toddler walked beside it, pointing a stick at her. "Bang, bang!"

Pull the trigger back nice and smooth.

Cady stilled, her mind unsuccessfully chasing the flash of memory. Maybe it was from her initial firearms training at the academy.

"Put the stick down, William. Let's get back in the stroller." The boy's earsplitting scream when he was disarmed had her focus shifting back to the job.

It took a few minutes to find Tina Bandy's most recent address and key it into her phone's GPS. Taking another gulp of coffee, she started the vehicle. It was a quarter to four. Schools were out. If she was lucky, she might find the boy at home. Possibly his brother as well.

Twenty minutes later, staring at the small, neat house with bright-yellow paint and a red front door, she revised her earlier thought. The place looked deserted. The home and detached single garage sat back from the road, shielded from view by fat pines and untrimmed brush. There was no sign of a vehicle from the graveled drive she'd pulled into. The shades were drawn in all the windows. According to the file, Tina Bandy worked at a local grocery store, although there'd been no information regarding her schedule. She got out of the Jeep to approach the house.

Climbing the three concrete steps, she opened the screen to pound on the windowless front door. A judas hole punctuated its center. When there was no answer, Cady knocked again. Waited. Just as she was about to give up, a slight sound on the other side of the door alerted her. Turning back, she partially unzipped her coat to withdraw her credentials and flipped open the case, holding it up in front of the peephole in the door. "US Marshals Service," she called.

She heard the lock being disengaged, and an instant later, the door swung open to reveal a teenage male. The shock of blond hair had darkened a bit, Cady noted as she tucked away her credentials. He was taller and wider in the shoulders than the boy in the interview clip she'd watched this morning, with an expression far more guarded. But it was easy to see the boy in the teen.

He stared at her for a full minute before surprising her by saying, "You're Katy Maddix?"

"Cady." She gave him an easy smile, noting the opened can he held in one hand, a spoon sticking out of it. Pork and beans. She suppressed a shudder. "You must have spoken to Special Agent Davis."

Wordlessly, he stepped aside, an invitation for her to enter. She did so, swinging the door shut behind her. "Not him. The other one. The woman."

"Special Agent Rebedeau."

"Yeah." Now that he'd allowed her inside, the boy didn't appear to know what to do with her. "Are you taking over for the SBI?"

"I'm charged with finding Eric Loomer and Bruce Forrester." It would have been impossible to miss the flicker of fear in the boy's gaze. "Is your mom home?"

Dylan shook his head. "She's at work. She won't be back until late."

Cady looked beyond him into the small living room and adjoining kitchen. Sparsely furnished but neat enough. The TV was on. "What about Colton?"

"He's not here, either."

She returned her attention to him. Nodding to the can, she asked, "Is that supper?"

He shrugged, scooping up another spoonful and shoving it into his mouth. "Lunch," he said around the mouthful. "Mom keeps forgetting to put money in my school account."

His words summoned a familiar recollection. There'd been no hot school lunches when she'd lived with her grandfather. He'd grudgingly made sure there'd been bread and peanut butter in the house most of the time. If she'd dared take any of the other food, punishment had been a stint locked in the root cellar.

Are you afraid of the dark, girlie?

She elbowed aside the mental snippet and eyed Dylan's skinny form. His natural build, maybe. Or it could be due to irregular meals.

"C'mon," she said. "Those beans aren't going to last you long. Let's go get cheeseburgers."

He looked up. Stared. "Serious?"

"You're not the only one who missed lunch."

"You left the note where your mom will see it?"

Dylan swallowed his bite of burger before answering. "Yeah. Like I told you, though, she won't be home. She works till ten, and then she usually hangs with friends for a while."

Meaning Tina Bandy had no intention of returning late to prepare a meal, either. Cady tried to reserve judgment. She had no idea what the woman's work schedule was, and a fifteen-year-old was plenty old to fend for himself when needed. If there was food in the house.

They were silent for a few minutes. Cady watched the kid eat with a sense of awe. Teenage boys were supposed to be legendary for their appetites. But she had no idea where he put the food. When he'd dithered between two different king-size burgers, she'd encouraged him to order both, thinking it wouldn't hurt for him to have some extra food to take home. Now she doubted there'd be a crumb left over.

She finished her more modest sandwich and picked up her diet soda. When he appeared to be slowing down, Cady asked, "Do you have a cell phone?" If so, he could text his mother without bothering her at work. Despite his assurances, she wanted to be sure the woman didn't miss the message about her son's absence.

Reaching for his chocolate shake, he shook his head. "Just the one the agents gave my family for emergencies. And when they want to get in touch with us. That's what Rebedeau called me on earlier." With a last slurp, he set the glass back on the table. "I just take it with me to school and stuff. It's in my backpack. Mom has a TracFone, because there's no expensive plan."

"What about when you hang out with friends?" He should have had the phone with him at all times.

His expression closed. "I don't have friends."

Cady sat back. The statement might have nothing to do with the subject of her warrants, but she couldn't leave it alone. "It's tough moving around this much, huh? Especially at your age."

"Tougher for the people who got killed because of me." Dylan's gaze was on his fries, which he'd topped with a liberal dose of ketchup.

"You're not responsible for their deaths. Their killer is."

The set of his jaw shouted disagreement, but he remained silent, shoving fries into his mouth as if he hadn't just demolished two king-size cheeseburgers. There was something going on under the surface, Cady thought, and why the hell wouldn't there be? The kid had had trauma layered over trauma in his young life. "You ever see a counselor about any of this? To help you work through it?"

"When I was a little kid, for a few days back when Trev died. Not anymore. Mom says that kind of thing is for pussies."

She was really starting to dislike Tina Bandy. With effort, Cady tamped down the reaction. She wouldn't allow it to affect the way she did her job. Reaching for one of the fries on her plate, she said mildly, "I don't know about that. Cops—detectives, marshals, FBI agents, whoever—have to see counselors after they experience traumatic events on the job. It's mandatory if they want to get cleared to go back to work."

Finally, his eyes met hers. "Yeah?"

She nodded, chewing on the fry.

"Have you ever had to see one?"

They'd entered personal territory. But she'd led them there. She forced herself to answer. "Once." Every job-related shooting required desk duty and a counselor while awaiting an administrative investigation of the event. The kid looked like he was mulling over the information. She made a mental note to talk to SBI agent Rebedeau about pushing the issue of counseling with Bandy. Keeping Dylan and his family alive was paramount. But letting the kid carry this kind of emotional baggage was guaranteeing a screwed-up adult in a few years.

"I realize this is the last thing you want to talk about, but I need to ask you about Bruce Forrester." Dylan dropped the fries he'd been carrying to his mouth. Looked down. Cady's voice softened. "You saw him in Greensboro."

He gave a short jerk of the head.

"When was that?"

Swallowing hard, he lifted a shoulder. "A couple of days before—" He broke off then. Took a moment before he continued. "It was before Ethan was shot."

"Then you saw him in Ayden. SBI said you reported both sightings."

"Fucking good that did," the kid said bitterly.

"And later he appeared in Raleigh?"

He hesitated. "I thought so. But no one was . . ." *Killed,* she filled in silently. "We left town pretty quick after that," he finished. "It got to where I was seeing him everywhere. He murdered two of my friends; you get that? He was every driver who went by too slow. Every guy walking his dog down the street. I was scared to death. Sleeping with the light on."

"And what about now?"

He looked away. "I said I was scared then. I'm not scared anymore."

She studied him closely. Bravado or something more? "How do you think he found you two or three times?"

"Isn't that what you guys are supposed to find out?"

"Yeah." She paused to take a sip of her soda. "But you're fifteen. You're not a kid anymore. I'm sure you've given it some thought."

His expression stilled. "I got nothing to do but think. I can't have friends anymore because they might end up dead like Trevor and Ethan. I don't go anywhere. Do anything. I go to school. I sit at home. That's it."

The picture he was painting was bleak. But she focused on his first words. "So you've considered it. What'd you come up with?"

For the first time that day, he appeared animated. In between polishing off more fries, he said, "The schools issue us a computer. All the social media and gaming sites are blocked on it—don't worry. Not like I'd have anyone to talk to online anyway. But I took a programming class. For coding and stuff. And I was thinking maybe Forrester knows something about computers too. Or he knows someone who does. Because the quickest way to find us would be to hack into the school's database and find their list of students. It's not like our names have been changed."

There was no official state law enforcement protection service in North Carolina, which meant no funding sources. The SBI agents deserved credit for repeatedly relocating the family and, she presumed, helping them find housing and a job for Tina Bandy. Providing them with new identification would not fall within their purview.

She considered the boy's theory. "There's nothing in Forrester's history that would lead us to believe he has those skills."

"He's a drug dealer," the boy said stubbornly. "He probably knows lots of scumbags. One might have the know-how."

The hacker would have to be skilled *and* have plenty of time on his hands. She didn't know how many school districts North Carolina had, but they had to number more than a hundred. If Dylan was correct and had spotted Forrester three times since Boster's death, the man would have to know they were in the state. Which again raised the question of *how*. "That's a possibility," she finally said noncommittally as the waitress headed their way, a determined smile on her face.

"Anyone interested in dessert? Pies are baked fresh every day."

Noting the interest in the boy's expression, Cady said, "I could make room. How about you?" They spent a couple of minutes making their choices. As the server moved away, Cady returned to their earlier conversation. "The boy who bought your bike, Chad Bahlman, was older than you. So you hadn't outgrown it?"

He hesitated, then looked away. "No."

She waited, but when he said no more, she guessed. "Maybe you didn't ride it anymore."

"After Ethan, I didn't go out much." His earlier animated tone vanished. The words were flat. "And money gets tight sometimes. My mom don't make much. Next year, if this is over, maybe I can get hired at a restaurant or something. Help out a little."

"Does Colton work?" He'd be nineteen now, according to what she'd read.

"I don't know. I don't think so." The teen looked up with anticipation when the waitress returned with their desserts. "I haven't seen him in a while."

She dug a bit more as he polished off the pie. Little by little, a clearer picture of the boy's life emerged. Colton and Tina Bandy argued a lot when Dylan's brother was home. Colton had been out of the house months before they moved to Asheville. Probably stayed at friends', Dylan guessed. His mom took off for the weekend, too, sometimes, with a boyfriend, but that was no big deal. Dylan was plenty old enough to take care of himself, and she usually left him pizza money. Tina didn't like the job she'd gotten in Asheville. She always seemed to get jobs with jerk bosses. Recalling the woman's attitude in the interview clip Cady had viewed, she suspected the opposite was true.

Because the boy hadn't been able to decide between pecan and peanut butter, she'd ordered a slice of both for him. He'd cleaned both plates by the time she'd finished her wedge of banana cream.

On the way back to his house, she dug in her pocket and pulled out one of her cards. Handed it to him. "Add my number to the contacts on the cell SBI gave you. Just in case you ever need it."

"Yeah. Okay." It disappeared into the boy's jacket pocket.

"How did you know about Forrester's background?" Cady asked. When Dylan just looked at her questioningly, she went on. "I saw the interview you gave to the sheriff's office. You said he'd been in prison and was a drug dealer. How did you know that?"

"Everyone knew." His tone was as good as a shrug. "I went to the store once with Trev and his mom, and he walked by. She told us about him and said how we should always stay away from him. I saw him one other time. I wasn't s'posed to go to town on my bike, but once Colton and me rode in for some ice cream. We went by this bar, and there were people gathered all around. Two guys were fighting. They both had a knife. One was Forrester. He cut the other guy real bad. Colton and I had stopped to watch for a few minutes, but after that, Colton made me leave. He said the cops would be coming."

The assault charge was listed in the file, Cady remembered. It'd been bumped down to disturbing the peace because witnesses had backed up Forrester's claim that he'd been defending himself.

All told, that made five times Dylan had seen the man. But as he'd mentioned, trauma could have his mind playing tricks on him, causing him to see Forrester everywhere. She was still mulling his words when she pulled into the drive of his home. It was problematic if it was Forrester who kept finding the Bandy family. But not as troublesome as the thought that three boys were dead, and their killer hadn't yet been apprehended.

Chapter 5

The effects of the caffeine had dissipated by the time Cady pulled into the graveled drive of the acreage she rented and got out to open the decrepit wire gates and drive through. As usual, Hero bounded across the yard to greet her, but this time, after she'd closed the gates behind her, she couldn't urge him into the Jeep to ride up to the house, as was their custom.

Cady parked her work vehicle behind her car, which was under the carport. Hunching against the bite in the air, she strode to the front of the house, climbed the tiny porch, and unlocked the door. Stepping inside, she toed off her boots as she swung the door closed behind her. Habit had her doing a quick walk-through of her home. The intruder she'd had a few months back still had her paranoia churning. Even if the trespasser was currently back in lockup for his efforts.

Satisfied the home was empty, she set her briefcase next to the recliner she'd recently purchased and shrugged out of her coat as she walked back to the hall closet to hang it up along with her purse. After crossing the room, she dropped into the recliner and took out the file Special Agent Davis had given them.

She turned first to review the background on Bruce Forrester. Born in Winterville but ended up being raised by his maternal grandmother in Louisiana by the time he was five. He'd become a ward of the state at eleven when he was discovered living in a shack on a bayou with the grandmother's corpse. Cady's flesh prickled. The woman had died of a cardiac infarction. The coroner's report estimated she'd been gone two weeks before someone had discovered her death and alerted the authorities.

And how had that experience shaped the boy into the man he'd become? Because Cady was certain it'd played a major role.

She returned to reading. Forrester's mother had never been found, and eventually he'd been returned to Winterville, upon his father's release from prison. The older man had been incarcerated for possession with intent. The apple hadn't fallen far from the tree there. Witness statements attested that Carl Forrester had found religion in prison. He and his son were often seen at the Baptist services in town. But the old addiction soon reared its head. Carl was dead of an overdose a few years later, when his son was eighteen. In another five years, Bruce was in prison.

A sad but all-too-familiar family history. Cady pressed the "Recline" button on the chair. The background summary was only an outline of the man she was hunting. It didn't fill in the details. Like the value system the life experiences had embedded in Bruce Forrester. What drove him? Money, greed, revenge? Discovering that would be key to understanding him. And knowing the man was the first step toward finding him.

She flipped to the next page and read until her vision began to blur. The folder went still in her hands as the creeping tide of exhaustion swamped her.

A sound at the front door roused her, muscle memory leading consciousness. By the time she recognized the dog racing into the room and the man turning to close the door behind him, her weapon was in her hand, trained on the human interloper. A moment later, mortification filling her, she pushed out of the chair and reholstered her weapon, but not before Ryder Talbot spied it.

He raised his hands in mock surrender. "I confess. I'm guilty of being a dutiful dog-sitter. Do with me what you will."

She stood, unbuckling her holster. "Breaking and entering will get you six months. Lucky for you, I'm grateful enough not to press charges."

"I'm guessing the sheriff will go easy on me." He came farther into the room, pausing to lean down to swipe a quick kiss before he continued into the kitchen. Hero beat him there, lapping up water as if he didn't have a pool out in the doghouse. "I didn't hear from you, so I swung by to make sure you'd gotten home. Hero was still outside."

Cady glanced at the clock on the wall. It was close to six. "Sorry. I forgot to let you know. I fell asleep." She went to join him in the kitchen, where he was already taking out dog food and pouring it into the animal's dish. She stopped, a sliver of unease stabbing through her at the familiarity in the action. Cady shook it off. Her inner defenses were daunting. She was still deciding how far to let Ryder Talbot through them. Sometimes she wondered if that decision was completely in her hands. "You must have worked late. And on a Friday night too." He was still in uniform. He'd come from the office.

Hero fell on the food like a ravenous wolf while Ryder put the sack back in the cupboard. "The porch pirate is hitting again. I thought I was done with that shit at Christmas, but I got two more calls today. Police chief is having the same problem."

"What do they do, patrol the city limits waiting for UPS and FedEx trucks to drive by?"

"Hell if I know." Ryder rose, propping a hip against the counter, facing her. "Your arrest go okay?"

"Yeah, we . . ." Her attention was diverted by the dog. Having gobbled up every last morsel, he picked something up from the floor and turned toward them. Her gaze narrowed. "What's he got?" Horror filled her. "Is that a . . . Did you give my dog a *clown*?"

"What? No. It's a rag-doll thing."

She jabbed a finger at the offending item. "With a round red nose and a painted face and mouth?"

He turned to inspect the toy more closely. Then grinned at her. "You afraid of clowns, Cady?"

"Do not," she warned him, "make this about me." She wasn't. Of course she wasn't. That didn't mean she wanted one in the house. The damn thing was creepy.

"I took him to my place for a while last night so he could play with Sadie." Sadie was his yellow Lab. "She gave it to him. He's been quite taken with it."

Cady turned her reproachful gaze on Hero, who'd sat and dropped the toy, thankfully, but kept one paw possessively on top of it. He must have had it in the doghouse. "So this is the reason you wouldn't come into the house? Burglars aren't going to take you seriously if you carry that thing around. The optics are terrible."

Seeming unconcerned, Hero picked up the clown and ambled into the living room.

"I'm having second thoughts about your dog-sitting ability," she told Ryder.

A smile lurked at the corners of his mouth. "I guess you need to be more specific about the necessary qualifications. It could have been worse. It could have been a mime."

She didn't shudder. But it was close. "Do those teardrops painted beneath its eyes have the same meaning as they do on prison tats?"

He laughed out loud at that, genuinely amused. "We can discuss it over a beer downtown if you like."

Cady hesitated, tempted, before shaking her head. "I'd probably fall asleep before I finished it. And I really need to familiarize myself with the background on a warrant I was recently assigned. Lots of history. Not many leads."

"Yeah?" Ryder followed her out of the kitchen to the tiny living room. "Anything interesting?"

Cady picked up the holstered weapon she'd abandoned and went to put it away in the bedroom, calling over her shoulder, "Drug dealers. One's wanted for questioning in three child homicides."

"Oh sure. What's his name? Forrester?"

Stunned, she walked back out toward Ryder, who'd moved the folder off the recliner and sat down. "You read the file? When?"

"Nope. We've gotten plenty of BOLOs about him, though. The guy seems to be a ghost. Is that the meeting you were pulled into today?"

Nodding, she perched on the edge of the couch next to the chair. "Yeah. I have to dive into the investigation this weekend to see if I can find a rock they haven't turned over trying to find him."

He looked good in the recliner. It seemed churlish not to acknowledge it. The soft leather that had enticed her to splurge had been called "rawhide brown" and was nearly the same streaky color as his hair. His broad shoulders filled it in a way hers never would.

Cady scrubbed both hands over her face. She was more exhausted than she'd thought if she was dwelling on Ryder Talbot's physical attributes. Although she'd spent more than a few pleasurable nights exploring them.

"You're dead on your feet. You'll be better off grabbing some sleep first. If you don't spend every minute on Forrester this weekend, you could drop by my place sometime. My sister and nephews are going to be in town. Not her husband, though, since he's already made an excuse, lucky bastard," he said amusedly. Cady stilled.

She had enough trouble navigating her own family. Although she had nothing against kids, she had about as much experience with them as she did alternate life-forms. It came, she supposed, from being deprived of a childhood herself.

When she dropped her hands, he was regarding her with a slight smile, accompanied by the ever-watchful look in his eyes. It took more effort than it should have to keep the edge of panic from her voice. "I spend Saturdays with my mom, remember? Then I plan to work on getting up-to-date on Forrester."

He was already nodding. "Figured as much. Just looking for a buffer. My mom and sister can be a bit overpowering when they get together and start in on my social life, and the boys have an affinity for wrestling. You could help me tag team them."

Her tension was already easing at his indulgent tone. She had the feeling that he'd noted her discomfort and set out to defuse it. "That does sound delightful," she managed wryly. "But I already took one skull to the face this morning." She tapped her eye, which, at last examination, had turned a fashionable shade of maroon. "I might give wrestling a pass for a few days."

"I noticed but was too gentlemanly to call attention to it." He shoved out of the chair and stretched.

"Another reason to thank you." Cady rose as well and walked him to the front door. "In addition to your dog duties."

Ryder zipped up his coat. "You've done the same for me." He nodded in the direction of Hero, who was stretched out on the floor, spooning that damn clown. "Wasn't sure you were in a grateful mood, seeing his new friend."

"It tempers my appreciation somewhat," she allowed. Hopefully the dog would get tired of it. Or better yet, she could replace it with something else. Squeak toys were out. Every one she'd brought home for him had been destroyed in a matter of hours while he removed the noisemaker. The clown doll, though, he protected like his long-absent doggie jewels.

Upon reaching the door, Ryder turned, pulled her close, and kissed her again, this time more thoroughly. When he lifted his head, he ordered, "Eat. Tend to your eye. Sleep. And have a little pity and give me a call this weekend. It'll be a welcome reprieve from the female interrogation and hooligan guerrilla warfare."

Cady's smile lacked sympathy. "Better you than me, pal."

Chapter 6

Dylan froze as a noise sounded outside the darkened house. When it wasn't repeated, he got up and went to the blinds at the big picture window. Peeked through them. He saw nothing. No movement. No lights. No traffic on the road beyond the drive. He dropped the blind, still rattled. He'd found a small stash of weed in the back of one of Colton's dresser drawers earlier and rolled a joint. It had chilled him out for a while, but now he just felt paranoid.

The only light inside the home came from the TV screen. He'd been playing *Call of Duty* for hours. He looked at the time on the screen. Nearly eleven. Mom should have been off almost an hour ago. But like he'd told that marshal, she didn't always come home right after work. Not till the bars closed mostly. What he hadn't told Marshal Maddix was that a lot of times, his mom didn't come home at all.

To distract himself, he went to the small kitchen and pulled open the door of the refrigerator, as if it had magically filled itself since the last time he looked. Three eggs. A bunch of yogurt and a twelve-pack. He should have asked that marshal to let him order some takeout. She probably would have. Maybe they had an expense account for that sort of thing. The cheeseburgers and pie he'd had hours earlier were a dim memory. He had the munchies something fierce.

Dylan was scavenging fruitlessly through the cupboards when another sound brought him up short. This time it was right outside the kitchen door. He made a move toward it, then stopped. What the hell would he do if he lifted the shade and there was a face looking through the glass at him? Forrester's face?

This was stupid. He was being a pussy. The self-castigation didn't stop Dylan from sprinting across the kitchen to a drawer. Grabbing a knife from it. It was barely sharp enough to cut through a burger. He tossed it back inside and reached for the scissors instead. At least they looked like they could do some damage. He could stab an intruder in the eye with them.

A lot of good a pair of scissors would be against a high-powered rifle. The thought kept him rooted in place. No one ever told him anything, but he'd heard his mom talking. Ethan and Chad Bahlman had been shot in the head with a semiautomatic. He'd looked up images on the web of what weapons like that did. He regretted it now. The pictures had lodged in his mind, and when he got worried about Forrester—like now—the fear came with its own illustrations.

The scratching sounds were getting louder, weren't they? Dylan imagined Forrester, just outside that door, waiting for Dylan to come lift the shade and look out. Imagined seeing the muzzle of that rifle on the other side of the pane if he did.

The thought had him bolting from the room. If he was going to be on his own all the fucking time, he should at least have something with which to defend himself. He ran past the bedroom he shared with Colton—when he visited—to his mom's. She had a handgun. He'd seen it in her purse before. He didn't know what the hell good it did her. She wasn't the one Forrester was looking to kill. And if he ever found this house, chances were she wouldn't be around for protection anyway.

Dylan rifled through the clothes in her drawer before turning his attention to her closet. Nothing there, either. She was probably carrying it with her. Unless she'd left it in another purse. She had gobs of them.

Why the hell did a woman need that many? He rummaged through them, coming up with enough loose change and bills to fill his lunch account for another week. He shoved the money into his pocket before turning his attention to the bed. Dylan checked beneath the mattress. His fingers closed around something, and he drew it out. When he saw the object, though, his frenzy turned to confusion. It was a cell. It looked exactly like the one she carried, another TracFone. But she didn't keep her phone under the mattress when she slept. It was always charging on the tiny table next to the bed.

He turned it on. The phone was activated and three-quarters charged. He sat back on his heels, his hand still clutching the cell, a sense of aggrievement filling him. What did she need two phones for when he didn't even have one? At least not one he could use for anything personal.

Replacing the cell, he searched the rest of the room, finding nothing. Waste of time.

Dylan was feeling a little foolish when he reentered the living room. Until twin beams of light speared through the darkness of the room. A car was coming up the drive. He dashed to the front window, yanked the blind aside. The vehicle continued up to the house and was lost from sight, but not before Dylan identified it as his mom's piece-of-crap Corolla. Relief streamed through him.

When her key sounded in the lock of the kitchen door, he walked into the room, more than a little surprised to see her not only home on a Friday night but also carrying a few bags of groceries. His disgruntlement fading, he leaped forward to take the sacks from her. "Hey, Mom."

"Hey, yourself." She shut the door behind her and took an exaggerated sniff. "Smells like pot in here."

He was too interested in the contents of the bags to lie. Carrying them over to the counter, he withdrew the contents, taking inventory. Hot damn, popcorn. Frozen pizza. And enough soda to tide him over for a week. "I smoked a joint earlier."

The whack on the back of his head wasn't totally unexpected. "And just where did you find that?"

"In Colton's dresser." There were cookies in one of the bags. Tina had gone all out. Ice cream. Frozen corn dogs. Dylan stared at the box in delight. He hadn't had a corn dog since he was a little kid. There'd been a carnival in town, and his mom must have been feeling flush. She'd given Colton and him ten dollars each to go to it. He'd stuffed himself with corn dogs and cotton candy and then used most of the rest of the money to buy her a necklace with her name spelled out in metal beads. His mom had yelled at him for wasting the cash on her, but she'd worn the necklace. At least for a while.

"If Colton comes back and finds it gone, don't expect me to step in for you. You'll deserve the ass whipping. Put that away for me, will you? I gotta pee something fierce." She sprinted by him toward the bathroom.

He had a belated twinge of nerves at the mention of Colton. His brother's temper was near 'bout as bad as his mom's. But who knew when he'd show up again? After dealing with the groceries, he served himself a big bowl of ice cream. He'd just dug into it when he heard his mom yell, "Dylan Ray! Have you been in my bedroom?" She marched to the kitchen with fire in her eyes, near spitting in fury. "My drawers are an absolute mess! How many fucking times do I have to tell you to stay outta my things?"

He spoke around a mouthful of chocolate fudge ripple. "I was looking for your gun."

"You . . ."

He swallowed and ducked as she came to his side, her arm raised threateningly.

"I thought I heard something outside the house. And then I started thinking it was him. I was looking for a weapon. Something I could protect myself with."

"Oh, baby." Her temper evaporating, she tousled his hair instead of delivering the slap she'd been poised for a moment ago. "No damn way I want you touching a gun. You ain't never been trained, and besides, I can protect you."

"When you're here," he muttered, and her expression darkened again.

"Well, there's more than one way to protect you, ain't there? I'm doing right by you every minute of the day, not just when I'm standing by your side. Where'd you put them chips?" He pointed at the cupboard he'd stowed them in, and she headed toward it. Snatched out a bag.

For the first time, he noticed the duffel she was carrying. "Now where you going?"

She ripped into the snack bag and stuffed some chips into her mouth before answering. "I gotta go visit a friend. Just till Sunday because that fucking Steve gave me hours even though I fucking told him I was going to be gone all weekend."

Steve had apparently known about her trip before Dylan had. He kept the thought to himself. At least he'd have food. It wasn't like his mom spent much time at home, whether she was around or not.

"You'll be okay, right, baby?"

His teeth clenched. He hated when she called him that. As if he were another nameless stranger who'd followed her home from the bar after closing.

"I don't want you to worry about that fuckin' Forrester," she continued, dragging out a chair beside him and dropping into it. "Didn't I make them agents move us again? You're safe here. All the cops in Asheville are probably watching out for us."

"Got a US marshal looking for Forrester too." From the expression on his mom's face, she hadn't known that. "Came here today." He considered whether to tell her that they'd gone out for lunch. Decided not to. Tina had a short fuse, and he never knew what would set her off.

"He came here? Without talking to me first?"

"She." Dylan scraped the leftover ice cream from the bowl, then got up to rinse it out before setting it in the sink for later. He hated washing dishes, but they wouldn't get cleaned otherwise. "Katy . . . *Cady*"—he corrected himself—"Maddix. I think she was looking for you, but you weren't here."

"A marshal, huh." She chewed a few more chips. "That's sorta like a sheriff."

"No, marshals are federal." Dylan knew that from TV. "She's supposed to bring in Forrester."

"Her and a hundred other cops." His mom popped up again, twisting the top of the bag closed before putting it back in the cupboard. "S'pose it don't hurt none to have another one looking for him, not that it's done much good so far. Is she anything like that twit Rebedeau?" Tina didn't have much faith in any of the cops helping them, but she seemed to dislike the females the most.

He lifted a shoulder. "I dunno. She's younger. Blondish-reddish hair." There was probably a name for that color, but he didn't know what it was. She would actually have been sorta hot, if not for the look in her pale-green eyes. It shouted "cop" as loud as a billboard. "She was . . ." *Nice,* he finished silently, *in a no-nonsense sort of way.* She hadn't talked to him like he was a dumb-ass kid. He appreciated that almost as much as the lunch.

"Probably a bad dye job," his mom was saying. Dylan wisely refrained from looking at the black roots splitting her blonde hair. She looked at the Apple watch on her wrist, the one she'd claimed a "friend" had given to her. "I gotta go. Stay outta my room from now on. I keep the gun with me anyways, and you'd probably shoot your own dick off. We're safe. Forrester ain't gonna find us here."

Dylan didn't ask her what made her so sure, since the man had found them before. He knew she'd have no answer. And a part of him didn't see the point. It was enough that he spent half his days certain a bullet was going to come out of nowhere and tear a hole through his skull. No use both of them living in fear.

"I should have a cell." He brought a damp cloth back to the table and scrubbed where they'd been eating. "Not the one the staties gave me. I mean one I can use to keep in touch with you. I would have let you know the marshal was here if I could."

"We'll see. Maybe next time I get paid." She picked up her duffel and headed for the door. "I probably won't see you until after work Sunday. Don't leave the house."

Where the hell would I go? Dylan thought gloomily, locking the door after her.

He went back to his game. But he couldn't concentrate and got killed when he made an amateur move. Disgusted, he threw down the controller. Brooded for a while. Mom had probably been lying about getting him a phone, he decided; otherwise she would have told him she had a second one she wasn't using. Getting up from the floor, he went back to her room, determined to look at it more closely. Maybe he could figure out the password. It wasn't like he didn't have time on his hands.

But when he reached beneath the mattress, he found nothing. Dylan picked up the edge, peered beneath it. The space was empty. He poked around the room again, being more careful this time to see where she might have stashed it. But he didn't find the phone.

Wherever Tina had gone, she'd taken the extra cell with her.

Chapter 7

Tina Bandy shoved open the bedroom door. It bounced against the opposite wall, bringing the couple in the bed upright. "Jee-zus." She clapped a hand over her eyes until they yanked up the covers. "Get some pants on, Colton. I need to talk to you."

"Mom? What the fuck?"

"Hey, Tina." Mya rolled out of bed like a buck-naked goddess and took her time pulling on her clothes. "Didn't know Colton was expecting you."

"'Cuz I wasn't," he muttered.

"Obviously. Place is a mess." Tina came farther into the room, eyeing her son. "You gonna get dressed or not?"

"I'm trying." He stuck an arm out from under the sheet, snagging his jeans from the floor and wiggling into them. Then he slid out of bed and grabbed his T-shirt, pulling it on as he walked barefoot past her. "I ain't having no conversation with you in here."

"Mya." Tina followed him into the small front room. "Find somewhere to go. I gotta talk to my son."

"She can stay if she wants!" Colton exploded. "This ain't your house."

"I asked nicely, didn't I?"

"It's okay. I gotta meet someone anyway." Mya slipped into a coat she'd slung over the back of a chair and headed out the kitchen door, Colton scowling after her.

"So." He dropped down into an easy chair. "What's new?"

Tina sat on the couch facing him. "You talk to your brother lately?"

"How the hell am I supposed to do that? Unless you finally got him a phone."

When she looked away, he swore. "I've been telling you for months. You can't keep him locked up forever. No way could I have handled that at his age. I'd have exploded."

"Yeah." Colton had actually realized that before she had. "Well, he ain't you. But you're right; he ain't a little kid anymore. And this last move . . . it's been tough on him. But what the fuck am I s'posed to do about that? Cops still haven't found Forrester. Bunch of incompetent assholes. Now they brought in some federal marshal, and she'll probably be just as worthless. I still have to worry about Forrester, on top of whatever stupid thing your brother might do if he can't take it no more."

Colton cocked a brow in that smart-ass way he had. "You askin' for my advice?"

She wasn't. Not exactly. "I've been thinking. We might have to step things up a notch."

His expression closed. "What's that mean? And who's 'we'?"

She'd spent the car ride thinking it over. She laid it all out for him. He gaped at her for a moment. Then shot up from the chair like his ass was on fire. "The fuck you are! Are you crazy? That's a terrible idea!"

Tina's temper flared. "Do you want to protect your brother or not?"

"Hell no, not like that!" He paced around the small room, grimacing when he stepped on something embedded in the worn carpet. "You think you can control everyone, but you can't. Why don't you let the cops just do their jobs?"

"Because they ain't doing it!" She stood as well. "And waiting on them will probably get us all killed. Or do you think Forrester plans to stop with your brother?"

That shut him up. Colton swallowed hard. "It's too risky. Let the cops manage things."

"Like that's worked so well in the past."

He disagreed with her, of course. Seemed like the kid had been born arguing. But after an hour of her laying it all out for him, he stopped to think for a minute. Then he said slowly, "I'm not sure if you're out of your ever-fucking mind or if you just might be a genius."

Chapter 8

It was barely 8:00 a.m. when Cady walked across the parking lot to the Buncombe County Detention Center. Before her plans with her mom this afternoon, she hoped to get in an interview with Michael Simmons. Maybe he was feeling a bit more cooperative today. The conversation she'd had with the deputy on the phone before driving over hadn't given her reason to be hopeful. Apparently Simmons wasn't playing well with others in lockup.

Thirty minutes later, the man was glowering at her from across a table, giving no indication his mood had improved. He had the beginning of a bruise beside one eye that could be a twin for the one he'd given her yesterday. *Karma,* Cady mused silently, *can be a bitch.*

"Bruce Forrester." Wasting no time on small talk, she returned to the subject of yesterday's questioning. "What can you tell me about him?"

"Same thing I told you yesterday. Jack shit."

She studied him through narrowed eyes. "Have you heard from him since he was released from prison?"

Silently, Simmons folded his arms across his thick chest, the chains on his wrist manacles jangling.

"So he didn't call, didn't write. It's almost like he doesn't care. That's harsh, Michael, after all you guys must have meant to each other." She leaned forward, lowering her voice conspiratorially. "Arraignment's Monday, right? Wouldn't do your case any harm to have a written message from a federal marshal noting your cooperation on an unrelated federal warrant."

Interest flickered in his expression. "I want a deal."

"That's not the offer on the table. I'm not talking to the DA on your behalf." She waited a minute, but when the man didn't answer, she stood. Went to the door.

"Wait."

Cady turned.

"I know Forrester had a job waiting for him in Mars Hill when he left prison." That much was true. It'd been in the digital case file. She went back to the table. Sat. "He was from Wilson. Winterville. One of them. Maybe he's still there."

He wasn't, but at least she knew Simmons was giving her factual information about his former cellmate. "The two of you must have gotten along." They'd been cellmates most of the time Forrester had been inside.

"If we hadn't, we'd have put in for a switch."

"So what was he like?" She had details of Forrester's upbringing. His crimes. But discovering what drove the man would have to come from people who knew him.

Simmons scratched his jaw, as if the question mystified him. "Like most of the guys inside. Don't piss him off and you might be fine. Do him dirt, you're probably going to have a bad accident."

So Forrester was violent. Not exactly a news flash, given what she'd learned about him. "Do you know of anyone inside who 'had a bad accident' at his hands?"

The man's expression closed. "I ain't a snitch. And I don't know nothing for sure anyway."

Intrigued, Cady pressed him. "Then you aren't snitching, are you? Maybe he just mentioned something, like people do. Doesn't mean he acted on it, right?"

Simmons seemed to mull over her words for a moment. "Yeah, that's right. Can't arrest someone for talking. So there was a guy, Gordy the Ghost we called him, 'cuz he had really white skin and light hair. Bruce called him a vampire. While we was inside, Bruce could arrange for, uh, some conveniences, and Gordy ran up a bill, then never paid. Bruce talked about catching up with him on the outside. If they ever found some pale-looking piece of shit with a stake through his heart, maybe ol' Bruce tracked him down." He cackled, seeming genuinely amused.

There were ways to verify the story. And to check on the welfare of "Gordy." Cady let the thread go and continued to question Simmons, but it soon became clear he had nothing else to offer. She rose to leave.

"Don't forget to write that letter. I helped, right?"

"I won't forget." She turned toward the door.

"What's he done? Bruce?" the man called after her.

Facing him again, Cady replied, "He's wanted on an abduction charge. He kidnapped a woman." Simmons smirked. "That amuses you?"

"Don't surprise me none."

"Why not?"

Shrugging his beefy shoulders, he said, "Guy like him wants to be in control. He'd rather take it by force than have it given free."

It. A thread of revulsion skated over her. But the man was still talking. "He had this thing he liked. Can't remember what they call it, but . . ." He put both hands to his throat and squeezed lightly.

"Erotic asphyxiation?"

"Yeah. 'Cept he didn't do it to himself. He liked to watch."

◆ ◆ ◆

Cady sat in the jail parking lot for a moment, her mood grim. Forrester had grabbed Cassie Zook six weeks ago. There'd been nothing in the woman's history to suggest the two had been acquainted before the abduction. Given what Simmons had just revealed about the man's fetish, the woman's chances of being found alive—already slim—had just worsened.

Her laptop sat on a swivel attached to the dash. She turned it toward her, booted it up, and waited impatiently until she could look at the digital file again. As Simmons had mentioned, Forrester had had a job waiting for him nine years ago upon leaving prison. He'd been hired as a mechanic at Pete's Garage in Mars Hill.

His employer and fellow employees from the time were listed in the file, as well as the date they'd last been contacted. Forrester had worked there almost two years. His final day on the job corresponded with an arrest date on his sheet. He'd spent a few days in the Madison County jail for assault.

She called the number for the garage, pleasantly surprised when a gruff voice answered. "Pete's."

"This is Deputy US Marshal Cady Maddix. I'd like to speak to Peter Benson."

"That's me."

From the corner of her eye, she watched a man get into the car beside hers, which was parked too close to the Jeep. "I'm calling about Bruce Forrester, a former employee of yours. What can you tell me about the time he worked for you?"

"Same thing I told the cops when they were here years ago, asking." Under her watchful gaze, the driver next to her carefully maneuvered from the spot, with only inches to spare. "Decent mechanic. Rough around the edges, but that's to be expected. Did what he was told and didn't cause any problems, at least at work."

"There were problems elsewhere?"

"Must have been, for him to be arrested. That violated the agreement I had with the fella at the prison who places the ex-cons. I'll give 'em a chance, but I don't want trouble. Never saw him after that."

"Do you know anything about his relationship with women? How he treated them?"

"I didn't spend any time socializing with him, and we keep the chitchat to a minimum when we're working."

"Is there anyone else employed there who would remember him?"

A bark of laughter sounded in her ear. "Marshal, why do you think I hire ex-cons? I can't keep help here to save my soul. Soon's I train them, the guys move on. Only one from that time still here is my son, Jeff. Don't know that he could tell you any more than I did, but you're welcome to talk to him."

A moment later, a new voice sounded. "Dad says you want to know about Bruce Forrester."

"That's right. I know you've both spoken to the police about him before—"

"At least twice. But not recently. I'll tell you what I told them. I didn't like the guy. I didn't trust him. Not just because he was an ex-con—I don't like my dad hiring them, either, no matter what kind of kickback he gets for it—but this guy had trouble written all over him. I was glad when he was gone, although it was just a matter of time. Guy was a powder keg. Someone finally lit the match."

Jeff seemed to have pegged Forrester correctly. "Did you ever hang out with him while he was there? After hours? Meet for drinks?"

"Nope. My dad never wanted me mentioning this to the cops, because I didn't have proof. But I'm going to tell you: I thought he was dealing drugs even at work. I wanted him gone."

Cady wondered if drugs were the "conveniences" Simmons had referred to. "What made you think that?"

"He disappeared most lunchtimes. Nothing wrong with that. But employees rarely get visitors at work. Forrester did, once or twice a week. Always on his break. Usually guys, but some women. They'd huddle in his vehicle for a couple of minutes; then the visitors would leave. I confronted him, and he said they were from his AA group. Just members offering each other support."

"But you didn't believe him."

"Because I'm not stupid. I told him we didn't want people on the property who weren't customers and to knock it off. He gave me that cold-ass stare of his, but after that, the visits ended."

She asked the question she'd put to his father. "What was his relationship like with women?"

"The guy liked his porn—I remember that. But that wasn't my beef with him."

Cady sat for a moment after the call was ended, impressions from today's conversations careening and colliding in her mind.

He liked to watch. Simmons's words sounded in her mind. Drugs. Porn. Fetishes. None of what she'd learned today was positive news for Cassie Zook. And given the man's propensity for revenge, if Forrester really was after Tina Bandy's family, it didn't bode well for them, either.

Chapter 9

"Your mom's still getting ready." With visible reluctance, Cady's aunt stepped aside to allow her into the cabin. If Alma Griggs had been able to, she'd forbid her from the property. But since Cady paid her to care for her mother, that option wasn't feasible.

But she showed her disdain in other ways. Turning her back, she stomped into the kitchen, hostility emanating from her.

Cady followed her, going to the counter to pluck the notebook from the small bookcase there. In it, she'd find a thorough accounting of her mom's days since she last visited. That was part of the caregiving deal she and Alma had struck after Hannah Maddix had received the early-onset Alzheimer's diagnosis that had precipitated Cady's transfer from the Saint Louis office. No one knew how long her condition would allow Hannah to be cared for at home. But Cady recognized that keeping her in familiar surroundings as long as possible would be helpful.

The cabin had been their home on and off when Cady was growing up. They'd landed here when Hannah was between jobs or, more often, when one of her worthless boyfriends had absconded with the rent money. It obviously held more pleasant memories for her mother than it did for her.

"It looks like she had a good week," she said finally, replacing the notebook on the shelf.

"She did." Her aunt's voice was grudging. "Until this morning. She forgot how to dress herself."

The news hit Cady with the force of a sneaky left jab. One hand crept to the edge of the counter. Clenched. "What happened?"

When Alma turned around, there was concern in her expression as well as the condemnation she reserved for her niece these days. "We'd picked out her clothes, and I laid them on her bed. Gave her a few minutes, and when I went back in, she was standing in the same spot, just staring at them. Said she didn't know what to do first."

A fist gripped her heart. Squeezed. Those episodes were to be expected. Logically, Cady knew that. They were still relatively infrequent. But each time one occurred, it ignited a fresh flare of panic inside her, reminding her that it was only a matter of time before the one person in the world she loved would no longer remember her.

"I reminded her of what to do, and she was fine."

Cady's gaze traveled to the bedroom door. "Is she . . ."

"Oh, she's ready to go. She's just doing a bit of primping."

"Remember to write it in the notebook the doctor gave us. With the date."

"I know how to take care of my kin, missy." The moment of concern had passed. Alma had taken up verbal arms again. "More'n I can say for you, that's for sure."

"I'm not going to have this conversation again." Cady pushed away from the counter.

"Yer cousin is sitting in a jail cell, and you could get him out if'n you wanted."

"I told you before—I'm not paying Bo's bail. You remember *why* he's awaiting trial, right? For breaking into my house? And the office of my landlady, Dorothy Blong?" Her intruder a few months ago had been none other than her no-good cousin. His antagonism was a carryover from when they were kids. So was his stupidity.

"I'm not talking about the bail. You mighta been right before. Do him good to think on his behavior."

That was a first, Cady noted. Alma had been making excuses for her boys since they were in diapers.

"I talked to that public defender of his. He said you could probably have them charges dismissed."

"I . . ." Cady shook her head in frustration. "You need a different attorney. That's ridiculous."

"You got yourself that federal job, don't you? Fed outweighs state, don't it?" Alma planted both fists on her ample hips, a mama grizzly in a man's flannel shirt and jeans. "If you didn't press charges, they'd let him go."

"I seriously doubt anyone with a law degree told you that." Cady drew a breath. Counted to ten. Alma apparently didn't think Bo stealing the key to Cady's house and leaving a window unlocked in her home after he'd trespassed was a sign of ill intent. But she'd learned as a kid just what her cousin was capable of. "With his latents found at my place and at the landlady's office, law enforcement has him dead to rights on burglary charges. It has nothing to do with me."

"But you could put in a good word for him," Alma pressed. "It'd go a long way with the judge, a marshal speaking up for him."

"Using my position to intercede for a relative would be a good way to get myself fired, even if I were willing to do so. I'm not." She'd never shared Alma's rosy perception of her sons, Bo and LeRoy. Cady knew from experience how dangerous they could be.

"I swear, if you wasn't Hannah's daughter," Alma said between gritted teeth. "Ain't like you never did nothing wrong. With your history, a body'd think you'd be a bit more sympathetic."

Alma's words rocked her, evoking the memories that were never far from Cady's mind. *The sound of the shot. The spray of blood.* With long practice, she'd learned to shunt them aside. But they weren't so easily avoided. Childhood trauma had sculpted the ghosts that haunted her into adulthood. It was a moment before she could fashion a response. "Bringing up my past isn't exactly a way to elicit compassion."

"Just because you don't wanna remember it don't mean folks 'round here have forgotten."

Smiling thinly, Cady retorted, "The reminder still won't get your son sprung from jail."

"Alma, you should have told me Cady was here." There was no reproach in Hannah's voice as she practically danced into the room. "I didn't even realize she'd arrived until I heard her voice."

Relieved, Cady walked to exchange a hug with her mom, who was a stark foil to Alma in almost every way. She was as pretty and slim as ever, her ethereal air and bright smile causing most of the world to smile back. She possessed an almost naive sincerity, a contagious enthusiasm for life and appalling taste in men, including Cady's father. *Especially* him.

"Bye, Alma," Hannah sang over her shoulder after slipping into a winter coat draped over the back of a rocker. "Let me know if there's anything I can pick up from town."

"Probably headed there myself to buy a few groceries."

Hannah linked arms with her daughter. "I just love our Saturday adventures."

Their outings did not, by any stretch of the imagination, meet Cady's definition of adventure. They usually included all the things Hannah enjoyed most—hair, makeup, nails, and shopping. But she treasured the time spent with her mom. More so, knowing days like these were numbered.

Cady returned her smile. "So do I."

It was dark when Cady pulled into the cabin's drive again. She shot her mom an assessing look. Maybe they'd overdone it. After Hannah had gotten her hair colored and wheedled her daughter into agreeing to pedicures, they'd strolled through every shop in Waynesville before Cady had noted the other woman's flagging energy. She'd persuaded her to stop for salads, which they'd followed with malts. Hannah had regained her normal vivaciousness over the meal. Or so Cady had thought. But now it would be difficult to miss the fatigue in her expression.

Guilt surged. "Maybe we did too much today."

"I loved every minute." Hannah touched her shoulder lightly. "I don't get enough time with my girl."

"Still, I'd feel better if you promised to turn in early tonight. Maybe watch TV in your room until you fall asleep."

"I'm not going to lie—that sounds tempting. And I'm going to wear that new nightgown you bought me today too. You know I have a weakness for pretty, frilly things. You're just so sweet to indulge me like you do." She gave Cady's arm a squeeze. "We missed these moments, you and I, after you went to live with your grandfather."

Tension shot through Cady's muscles at the mention of Elmer Griggs. She'd come to terms with her mom sending her away after Bo had attempted to sexually assault her when she was twelve. A woman with almost no support system, Hannah had sought to protect Cady, without considering *whom* she was sending her to.

Without considering that abuse could take different forms.

"Before I knew it, you were off to college and then Saint Louis," her mom continued brightly. "I just didn't get to see you near enough, except for quick visits. I'm so thankful to have the time now."

"Me too." Cady pulled to a stop in front of the cabin, her throat full. The moments were bittersweet. More so when she acknowledged that if it weren't for her mother's diagnosis, nothing would have brought her back to North Carolina. She'd grown adept at burying her past, but the memories seemed closer here. More vivid. Life was a series of trade-offs. This one was worth it.

They got out of the car, collecting the bags, then climbing the steps to the cabin. The door swung open before they reached it. Alma's girth filled the doorway. "I was 'bout to call. What on earth kept you?"

"Oh, Alma, we just had the best time." But even as Hannah launched into a recounting of their day, her sister sent Cady a condemning look. Not unusual, but in this instance her disapproval had some merit.

When Hannah paused for a breath, Cady said, "We've eaten. Mom has agreed to rest now. Maybe turn in early tonight."

"Which bag has my nightgown?" Hannah rooted through them as she and Cady walked toward her room. "It's just the prettiest thing, Alma; you'll have to see. It's white and sprinkled with rosebuds. Cady has one too. She looks so cute in it."

The words rocked her back on her heels. She could recall the garments her mom was describing in detail. The pink ribbon that threaded around the neckline. The delicately scalloped hem. It took effort to maintain a matter-of-fact voice as she guided Hannah into her room. "The one we bought was turquoise, Mom, remember? Your favorite color."

"Oh, you're right." Hannah sat down on the edge of her bed and reached into a bag. Drew out the nightgown. "It's so lovely." But then she frowned, confusion tingeing her tone. "But I had that white one. I haven't seen it in a while. I think it got ruined, but I can't quite recall how. Why can't I remember?"

Blood spattered on Cady's pretty printed nightdress. Little pinpricks of crimson making their own pattern along the rosebuds. And her mother's matching gown. Soaked with blotches of bright red.

"Because you're trying too hard," Cady said, slamming a mental door shut against the specters from her past. "Put it out of your head. It will come to you when you least expect it." She knew that from bitter experience. But with any luck, her mother would forget the entire conversation in minutes.

She stayed while Hannah readied for bed, wearing the new nightgown. Got her tucked in with the TV on and the remote nearby. Cady thought she was nodding off and rose silently, preparing to leave. Before she got more than a step, Hannah's eyes opened, an expression of misery crossing her face. "I'm so sorry, Cady. If only I could go back and change things. We never should have let you take the blame. That was so wrong. You were only four! How could we have done that to you?"

The words were sharpened little darts, each sinking deep, spreading their poison. But Cady ignored them for the moment. Concentrated on soothing her mom's sudden agitation. Distracting her with memories of their day. After an hour, when Hannah seemed to doze off, Cady silently left the room and eased the door closed.

Alma surged up from the rocker she was sitting in, her expression thunderous. "She had an episode, didn't she? And it's all yer fault for running her about until she's near faint with exhaustion."

Cady moved farther into the room, her voice quiet. "We didn't do any more or less than most weekends, but maybe there's been some progression in her condition. I'll call Dr. Baker Monday and discuss it with him. I wanted to ask you about something she said, though. She was talking about that day." The flicker of recognition on Alma's face told her better than words that the woman knew exactly what she was referring to. "She kept saying *we*. '*We* never should have let you take the blame. How could *we* have done that to you?' Was there someone else involved? Someone there, or maybe later . . ."

Alma's mouth flattened into a thin, hard line. "Only people in the kitchen that night were you, your mama, and Lonny Maddix. Don't go looking for anyone else to cast the blame on, missy. You mighta only been four, but you was the one who picked the gun up off the table and shot your daddy dead."

Chapter 10

"What's got you in such a good mood?"

When Eric's voice sounded next to him, Bruce Forrester quickly closed out of the message he'd been reading on the computer screen. "What're you talking about?"

The other man dropped into a chair next to him at the table. "Something had you smiling. Good news? Did Cortez agree to increase our next shipment?"

"Yeah," Bruce lied. "Possibly."

Eric gave a self-satisfied grin. "Told you it wouldn't do no harm to ask. With more product, we can expand our territory."

Anxious to be rid of him, Bruce asked, "You finish the packaging?"

"Yeah." Eric's eyes slitted. "I ain't a kid. You don't need to be reminding me every ten minutes."

"No reason you can't take the night off, then." Bruce knew exactly how to keep him happy. And get him out of his hair for a few hours, which was even more important.

Shock flickered across Eric's face, but he rose fast enough to almost topple his chair. "I'm not going to say no. Need me to get anything from town?"

Itching to have him gone, Bruce said, "Beer, maybe."

"Okay, see you later."

He waited until the door to the room closed behind Eric before turning his attention back to the computer. He clicked on the direct message to read it again. Found your runners. They're in Asheville. The mom's working at a Food Mart this time. 2nd half of payment is due.

A broad grin crossed Bruce's face. The hunt was on. Again. And the only thing he liked better than hunting was watching the death throes of his prey.

Chapter 11

Cady fed Hero the next morning, surreptitiously sliding the clown under the dog's bed while he ate. His affection for it seemed as strong as ever. Maybe if it was out of sight, he'd forget about it.

She went back to the recliner where she'd left the computer she'd been engrossed in last night. Turned it on. She'd worked until well after midnight, the time interrupted only by a quick call to Ryder. Delaying sleep sometimes prevented the nightmares that visited too frequently, an unwelcome montage of events from her past. Total exhaustion had successfully warded them off.

She'd worked her way through the case summary Davis had given her and then started delving into the more complete digital file, making notes on avenues taken to track down Forrester. Friends, family, acquaintances. At the end of her research, one thing had been apparent: the search for Bruce Forrester had been depressingly thorough.

Hero went to the door and whined politely. Cady glanced up, her brows coming together. He was carrying the damn clown doll again. "I'm embarrassed for you. Really." She let him out and fixed herself a couple of slices of toast and coffee before returning to the laptop.

It wasn't long before she was engrossed in the digital file again. She found notations of other arrestees, contacts, visitor logs, and phone calls for his stays in the Hope Mills police station and Cumberland County jail. But there were no such records for his lockup in Madison County. She checked to see if the county provided online access to old arrest records and struck out. Some of the smaller ones didn't provide that service. Which meant she'd have to drive over and go through the records herself.

Cady considered the task with a decided lack of enthusiasm. But Marshall, the county seat, was only an hour away. She called the office and waited to be connected with the detention lieutenant on duty, Ken Goldman.

"Oh yeah, we remember Forrester around here," he said after Cady introduced herself and gave her reason for calling. "We still get the BOLOs for him but haven't had a confirmed sighting since he moved out of the county."

"I have the dates he was held in your jail. Is there an easy way to cross-check them to find who else might have been locked up with him at the time?"

"It's possible. Takes a while, though." Cady's heart sank. "We're set up to search by name, but you can't check by dates per se. There might be a work-around, though. Give me a date range." She waited several minutes, which were interrupted only by the man's occasional soft curses. "Okay, here's one," he said finally. "What I have to do is scroll through the inmate list for the given year, which is in alphabetical order, until I find a date that at least partially corresponds. Evan Gosch. Big surprise, he happens to be a guest of the county again this weekend. Guy's such a regular, we should put his name on one of the cells."

"He'll be there overnight?"

"Just picked him up Friday for using a stolen ATM card. I don't see him going anywhere until after the court hearing Monday."

"I can be there in an hour. I'd like to talk to him."

A shrug sounded in Goldman's voice. "You're welcome to him. If I get any free time before my shift ends, I'll take another look at the database."

Knowing how full the deputy's schedule probably was, Cady appreciated the offer, even while she didn't pin her hopes on it. "Thanks. I'll see you later."

She got up and retrieved her weapon and credentials, then selected a jacket from the hall closet. She'd give her mom a call on the way to see how her day was going. Locking the door behind her, she jogged down the front steps and made a mental note to call Dr. Baker tomorrow.

Hero raced up to her, the toy in his jaws, and trotted along at her side until she reached the Jeep, when he loped back to the other side of the house. Temperatures had returned to a more normal midforties. The light snow on the ground had already disappeared. He'd enjoy the time outside and probably be a muddy mess when she got back. With any luck, he'd lose the damn clown in the muck before she returned.

Marshall was a historic town nestled between the Appalachians and the French Broad River. The sheriff's office was a newish building and one she hadn't had occasion to visit. She rang the buzzer at the door in the rear of the building and waited a couple of minutes for someone to answer it.

"Cady Maddix?"

She offered up her credentials, to which the deputy gave a cursory glance.

"The lieutenant is expecting you. Follow me."

She trailed him silently through the building to the detention center, where he turned her over to the lieutenant. "Marshal." Goldman got up from behind a desk to greet her. "I alerted the jailers. Your guest of honor should be ready. I'll show you to the conference room."

"Thank you." As they walked, he continued. "Sorry I never got back to that database. They brought in two dozen extended family members from a reunion that turned violent. Over a college basketball game, no less."

"That's okay. I'll take a look at it myself when I'm done with Gosch, if you don't mind."

"I'll keep the jailer posted outside until you're done." Goldman stopped at a door on his left. A female jailer in her midforties stood next to it. "Gosch shouldn't give you any problems, but holler if you need help." He opened the door to the room, and Cady saw the occupant sitting at a table inside wearing a bright-orange jumpsuit with shackles on his wrists and ankles.

"I appreciate it. Thanks."

She entered the space and pulled out a chair opposite the inmate. The door closed behind her. "Evan Gosch?" She sat. "I'm Deputy US Marshal Cady Maddix."

"Well, day-um." Gosch flashed a smile, revealing a missing upper incisor. "No one said my visitor was a woman. Guess my luck is changing."

"I have a few questions for you, Mr. Gosch."

"Call me Evan, sweetheart."

Her gaze narrowed. "You can call me Deputy Marshal. You've been an inmate of the county before, haven't you?"

He lifted his manacled hands to scratch his grizzled jaw. "Been here a few times, nothing serious."

"In fact, you were here seven years ago." She recited the date for him.

His mouth twisted. "I don't keep a diary. I might've been."

"Do you recall the names of any other inmates here then?"

"Swee—Marshal, seven years ago? My memory ain't that good."

"A man named Bruce Forrester was also locked up at that time." Cady took a picture of Forrester from her pocket and slid it across the table to Gosch. "Do you remember him?"

He tapped the photo once. "Yeah. Yeah, I do. Mostly 'cuz I heard 'bout what he done later. Killing that kid and all. Knew at the time there was something wrong with him. Did he molest the boy before he killed him?"

Cady blinked. "Why would you ask that?"

Gosch leaned forward, lowering his voice. "There was this other guy in here at the time. Byrd. He was kept isolated, in his own cell, as far away from us as possible. Sort of funny, he was a bird in a cage, get it?" Finding no answering amusement in Cady's expression, he went on. "I figured he done something big, but then one of the guys said he was one of them pedos."

"A pedophile?"

"Yeah. So some of the guys were yelling things, y'know. 'Bout what you'd 'spect. Jailer came in to quiet us down a time or two, but then it'd start up again. There were just a few of us in there until late the next night when a whole shit ton of people got hauled in. Jailers shifted people around some, but Forrester, he *asks* to cell with him." Gosch sat back, gave her a knowing look. "Forrester is one of them guys you give a wide berth. What would he want with someone like Byrd? The rest of us, we just waited, expecting a bloodbath. Ain't no one got time for a fucking pedo, and we figured Forrester would half kill him before the jailers could separate them again."

That was the impression Cady had formed of the man as well. "But he didn't?"

Gosch shook his head slowly. "Nope. Byrd acted afraid of Forrester at first, but pretty soon, they had their heads together, whispering. And that's how it was until I got released. They was always just talking real low, like the best of buds. Only thing I can figure, Forrester might have the same interest in little kids that Byrd did. Wouldn't be surprised. Some guys act tough but they're really just perverts in the end."

The man's impression of Forrester rocked her. Nothing she'd learned so far had indicated that particular paraphilia. She tucked it away and probed the prisoner for a few more minutes. Finally deciding he had nothing more of interest to share, she slipped the picture back in her pocket and rose. "Thank you for your time, Mr. Gosch."

He shrugged. "I got nothing but time in here."

She left the room and found her way back to Goldman's office. He jumped up when he saw her in his open doorway. "You still want to look at those old records?"

"I don't think *want* is the operative word, but yeah." He rounded his desk and showed her to an empty cubicle and turned on the computer there. While she waited for him to bring up the database, she asked, "So you were around when Forrester was arrested back then?"

"Sure was."

"Gosch recalled there was someone in jail at the time by the name of Byrd. He claimed the man was a pedophile."

The deputy straightened. "That I don't remember, but you'll be able to verify it in these old arrest records."

Her gaze went beyond him to the screen he'd brought up. "He said something else. That Forrester requested to be placed in a cell with Byrd. He seemed to think that meant he might have similar interests."

Goldman snorted. "Forrester? He'd be more likely to beat the hell out of the guy. We keep the sexual offenders by themselves if we can. No one has time for a kid molester. Even dirtbags have a pecking order. If Forrester was placed in a cell with Byrd, that would have been a violation of protocol. But it was before my time supervising the detention center." He proceeded to explain how to find the call and visitor logs she was interested in and excused himself.

Cady sank into the seat in front of the computer and immersed herself in the task at hand. It was tedious, but after a couple of hours, she'd gotten the information she'd been looking for. Gosch had been correct in some of his recollections. The number of inmates did explode the second night Forrester was locked up. And Reginald Byrd was an inmate at the same time.

She made a depressingly long list of names of people who had been locked up during the duration Forrester was there before checking the logs. The only person who'd called or visited Forrester was his public defender.

She got up and stopped by the lieutenant's office to thank him before making her way back to the parking lot. As she got into her Jeep, she noticed the jailer she'd seen earlier grinding something beneath the toe of her boot and heading back toward the building. Cady returned the woman's wave before turning on the Jeep's swivel-mounted laptop.

It took only a few minutes' search to find a Reginald Byrd on the sexual offender registry, still living in town. She took another half hour to read about the man's arrest, trial, and sentencing before setting out for his home. Cady found the address easily, a small, neat white home with green storms in grave need of paint. Spying a gentleman shuffling toward the house from the detached garage, she got out of the vehicle. "Excuse me. I'm looking for Reginald Byrd."

His guarded look might have been from being accosted by a stranger. Or perhaps he'd acquired it in prison.

She drew closer and presented her credentials. His expression closed. "Don't you people have better things to do than pester a dying man?"

Slipping the ID back into her coat pocket, she reassessed him. She knew he was in his midfifties but his face was haggard, the skin gray and sagging.

"I just want to ask you a few questions, and then I'll be on my way," she promised.

Byrd moved slowly past her, his gait torturously slow. "We can talk inside. I need to sit down."

Minutes later, Cady was seated in a darkened room in the house. It smelled musty, an odor derived not from uncleanliness but age. It reminded her, oddly, of her grandfather's home. The place had seemed to absorb the man's bitterness, exuding a stale scent of recrimination and disappointment. The recollection swiped across her nape like an icy finger.

"How long have you been out of prison?" she asked bluntly.

With sluggish movements, he shed his coat and took off the stocking hat, revealing a bald head. In the photo she'd seen on the database, he'd had thick gray hair and a mustache. He looked as though he'd aged twenty years since it was taken.

"Three months." He eased himself into a chair. "Got released just in time to go home and die. Stage-four liver cancer. Already spread to my lungs. Maybe if my treatment had been more aggressive in prison, it wouldn't have gotten this far." The acrimony in his tone would be difficult to miss. "And you don't give a shit about that. What do you want? I've been harassed by about every law enforcement agency there is."

She supposed she should have more compassion for a dying man. But after reading a bit about his conviction for possession and receipt of child pornography, she was hard-pressed to find any. Cady made sure her voice was impassive when she said, "When you were first arrested, you were taken to the county detention center in Marshall."

"You asking or telling?" Byrd said with the first hint of spirit he'd shown.

She went on. "There was a man by the name of Bruce Forrester locked up at the same time." Recognition flickered across his expression. "You two ended up in the same cell. I'm told you grew friendly."

The man snorted. "Nothing friendly about a guy like Forrester. He was a brute. A thug."

"Which makes me wonder what the two of you talked about while you shared that cell."

Byrd's gaze slid away.

"Did he share your interest in child pornography?"

He was silent a long time. "Maybe. I thought so. He kept asking questions about where I'd found it. How the deep web worked. How to get on the Tor network. How the forums were set up on the websites I visited. How I stayed anonymous."

That last was ironic, given that Byrd had been swept up in an FBI cyber investigation and his real identity discovered. "Why do you think Forrester was interested in those topics?"

Byrd shrugged. "I was less concerned about that than staying alive. People like me don't do well in jail, Marshal. If answering his questions meant he wasn't going to pound on me, I was relieved enough to tell him whatever he wanted to know."

"Have you seen or heard from him since then?"

"No. Why would I?"

After a couple more minutes of questioning, the man's fatigue was easy to read. She handed Byrd one of her cards and rose. "If you should see or hear from Bruce Forrester, give me a call."

She got as far as the door before he spoke again. "I never laid a finger on a child that way, you know. Not my nieces or nephews. Not a neighborhood child. All I did was . . . look."

Revulsion snaked down her spine. Cady turned. "And how many kids were exploited so people like you could pay to 'look'? Seek absolution from your pastor. You won't get it from me."

Chapter 12

It was just after six that evening when Cady's phone buzzed. Ryder's voice sounded in her ear. "Pizza."

"When?"

"Forty minutes."

"I'll be there. Do I need to bring pain relief ointment for the aftermath of nephew-uncle warfare?"

"Only if that's a euphemism for an intimate massage."

"Not sure I'm the right person for that." A bit of the day's tension seeped from her shoulders at their banter. "I have a tendency to rub people the wrong way." His laugh had her lips curving. "See you soon." She disconnected and rose to set her laptop on the couch. She'd been poring over the digital case file long enough to have her eyes burning. A break sounded perfect.

"C'mon, Hero." The dog lazily got up from beside her chair and stretched. "We've got a dinner invite, and it'd be rude to show up empty-handed."

Thirty-five minutes later, she and the dog arrived in Ryder's drive as the pizza delivery man was pulling away from the curb. Ryder waited for them to enter the house before shoving the door closed with his foot.

"Beer." She held up the six-pack she carried.

"A perfect companion to any meal."

She followed him to the kitchen as Hero loped over to Sadie's side. "Your house doesn't show the devastation one would expect from two small boys."

"I've had time to shovel through the mess." Ryder served up two slices apiece on each of their plates and pulled out stools from the counter.

Cady twisted off the tops to a couple of bottles and handed him one, carrying the other to her seat. Sitting, she reached for a slice. "I haven't eaten since breakfast. You've been warned. When did the troops leave?"

"About four. I have new sympathy for my mom, who usually hosts them. Must take her a week to pick up afterwards."

"Maybe she just pretended to be painting the interior of her house."

"Wouldn't blame her." He took a bite of pizza. Chewed. A moment later, he said, "She sort of dropped a bomb on my sister and me. Told us she's in the process of becoming a foster parent."

Cady's gaze flew to his. "Really? And you didn't know anything about it before?"

He shook his head. "She's a softy. I guess I can see why foster parenting would appeal. But there's a lot of heartache in the job too."

"And you'd like to protect her from that." Cady could understand the sentiment. She spent a lot of time doing the same for her own mother.

"Yeah. Don't get me wrong—any kid would be lucky to land with her. But how is she going to handle it when they go back to their homes? Or when they're adopted?"

"She could do a lot of good." Instead of foster care, she'd landed with an emotionally abusive grandfather. Cady knew from personal experience how much damage the wrong placement could inflict on a child. "You're right. Kids would be fortunate to live with her. But I understand your concern."

They watched the dogs' antics as they ate. "I expected you to have a word with Sadie about her gifting choices," Ryder said. "I see Hero brought the clown with him."

"I'm convinced she gave it to him because it freaked her out to have it around." With delicate greed, Cady made short work of the first slice of pizza. Picked up the second from her plate. "I had hopes of him losing it in the mud today, but no such luck."

Between them, they polished off the entire pie before spending a mindless couple of hours watching TV. It was difficult for Cady to ever completely relax. But she leaned companionably against him on the couch while they drank their beers and poked fun at a pointless reality show. She'd never understand the appeal of watching a bunch of strangers' manufactured drama play out on the small screen. She got more than enough of that in her job.

"Do you have online access for law enforcement to check old inmate information in your county?" she asked suddenly.

"Yeah, why?" He turned to look at her.

Instead of answering, she said, "How far back does it go?"

"I'm not sure. Ten years or so. Well before I became sheriff, anyway."

Which meant the former sheriff had implemented it. Butch Talbot, Ryder's father. Cady mentally dodged the memories that name elicited. "What about the older records? Are they digitized?"

"Yes. It's been a process." His expression was quizzical. "My dad had them on microfilm, and we've since converted them to Digital ReeL. That's an imaging service that scans the files so they integrate with our records management system. They're text searchable now. Half the basement is full of file cabinets because Dad maintained paper files as well. I've had Stacy—she works the front desk—slowly matching the old files to those on Digital ReeL. If anything's missing, she scans it into the system. Then the physical paperwork is destroyed. Eventually we'll be paper-free, but it's a huge time suck."

Cady went silent for a moment, reluctance filtering through her. She'd spent a lifetime building her inner defenses brick by brick until they were fortress strong. But lowering those walls didn't come easily. Intimate exchanges were expected in a "normal" relationship. She was still uncertain how she'd found herself in one.

Her gaze remained fixed on the TV screen. "We've never discussed it," she finally said, still not looking at him. "But being from the area, you've probably heard about my childhood."

Although she didn't look at him, she was aware of Ryder carefully setting his empty bottle on the end table. "My investigator, Jerry Garza, mentioned it when we were working the Aldeen case. I was a few years older than you in school. Never recall hearing about it when I was a kid."

Cady gave a humorless laugh. "I wish I could say the same about my classmates. I bounced in and out of school districts a lot, including the one here. You could say the event sort of defined my childhood." *Defined my life,* she mentally corrected herself. It didn't take a psychologist to understand that her path to the USMS Academy had been paved by the marshals' failure to apprehend her father for bank robbery.

She slipped her thumbnail under the bottle's label, loosening it. "I don't remember much of the scene. And I can't be sure whether the recollections I have are mine or planted by others' retellings." When she'd peeled off the label, she busied herself folding it into little squares. "But my mom had an episode yesterday and mentioned something. I'm unsure whether what she said is new information or the result of her confusion. So I'd like to look at the case file. The incident report and the statements. See if there's anything there that wasn't released to the press."

"If we get an early start tomorrow, you might even have time to look in the morning."

The tightness in her chest eased a bit at his words. He was making it easy for her. Cady was well aware of how often he did so.

"People might start to talk, though," he added. She met his gaze. Recognized the wicked gleam in his eye. "They could say your primary interest in me is my musty archives."

She smiled, as he'd meant her to. Her free hand sneaked over to cup him intimately. "I'd never refer to your 'archives' as musty. And given your looks, I'm sure most people would realize that my interest in you is purely sexual."

Chapter 13

They'd gotten an early start Monday morning, one that would have been even earlier if Cady hadn't let Ryder convince her that showering together would be more economical. It was still dark when they pulled into the parking lot of Haywood County's law enforcement center. In the daylight, it was the spectacular backdrop of the Blue Ridge Mountains behind the building that would draw the eye. But right now, Cady doubted even that would have distracted her. Her entire life—in one way or another—hinged on an event she could barely recall. Her most vivid memories were from the nightmares that plagued her, which further muddied her memory. Police incident reports and witness statements could be relied on to supply fact without the accompanying emotion.

That didn't account for the trepidation that was knotting her gut. Best-case scenario was the reports would color in specifics to the scene that had haunted—and eluded—her for years.

But they would also supply her subconscious with even more details with which to torment her.

"Shouldn't take us too long to pull up the file." Ryder unlocked the door and ushered her inside. "I've got a coffee maker in the office preprogrammed. Want to grab a cup?"

She shook her head. "I still have to pick up Hero at your place, go home and change, and get to work." Allen didn't hound them about their hours, and she'd put in extra time yesterday. But she had a full day ahead of her. Tina Bandy would likely have heard that she'd spoken to Dylan. Making another attempt to talk to the woman was a priority.

Ryder greeted the few employees present and led Cady to his office. Her gaze immediately went to the area behind his desk where the portrait of Butch Talbot had once hung. It'd been replaced with one of Ryder and his staff standing in front of the building.

When he sat down behind his desk and turned on his computer, she moved to the coffee maker he'd mentioned and poured him a cup. Set it next to him.

"Huh. Weird." He frowned at the computer screen. "Your dad's name doesn't come up when I search. Your mom's does, though."

"My mom?" Cady looked over his shoulder. This was news to her. "For what?"

She scanned the documents as Ryder brought them up. "Looks like she made a complaint six years ago. A former associate of Lonny's looked her up. Made some threats."

They exchanged a glance. Six years ago, Cady had been assigned to the Saint Louis office. "She never mentioned a thing." It was a kick to the chest to realize just how much her mom had kept from her over the years. How much she'd struggled through on her own. Ryder flipped to another document, and she began reading. Stan Caster. The name rang a bell, although she couldn't put her finger on the memory.

"Caster was Lonny's accomplice in the bank robberies they were charged with."

Of course. She'd read his name online, as well as the details of the crime. Earlier in his criminal career, Lonny Maddix had confined himself to petty larceny. B and Es. But bank robbery had elicited a federal warrant.

"So what happened?" He was scrolling through the file too quickly for her to follow along.

"Not much more in here. Caster seemed to think Lonny had hidden the money and wanted it. Most of it was never recovered. He was picked up after your mom called in. The incident landed him back in prison for a parole violation. It'd be interesting to know if he's still inside."

Her gut clenched. The problem with sticking her hand into the darkness of the past was she never knew what she was going to find.

"What year did your dad die? Maybe I can pull up that case by date."

Cady told him. A moment later, she added, "It was March." She'd turned four a month earlier. What did most people remember from that age? Birthday parties? A family pet? Most of the memories from her earliest years had always remained stubbornly blank.

He remained intent on the screen for fifteen minutes before looking up with a puzzled frown. "That's weird. I can't find any information about it at all, and I cross-referenced search terms." He sat for a moment, thinking. "I guess it's possible some files got missed when my dad had them put on microfiche." He grabbed the cup she'd poured for him. "C'mon. Maybe those damn files in the basement will come in handy after all." She followed him out of the office toward the front door.

The entrance to the basement was inside the foyer of the building. Ryder unlocked the door and snapped on the light. Once downstairs, she could see that the vast majority of the area was taken up by storage. At least a third of it was devoted to file cabinets.

"How far has Stacy gotten with the file comparison?"

"The most recent decade or so." He searched the labels on the cabinets until he found the year in question. Then he pulled out a drawer. Began to thumb through the folders.

She watched him for a few minutes. When he slammed that drawer shut and opened the next, Cady turned away. Tension had been growing inside her since entering the building, and it was crying for release. She had to move.

She'd gotten only a few steps before she came face-to-face with a large framed photo leaning against the wall. Butch Talbot. When Ryder identified it the first time she'd visited his office, she'd finally had a name to go with a snippet of memory that occasionally surfaced before becoming fuzzy and indistinct.

She'd been about six. Cold beneath the too-thin blanket that covered her bed. She'd slipped out of it and padded barefoot to the kitchen. She could still feel the chilly plank floor beneath her bare feet. Cady could see the girl she'd been standing in the doorway of the kitchen. She couldn't peg which house it had been. There'd been different ones every year, with enough similarities to meld together. All had cracked linoleum. Sagging countertops. Unreliable appliances.

And that night, a man had been sitting in one of the kitchen chairs, with her mom on his lap. His uniform shirt was partially unbuttoned and his hand was inside Hannah's blouse. Shock and fear had held Cady rooted in place.

Her mom had tried to rise. The man's arm tightened around her, preventing it. Hannah had brushed the hair back from her face and attempted a smile. "Go on back to bed, baby. I'll see you in the morning."

But she hadn't moved. Couldn't.

"You heard your mama. Get."

The man's rumbling tone had held a command, one the child in her recognized and obeyed. She'd run back to her bedroom and dove under the covers.

Seeing this portrait in Ryder's office months earlier had been a shock. She'd since learned that while Ryder worshipped his mother, he was more closemouthed about his father. She had the impression their relationship had been difficult. She recalled him saying Butch and Laura Talbot had celebrated their fortieth anniversary before his death. Which meant the day Cady saw him in their kitchen with her mom, he'd been married.

"How long was your dad the sheriff here?"

Ryder's head was bent over another drawer's contents. "Thirty-five years or so, I think. Deputy for a few years before that."

So he'd been in office when he'd carried on an affair with Cady's mom. There was no reason to share that memory with Ryder. No reason for her dysfunctional childhood to splash its darkness onto his, which, despite the problems, looked to have been fairly normal in comparison.

Normal was not an adjective that remotely applied to her past.

"Well, shit," he said as he straightened from the bottom drawer of a cabinet. "I've gone through two of these and can't find the case file. I tried the year before, as well, thinking it might have gotten misfiled."

"Oh." Was that relief mingling with disappointment? She was nothing if not a study in contrasts.

"It's got to be in one of them. How much time do you have this morning?"

"Not much more." She pulled out her cell and looked at the time. "Not any," she amended. "I appreciate you looking, though."

They headed for the stairs. He turned off the lights in the basement before they ascended. "I'll have Stacy check for it."

"All right." Her cell buzzed in her coat pocket. Taking it out, she saw "State Bureau of Investigation" on the screen. "Sorry, I have to take this." They entered the foyer, and Ryder relocked the door as she answered. "Maddix."

He gave a nod of understanding. "See you later." His casual pat on her ass would have earned him an elbow to the gut if he wasn't already moving out of range. Judging from his expression as he strolled away, he knew it too.

The voice on the other end pushed all thought aside. "Marshal? This is Tina Bandy. You and me need to talk."

Chapter 14

"I'd hoped to find you home when I was here Friday." With a sense of déjà vu, Cady stepped inside the door into the small dark hall where she'd first spoken to Dylan.

"I work most days."

Cady's first thought was the last five years had been unkind to Tina Bandy. In the interview clip, the woman had looked jaded. That edge was more pronounced now. She was still slight, with the same partially grown-out dyed blonde hair. But creases bracketed the woman's mouth, and new wrinkles fanned from the corners of her eyes.

Tina studied her. "You ain't what I pictured."

Unsure what to do with that statement, Cady ignored it. "As I told Dylan, I'm working the warrants for Bruce Forrester. I wanted to get both of your perspectives about the investigation to this point."

Tina narrowed her heavily made-up blue eyes. "What the hell is that supposed to mean? Damn state and local cops are worthless— that's my *perspective*. Five fucking years and all they got to show for it is two more dead kids and adding a Fed to the mess? How the hell is that s'posed to help? We've moved four times. Forrester keeps finding us. So my perspective is maybe you could figure out how that keeps happening."

While the investigation hadn't come up with definitive proof that the man was behind the teens' homicides, Tina appeared convinced of it. "How do *you* think he's found you every time?" She'd posed the same question to Dylan, and while his answer was improbable, it was at least reasonable.

Tina moved closer, her expression ugly. "You think we're doing something to lead a killer straight to us, time after time?"

The woman was as volatile as she'd been in the clip. "No, I'm asking for an opinion." Although Tina had touched on a possibility. The most likely explanation was a leak in the investigation or one inside the family. *There are infinite ways to leave tracks,* Cady mused as she watched the woman mentally wrestle with the question. It could be as simple as trusting the wrong person. Being careless with what they said and whom they spoke to. But a continual lack of caution would be mind-boggling, especially with the SBI agents advising and monitoring them.

Tina turned away, crossing her arms over her chest. "He musta been a bigger dealer than anyone ever knew. Guys like that can have spies all over."

Cady hadn't gotten that impression of the man's network, but she made a mental note to check with DEA agent Weddig, who would be delving into that side of Forrester's past. "Would he have known about your sister? That's the first place you went, right?"

"Right. Tami. Christ, I need a cigarette." Tina walked into the living area and picked up a pack from an end table. Lit it and walked back, inhaling deeply. "We stayed with her in Greensboro first off. Until Dylan saw Forrester in that truck and another kid ended up dead."

"Did your sister know Bruce Forrester?"

Tina choked before exhaling. "Tami? Only if she met him in one of her bible classes. Truth is, we'd have been heading out even if Forrester hadn't shown up. Me and my sister don't exactly have the same views on things."

Cady could imagine. She discounted Tina's idea of Forrester having a vast network of informants. But family. That would have been easy enough for him to discover through any mutual acquaintances in Hope Mills. Tina had frequented the bar scene. Regulars or even bartenders might have overheard that information.

"Do you stay in contact with your sister?"

"Some." Tina lifted a shoulder. "Like I say, we don't have much in common. But she don't know where we are. Agents said not to tell no one, not even family. It's not like she'd want to come visiting."

"What about your parents?"

"My mom's dead. Going on fifteen years now. Pancreatic cancer. My old man took off when I was young. No idea what happened to him."

"And other siblings?"

"It's just Tami and me." She drew deeply on the cigarette again. Blew a perfect ring.

"Is there anyone in Hope Mills you stay in touch with?"

She shook her head. "Friends I had there ain't the staying-in-touch type. 'Sides, the agents said no on that too."

"Has Dylan maintained contact with any friends?"

"How, by carrier pigeon? We don't got internet, and he don't got a phone. Just the one SBI gave 'im, and since they pay the bill, it's for emergencies only. He added your number to it, like you told him."

"What about school?" From what Dylan had said, Cady had the distinct impression he was avoiding making friends there. Which had her wondering about his emotional state.

"I dunno. He don't mention no one. And he don't go nowhere." She stabbed a finger toward Cady. "And that's the only reason I wanted to talk to you today. Dylan was in a bad way when the cops found him after Trevor's murder. He was barely able to talk at first. Shrink said he was in one of them fog states."

It took Cady a moment to interpret. "A fugue state?"

Tina jutted her chin. "What I said, ain't it? For years after, he had bad headaches. Now those are better, but I'm still worried about my kid, and not just when it comes to getting his head blowed off. This life he's living ain't exactly normal, and he's a regular teenager. I don't know how much more of this he can take. He's jittery as a cat on its ninth life. He knows what's gonna happen if Forrester finds us. First, he'll take out the only witness to Trevor Boster's murder, right? And I'm not so sure he'll stop there. From what I know about him, he might just wipe out the whole family while he's at it."

Chapter 15

Dylan hunched behind his school laptop in American history class and did the same search he did every Monday. First, he googled Forrester's name. Then Trev's. Then his own. It was stupid. If there was anything new, he'd probably hear about it before the media would. But he couldn't help himself. The agents never gave them in-depth info about the case. They mostly did what that marshal had. Asked questions. Told them what to do.

He closed out of one search window and opened another. Maddix hadn't been bossy, though. She'd listened. Probably the only one who had since they'd moved here. He cast a gaze around to peg how close Mr. Lawson was. They were supposed to be working on their paper for the class. "How America's Founding Principles Manifest Themselves in Current Times." Typical school bullshit. It sucked how the only hours he got out of the house were when he was at school, which he hated anyway. Bouncing from one district to another meant walking into buildings every day where he didn't know anyone. And after what had happened to Ethan and Chad Bahlman, it was best to keep it that way.

But for all the time he spent alone at home, somehow it was lonelier at school with a bunch of strangers around. And that was seriously messed up.

Lawson was bent over a student several seats up, so Dylan went back to his search. He was always careful to delete the history afterward. IT gathered the computers sometimes to upload new firewalls or just for random checks that students weren't violating the code-of-use policy.

He scrolled quickly, noting nothing new in the articles that popped up. There never was and that was a good thing, he guessed. His name hadn't been mentioned, even in the first ones back when Trevor was killed. His throat went tight, the way it always did when he thought of his friend. If Dylan hadn't insisted, they'd never have gone to the creek that night. Maybe he and Trev would still be friends. Maybe even living in those same houses.

One thing was sure; Trev would still be alive.

My fault. My fault. My fault. The words pounded in his brain, a familiar mantra. Didn't matter what anyone said. The only reason Trevor had been at the creek that night was because of Dylan. A familiar throb started in his temple. It happened every time he remembered what happened back then. He used to think if he concentrated hard enough, thought long enough, he'd be able to come up with the exact detail the cops needed to find Forrester. The pain shifted then and took up residence behind one eye. Blinking rapidly, he forced his mind elsewhere before it turned into a full-blown migraine. He didn't have medicine for the headaches anymore. He'd run out, but Dylan hadn't told his mom. He knew what a hassle it always was to find a new doctor, and they didn't have the money, anyway.

The doctor he'd seen those first few days taught him about positive association. So whenever the memories started the pain, he'd fix on that rope swing they'd seen in the clearing before Forrester chased them.

Dylan imagined what would have happened if it'd just been him and Trev in that clearing, taking turns and swinging through the trees out over the creek, not a care in the world.

He caught a blur of movement from the corner of his eye and deftly closed the window, leaving the one visible with the search results for the Bill of Rights Institute.

"How are you coming on your sources, Dylan?"

The blank notebook next to him was a dead giveaway, so he shrugged. "Not good. I mean, I know where to get information on the Bill of Rights and the Constitution. I don't really get the rest of the assignment, though."

"Apparently, you're not alone there." Lawson grinned. He wasn't bad, for a teacher. He was sorta young, with a beard and framed glasses. This was the lamest assignment he'd ever given.

"All right." Turning toward the class, he announced, "Odd-numbered rows, move your desk to the left. Other left, Brian." Some kids laughed. There was a lot of scraping of chairs. Dylan counted over. His was an even row. Which meant . . . He eyed the girl who shifted her desk toward his.

"Hey. I'm Grace." She smiled at him. "You're kind of new, right? I mean, you didn't start the year here?"

He shook his head. He wasn't good with girls. He never knew what to say, and it wasn't like they tripped over themselves to talk to him, either. "I'm Dylan."

"I know. This assignment is the worst. Maybe having a partner will help."

"Share the pain."

She laughed. "Right?" She pushed her long hair back over her shoulder, revealing triple piercings in her ear. Dylan never understood why girls did that. Why wasn't one enough? She also had a stud on the side of her nose that was so small, he'd almost missed it. Which raised more questions.

"Okay, folks, listen up. You're partnered for the rest of the assignment. You have the next two days to work on finding sources."

There was a chorus of cheers from the students. Dylan slid a glance at Grace. "So how d'you want to do this? You look up founding principles and I look for the rest?"

"I think that's why I got stuck earlier. We need a better way. I wrote down a list of the basic principles." She handed her notebook to him to scan. "I think we also need to be careful of partisan bias when we look for sources."

"You still speaking English?" She had a dimple on one side that showed when she smiled. Dylan found himself fascinated with it. She wasn't pretty, exactly, but her personality made up for that. Bubbly.

She shoved lightly at his shoulder. "You know. Make sure they aren't political. Too far right or too left."

What he knew about politics he could fit on the head of a pin. But he was willing to take her word for it. "Yeah, you're right."

"Here. Copy this URL and start there, and I'm going to head in another direction."

While he obeyed, she said, "Were you at Merrick's party last weekend?"

Dylan's weekend had definitely not included a party. Party of one, maybe. "No idea who Merrick is."

"I'm pretty sure half the people there didn't know him. It was packed. I thought maybe you were there and I missed you." She had no trouble keeping up a running conversation and working at the same time. She was typing, scrolling, scanning articles, closing out of them, and going on to the next. Dylan was still on the first one that had popped up on the page.

"It got totally out of control. People were puking all over, and someone broke a window. That's when I left. I knew it was going to get raided, and my parents would strap a shock collar on me if they found out I was there."

He stopped pretending to work. "Did it? Get raided?"

Her dimple flashed again. "That's what I was going to ask you. But yeah, I think so. I saw police cars going in that direction while I was walking to a friend's house before calling for a ride."

He could just imagine what the local cops would have to say if they found him at a kegger. Davis and Rebedeau would lose their shit. His mom's reaction would be far worse. A familiar dark cloud of depression settled over him. Hanging out with friends, dating, parties . . . that was normal high school. Nothing about his life was normal. Sometimes he thought it never would be.

"When's your study hall?" Grace asked.

He told her, and she shook her head. "I'm in chorus then. Maybe we could work on this after school."

"I'm a busser." But the thought of being alone with Grace, talking while they worked, was a hell of a lot more appealing than going home to an empty house. Almost anything would be. He mentally calculated how far it would be to walk home. Too damn far.

"Shit, you poor thing. I would be, too, if my mom worked." She rolled her eyes. "She thinks the bus is too dangerous, because she watches too much talk TV. Anyway, she could drop you at your place after. Or better yet, you could come over and we'd work at my house. And snack. I'm absolutely starved after school."

Temptation nearly swamped him. It was like Grace was offering everything missing in his life in one neat package. Mutiny rose inside him. What harm would it do? He could direct her mom to another house, a road over from his. Then, when they left, he'd cut across the field to his place. Everyone else in his family had a life. Walked around free as birds.

It was like there was an angel on one shoulder and a horned beast on the other, each whispering in his ear. And he knew which one he should listen to. As hard as it was to admit, he really had no choice. He opened his mouth to answer. But what came out was, "Sounds good."

Chapter 16

Cady went through the security check to get into the parking lot at the federal courthouse and made the call to the doctor, leaving a message. Then she headed inside. Dylan had ID'd Charles Weber and Stephen Tillis as being in the woods five years ago. Setting up conversations with them felt more pressing at the moment than did tracking down the seventy-plus inmates who had been in the Madison County jail at the same time as Forrester. Almost anything would.

She mentally chastised herself for not hitting a drive-through on the way to work. Once inside, Cady did a detour by the coffee machine and found it nearly empty. Her mood notched darker. All in all, it'd been an inauspicious start to her day. Going without caffeine was merely the clincher.

She spent an hour at her desk following up on Simmons's story about Gordy the Ghost. Cady sat back in her chair, troubled. She'd gotten Gordon Melbourne's name from the prison officials, but her attempt to track down the man had been fruitless. Melbourne had gotten out a year after Bruce Forrester, but the last sighting of him had been three months after his release. His family had filed a missing persons report on him around that time. It didn't prove Simmons was right about Forrester's revenge plot against the man, but it was concerning.

Cady went to Allen's office, where she stuck her head inside the door. "I'm heading over to Wilson to interview one of the bandit's old drug associates."

He waved her inside without lifting his gaze from his paperwork. After a few moments, he looked up. "Wilson. That's four hours away. You wouldn't get there until midafternoon."

"Four and a half, but yeah. I know where he's working, and I've verified he's there now."

"Sit down. Catch me up."

Cady dropped into a chair in front of his desk and gave the supervisor a rundown of how she'd spent her weekend. "I'm starting to get a picture of Forrester," she concluded. "But I'm not quite sure how all the pieces fit together. Byrd's statement is sort of an outlier. I want to check it out with people who knew Forrester. I'm trying to get a better idea of what motivates him."

"Sounds sensible. You won't get back until well after hours. Why don't you wait until tomorrow?"

"Cassie Zook has already been missing six weeks," she reminded him. "And then there's the boy. Dylan Castle. The last five years of his life have been put on hold. Both of them deserve some urgency in this case."

"All right. Take Rodriguez with you."

"Okay." She rose and went to find Miguel. He'd be thrilled to learn he wasn't going to make it home much before eight tonight.

Shit. Neither was she. Cady pulled out her cell and texted a familiar message to Ryder. Having him step in for dog duty was getting to be a habit. She'd done the same for him but much less frequently. When she finished, she slipped the cell in her pocket and stopped in front of Miguel's desk.

"I talked to Gant. You're with me. Road trip."

He looked up from his computer and clasped his hands prayerfully. "Mom. Are we finally going to Disney?"

She stifled a grin while she grabbed her coat and packed up her laptop. Unlocked the drawer of her desk and took out her purse. "Not quite. But if you're good, I promise to get you some Mickey Mouse ears."

When they were heading across the parking lot, she dug in her pocket and withdrew the keys. She threw them to him after unlocking the Jeep. "You can drive. I control the temperature and the radio."

"I know the rules." He did. But it paid to remind him. "Want to give me a summary of the warrant?"

"I will on the way." She'd also make a stab at tracking down the dozens of arrestees from the time Forrester was in jail in Marshall. Four and a half hours there and back. She heaved a mental sigh. But it was better than wasting office time on the chore. "Let's find a drive-through first. I'm going to need a gallon of coffee."

Chapter 17

Cady eyed Charles aka Charlie Weber as he gulped from a can of soda he'd grabbed on the way out of the building. "So you've been out for . . . how long?" He was about five eight, with a face like a road map, despite being only in his midforties. Prison aged people, she supposed. He looked like he'd spent his time inside bulking up.

"Got out couple of years ago. Thereabouts."

Eighteen months, according to the file. Although Weber had initially lied on his statements to the Cumberland County sheriff's office, he'd eventually become more forthcoming about the details of Forrester's drug operation. His cooperation had earned him a deal from law enforcement. Five years, of which he'd served 60 percent.

"We're here to ask you about Bruce Forrester," she began. "Have you heard from him since your arrest in Hope Mills?"

Weber squinted, as if the question required a major source of brainpower. "No. Why the hell would I?"

"Did he ever mention places he's lived? Places he'd like to visit?"

"No." He'd come out without a jacket and seemed perfectly comfortable, despite the wind that whipped around the corner of the building. "Not to me anyway."

"Did he have fetishes? A sexual interest in kids?"

Weber stopped midway in the act of lifting the soda to his lips, his mouth agape as he stared at her. "Him? Guy like that would get killed inside. I don't care what he done, shitting on a guy's reputation like that sucks."

He has a unique concept of right and wrong, Cady mused. "So that's a no. Did he ever mention pornography to you?"

He drained the can and then crushed it in his fist. "What guy don't talk about porn?"

Cady resisted the urge to slant a gaze at Miguel, who stood silently next to her. "You tell me. What'd he talk about?"

Weber shrugged, a quick bounce of his shoulder. "He liked the rougher stuff. Tying chicks up and shit. Wasn't that big a surprise, tell ya the truth. He was the type of dude you don't mess with. You do him wrong, he'll do you twice as bad."

Simmons had said much the same thing. "What do you mean by that?"

"Just that he had a rep. I seen his temper a time or two. Wouldn't want to get on his bad side."

"Ever know anyone who did?"

Weber snorted. "Plenty. Most regretted it after. Heard of one fellow. Jumped him outside a bar with a knife. Cops broke it up, but couple of weeks later, the guy who started it was out on bail and poof." He made a gesture with his fingers.

"He disappeared?"

Lowering his voice, Weber said, "Way I heard it, Forrester caught up to him. Used a chain saw on him, then got rid of the pieces."

The skin on the back of her nape prickled. The story was much too similar to that of Gordon Melbourne. Violence and revenge were recurring themes with Forrester. Dylan had mentioned witnessing Forrester and another man engaged in a knife fight in Hope Mills. She'd track down the other party's name and try to substantiate the rumor.

Cady thought for a moment. Byrd had mentioned the man's interest in the deep web. If Forrester didn't share Byrd's pedophilia, she was
no closer to discovering the reason for his curiosity. "Was he good with
computers?"

"How the hell would I know any of that? I wasn't his guidance
counselor."

"He was running a fair-size drug ring in the area," Miguel put in.
Cady had filled him in on the highlights of the case on the long trip
over. It had given her a break between running down the Madison
County inmates. "That takes some organization."

"I don't know. Loomer seemed more into the geek than Forrester."

Here, at last, was new information. "What makes you say that?"
According to the statements she'd read, Weber had denied knowing
Loomer well.

"I played video games with him a few times. He said he'd made one
once. That he'd done the programming and tried to sell it, but some
company stole his idea." He turned and threw the crushed can toward
a dumpster. It fell well short of it. "Figured he was full of shit, but he
did know a lot about how the games were made. How it worked to get
them online, y'know, where you can play with people who aren't there
with you."

There was a thrum of excitement in Cady's chest. "So *he* was good
with computers?"

"Never saw him with one. But he'd have to be to do programming,
right?"

"And you haven't seen him since you got out of prison?"

"He was one of the lucky ones. Cops never did catch up to him."

"Where'd you play video games together?"

"My place." He pulled his phone out of his pocket to check the
time. A busy man, apparently. "Or sometimes his. He didn't really own
the cabin, I guess. Belonged to an uncle or something."

"Around Hope Mills?"

"I don't recall exactly. Near Vander, that's all I remember."

It was more than he had "remembered" to include in any of the statements he'd given to the investigators, Cady noted. She said as much to Miguel a few minutes later when they were walking back to the vehicle.

He shrugged. "He changed his story a lot in the series of interviews he gave, you said. He doesn't have to keep facts straight anymore. Nothing hangs in the balance for him."

She sent another last look over her shoulder before getting into the vehicle again. Weber hadn't returned to the building. He was standing in the same place, watching them. They got into the Jeep. "Loomer's uncle lives in the Vander area." She recalled the fact from the digital file. "I'll bet that's where they played video games. Let's pay the uncle a visit."

"How far is it?" Miguel started the vehicle.

"An hour or so," she said, purposefully vague.

"We're halfway to Florida already," he muttered, pulling out of the lot. "At this rate, I'll be lucky to get home before work tomorrow."

She knew the man well enough to be familiar with his moods. "Why don't you hit a drive-through and pick up some food on our way out of town?"

Miguel visibly brightened. "Navigate us to the closest one. But that doesn't mean you're off the hook."

"Then I won't bother offering you the toy from my Happy Meal." She did a search on her cell, gave him the route, and then turned her attention to the file on her laptop to look for the number to the Cumberland County sheriff's office. They needed some background on the Loomer relative before arriving on his doorstep.

Chapter 18

Bruce pulled his Malibu into a slot in the Asheville Food Mart parking lot and turned off the ignition. According to the in-dash GPS, there were five of the grocery stores in the city. He scanned the lot, looking for Tina Bandy's beat-up white Impala. His anonymous internet source hadn't found a different vehicle registration in her name. Hopefully that meant she hadn't changed vehicles. He couldn't exactly walk into the store and look for her. Damn places had cameras and security she could call for help.

But if he spotted her car, all he had to do was wait around and follow her home. Catch the whole fam-damily in one place. Then . . . A nasty grin split his face. Then the fun would start.

His TracFone rang. When he read the identity of the caller on the screen, a slow thrum started in his veins. He answered. "Well, well. Been a while."

"I . . . I have news for you. But if I share this, we're even. You leave my family alone."

Too late for that, bitch. The thought remained unspoken. "Look at you, thinkin' you make the rules here."

When the woman on the other end hesitated, he said, "Tell me what you got. I'll tell you what it's worth to me."

"They've added a federal marshal to the hunt for you. A woman. Name of Cady Maddix."

The news hit him like a brick. He cursed mentally. Bringing in a Fed meant either the drug charges had been kicked from state to federal or they knew about the woman he'd snatched. But how could they? There'd been no one else in the parking lot. He'd made sure of that before approaching her. The marshal obviously hadn't learned jack shit, though, or else he'd be behind bars already.

Feds had different tools they could use. He knew that much. Which meant the marshal could be a problem. And a woman, to boot. The fact ignited a little hum in his blood. Some possibilities there. He'd have to think it over.

"So that's worth a lot, right? I might've saved you from getting caught."

"Might be worth something. Don't wipe out the trouble your family's caused me, though." He interrupted the woman's protest with, "What else do you know?" And waited for her to grudgingly give up more details.

"We're even now after this. I don't give a shit what you say."

They were a long way from even. She'd learn that the hard way. "You want to be even? Get me the marshal's address." He hung up on her screech of dismay and returned his gaze to the parking lot. When he didn't find the crappy Impala, he punched in the next address on the GPS. Started the engine. The tedium of the hunt made the final payoff that much more rewarding.

Chapter 19

Stacy appeared in the doorway to Ryder's office. "Much as it pains me to admit it, you were right."

Ryder looked up from the pile of paperwork that seemed to multiply overnight. "About? Oh yeah. The Maddix file."

Stacy stepped farther into his office. "It's not documented in the database. That means it was never on the microfiche at all. Or," she corrected herself, "if it was, it was too damaged to be transferred."

He'd reached a similar conclusion this morning but had double-checked with the vendor for Digital ReeL. The man had said much the same thing. They could digitize only the information given to them. Other files dated around the same time as the Maddix case were present.

"I did some digging. The office started converting paper files older than five years onto microfilm thirty years ago. They stopped about a decade ago because they were planning to upload them to a computer system instead. But nothing got done until you made that decision." From the expression on Stacy's face, he'd gotten her intrigued.

"I can't figure out a way I'd know if any other files are missing."

"Neither can I," she admitted. "But I'll keep checking the newer files downstairs and see if it shows up there."

"Thanks, Stacy." She exited the room, and Ryder leaned back, brooding. After Cady had left this morning, he'd done some online research. The Maddix case would have been big news in these parts. Maybe even across the entire state. Which made it more than a little strange that there was no trace of a file, physical or otherwise.

It was possible that it could have been checked out for some reason when others the same year had been converted, and the mistake had never been caught. Stuff like that happened. It was harder to imagine it being destroyed, however, before double-checking that a microfiche copy existed. Ryder reached for the coffee sitting on his desk and took a sip, wincing when he found it cold.

His dad had died suddenly, from a type of heart attack the pathologist had called the widow-maker. After nearly five years, Butch's clothes remained in the bedroom closet he'd shared with Ryder's mom. His tools still hung on the pegboard in the garage. His car sat next to them, idle. Because Ryder wasn't the type to tell someone else how to grieve, he'd never mentioned any of that to his mom, even if it was a shock to hang up his coat and still find his dad's in the closet.

As usual, thoughts of Butch Talbot brought conflicting emotions. Ryder had long ago come to terms with the fact that loving a person didn't necessarily mean liking him. His parents had had a happy marriage, partially because of the years Ryder had spent protecting his mom from some of her husband's secrets.

He couldn't imagine a reason for his dad having an old file at home, but with Stacy taking care of the search downstairs, he supposed it was worth looking around his mom's house the next time he went by.

Ryder rolled closer to the desk and picked up his pen. If finding that damn file was going to bring Cady some closure, it was worth the effort to locate it.

Chapter 20

Breathing hard, Dylan unlocked the front door and let himself into the house. He'd checked the garage first to make sure his mom's car wasn't in it. She was supposed to be at work. But all sorts of crazy possibilities had flashed through his mind after he'd waved goodbye to Grace and then ran a mile and a half home after her mom had driven away. Tina could have had a squabble with her boss and quit. She could have gotten sick and gone home. There could be cops looking for him right now. The sweat snaking down his back was only partially due to his exertion.

The house was dark when he slipped inside. Quiet. Unconvinced, Dylan did a walk-through, his heart hammering in his chest. Only when he convinced himself that the place was empty did the sense of foreboding lift.

A broad smile crossed his face. He'd gotten clean away with it. He did an enthusiastic fist pump. He couldn't recall the last time he'd done something—gone somewhere—other than school where his mom didn't accompany him. Or the law.

Jubilant, he let his backpack slide down one arm and dropped it on the couch before heading to the kitchen. It'd been weird, being in Grace's house. The place was huge, and almost everything inside was white, black, or glass. But her mom had been okay and didn't hang around like she was worried they'd mess stuff up.

He opened the refrigerator and pulled out a carton of milk. Because no one was around to tell him he couldn't, he chugged it straight out of the carton before wiping his mouth on the shoulder of his jacket and putting the milk away. Then he went to the cupboard and snagged the last bag of chips to take with him into the other room. They'd had plenty to eat after school. Grace's mom had kept offering until Grace told her to leave them alone so they could concentrate. And he hadn't wanted to eat that much there anyway. He didn't want them to think he didn't have manners.

He turned on the TV and settled down on the pillows on the floor in front of it. Grace hadn't just been blowing her mom off, either. They'd worked. They'd talked and stuff, too, but she kept saying the sooner they got their sources lined up, the less pressure there would be in class tomorrow. He'd gone along, because she did have good ideas. And he really didn't have any.

Dylan flipped through the channels. Cable was about the only thing that made living here bearable. Settling on *Terminator 2*, he reached for some chips. Munched loudly.

He felt lighter somehow. Like the familiar weight of responsibility had lifted. He watched the bar scene in the movie, more relaxed than he could ever remember being. It was a weird feeling, one hard to identify.

He almost felt . . . happy.

Chapter 21

"Okay. Thank you for the offer. We'll reach out again if necessary." Disconnecting the call, Cady turned her attention to bringing up GPS for the address the Cumberland County deputy had provided her. "Larry Loomer is Eric's great-uncle on his deceased father's side. The sheriff's office has been out to his place half a dozen times looking for Eric, beginning right after Boster's death. They haven't found Larry to be especially cooperative. The nephew has never been discovered on the property." Her tone went dry. "The deputy warned me that the elder Loomer is a war vet with EOD training. We should approach the property with caution."

"You always take me to the nicest places." Miguel took the sunglasses from his nose and folded them, sticking them inside his jacket. "Do we need to bring the bomb squad?"

"Just keep our eyes open." The sandwich stop hadn't effected as much of a change on Miguel's attitude as Cady had hoped. She should have suggested pizza instead.

A half an hour later, he slowed in front of an overgrown drive. "This looks like a GPS drive and drop."

Cady mentally agreed. Vander was a rural, unincorporated community. She eyed the drive dubiously. The Jeep would fit up it, barely. The brush crowded both sides of the rutted path, the bare branches stretching over it like black skeletal fingers. Between the stands of bushes and the twists in the drive, any potential dwelling ahead was obscured, if indeed they were in the right place. "I'll walk ahead and scout it out."

"That might be easier. It's not the getting up there I'm worried about; it's getting turned around and back down."

Cady got out of the Jeep and started walking. Ten minutes later, she still hadn't reached the house, although she could see a thready plume of smoke emanating from what might be a chimney. As she moved farther up the drive, even the sound of the occasional passing car was muted. There was only her breathing and footsteps. An infrequent birdcall. The silence was a bit unnerving.

It also gave her too much time to think. The earlier return call from her mom's doctor swam across her mind. They'd had a brief discussion, and Cady had detailed the events of the last few days.

One incident is concerning, but it's the frequency of incidents that will help us determine whether there's a deterioration in your mom's condition. Given Hannah's earlier confusion over getting dressed, Dr. Baker's words brought Cady no comfort. Reminders of the disease's inevitable progression carved a furrow through her chest.

Thoughts turned inward, she almost missed what was right in front of her. She stumbled to a halt.

A thick cord stretched across the bumpy drive. No, not a cord, she saw as she crouched for a closer look. A length of rubber hose. The kind gas stations used to have to alert clerks they had a customer. She followed it as far as she could into the brush. If it served the purpose she assumed, it'd be rigged to a bell or an alarm. She took several more minutes to examine either side of it as far as she could without crawling through the bramble of bushes. Once she'd satisfied herself there was no danger, she stepped over the hose and continued up the path.

Several minutes later, the path curved yet again, and she walked into a clearing. There was a small cabin butted up against the base of a steep rocky bluff that towered above it.

A lean-to was built against one side of the home. A dilapidated carport sat on the other. It was empty. Other than the smoke rising from the chimney, there were no other signs of life on the property. Her cell buzzed.

"Did you take the scenic route?" Miguel's voice sounded in her ear as she spotted something on the ground. Squatted to get a closer look.

"There are definitely items of interest along the way." She told him about the hose she'd seen halfway up the drive, finishing with, "There's a cabin up here. Problem is, there's a half-hidden wire running across the front access to it."

"I'm coming to join you. Try not to touch anything. You hit your quota for getting blown up a few months ago."

Cady made a face as he disconnected. Funny guy. She could have pointed out that if Miguel had been a faster runner, he'd have been first to near the rigged car that had detonated during the Aldeen case. She'd looked—and felt—like the walking wounded for a couple of weeks, but she'd fared far better than the suspect they'd been chasing.

She backtracked, retracing her footsteps to the previous bend in the path, out of sight of the cabin. Miguel appeared in minutes. He must have jogged. "Did you see it?" she asked.

"The hose? Yeah. I think you're right. Some sort of alert system, maybe. Makes sense, living clear out here."

Silently, she led him to the wire she'd discovered earlier, half-hidden beneath loose gravel and dirt. He bent to examine it. "You take the right side; I'll check the left. See if these wires run from that hose we saw farther down."

But before they could move, the cabin door swung open, and the barrel of a shotgun emerged. It was followed by a tall, bent man of indeterminate age. "That's far enough. Stand up. Both of you."

Cady slowly rose. "Larry Loomer? Deputy US Marshals Maddix and Rodriguez. Lower your weapon."

"Don't think I will quite yet. You got that idjit from the sheriff's office with you? Least I'd recognize him."

"No, sir. Put the gun down and we'll show you ID."

Loomer hesitated for a moment before lowering the weapon. He picked his way down the steps and headed toward them. "Don't mind that wire you was so interested in. Just tells me someone's heading up this way. Man out in these parts by himself can't be too careful." He halted a couple of yards from them. In a synchronized movement, she and Miguel reached for their credentials. Held them up. The elderly man squinted, craned his head forward. "Got warrants?"

"Is Eric Loomer inside, sir?"

The man snorted at Cady's question. "No. You can look for yourself, if'n you don't believe me." If the wire she'd spotted was linked to an explosive device, Loomer was standing close enough that he'd be caught in the blast too. Cady moved toward the cabin. It was unlikely they'd get another invitation, and she wanted a look at the place where Weber had claimed he'd hung out with Eric Loomer.

The inside was open, compact, and surprisingly neat. A bed was notched into a corner next to a wooden wardrobe and a chest of drawers. The front of the cabin was a small kitchen, with the rest devoted to a midsize TV and a couple of easy chairs. "Bathroom's that way." He jerked his head toward a small door that would lead to the lean-to Cady had noted earlier. She walked over to check the small space. It was empty.

It soon became apparent that Loomer had had an ulterior motive for inviting them inside. "Maybe you can give me a hand with this," he was saying to Miguel when she returned. There was a small lamp on the table. "Damn switch doesn't work anymore. I got the parts right there but can't see well enough to put them in. Macular degeneration."

In the manner of men everywhere, Miguel went over to poke around a bit. It was a few minutes before he finally admitted, "Ah . . . I don't really know much about this sort of thing."

"Let me see." Cady crossed to the table. The base of the lamp was already apart. Quickly, she switched out the faulty parts and replaced them with the ones on the table. She tested the switch before putting the lamp back together. Once her grandfather had gotten too feeble to take care of small repairs around the house, he'd stand over her, giving step-by-step directions so she could make them. The skills were the only useful ones she'd learned during her time living with him.

Loomer reached over and tapped the switch. "Not bad," he said when it turned on.

"When's the last time you saw your nephew Eric?" she said, straightening from the task.

"I tell the deputy every time he comes out here. Haven't seen him for more than five years now. Don't know exactly what he done, but guessing he took off."

"Have you ever met any of your nephew's friends?"

"No reason I would." The man crossed to the decades-old refrigerator and set the shotgun on top of it. "He didn't live here. Used the place a few times when I was gone, and I gave him hell about it too."

"Did he ever mention Bruce Forrester?" Cady asked.

"Nope."

"Charlie Weber? Stephen Tillis?" Loomer gave a headshake each time.

"How did he spend his time? What was he interested in?"

"Not much but computers and video games." The words were spoken with obvious disgust. "Useless time wasters, you ask me. Didn't have a thought in his head that didn't involve one or the other."

"How about girlfriends? Did he mention any?" Although the investigators hadn't learned of a woman Loomer was involved with, his uncle might know more about his nephew's personal life.

The man shrugged. "Liked women as much as the next guy, I 'spect. Never brought one here. Least, not when I was around." He walked to the door, clearly ready to have them gone.

"How much time did he spend here?" Miguel asked.

"He came every month or so. Used to bring my groceries and medicine from Hope Mills. Now I use a delivery service twice a month. Got some damn outreach program from a church in town poking their nose in now and then. If I need a ride for anything, I can send a note to them."

"What did you and Eric do when he was here?"

"I taught him some real skills. How to fish and hunt. How to dress a deer. Thanks to me, he knows how to live off the grid without worrying about anyone sneaking up on him."

"You mean like the alert system you rigged on your path?" When the older man's gaze slid from hers, Cady recalled the deputy's warning earlier. "Mr. Loomer, did you teach him about explosives?"

His jaw jutted. "Man's got a right to protect himself."

Cady and Miguel exchanged a look. The news was ominous. "Do you have any idea where he might have gone, if he was intent on hiding out?"

"How would I know? He was raised 'round these parts, so makes sense to go somewhere he's not known." Clearly having reached the limits of his hospitality, Loomer opened the door. "I'm done talking."

They left the house and walked toward the drive that would lead them back to the Jeep. They lost sight of the man behind as they passed the clearing and started down the path toward the vehicle. Then an explosion ripped through the air.

"Get down!"

Cady was already diving for cover when she heard Miguel's warning. She hit the ground. Rolled and came to her knees with her weapon drawn. The smoke made it difficult to immediately discern what had happened. She scrambled to her feet, jogged back to the clearing. There were bits of carcass and blood strewn along the left side of Loomer's cabin, no more than thirty feet from where they'd passed. An instant later, his door opened, again with the shotgun barrel jutting out. Then the man himself sidled out onto the porch. Lowered the weapon and heaved a sigh of disgust. "Damn deer."

He had the property booby-trapped. Adrenaline doing a fast sprint up her spine, Cady looked over her shoulder for Miguel. He was stepping into the clearing, brushing off his clothes. They approached the cabin again, weapons drawn.

"Mr. Loomer. Set down your rifle," Miguel called. With her free hand, Cady took her cell from her pocket. They'd require assistance from the Cumberland County sheriff's office after all.

But as they assumed control of the situation, it wasn't their close call that had Cady most worried.

It was Loomer's tacit admission that he'd taught his nephew similar skills.

Chapter 22

"How are you coming down there?" Laura Talbot called from the top basement step.

"I'm done," Ryder called back. After feeding Cady's dog, he'd been at loose ends. He hadn't heard from her since her text saying she was heading to Vander and wouldn't be back until after dark. That wasn't uncommon. But a thread of worry nagged at him anyway. He hoped she'd taken someone along with her, whatever she was working on. Not that he'd give voice to his concern. They'd grown closer in the last three months. But the unspoken no-trespassing signs she posted were unmistakable.

He got to his feet and dusted off his jeans. His trip to his mom's to start looking for the missing files had morphed into a handyman session. First tightening a leaky pipe under the kitchen sink and then switching out the furnace filters. He carried the old ones to the door of the storage room and stepped inside it. After scanning the rows of neatly labeled plastic bins, he backed out the door again.

Going through each of the tubs would take far more time than he had at the moment, since he'd already spent a couple of hours here. He headed toward the stairs, filters in hand. If Butch Talbot had brought home the Maddix file to peruse at his leisure, one would think it'd be in his den. But Ryder had thoroughly searched the file cabinet and desk when they'd looked for property and financial documents after his dad's death. He'd recall if it had been in either.

He climbed the steps and set the filters by the garage door. He'd take them with him and discard them for his mom later. Without conscious decision, he moved toward the den. Stood in the doorway. Meant as a bedroom, it had always been his dad's domain. The large hickory desk with matching file cabinet sat against one wall. A recliner and end table next to a window. He went to the closet and opened it. Found it filled with more of his mom's clothes. He checked the bookcase on the opposite wall and the TV stand.

"Honey? Are you looking for something?"

Feeling foolish, he jerked around. Smiled at his mom. "Did Dad ever bring work home?"

She rolled her eyes. "More times than I like to remember. If I saw him at his desk paying bills, I always tiptoed on by. But if he had folders open, I knew I'd need a bullhorn to get his attention. When something from work was nagging at him, he was like a dog with a bone."

Had something caught the man's attention in Lonny Maddix's case? Ryder considered the idea. No way to discern what it might have been without the file itself. And he could be fairly certain it wasn't in this room. Which left only one place to look.

"I'm going to poke around in the garage a little bit. I'll put the wrench away."

"Thank you, Mr. Fix-it." She smiled up at him, a petite woman, her blonde hair and makeup still immaculate despite the hour. "You must have gotten your skills from your dad. He was handy, too, but I swear sometimes the roof had to practically cave in before I could get him to take the time for a few repairs around the house."

Tension seeped into his shoulders. "I learned a lot from him," Ryder said impassively as they walked from the room and through the house.

Memories of his dad would always be marred by the less-flattering things he'd discovered about the man. He still hadn't figured out how to untangle the good from the bad. His mom followed him to the kitchen, where he retrieved the wrench he'd used earlier. "Is the painter all done?" he asked.

"All that's left are the bedrooms."

He stopped at the door to the garage and dropped a kiss on top of her head. "I'll see you later."

"Come for dinner sometime. Bring that woman you were so cagey about last weekend."

Ryder halted. Narrowed his eyes. "I wasn't cagey. You and Ronda were just nosy."

His mom looked satisfied. "If there wasn't a woman, you would have denied it flat-out. Instead you danced around our questions like you were hopping on live coals. I might not be an experienced cop, but I can read people, especially my son. There's someone. I don't know why you're being so closemouthed, but I figure that means something too."

"It does." He waited for her gaze to fly to his. "It means you have an overactive imagination." He ducked the light swat she aimed at him and grabbed the filters, letting himself into the garage and flipping on the light.

"I'll find out. I have my sources." His mom gave what could only be described as an evil laugh before shutting the door. Ryder shook his head. It was probably best that Cady had had other plans last weekend. The grilling she would have faced would quell hardened criminals.

Quickly, he crossed to his dad's workbench and replaced the wrench on the pegboard that hung above it. Not that Cady wouldn't be up to the task. He hadn't noticed much that daunted her. Given the grimness that had dogged her life, that was no surprise.

You could say the event sort of defined my childhood. The mental snippet flashed across his mind. Of course it had. And he knew the impact lingered.

He scanned the garage's interior, doubt creeping in. If the file had been brought home and not returned, it should be in Butch's den. There would be no reason for it to be in the storeroom or here. Knowing that didn't keep Ryder from swiftly going through the drawers of the workbench and tool chests. Eliminating the unlikely was a necessary part of the search too. If the file wasn't located soon, maybe he'd mention it to Jerry Garza, his investigator. Although Garza's time with the sheriff's office didn't stretch back decades, he had worked for Ryder's dad.

Finished with the drawers, he went to the shelves lining the wall in front of his dad's car. They were stacked somewhat neatly with the same stuff found in Ryder's own garage. Spare parts. Gasoline containers. Cans of oil. Extension cords. Portable lights. He shifted everything he couldn't see behind and then replaced it as he moved on, already preparing himself for failure. He'd head home after this, give it more thought over a beer. He'd missed the Hornets game Saturday night. Maybe something would come to him as he watched the recording.

He dragged over the stepladder and climbed it to check the highest shelf. He shoved aside a plastic tote that reached the ceiling, then righted it again and started to move on. Belatedly, comprehension clicked in. He took the tote off the shelf, balancing it on the top step of the ladder. The drywall in the ceiling above it had been scored into an eighteen-inch square. Ryder traced the seam with his index finger. Found a rough spot where some of the material had been chipped away. He pressed his palm against the center of the Sheetrock. It shifted inward.

Foreboding knocked at the base of his skull. He dug in his pocket for his penknife and flipped out a blade. Slipping it inside the seam, Ryder pried the piece off and set it on top of the tote. He shoved his hand up in the area, fingers searching blindly. There was a flat shelf wedged between the rafters on one side of the opening. Something rested on top of it.

Ryder withdrew a black expanding file. Looked inside. He wasn't totally surprised to find a file folder in it. But he hadn't counted on finding six of them.

Chapter 23

Cady would have had to be comatose to sleep through Hero's raucous barking. She bolted upright in bed, scrubbing her hands over her face. Picking up her cell from the bedside table, she checked the time. Just after three. She pushed the covers back and swung her bare legs over the edge of the bed. Went to find the animal.

He had his front paws on the sill of the picture window in the front room, baying for all he was worth at something he'd seen or sensed outside.

"C'mon." She took him by the collar and dragged him away only to have the dog duck free and return to his ruckus. Cady got a firmer grip and pulled him toward her bedroom. She knew better than to let him outside. If a deer had jumped the fence or another critter was in the yard, closer proximity would only prolong the racket.

She grabbed the discarded clown on the way and shut the bedroom door behind them. "Here. Take the damn thing and calm down."

But Hero went to the window instead, letting out short staccato barks. The room didn't have a view of the front of the property. Cady got back in bed and aimed a gimlet stare at the dog, who was still growling and pacing. "Hero! Quiet!"

Finally, the animal quieted but remained alert. That was fine with her, as long as the din stopped. She didn't have much hope of falling back to sleep, but at some point, she dozed fitfully. And this time an all-too-familiar nightmarish montage followed.

A shadowy figure. Unidentifiable. "Only point it at bad guys." The words swirled through her mind like an icy breeze. "You don't like bad guys, do you, Cady?" Then, like a disjointed scene in a spliced movie, she was suddenly at Larry Loomer's house, but this time the explosion was closer. More violent. The dream morphed again, and she was transported to Charlotte. Her body was hurtling across an alleyway to slam against a brick wall, debris raining down on her. Her grandfather's face superimposed over the destruction. "You mess with the bull, you get the horns." Darkness swallowed her up. Her body shook. His root cellar again. The scent of the earthen walls filled her lungs. The cold dampness crept into her bones. Her grandfather's voice whispering in her head. "You afraid of the dark, girlie?"

She wrapped her arms around her middle, chilled. And still the nightmare reel continued. A spotlight split the darkness. Filled it. And Cady wasn't in the cellar anymore. She was in the kitchen. The cracked linoleum beneath her feet. Blood on her mama's face. On her nightdress as she huddled on the floor against the old refrigerator, Cady's dad looming over her, his features blurry and indistinct. Her hand creeping toward the gun on the table. The weight of it in her hand. The shot deafening in the small room . . .

She came fully awake, her heart beating a frantic rhythm in her chest. Cady leaped from the bed, anxious to leave the remnants of the nightmare behind her. Her actions roused Hero. He padded over to her, nosed her hand. She hauled in a deep breath, then another as she petted him, his warmth and nearness calming her in a way nothing else could. "I'm okay. It's okay. Guess we're even now, huh? We're both sleep wreckers." Straightening, she grabbed her phone to check the time. Five thirty. Allen wouldn't expect her in first thing this morning because of the long hours they'd put in yesterday, but she had no intention of taking leave. There were multiple threads she wanted to follow up on. She also needed to take a stab at contacting the Madison County inmates she'd run down yesterday.

She fed Hero and let him outside. Changing into shorts and a sports bra, she headed to the treadmill in the second bedroom. A forty-five-minute run successfully banished the dark, sticky remnants of the dream. She showered, dressed, and ate breakfast, finally feeling human again despite the lack of sleep.

Cady loaded her laptop into its case and set it next to the breakfast bar. Then she went to find her phone. She shoved it into her jeans pocket as she walked back into the living room. Blew out a breath when Hero's frenetic barking started up again. He hadn't carried on this much since he treed an opossum last fall. She got a coat and jammed her feet into boots, letting herself out the kitchen door that led to the carport.

As she continued past the car toward the Jeep, the motion lights mounted on the house switched on, illuminating her way. Hero was still raising havoc. Cady scanned the yard, trying to spot him.

There. At the fence line on the other side of the drive. Her property butted up against an empty field that had been unused for as long as she'd lived here. It was the same area that had been the animal's focus last night.

Trepidation rose. Cady reached the rear fender of the Jeep, about to round the bumper when the dog bounded over to her. She leaned down, making a grab for his collar before the animal dodged away. A loud report sounded, and instinctively she hit the gravel drive, scrambling behind the front wheel well. Hero raced toward the fence, barking and lunging at something.

She started to raise her head cautiously, intent on looking across the hood toward the neighboring property. There was another shot, followed by the sound of shattering glass from a nearby window.

"Jesus. Hero!" She shouted for the dog futilely as she ducked, her fingers scrabbling for the cell in her pocket. Another bullet tore through the vehicle, exiting inches away from her. Cady huddled behind the axle as she punched in Ryder's number. At the first sound of his sleepy voice, she said urgently, "I'm under fire. High-powered rifle." She stopped as several more shots riddled the Jeep. Glass sprayed down on her. She shook it off. "Shooter's on the property east of mine."

To his credit, Ryder didn't waste time on questions. "Be there in ten. I'll try to get a car there sooner. Stay. Down."

She smiled grimly as she shoved the phone back in her pocket. Cady unwrapped her body until she was lying directly behind the Jeep's front tire. Vehicles made notoriously poor cover. The best chance she had was putting the engine block or an axle between her and the shooter, then hoping for the best. She peered cautiously around the side of the wheel. There was a large fir situated about halfway across the field next door. The shooter was likely hiding behind it. She could see the dog was focused on that spot. She needed to get to the house and retrieve her weapon. She rose to a crouched position. Then flattened again when a volley of shots sprayed the Jeep and the house behind her.

Her pulse hammered in her ears. Distantly, she heard a siren. Cady rolled to the other side of the tire so she could see beyond the vehicle, straining to glimpse signs of movement near the fir. Then terror gripped her. Hero had jumped the fence and was galloping toward the evergreen. She screamed for the dog.

The neighboring property was unfenced in back and had the same thick stand of brush and volunteer trees bordering the rear as hers had. Cady rose to look over the Jeep's hood. She was able to make out a silhouette moving quickly away from the fir toward the trees. She raced into the house and then sprinted back outside with her weapon. Cady was running toward the fence as a sheriff's car crashed through the gate at the entrance of her drive.

"It's Maddix!" she yelled at the deputy lunging from the vehicle. "Shooter heading toward the southwest side of the property." Her heart dropped when she saw Hero gaining ground as he galloped after the figure.

She heard the deputy speaking into the radio as she reached the chain-link fence. It was ancient and not particularly sturdy. She bent it down far enough to climb over it and sped across the field. The shooter and the dog were lost from view in the wooded area.

Moments later, a shot sounded.

A frigid bolt of fear twisted through her. Cady's knees pumped faster. The morning air sliced her lungs. She took cover behind the random stands of nude bushes as she approached the woods. In a crouched run, she dodged from one bunch to another as she drew closer.

She squinted, searching the shadowy woods for signs of the animal. She heard the dog's whining, but it was another moment before she spotted him on the leaf-strewn ground, at the base of a fledgling oak. Her blood chilled.

An engine sounded in the distance. She heard the faint sound of spraying gravel. "Shooter's in a vehicle heading east," she called back to the deputy who was running toward her. And then she dropped to her knees. Hero whimpered. Tried to crawl toward her. "It's all right. It's all right." She whispered the lie and wished it were true as she ran her free hand over the dog. Felt the wet, sticky substance that confirmed her worst fears. Reholstering her weapon, she pulled off her coat and struggled out of her shirt before redonning the jacket and zipping it up. Grabbing for her cell, she turned on the flashlight app, her breath catching at the sight of the wound. Blood oozed from his left rear flank. Gaping muscle was visible. Swiftly, she used the shirt to fashion a tourniquet and applied pressure to it.

The deputy jogged past her and was lost from sight. Multiple sirens wailed and were abruptly cut off. The sound was close. At her house, maybe. But she didn't raise her gaze from the animal as she attempted to keep him from struggling to his feet. "It's going to be okay, buddy. It's okay." She stroked the animal's head, waiting for the deputy to return. She'd be unable to lift the animal without his help.

The dog nuzzled her knee, and her breathing stopped for a moment. "What's this? Let go, boy. Drop it." Hero wearily lay his head down and loosened his jaws enough for her to remove the scrap of fabric from his mouth. It was some sort of dark nylon.

A minute later, the deputy was making his way back toward her. "I think the dog might have ripped a piece from the shooter's clothes. His jacket or pants." She looked behind her, trying to approximate the exact spot where the contact could have been made. "Maybe there are more pieces." And maybe—if they got supremely lucky—there'd be DNA.

The deputy slowed, taking a Maglite from his hip and turning its beam on the area. She looked over her shoulder to watch his progress. "Wait. Move the beam back to the right. Farther. There. What's that on the ground? A branch?"

The man walked toward the object she'd pointed out. Crouched. "No, ma'am," he said, rising and reaching for his radio. "It's a rifle."

Chapter 24

"We totally rocked it." Grace nudged Dylan as they were filing out of history class.

He grinned. "We both know it was mostly you."

"Not true." She paused a minute before adding with a laugh, "But I do have good ideas."

He couldn't disagree. They'd pretty much done today's work last night at her place, so they'd spent a lot of time talking today about things other than the assignment. Movies, sports—which he couldn't believe she liked too—and music, which he knew nothing about.

She turned around to face him, walking backward despite the mob of people. "I've got a unique idea for our presentation too. One of us can dress up as a founding father, say Ben Franklin, and the other like one of the Supreme Court Justices . . ." He reached out to steady her when she nearly tripped over someone behind her. She stopped.

"Ehh, I don't know." He had no idea where he'd get a costume, for one thing. He'd almost been late for the bus this morning because he couldn't even find a clean shirt and had to rummage through Colton's drawers for something. And he didn't want to look stupid. Just standing up in front of everyone was going to be bad enough. Then she flashed that dimple again, and his reluctance faded away. "Maybe. We'll see." Dylan couldn't believe the words coming from his mouth.

"Great. Can you get together again after school? We should really get started. Two weeks isn't that long to get the paper written."

"Yeah." The word was out of his mouth before he even thought about it. "Your mom won't care?"

"No. Comes from being the only kid still at home." Grace rolled her eyes. "She *hovers*, you know?"

Dylan wondered what it was like to have a mom who *hovered*. One who didn't have to work and liked it when kids came over. But even more interesting, he wondered how Grace got her hair so shiny. Its color reminded him of the river otter's coat he and Trevor had seen once at the creek. Dark brown with highlights that glinted under the overhead lights.

"Great! Meet you at the same door after school." A warning bell rang. They had only a minute to get to their next class.

"Okay." But she was already moving swiftly away. His next class was shop, and it was halfway across the building. Dylan spent the time trying to recall what his mom's work schedule was. She usually went in at one, and the store closed at ten. But if she was on over the weekend, she didn't work every weekday.

He'd borrow a cell from someone and call the store, ask if she was there. He broke into a trot when the tardy bell rang. He needed to get her schedule memorized if he wanted to have a life outside home and school. The thought felt novel. Foreign.

After yesterday, he could almost taste the freedom.

He could hear yelling as he rounded the corner to the shop room's hallway. Dylan recognized the two kids pushing each other. One was in shop class with him. Benny. He was a real dick.

"Give me my backpack, you fucker!" the other kid yelled.

Drop that backpack, you little fuckers, or I'll drown you both! The words arrowed across Dylan's mind, as real as the ones shouted a few feet away from him. He froze, his head beginning to throb on cue. The shop teacher ran out of the classroom and down the hall, yelling at the kids who were now throwing punches.

But Dylan wasn't in the hallway anymore. He was ten again, back in the woods running for his life. Tripping over rocks and logs, panic balled up in his chest until it felt like it was going to explode.

With Bruce Forrester gaining on him.

Chapter 25

"The weapon was an AR-10. Unless he used gloves and wiped down the weapon, we may get lucky and pull some prints from it," Ryder was saying as Cady rejoined the group in his office's conference room. It was just after noon, and she'd taken a call from the vet. Hero was out of surgery. The weight of worry she'd been carrying since one of the deputies had helped her transport him to town was only slightly relieved. Her assailant and the animal had both been running when the shot was fired, so it could have been far worse. The dog was stable, for now. But anxiety over his wound would continue to gnaw at her until she could check on him for herself. She slipped back into her chair at the table.

This summary was for her supervisor's benefit. Allen had headed over after she'd reported the incident hours earlier. "We had several people in the area report that they heard shots fired, but only the neighbors directly north of Cady's place had an approximate estimate of where they were coming from." Ryder was in uniform but unshaven. "A motorist reported a speeding vehicle on the road in front of Cady's neighboring property, a few miles east. He couldn't give much of a description, other than it was a dark-colored pickup."

Cady stilled. "Did he give any clue as to the make or model?"

"No. But from the shape, he thought it might be an older vehicle." His gaze remained on her. "Does that sound familiar?"

Allen said, "Old-model green pickup. Wasn't a similar truck driven in those last couple of homicides in the Forrester case?"

"We don't have anything solid connecting him to those murders." But if the ballistics from today matched those from the Matthis and Bahlman scenes, *and* if Forrester's latents were pulled from the weapon, the evidence would be damning. It'd also effectively sideline Cady. She knew the protocol. If the shooter today was proven to be the subject of her warrant, it'd be handed off to someone else.

She'd ping-ponged between concern and rising fury all morning. She'd need time to shake free of emotion and start making sense of the avalanche of questions cascading through her mind. For once, she wouldn't be impatient about the time it took for lab results. Until and unless they came up with inculpatory evidence pointing to Forrester, she'd remain on the man's trail.

"My team gathered brass, all scattered near the evergreen where Cady thought the shots were being fired from. There were more bullets, badly damaged, dug out of the ground. We found some smaller pieces of fabric that look to match the bit Cady recovered from the dog. No noticeable bloodstains were discovered during the search."

Which likely means retrieving DNA will be a bust, Cady mused. But a print could provide ID, as well, if its owner was in the IAFIS database.

To Allen, Ryder said, "Cady's work and personal vehicles and all physical evidence will be transported to the Western Regional Crime Lab in Edneyville."

The Jeep had gotten the worst of it. But her car had also taken a couple of bullets before she'd dove for cover. Which meant she'd have no vehicle at all for the foreseeable future.

"The east side of the house sustained serious damage," Ryder continued. "The gate and a portion of the fence are toast."

"We'll go through Cady's assignments since she's been stationed in Asheville. See if we can come up with anyone who might have had cause to be involved." Allen looked at her. "You've covered a lot of ground on your current warrants since you were assigned them a few days ago. Anyone you talk to stand out as a suspect in this?"

She shook her head slowly. "Not really. I sent a request to the warden at Craggy Correctional for an interview with Stephen Tillis a couple of days ago but haven't heard back yet. We spoke to Weber, who flipped on Forrester five years ago. He stated he hasn't seen or heard from either him or Eric Loomer since then. Loomer's uncle made a similar claim about his nephew. The two men I interviewed on Sunday in Madison County said the same. And the million-dollar question is how the shooter discovered where I live. Hero started going crazy at about three in the morning. The intruder may have been casing the property then. When I let the dog out this morning, he immediately raised the alarm." And had been shot for his efforts. Cady tamped down the surge of anger at the memory. "Obviously it's someone skilled with weapons. That tree he took cover behind was a hundred, hundred fifty yards from me."

"One hundred forty-one, to be exact." Ryder's tone was grim.

She thought for a minute. "I don't have a view of the front of the property from my bedroom window. If the security lights came on after I went to bed, I wouldn't have noticed." But she bet the shooter had. A spear of fury arrowed through her. He would have known she'd be a sitting duck heading to her vehicle in the morning.

"Your dog lived up to his name, at any rate."

She managed a smile at her supervisor's words. "He did. As I was trying to get a clear shot, he sailed over the fence and was chasing the punk down." For the first time, the full implication of Ryder's earlier words hit Cady. Her gaze shifted to him. "The house is still livable, right?"

He shook his head. "I don't think so. It'll take new Sheetrock, windows, carpet . . . I'm guessing it will be weeks to get the work all done."

Weeks. The word slammed into her with the force of a blow. She'd have to move. Her landlady, Dorothy Blong, had a number of other rental properties. Maybe another would be available. Cady needed to stay in the area to keep an eye on her mom's condition while in Alma's care.

As if reading her thoughts, her supervisor said, "Obviously you need a new place to live. That's first on the list. But today's attempt on your life means we also call in a USMS countersurveillance team to keep an eye on your new home. You'll be partnered on every aspect of the case that takes you outside the courthouse."

Cady accepted the news with a mental sigh. It wasn't unexpected.

"And," her supervisor continued with a glint in his eye, "you'll wear a vest at all times. If your new living quarters don't have decent security, we'll have to see to that too." With a look at the clock on the wall, he stood. "I don't want you back at the office today."

She didn't argue. Cady had a number of things to tend to, starting with packing a bag and finding a place to stay. A motel might serve for the night, but she'd need a place she could take Hero to when he was released from the vet.

Allen stood. "We'll pull your files this afternoon, and I'll contact you if someone pops."

As he left the room, Cady's mind flashed to Larry Loomer. He said he'd taught Eric to shoot. She wondered now just how skilled the two men were.

Ryder interrupted her thoughts by asking, "How's Hero?"

"Holding his own." She released a long breath. "He'll stay at least overnight. Maybe longer. I need to stop by today before the office closes. The bullet hit him on his left rear flank, but the vet didn't think it would impact his ability to walk once it's healed." She'd never had a pet before. Was still taken aback at how one could wind around her heart and settle so seamlessly into her life.

Ryder had shoved away from the desk as she spoke. Then he was in front of her, grabbing her hand and pulling her up and into his arms. Cady stood stiff and still for a moment before allowing herself to melt, just a little, returning his hug. "It's been a helluva day."

"Longest thirteen minutes of my life was between your call and pulling into your drive this morning."

"That tops my list too." When his fingers rose to toy with the zipper of her jacket, she slapped them away. "That's a good way to lose a hand."

"I have a spare."

She stifled a laugh. "I need to grab another shirt before I do anything else." She hadn't had time after using hers to bandage Hero.

They stepped apart, but he stayed her with a hand on her arm. "Here's why you should stay with me." Her rejection of the idea must have shown in her expression, because he raised a hand. "Hear me out. I have no close neighbors on my cul-de-sac. Big fenced-in backyard where both dogs can be outside. Decent security, including alarms and video cameras. And when Hero is released from the vet, you're going to want someone who can check up on him a few times a day."

"You don't have the time for that," Cady scoffed.

"Nope. But my mom would love to be asked. She's never happier than when she's fussing over someone or something."

The simple logic of his words didn't silence the unease skittering through her. "I can always find a motel until he's released. Who knows, my landlady might have something available."

"She might." She wasn't fooled by his agreeable tone or amiable expression. They were both tools that had wedged holes in her resolve in the past. "We can swing by the vet, and then I'll follow you to your place so you can pack."

Damn. How could she have forgotten, even for a moment, that she no longer had a vehicle? The USMS had several for marshals' use, and they sometimes traded with each other when one better fit the need of the investigation. There were probably a couple of extras. She had no idea which one might be assigned, but she hoped like hell it wasn't a soccer-mom minivan. "I've sucked up enough of your day. I can get a Lyft."

"No, you can't. Because you aren't going back to your place without backup."

She opened her mouth to protest. Closed it again. She'd better get used to it. She was going to have company until today's shooter was jailed.

"Fine. Vet first. Then home." She turned toward the door.

"Food first. Vet, then home," he countered.

As they walked out the door, her cell rang. Pulling it out of her pocket, she checked the caller ID. Frowned. Madison County sheriff's office. Answering it, she continued walking down the hall and toward the facility's entrance. "Maddix."

"Marshal, this is Sheriff Jon Crawley. We haven't met, but it's my understanding you were here last weekend."

Mystified, she replied, "That's right. I spoke with Lieutenant Goldman on Sunday."

"Well, he and I have been doing a little investigating, and it's come to our attention that one of our longtime jailers has been snooping around in our most sensitive computer files. And she may also have accessed your contact information."

Chapter 26

"The cleaning staff reported Suzanne Fielding's presence in Goldman's office when the deputy had stepped out for a few minutes." Sheriff Jon Crawley's drooping white mustache matched his bushy brows that were currently knitted together above his dark eyes. "It seemed apparent she was checking the phone's caller ID log and making note of the numbers. We've had a problem with the office computers for months, which we suspected was due to unauthorized access of our most secure files. It's taken a while for our IT person to set up a firewall and an accompanying alert when there's a hacking attempt. Monday, we traced the breach to the computer used by the jailer."

Cady felt Ryder tense beside her. "And what's in your most secure files?" she asked, already knowing the answer.

"Ongoing multiagency investigations. Bruce Forrester is the subject of one of them. But let me backtrack a bit." The sheriff settled his bulk a bit more comfortably in his massive leather desk chair. "When we nailed Fielding for accessing those files, a lot of pieces clicked into place. For one, she was disciplined seven years ago for breach of protocol while Forrester was jailed here."

Cady's gut clenched. "For placing Forrester and Byrd in the same cell?"

Crawley looked surprised. "You got it. Standard procedure is to keep child sexual offenders in solitary occupation because of the heightened threat of violence against them. We had a big influx of inmates that night, but it wouldn't have necessitated doubling up occupancy with Byrd. That was a major strike against Fielding. But . . ." He lifted a beefy shoulder. "Up until that point, she'd been employed ten years with us with no complaints. She was suspended without pay for a week, and that was the end of it."

Cady thought for a moment. "Shortly after his release here, he ended up in Hope Mills, where he was linked to a drug operation. Any chance that's the hold he had on Fielding?"

"She's never failed a drug test," the sheriff replied.

"Does she have older kids? Husband? Other family?" Ryder asked.

"Two daughters. Twelve and six. Suzanne's divorced. Has been for a few years now. Her folks live in town. Her brother used to as well. He moved to Weaverville several years ago. Works in the IT department for a business there." Noting Cady's heightened interest, the sheriff nodded. "It would have taken expertise to get by the firewall to access those files. We got a warrant for her cell phone. She refused to give us the password, but Kathy, our IT gal, cracked it." He half turned to reach for a phone on the table behind him. Set it on the desk. "Call log was deleted. Wouldn't take the crime lab long to retrieve it, but who knows when they'll get to it. She's not going to admit to having had contact with a felon."

Cady eyed the cell. Since it might be a link to Forrester, the Greensboro lab would expedite the cyber forensics. "Maybe I can offer some context for further questioning," she said grimly. "Let me brief you on the events of the morning."

◆ ◆ ◆

Two hours later, Ryder and Cady were seated next door to the interview room, watching the proceedings on CCTV. Crawley was speaking.

"Thank you for agreeing to come in again today, Ms. Fielding." He nodded to the woman beside her. "Ms. Stanton." He didn't indicate the reason for the other woman's presence, so Cady assumed she was Fielding's attorney. "I just wanted to update you both on where we are in our investigation."

"As long as you realize there is no new information to be had here. My client has been as forthcoming as possible in our previous meetings."

Crawley asked, "Ms. Fielding, can you tell us where your brother is?"

The woman looked shocked. "Tim? Why? He has nothing to do with this."

"You don't know where he is?"

"I . . ." She looked at her lawyer. "He's in Vegas, I think. At an IT convention."

"How does he know Bruce Forrester?"

Suzanne's chair scraped as she half rose from it. "That's crazy. What does Forrester have to do with any of this?"

"We obtained a warrant for your cell phone." At the sheriff's words, the blood drained from the woman's face, and she slowly sank back into her seat. "You deleted the call log. Figure you might have a reason for doing so. Doesn't mean it can't be recovered, of course. Folks in the state crime lab are pretty good with that sort of thing. You can make us wait however long it takes for the cyber forensics folks to tell us what you don't want us to know about your phone. In the meantime, you got no pay coming in. No way to take care of your kids. And attorney fees on top of that. So how 'bout you just tell us now if the lab is going to find a call to or from Bruce Forrester on your cell."

"Who is this Forrester you're referring to?" Stanton asked. "You understand it's not my client's primary concern to save your office time and resources."

"Bruce Forrester is a fugitive, ma'am. He has outstanding warrants for kidnapping and drug charges. And he's wanted for questioning in three homicides." Crawley let the silence stretch before adding, "He was also the inmate your client broke protocol for seven years ago or so. My question to Suzanne is, did you contact Forrester with information on Deputy US Marshal Cady Maddix?"

"I need to confer with my client. Please show us to a secure room." At Stanton's demand, Crawley got up and rounded the table, and the CCTV feed went fuzzy.

Cady pushed back from the table. Rose to pace the small area. "Why else would she be interested in my number and the Forrester files if she didn't have some connection to him?"

"Exactly." Ryder's tone was hard. "Given her employment, she likely knows the marshals serving this area of the state are located in Asheville. It would only take someone armed with your description to surveil the courthouse and follow you home. Or . . . it was Sunday when you went to the jail. Her brother wouldn't have been working. She could have had him trail you."

Insulted, she snapped, "Like I wouldn't notice a tail."

He held up his hands in mock surrender. "I'm just throwing out one possibility."

She thought again of Larry Loomer. The guy was clearly a loose cannon with an alarming knowledge base. But even if it were plausible that he'd lied about his eyesight and had the will and concern for his nephew to follow them, he'd been tied up with the Cumberland County deputies until well after they'd left.

The TV flickered to life again. Stanton was speaking.

". . . client has been under great duress, fearful for the lives of her loved ones. That factor has caused her to go to unnatural lengths, to take actions she'd normally never dream of, all in the interest of keeping her family alive."

"Tell us, Suzanne." Crawley's expression was sympathetic. "Have you been aiding Bruce Forrester?"

"I . . ." The woman swiped at her eyes. "It's Tim. He got in trouble years back. Drugs. He owed a lot of money to Forrester and then couldn't pay it. Forrester threatened to kill me. Kill my kids unless he got the cash. I tried to help, but I just get by on my paycheck. My ex doesn't work. I sold some furniture . . . I didn't know what else to do. If word got out about Tim's drug problem, he'd lose his job. Maybe even go to jail." Her voice hitched.

Cady's mouth flattened. It was the same scenario with monsters everywhere. Exploit the vulnerable. Threaten their loved ones. And too often, fear kept the innocent from going to the police.

"Then one day, Forrester calls and says I can work off the debt by giving him information when he wants it. Doing him favors."

The mask of sympathy had vanished from Crawley's face. "What type of favors?"

Fielding looked down at the table. "Alerting him to dispatch calls that might concern him. I don't know what he was doing, what he was involved in," she added quickly. "When he was arrested that time and wanted to be moved in with Byrd, it was really only the second or third time I'd spoken to him."

"And how often have you talked to him since?" The sheriff asked the same question Cady was wondering.

"I'm not sure. A half dozen or so. All after that deal in Hope Mills."

"Did you always contact him, or did he call you?"

She took a deep, shuddering breath, and her attorney placed a reassuring hand on her arm. "He'd reach out wanting updates on anything that came through the office concerning him. If I didn't report back, he'd call again, making threats. I lived in constant fear. When Maddix came Sunday, I . . . I thought maybe I could wipe out my brother's debt for good. Maybe we'd be safe at last."

"Didn't give a thought to your safety, did she?" muttered Ryder.

"You made the contact?" Crawley asked. The woman nodded miserably. "When did you delete the call information?"

She moistened her lips. "After you talked to me the first time."

"What information did you pass to Forrester regarding Marshal Maddix?"

"Just that a federal marshal was asking about him. I gave him her name and phone number, that's all! I swear! And it was probably a work phone anyway, right? I . . . I might have said she'd probably be out of the office in Asheville."

"It's like I'm a fortune-teller," Ryder said smugly. Cady elbowed him.

"Did you tell him about the kidnapping warrant out on him?"

Suzanne shook her head at the sheriff's question. "No. Just about the marshal, I swear."

"Clearly the circumstances of these communications were extenuating," Stanton put in. "My client fears for her family's life, now even more so. If Forrester learns she's been found out . . ."

"Maybe we make sure he doesn't discover that," Cady murmured. She straightened. "It shouldn't take the lab long to get the number she dialed." And with the number, they almost certainly could get a general location for Forrester. Adrenaline sprinted through her veins at the thought.

"Do you think he's in this area?"

She considered Ryder's question for a moment before shrugging. "He wouldn't have to be, since he has eyes here. He snatched Zook from Bryson City." That was an hour and a half from Marshall. Something was keeping Forrester in the state when it would be far safer for him to move away. Cady wondered again if that something was Dylan Castle. She returned her attention to the screen.

"Do you have any idea where Bruce Forrester is?" Crawley asked.

"No."

"Has he ever mentioned a place he's been?"

"No. We didn't have conversations like that."

"Did you ever hear anything in the background while speaking with him that would give an idea of who he was with or where he was?" Fielding was shaking her head. "I need an answer for the record."

"No. I never heard anything like that."

"Just a moment." Crawley pushed away from the table and left the room. A moment later, the door to their space opened. "Marshal. Do you want to talk to her?"

"I do." Cady followed the sheriff into the other room. Noted the emotions flickering across the woman's face. Shock. Fear. Shame.

"This is Deputy US Marshal Cady Maddix. She has a couple of questions for your client." Crawley said to Stanton as he sat back down.

Cady remained standing. "How many times have you seen Forrester face-to-face?"

"I . . . Just the once, I guess." Fielding looked down at her clasped hands. "When he was jailed here."

"When you contacted him, did he always answer right away?"

The woman looked perplexed, then thought for a moment. "He did this time. Sometimes, though, he didn't call back until the next day."

"Describe how he speaks to you. Does he repeat certain phrases? Are the threats always the same?" Knowing how he spoke to the woman might give Cady more insight into the way the man's mind worked. Were the threats sexual in nature? Directed at the children?

"Mostly he starts on what he'll do to my brother. I mean, Tim makes good money in his job now and could pay Forrester what he owes him. But Forrester keeps tacking on interest, so it's like no matter how much we offer, it's never enough. Then he starts asking about the girls."

A trickle of revulsion snaked down Cady's spine. Her mind flew to her conversation with Byrd. "Any one in particular?"

She shook her head. "Both. He starts saying . . . sick stuff."

"Sexual?"

"I . . . No. Like describing how he'd kill them. Horrific things. He always talks about how their lives are in my hands. I'm to blame if something happens to . . ." She broke down then, her words difficult to make out.

Violence. Revenge. Control. They were recurring themes in what she'd learned about Forrester. Cady didn't know yet exactly what the man was into.

But she knew more than she had this morning. And Fielding's phone might lead them right to wherever Forrester was hiding.

Chapter 27

When Ryder returned from putting Cady's things in one of his spare bedrooms, she was standing in the family room looking as lost as he'd ever seen her. She was familiar with his house—she'd stayed with him before, although they usually spent the night at her place. But things were out of her control right now, and he knew exactly what that was costing her.

He realized he owed her some answers about the files he'd found in his dad's garage but couldn't think of a worse time to broach the subject. It'd keep. He still didn't know what it meant, those files not being in the system. He could follow that thread on his own for a while longer.

Because he knew how much she'd hate it, he kept his concern for her to himself. "Lucky we stopped by the vet before heading to Madison County."

Mention of Hero, even indirectly, was enough to bring her around. "It was good to see him. I mean, the vet had said he'd probably be okay, but seeing for myself . . ."

He nodded, giving Sadie an absent pat when she nosed his hand. "You can take him his toy tomorrow. That'll probably make him feel better." They'd had the car packed up when she'd gotten out and dashed back into the house for it.

She rolled her eyes. "Unfortunately, you're probably right. And I'm at the place where I'm okay with that."

The vet had been cagey when they'd tried to pin him down on a release date. Ryder privately thought that the longer the animal stayed under the doctor's care, the better. Cady would worry more once he was back home. Or wherever she decided they'd be staying long-term. She'd been vague about her plans.

But she was here now. And so was a dark sedan belonging to the surveillance team, parked in front of his home. It'd serve as a constant reminder of how close a call she'd had this morning. And of the danger that persisted until the shooter was apprehended.

Habit had him picking up the remote and turning on the TV. They'd grabbed something to eat on the way back from Marshall. "What's your next step?"

Talk of work roused her, the way he'd known it would. "I called a task-force meeting for tomorrow. Crawley said he'd have one of his deputies deliver Fielding's cell to the Greensboro lab today. Hopefully cyber forensics will be quick."

"I should have the eTrace results for the weapon tomorrow. I'll email them to you." He'd submitted the weapon's model name, manufacturer, and serial number into the ATF's online site. A technician would trace the weapon to its first owner. "If the Edneyville lab fast-tracks the ballistics tests, they could forward the results to Greensboro. Maybe the recovered brass and bullets can be matched with the ones found in the Matthis and Bahlman homicides."

She still hadn't sat down. Ryder could feel the nerves radiating from her. He crossed to the couch and dropped down on it. "Have you called your mom since this morning?" As guilt flickered in her expression, he mentally damned his words.

"You're right." She drew her cell out of her jeans pocket. Checked the time. "I'd hate to have her hear about the shooting secondhand." She went into the room where they'd put her things. Shut the door.

Ryder flipped on a Duke game. By the time it was over, Cady hadn't returned. He switched off the lights and TV and headed to the back door to let Sadie out for the final time. His mind wasn't on the task. It'd been just after dawn when Cady had walked outside this morning on much the same errand. And almost wound up dead.

His fingers curled. Between the shooting and the Fielding bombshell today, he knew her investigation had taken a giant leap forward. It remained to be seen whether it could be solved before another attempt was made on Cady's life.

The dog bounded back up the deck. He stepped aside and let her in, locking up. It took more restraint than he would have imagined to walk past that closed bedroom door. To climb into bed alone. He hadn't expected to sleep. There were too many thoughts bumping and colliding in his mind, much like the clouds scudding in the night sky outside. But he must have. He had a sense that some time had passed when he came alert. The door to his room had opened.

She stood in shadow, but there was no mistaking her silhouette. Blood pooled in his groin. Without a word, he reached over and flipped the covers back on the bed. She padded across the room and slid between them. Their embrace was desperate. Urgent. Cady was often an enigma. But right now, Ryder knew both of them needed the same thing.

Chapter 28

"What are you still doing up?"

Dylan hid behind his back the knife he'd pulled from the drawer, feeling foolish. He hadn't expected his mom home at—he snuck a glance at the clock on the stove—eleven o'clock. He'd been so shocked by the headlights in the drive, he'd immediately assumed the worst. That Forrester had found him. That Dylan had only minutes to live.

His paranoia was probably made worse by that weird flashback he'd had on the way to shop today. Dylan had no idea if it'd been a real memory or not. But he assumed so, because he'd had a pounding headache like he always got when he thought too much about that night in the woods.

Tina walked by him into the living room, and he snuck the knife back into the drawer he'd gotten it from. "I was just going to bed." Surreptitiously, he eased the drawer closed. Followed her into the next room.

She obviously didn't realize he was lying. Or didn't care. His mom dropped her purse onto the floor and sat heavily on the couch. "Christ, what a fucking day. I got cramps and a headache to boot. Get me some Midol from the pink purse in my closet, will you, baby?"

Silently, Dylan did as he was told. He stopped in the bathroom for a glass of water. Handed both to her.

"Thanks."

"I cleaned the house today." He'd figured it would help to get his mom in a good mood. Which now looked like a waste.

"You do the bathroom?"

"Yeah." It had to be the grossest job in the universe. As much as Dylan disliked school, if a diploma saved him from a job like that, it'd be worth sticking it out. His mom hadn't seemed to care that Colton never made it through. Somehow he suspected it'd be different with him. Everything always was. "Do you have to work tomorrow?" It'd be a good time to try to figure out her schedule for the week.

"No, thank God. Not till Friday. Then Sunday again, because that fucking manager hates me."

His heart dropped. But better to know up front. He'd been turning over possibilities in his head all evening. He could tell Grace he was busy for a while. Or . . . "I have to stay after school tomorrow. Probably the next day too."

Hand on her forehead, Tina cracked open one eye to survey him. "No. You don't. You need me to call the school and tell them exactly that, I will."

That was definitely the last thing Dylan wanted. "It's an assignment. And I can't do it here because I need internet."

Her eyes closed again. "Do it in study hall."

"It's a paper for history. It's going to take a while. I have to get a couple of pages written every day if I want to be done by the time it's due." When she said nothing, he plowed ahead. "Could you pick me up around four thirty from school the next couple of days?"

"Sure, Dylan, there's nothing I want to do more than drag the laundry to the Laundromat tomorrow, spend hours doing the wash, do the grocery shopping, and then toddle over to your school to chauffeur you home. No. Take the bus."

His stomach clenched. Her answer was hardly surprising. "I remembered something about that night," he blurted out. Then stopped himself. Talking about what happened in the woods all those years ago just got his mom wound up.

Her eyes flew open. "What night?" When he looked away, she snapped, "Dylan Ray. You know what I told you. It ain't good for you to dwell on it."

Dwell on it. That was a laugh. Like the night of Trev's death was ever far from his mind. "I remembered a backpack." He studied his mom's face carefully. "Forrester was yelling about it when he chased us."

"First I ever heard about it. The cops didn't mention it, and you never talked about it to that doctor, neither."

Doubt filtered through him. She'd know. She'd been with him at every appointment and each time he'd talked to the deputies.

"Listen to me, now. I told you over and over. Try to forget that night. That's what the doctor said back then."

That wasn't exactly what Dylan recalled the doctor saying. But his mom was still talking. "You and me are a team, right? You do your part and I do mine. Don't forget it."

"Yeah, yeah." He turned to walk away. She'd been saying that for years now, but only ever to him. Never Colton. His older brother had always gotten special treatment.

"Get on back here. I ain't finished." Grudgingly, he faced her again. "It don't do you no good making yourself sick over trying to remember what's done. Gave yourself a headache, didn't you?"

Sometimes, when she bothered to look, she saw too damn much. "Yeah."

"This is the kind of thing I've been worrying about for a while now. It ain't healthy to have you here alone all the time. Or safe. I've invited Uncle Teeter to come stay for a while, for some extra protection."

"Huh?" It took a minute for him to comprehend. "Uncle T is coming here?" He'd been a little kid the last time he'd seen John Teeter. His memory of him was hazy, but he recalled that he was tall. And he'd always brought him and Colton presents when he came to visit. "Do the agents know?"

"No, and they ain't gonna."

Dylan sat on the arm of the couch. "What if they show up?"

"Why would they? They ain't exactly offering you around-the-clock protection, are they?"

"That marshal came last week."

Tina straightened. "He can sleep in Colton's bed." Dylan mentally groaned. Because one thing he did remember was that T snored like a buzz saw. "And he can keep his car in the garage during the day. Or in back of it. Even if someone comes, no reason they'd know he's here, and none of their business anyway."

The paranoia that had filled him earlier this evening came rushing back. "Why now? Did something happen? Was Forrester sighted in town?"

"Jesus, no, calm down. That's why you need someone else around. It ain't normal to think about this shit all the time." She leaned over for the purse she'd dropped on the floor and rummaged through it for a pack of cigarettes. Lit one. "When we left Hope Mills, I never woulda guessed we'd still be living like this after five years. All I thought about was getting you and Colton somewheres safe." She drew deeply on the cigarette and exhaled on her next words. "You're sixteen now."

He wouldn't turn sixteen for several months, but he knew better than to correct her.

"Boy your age needs people in his life. Time for horsing around with friends and whatnot. Guess you get some of that at school, but you're still alone too much."

He kept his head down, staring at the worn carpet. There was no point in telling her that he deliberately didn't make friends at his schools anymore. Being buddies with Dylan had signed Ethan's death warrant, all because they'd switched hoodies for a few days. Getting too close to

Dylan Castle—looking a bit like him—had gotten two kids murdered. Did she really think he'd chance that again?

"Maybe instead of having Uncle T come, Colton could just move back." Not that his brother and mom got along that well. This life hadn't been good for Colton, either.

"That ain't happening. He's got himself a girl. Couldn't blast him from her side right now. Anyway, he's a grown man. He should be living his own life, long as he keeps a low profile. Believe me, I check in regular to make sure he's doing just that."

It was the first Dylan had heard of it. "Where is he? Nearby?" Colton hadn't visited in months.

"Not too far. That ain't the point, though. If Forrester finds this place, it'd take a lot longer for the cops to arrive than for him to sh—" She broke off and amended, "For him to do the worst. You need more of a bodyguard. Someone who'd be here all the time even when I'm not around."

"I don't know. What if the agents get mad that we're not following orders?" They might just pull out, leave them to Forrester. Just the thought of the chance they were taking had his palms going slick. Yeah, they hadn't found Forrester yet, but he trusted them more than someone he hadn't even seen in years.

"They don't need to know everything," Tina snapped. She was smoking in quick little puffs, a sure sign she was getting pissed.

A sudden thought occurred. "Is he really my uncle? Or . . ." Distaste twisted through him. His mom had a habit of attaching the title to random guys who followed her home. And he knew for sure she and Tami didn't have a brother.

"As good as. My mom moved us in with his daddy and kids for a while when I was a teen. T's the only person in my life who's always been there for me. Once when I was in a heap of trouble for sneaking in way after curfew, he threw a baseball through the window so our parents would forget about being mad at me and yell at him instead."

"Why didn't he just help you think of a good excuse for being late?" Dylan asked logically.

"That ain't the point." She blew out a thin stream of smoke. Squinted at him through it. "He stuck up for me. He will for you, too, if it comes to that. He's been helping us right along, though you don't know it. It was T who found a different car for me when we moved here. I paid him, but this one's in his name instead of mine. So no one can use the DMV to find us."

As far as Dylan knew, only cops could access the DMV. But there was no point mentioning that or anything else. It wasn't like he had any real say in much that went on here. Then her earlier words belatedly registered. "T will have a car? So he could pick me up from school? Just till I get this assignment done?"

His mom shoved herself from the couch and started for her bedroom. "I s'pose. But he ain't taking you anywhere else. School and home. That much ain't changed."

It was enough. Dylan stared at her receding back. They didn't have to go to Grace's house. After tomorrow, he could make an excuse for working at school.

He still wasn't happy about having to share his bedroom with a man he barely recalled. But his mom was right about one thing. T coming might make his life a little more normal.

Just not in the way she thought.

Chapter 29

After failing to find Tina Bandy's car in the lots of any of the Food Marts, Bruce had picked one store and watched the doors all day to see if she'd exit. When she hadn't, he'd headed home, intent on trying another one tomorrow. He'd swung by the school, too, as it was letting out to see if he recognized the kid. If he had, he could have put an end to this mess in a hurry.

The hours he'd spent with nothing to show for it soured his mood. It was a long trek back to the cabin. Shifting his thoughts to the woman he'd taken cheered him. He'd followed a group of females home from a bar, hoping to catch one alone. But they'd stuck together all the way into the motel. He'd been about to leave when he saw the blonde getting out of her vehicle.

Happening upon her in that parking lot was a sign, his granny would have said. His mind wandered, as it often did, to his grandmother. She'd been a weird old gal. Given to believing she had powers like some sort of voodoo queen. The old bat had thought being deprived of oxygen brought visions. So sometimes she'd have him choke her unconscious. She'd taught him exactly where to place his hands and for how long. The memory flooded him with warmth.

Watching the consciousness fade from her eyes had always given him a woody.

She might have been half-loony, but she'd sparked a fascination that had lasted throughout his life. The act of dying was riveting.

And he liked to watch.

Chapter 30

"Forget a different vehicle," Miguel said when Cady walked into the office. "We're getting you an armored truck."

"You're just saying that because you're stuck riding with me for the duration." When Allen had said he'd name another marshal to attach to her hip for the foreseeable future, she'd figured it'd be Miguel. They often partnered together.

"I'm the obvious choice." His breezy tone didn't hide the worry in his gaze. "Bullets bounce off me. Seriously, though. Too damn close yesterday."

"No kidding." She draped her coat on the back of the chair. Sat.

"You'll be happy to know that while you were dodging bullets, I was doing the equally valiant but less attention-getting task of contacting those names from the Madison County detention center."

"From the night Forrester was arrested there? You're officially my hero." She hadn't made contact with more than ten people on the list yet, with zero results.

"That'd mean so much more if I didn't know how easily you throw that word around. How is the super canine today?" He handed her an untouched cup of coffee from his desk. Cady's brows rose. Solicitude from Rodriguez was almost—almost—worth getting shot at. She took a sip.

"Vet wasn't open today yet, but I saw Hero yesterday. He was still groggy from surgery. I expect he'll be raising hell soon about being kept in that kennel." At least she hoped so.

Miguel handed her a list, and she scanned the names he'd crossed off. Between his efforts and hers, they were almost through the Madison County inmates. "Did you get anything from these contacts?"

"Very little. A few remembered Forrester. A couple recalled him in the cell with Byrd. No one claimed to have spoken to either man."

It was about what she expected. The task was something to be checked off, nothing more. And now that they had a weapon—and soon cyber forensics on Fielding's phone—whatever information they might get from a former inmate on that list was likely to pale in comparison.

As if to underscore that thought, the cell in her pocket buzzed. She pulled it out. Checked the screen before answering. "Marshal Maddix."

"Marshal. This is Jim Upton at Craggy Correctional."

"Good morning, Warden." She turned toward Miguel, who was clearly eavesdropping.

"It's a bit of a surprise, but Stephen Tillis has agreed to your request for an interview."

Her brows rose. "Happy to hear that. Is he usually less cooperative?"

Upton gave a short laugh. "That's not an adjective I'd use in conjunction with him. Maybe his upcoming parole hearing is a factor in his decision. When would you like us to arrange the meeting?"

"Is an hour too soon?"

"I think we can manage that. I'll let security know that you're expected."

"Thank you." When she disconnected, Miguel was already up, reaching for his coat.

"If I have to wear a vest, why wouldn't you need one if we're together?"

Looking pained, he turned toward the door. "It's in my truck. I assume I'm driving again."

It was probably wiser than taking the car she'd rented and driven here today. But it meant shelving their usual turn-taking behind the wheel. "You've gotten lucky, Rodriguez." They jogged down the steps facing the parking lot, and Miguel used his fob to open the door. "Don't let it go to your head, though. Eventually, I will get another vehicle." She hoped.

Despite allegedly agreeing to this interview, Stephen Tillis did not look happy to see them. With shackles on his wrists and ankles, he was seated at a scarred table in a small interview room. When Cady and Miguel walked in, a guard stayed outside the door.

Tillis's shaven head gleamed under the lights. His dark mustache and goatee were shot with silver. He watched them impassively as they entered.

"Deputy US Marshals Maddix and Rodriguez." Cady pulled out a chair opposite the man. Miguel remained standing. "Thank you for speaking with us."

"Never heard of a woman marshal before."

"There are more of us than you'd think." She didn't flinch from the man's baleful gaze. "I'd like to talk to you about the events in Hope Mills five years ago. In Hanson Woods."

He blinked. "What for?"

"Because we're working a warrant for Bruce Forrester, and maybe you can help us find him."

"Shee-it. Wondered what marshals would want with me. I don't know nothing 'bout Forrester."

"You know him."

"Used to."

"How well?"

He stared at her for a long time and then away, as if making up his mind about something. "I told the cops everything back then."

"You weren't in those woods, you didn't know anything about the drug ring, you were fishing alone in the creek, and you didn't see anything."

He smirked. "Sounds like you read the statement."

"I also know you lied on it." Anger clouded his features. "Two witnesses place you in the woods with the other three men. Even more can attest to your friendship with Forrester and Loomer." A bartender and a neighbor had stated that the three had been seen together on more than one occasion.

"Don't mean we were together that night." He was silent for a minute. "Say I did hear something, though. Maybe I set my fishing pole down and went into the woods to see what was going on."

So he was sticking with the innocent fisherman story. Half-amused, Cady said nothing, although she wondered what the man had to lose by coming clean at this point.

"There was a clearing, like. That's where they were cooking. I got a pretty good look. Recognized the three men."

"Their names?"

"You know." He sounded impatient. "Forrester. Loomer. Weber."

"What else could you see in the clearing?" Cady asked.

He shrugged. "Stuff strewn around. What they use to make that shit."

So far, his big reveal was a bust. "Did you see anyone besides those three men?"

"No, but . . ." She waited for him to go on, but he was stroking his goatee, thinking. "Okay, there was a tent. Farther off from the clearing, but it had to have been theirs, because it was close enough that they'd see it."

Interest sparked inside her. Although Dylan had claimed to have seen a tan tent, Weber had denied one had been in the vicinity. "Describe it."

"Not a big camping tent. A pup tent, I guess you'd call it. Only fits one or two people, if they was to sleep in it."

"What color was it?"

He stroked his beard again. "Brownish. I don't know. It was moving around like someone was in there. I figured it was a woman, maybe a whore they'd brought along for later."

Everything inside Cady stilled. "Did Forrester frequent prostitutes?"

"He had a taste for 'em. Probably because they don't run to the cops."

He liked the rougher stuff. Weber's statement took on new meaning. "Did he ever express a sexual interest in children?"

"Not to me."

"There were two young boys in the woods that night. Did you see them?"

"Nope."

"Did you hear shouting? A commotion?"

"Like I told the cops back then, I moved down the bank some and didn't see or hear nothing else."

Cady tried a bit longer, but after a couple more minutes of questioning, it was clear they'd reached the limits of Tillis's cooperation. Finally, she rose. "Thank you for your time."

"What if I could tell you something else about Forrester?"

Exchanging a glance with Miguel, she sank back into her seat. "Like what?"

His wrist manacles clanked when he clasped his hands on the table between them. "Say I heard something once. Something no one else knows about."

"Like . . . ?"

"Like where he buried a body. Pieces of it anyway."

Her heart rate sped up. This was a new twist. "Who?"

"Guy by the name of Brady Boss. The guy tried to knife him. Forrester was waiting when he got out on bail." His lips twisted in amusement. "Payback time."

Cady's mind flashed to the conversation with Weber. *Used a chain saw on him, then got rid of the pieces.* "How'd he kill him?"

Tillis lifted a shoulder. "All I know—what I heard," he corrected himself, "is the body parts were dumped in Cutter's Swamp, between Hope Mills and Fayetteville." He sat back in his chair, looking pleased with himself. "You check that out and then tell the warden about my help."

Suppressing the excitement singing through her veins, Cady nodded. "I'll follow up. If what you say is true, I'll make a call to the warden."

The guard opened the door for Cady and Miguel to exit the room, and another one posted outside escorted them to the entrance.

"He's still pretending he wasn't in the woods that night," Miguel noted. "What would he have to lose at this point by telling the truth?"

"I have no idea. But that part about the body? It follows with what Weber told us about Forrester killing his attacker with a chain saw. I followed up with the Cumberland sheriff's office. The man charged in the knife fight was Brady Boss. He never showed up for court, and no one ever saw him around there again." Her thoughts flashed to what Simmons had said about Gordon Melbourne. Cady couldn't help but wonder if he'd met a similar fate.

They left the confines of the prison and walked toward the vehicle. With the ladder on top and various equipment in the back, it'd fit in at a construction site. Which was exactly the reason the USMS used it.

Miguel reached out a hand and remotely unlocked the pickup as she pulled out her cell and placed a call to the Cumberland sheriff to relay the tip. When Cady'd finished the conversation, she slipped into the truck, picking up the earlier conversation as if the interruption hadn't occurred. "Why would Weber deny seeing a tent in the woods when Tillis made it sound like it'd be hard to miss?"

Miguel started the pickup. "Both of them are motivated by saying whatever gets them what they want. A deal for Weber and now a good word with the parole board for Tillis."

"Definitely." But if the details about Brady Boss panned out, Tillis would have opened a whole new avenue of investigation into Forrester's past.

When Miguel reached for the thermostat control, she slapped his hand away. "You have to be watched every second." The rules were clear. The passenger ran the radio and heat.

"You keep it too cold in here."

She smiled. "You have the body temperature of a ninety-year-old." They pulled out of the lot and headed for the first of several security checkpoints. "Despite Forrester's deep conversation with Byrd in the Madison County jail, I haven't been able to verify that he shares the man's pedophilia."

"It might be the one vice Forrester doesn't have." Miguel took sunglasses out of his pocket and flipped them open, settling them on his nose. "Maybe his interest in Byrd was just the inside workings of the deep web and not necessarily the subject matter."

"Exactly." She sat back, satisfied. Cady didn't know what it all meant yet. But she had a theory to share with the task force when it convened later today.

She took out her cell and opened an email she'd received from Ryder. It was the eTrace results on the weapon found yesterday. She'd have to hustle when they got back to the office to get the information run off for the meeting later.

Noting she had a missed call, she checked the caller ID. Dread slithered into her gut when she saw Haywood County Detention Center. There was only one person it could be from. Her cousin Bo.

He'd tried to contact her before. She hadn't returned that call, either. He and Alma refused to believe Cady couldn't save him from the consequences of his actions.

And she wouldn't pretend to even want to.

Chapter 31

"You wanted to see me?" Jerry Garza appeared at Ryder's office door.

"I do. Shut the door, would you?" Once his chief investigator did so, Ryder waved him to a seat facing his desk. "Anything new on the porch pirates?"

Jerry shook his head woefully. He'd be about Ryder's dad's age, had Butch lived. Well into his sixties, Jerry showed no indication that he was considering retirement anytime soon.

"You've been here since, what? The eighties?"

"Came on in eighty-eight. Was a cop in Richmond prior." Garza hiked an ankle over the opposite knee. "You know that, though. Looking for some history?"

"More like solving something that's been puzzling me." Ryder hesitated. Loyalty to Butch Talbot lingered in the office. The man had been well liked by the crew here. The need for diplomacy was paramount. "I went to look up an old case file on the Digital ReeL and discovered it was missing. It's also not in the files downstairs."

The older man arrowed a look at him. "Seems to me there's nothing like having the physical file in my hands. Never did see the point in getting rid of them."

He'd kept his opinion to himself, Ryder reflected. Which was another reason the man was a trusted employee. "Digital ReeL transferred everything we had from microfilm."

"So it was never on microfilm." Ryder rarely had to waste time explaining things to him. Garza frowned, swiping a hand over his gray buzz cut. "Huh. You think it was lost or misplaced?"

"I did. Until I found it and a few others at Dad's place."

"Are they connected in some way? He might have wanted to take a closer look at them, look for a pattern."

"Not that I can figure out. There are six of them. Different types of cases, different people. The dates range from the mideighties to early two thousand."

"And none of them appear on the ReeL?" Garza rubbed his craggy jaw for a minute. "Well, there might be one thing. Your daddy ran unopposed most of the time, but every now and again some young upstart ran against him. A couple of times things got a little heated. What was that punk's name?" he muttered to himself. "Fitzgerald. Got himself elected as a county supervisor and was a real thorn in your daddy's side. Liked to stick his nose in where it didn't belong. Thought he'd take himself a run at sheriff. Couple other times we had a deputy who didn't see eye to eye with Butch do the same thing."

"You're saying my dad would have removed files of cases that might have reflected badly on him?"

"Not saying that at all." Again, Ryder was reminded that Garza and his father had likely been close. "I'm saying someone with the desire can twist the facts of a case to make it look any which way they want. The press covers the sensational and ignores the boring reality."

Since he'd had his own experiences with media, Ryder nodded. "They surely can." Nothing in the files had struck him as particularly sensitive. Even the Maddix case, while tragic, had appeared open-and-shut. "Doesn't explain why they were never converted to microfilm in the first place."

The man shrugged. "Sorry, Ryder. I just don't know what to tell you."

"No problem. At least I found them." But long after Garza departed, Ryder turned the matter over in his mind, forming and rejecting theories about the files that had been hidden in Butch's garage. His relationship with his father had never been an easy one. And maybe that fact was impacting the possible scenarios that occurred to him. Because none of them cast Butch Talbot in a particularly flattering light.

Chapter 32

Cady looked around the table at the task-force members present as she concluded summarizing the events of the last few days. "I have the warrant for Fielding's cell. Once cyber forensics is finished with it, we can get the provider to ping it for location data." It was just after noon. She wondered if they were destined to always meet over empty stomachs.

"The rifle will be a great lead too." ATF special agent Gabe Pearson held up the eTrace results she'd distributed to the group. "Too bad you nearly had to be killed because of it." There was a murmur of agreement from the rest of the individuals around the table.

"That's me." She tried to hide her discomfit with a light tone. "Always willing to take one for the team. The Haywood County sheriff's office is investigating the shooting. But ballistics will tell us whether the weapon links to the one used in the Matthis and Bahlman homicides. I'm hoping you can fast-track the rifle's line of ownership investigation."

"eTrace gave us the first owner," Gabe replied. "I'll see if it can be tracked from there."

The *if* in his statement was critical, Cady knew. If ownership of the weapon had been transferred, the trail could get snarled. Criminals rarely used weapons that could be traced directly to them. Private sales and theft could be insurmountable obstacles to ever finding the current owner.

"Ballistics will give us certainty as to whether the weapon was used in the boys' homicides as well as in the attempt on Cady yesterday," Gabe concluded.

"My supervisor dug up my former warrants in this office to see if anyone of interest pops. That was a bust." Cady hadn't expected any differently. Her mind went to the only bandit she'd killed in the line of duty when she'd worked out of the Saint Louis office. Little more than a boy, really. Her reaction when she'd rounded the corner of the house and found him with his weapon pressed against another marshal's forehead had been instinctive. Instantaneous. But knowing it'd been found a good shoot didn't banish the scene from her memory. His family likely held her more responsible than most. But they were also six hundred miles away.

DEA agent Curtis Weddig spoke up then. "I've been talking to fellow agents and drug task-force personnel around the state. While Loomer wasn't a known entity to those in Cumberland County, Forrester was. He had midlevel status when he lived in Hope Mills. But his name isn't on anyone's radar now. That might mean if he's still in the state, he's no longer involved in drug trafficking. Or he's doing so under an assumed name."

"Forrester has to be making a living somehow." Cady tapped her index finger on the table as she formulated her thoughts. "He could be operating out of state or has false ID, as Curtis mentioned. I initially thought Forrester's conversation with Byrd in the Madison County jail might mean he shared Byrd's pedophilia. But I haven't gotten any verification of that from our interviews. From Suzanne Fielding's statement, we know that Forrester went right back to drug dealing after his release from prison. If he's still at it, he could be using the deep web to sell his product this time. No one I've talked to claims that Forrester has computer skills, but two have verified that Loomer does."

"That's a lot of maybes," SBI agent Rebedeau noted. "And tracking anything on the deep web is like looking for a needle in a haystack. Especially without a site name or an IP address."

"Probably," she admitted. "But I know those who do monitor cybercrime often run across things they aren't actively investigating. They still might make note of it."

"DEA has cyber agents, right, Curtis?" Cady shifted her focus to Weddig.

He nodded. "I can ask Henry Dallas. Maybe he's aware of some drug sites that have been traced to this area."

It was clear he didn't put much stock in the idea. Cady didn't take offense. It was a long shot. And they were much more likely to catch Forrester by triangulating the location of his phone than running a drawn-out cyber investigation, even if one was warranted. She looked around the table. "Does anyone else have updates?" When no one spoke, she picked up the pen next to the yellow pad on the table in front of her. "We know we're only hours away before we have lab results on Fielding's phone, which will give us Forrester's number. Then we can start pushing his phone provider and, God help us, maybe get a general location. Let's brainstorm multiple strategies for various eventualities and the personnel needed for each."

The best scenario would be if Forrester had a fully equipped smartphone. Pinging sometimes gave an exact location. Other times, however, it narrowed the area to a few square miles. It didn't matter. Adrenaline kick-started in her veins. Soon enough, they'd have a place to start the search for Bruce Forrester.

Chapter 33

Dylan trudged up the overgrown drive toward the house. Riding the bus home had sucked more than usual after a couple of days away from it. He hated the noise. He hated the constant stops and the bus driver yelling at the students horsing around. He hated that few of the kids were even in middle school yet, and most of the laughing and yelling revolved around jokes about farts and belching. He could barely recall being that age. It was like he'd been put in a time capsule and forced to age in a bubble.

His mom's car was in the drive. Dylan was surprised and a little pissed. There was no reason she couldn't have come and gotten him at school like he'd asked. He could have spent a couple of hours with Grace, which would have been a hell of a lot better than the damn bus.

Out of sorts, he took the key from his pocket and unlocked the door. They never left it open, even when they were inside. Security was a way of life.

Tina sat at the kitchen table with an open beer in front of her. "I didn't expect you home," Dylan observed. "You said you wouldn't be."

"No, I said I wasn't gonna be your damn chauffeur. Come on in here."

Disgruntled, he let his backpack slide to the floor by the couch and went to the kitchen. He hoped she'd at least gone to the store today. "You still haven't given me money for my lunch account." And the spare cash he'd found scavenging through her collection of purses wouldn't last long. He'd given some thought more than once to smashing that big piggy bank on his dresser. T had given that to him when he was little. But his mom would kick his ass if he did, and it wasn't like there'd be much in it anyway. "By tomorrow, they probably won't let me eat."

"Jesus, you're in a mood today." She snatched up her purse, which sat on the table next to a pack of cigarettes, and rummaged through it. Brought out two twenties and slammed them on the table. "Take it and quit your bitching. Been working my ass off doing laundry and shopping today. A thank-you would be nice."

Guilt filtered through him. Dylan didn't ever recall when she hadn't worked full-time, or at least juggled a couple of part-time jobs to make ends meet. And he couldn't do much to help, other than to keep the place neat. "Thanks, Mom."

She grunted. "Welcome. Grab a soda or something and sit down here. We need to talk."

He pulled open the refrigerator and felt some of his ire fade away. It was stocked full. Selecting a Gatorade, he shut the door and twisted off the top of the bottle, flicking it into the trash in the corner before sinking into a chair next to his mom.

A man came around the corner into the room holding a beer. He must have been in the bathroom or one of the bedrooms. He grinned at Dylan, revealing a gold bottom tooth that winked in the light. "Hey, boy. Been a long time."

Recognition flickered. He was tall and built like a toothpick. Shaggy brown hair nearly reached his shoulders. "Hey, Uncle T."

Teeter bounded into the room, punched Dylan in the shoulder. "Hellfire, kid, stand up and let me get a look at ya." Grabbing him by the arm, he dragged Dylan out of the chair. Looked him up and down.

"Holy shit. You might get tall as me someday. Last time I saw you, you was barely to my chest."

Discomfited, Dylan sank back down again. "Well, I was just a kid. Five or so."

"No, you was older than that." Teeter sat down in the remaining chair and gulped from the can he held. "As I recall, it was right before the trouble in Hope Mills. You'd a been ten, I think."

Lifting a shoulder, Dylan brought the bottle to his mouth so he didn't have to respond. He didn't see how bringing T here was going to change much of anything. Unless . . . His gaze went back to the man. He wasn't armed. That didn't mean he didn't carry, though. And from what his mom had said, he must have a gun if she thought he'd be protection against Forrester.

"Like me and you talked about yesterday, Teeter will make sure no one comes nosing around," his mom said.

"Someone does, I'll make damn sure they regret it." Teeter's Adam's apple bobbed as he took a long swallow, then wiped his mouth on his shirtsleeve.

"Not a word of this to anyone," Tina said, getting up to grab a couple more beers out of the fridge. "We wanna keep this quiet." She sank into her chair again and slid one of the beers over to Teeter.

T winked at Dylan. "Your mom said you'll need a ride home sometimes. I'll be glad to do it. Long as I stay outside the school. Hated going even when I had to, y'know?"

Smiling slowly, Dylan nodded. "Yeah." Working at Grace's house would be out of the question now, of course, but they could still meet after school. He looked at the man thoughtfully. It remained to be seen if the freedom he represented outweighed having gained a warden.

Chapter 34

It was nearly seven by the time Cady pulled into Ryder's drive. She'd been in touch with the vet, and he'd promised to come in early tomorrow so she could collect Hero. He wouldn't be going home, though. Neither of them would. Then she'd made a quick trip across town to check on her mom, who'd seemed—much to her relief—back to normal. Not even to herself would she admit that she'd put off returning to Ryder's for as long as possible.

She turned off her rental car. Sat motionless for a minute. The surveillance team parked in the discreet dark sedan in front of the house was a stark reminder of how far things had shifted out of her control. Cady glanced at Ryder's home, lights aglow in its windows. It was a perfectly nice house, but it wasn't *hers*. She hated being dependent on someone else. None of the houses she'd shared with her mom had been permanent. They'd always been one missed rent check away from being homeless. And given her mom's taste in men, there'd been plenty of missed rent checks. Hannah had ping-ponged between relying on Alma's largesse when they'd occasionally lived with her and her boys and then sending Cady to spend years with a grandfather who'd hated the sight of her. And had shown it at every opportunity.

To be fair, Elmer Griggs had hated everybody. She'd just been the one unfortunate enough to be at his mercy.

Grabbing her laptop and purse, Cady got out and locked the vehicle.

Her gut clenched as she approached the front door. Did she knock? Walk in? A woman her age should have more experience with this sort of thing. In her adult life, she'd made damn sure she'd had her own space. She protected her privacy religiously.

In the end, she didn't need to worry. Cady heard Sadie barking, and by the time she reached the porch, Ryder was holding the door open for her. "Just in time. What do you know about cooking chili?"

"Ah . . ." Her mind went blank as she followed him inside, where she toed off her boots before trailing after him into the kitchen. "You open a can, dump it in a bowl, and warm it up in the microwave?"

"It's a sad day when my expertise in the kitchen surpasses yours."

She set her things down next to the breakfast bar. Spotting a Crock-Pot on the counter, she moseyed over as he was lifting the lid off it. The smell was heavenly. "Looks made."

"Not by me. I should have been more specific. Mom brought this over but said she was leaving me to season it myself. What does that mean? Do you put salt and pepper in chili?"

Her mouth quirked. "Maybe chili powder. Or red pepper." That was about the limit of her knowledge. "I think she might have meant season it to taste. How do you like it?"

"Hellfire hot." He cocked a brow at her. "And you?"

"Medium spicy. So season your bowl, not the entire pot."

He immediately started opening cupboards, muttering, "Do I have chili powder or red pepper?"

Amused, she said, "You do if your mom bought your spices."

"She likes to help."

"Uh-huh."

"Get some bowls and spoons, will you?"

Cady opened cupboards and drawers until she found both, plus a ladle. She set the bowls and ladle next to the pot, and spoons at the bar. She went to fetch glasses before hesitating. "What do you want to drink?"

"I'm having a beer. But there's milk in the refrigerator if you want some."

She snagged two bottles of beer and placed them on the bar. A moment later, he was setting two steaming bowls of soup on it, sliding one toward her. "Unseasoned. See what you think." With amusement, she watched him shake seasonings into his, pausing to bring a spoonful to his lips before sprinkling more. Cady sat down, twisted off the beer cap, and took a drink before picking up her spoon to taste. "This is fine." She batted away his hand when he reached to hover over her bowl, holding the chili pepper. "I can do without hellfire, thanks."

They ate companionably, conversation interspersed between eating. "Did you hear from the lab today?" Ryder asked.

"Cyber forensics came through. There were three different numbers on Fielding's cell that she indicated were Forrester's. The cell provider is pinging all of them, but the number he used recently is probably most viable. They haven't gotten anything yet. And as expected, no personal contact info was needed for ownership of the plans related to the numbers."

He paused in the act of raising a spoon to his mouth. Lowered it, all the while looking at her. "I'm more concerned about what he'd do with the information she gave him about your addition to the case." His intimation was clear.

"We don't have proof he was the shooter," she reminded him. It would boot her off the warrant if and when they received it. "What would killing me gain him? If I'm out of the picture, another marshal will take my place."

"Maybe he sees you as the first real threat toward his capture." Ryder resumed eating, his expression pensive.

"He's had SBI after him for five years," she scoffed. "My addition is hardly a game changer."

"It is when he just abducted Cassie Zook." Ryder pointed his spoon at her for emphasis. "He has to wonder if that's what brought you aboard, and if it did, how the cops ID'd him. If he's smart, he'll figure your appearance probably relates to fresh charges against him. That could have caused him to panic. Maybe he thought taking you out would buy him some time."

She couldn't refute Ryder's words. She was learning more about the fugitive but not enough to predict what he'd do if he felt cornered.

He liked to watch. Michael Simmons's words floated across her mind, leaving a chill in their wake. The only hard proof she had of Forrester's recent criminal activity was the grainy security footage of him shoving Zook into a trunk. The one thing she could be certain of was the man's propensity for violence.

Ryder got up and fetched soup crackers from another cupboard and sat down again, putting the package on the counter between them. Cady ate silently for several minutes before saying, "I worry that having three different numbers associated with him might mean he switches cells frequently. If we're lucky, he's still using the number Fielding called days ago. The longest she ever waited for a callback from him was a day. We'll get something. Soon." Any location information determined by his cell usage meant the noose was tightening.

Her thoughts shifted to Dylan Castle. His story had struck a sympathetic chord in her from the start. Cady's situation when she'd lived under Elmer Griggs's roof had been nearly as confining as the boy's was. Her world had included school, her grandfather's house, and the post-age-stamp-size backyard. Later she'd been able to escape to the library, and later still to a part-time job. But unlike Dylan, she hadn't spent her childhood fearing for her life.

They finished eating and cleaned up the kitchen, stacking the few dishes in the dishwasher while she updated Ryder on Hero's status. "I can pick him up tomorrow." She smiled. "He'll have to wear one of those cone things around his neck to keep him from bothering the wound for a while. He's going to hate that."

"I don't blame him. And I already mentioned your situation to my mom." He slammed the dishwasher shut and turned to look at her. "She's ready and willing to play nursemaid as needed. She said she'd be delighted."

Everything inside Cady shied away from the idea. Circumstances were forcing her hand, first into accepting Ryder's invitation and now his mother's help. There were reasons she'd avoided being drawn further into his family life. It was far easier to extricate herself from a relationship when there weren't other connections made.

"So you've had a helluva day." Ryder was fiddling with his bottle, the show of nervous energy unlike him.

"Better than yesterday by far."

"Goes without saying."

When he said nothing more, her instincts quivered. "Whatever it is you're worried about bringing up, just spit it out. You may not have noticed, but I'm not exactly the delicate-flower type."

He flashed a smile. "A massive understatement, but you're right. Just a minute." Mystified, she watched him go to the third bedroom, which he used as an office. He was back a moment later with a stack of folders in his hand.

The sight of them was like a fist to the belly. Her request to view the file on her dad's death had taken a back seat to recent events. "Are these all from . . . ?" She flipped through the folders. Noted the names on the tabs. "They don't all relate to my dad." Confused, she looked at him as he retook his seat at the bar.

"No, and I'll explain later. This is the one you wanted." He slipped one out of the pile and rested it on top.

Cady stared at the folder as if it were filled with vipers. For one brief instant, she regretted setting him on this quest. What difference would the contents make? She'd lived with the ramifications of that day all her life. Nothing would change by delving into the details. If anything, they'd just give her nightmares more material.

But her mom's outburst last Saturday had raised new questions. And she knew she wasn't going to be able to shunt those aside. Cady had never been a coward. Mentally steeling herself, she flipped open the folder.

The pictures were first. A mug shot of the man who'd fathered her. Lonny Francis Maddix. Her throat went tight as she studied it. The grainy police photo failed to conceal his handsomeness, the arrogance apparent in the jut of his jaw. Her gaze went to the identifying details below. She'd gotten her hair and eye color from him.

Turning to the next image, she recoiled a bit at the photo of her mom. She would have been around Cady's age at the time and was pretty, with the ethereal air that had attracted men all her life. There were spatters of blood on her face and in her hair. Her lip was split, and her eye had started to swell.

A vise tightened in Cady's chest as she stared at the image until her eyes began to blur.

"It doesn't have to be tonight." Ryder's voice was low. "It's a lot, with everything else going on. Might be best to put it off for a while."

He was handing her an out. Cady could only manage a headshake. She reached for a level of objectivism. Focused on the white nightdress her mom was wearing. The details of it were already etched on her mind, as if that, at least, had been safe to remember. The delicate ribbon that threaded the neckline. The scatter of rosebuds on the white fabric. The rivulets of blood staining it would have come from her injured lip. Or possibly a blow to the nose. Cady willed herself to remember. But she'd only ever recalled snippets of the scene. The shouting. Her mom's crying. The sound of the gunshot.

She forced herself to turn to the next picture. Caught her breath when she recognized the small weeping child in it in a miniature duplicate of her mother's nightdress. Her heart squeezed. What had happened later that night? Where had they gone? Who had helped? She didn't know. And Hannah had never said.

Next were crime photos. Lonny Maddix lying limp against the kitchen door in a pool of blood, eyes wide and staring, a hole in his chest. More images when the body had been taken away, replaced by *X*s and a chalk outline. The scarred wooden table.

She paused at the picture of the weapon. It was a small pistol but would still have been large for her four-year-old hand. Cady could almost—almost—recall its weight. The sound of the shot. Those details were constants in her dreams.

You don't like bad guys, do you, Cady? A shudder worked down her spine. The disembodied voice felt real, but when she tried to pull on that mental thread, she met a familiar blackness. With effort, she refocused on the file. It was a relief to be done with the images. Easier to tuck away the subjective and concentrate on the matter-of-fact police reports. A neighbor had reported the gunfire. That was new information. They hadn't always had a phone. She didn't know if that house had had one. Or whether her mom would have been emotionally equipped to call for help anyway.

Chief investigative deputy Harvey Klatt had responded, along with another deputy, Phillip Marlowe. Cady skimmed over the description of what they'd found at the scene. Slowed to read details of her mom's description of the evening. Lonny Maddix showing up. He'd been a wanted man at that point. She imagined the night had followed a familiar pattern. The drinking. The escalation of abuse.

She turned the page and stopped after the first paragraph, shock punching through her. The gun had been Hannah's. She'd had a permit. When Lonny had shown up, she'd run and gotten it. He'd taken it away from her. Slapped her and set it on the table. Dared her to pick it up.

It was hard not to focus on the terror her mom had felt that night. The helplessness. She'd been alone. Vulnerable, with a small child to protect. And still, every time Hannah drifted back to those days, she spoke lovingly of Lonny Maddix. As if after all this time she was still under his spell.

Cady was half-aware of Ryder moving to put his empty bottle in the recycling. She didn't look up. Couldn't. The report from the canvass done of the neighbors painted a sad and all-too-familiar picture. One statement after another revealed there'd been disturbances at the home before. Federal marshals had spoken to many of the people in the area, advising them to call if they spotted Lonny Maddix. Sheriff Butch Talbot himself had come by to tell them the same.

There was more. Much more. Numb by now, she flipped through autopsy reports. Hospital records. Hannah had been treated and released the same night. Cady slowed again at the report of the gunshot residue test on the hands of Cady Maddix. Read the particle count. There could be no doubt she'd been the shooter.

Don't go looking for anyone else to cast the blame on, missy. You mighta only been four, but you was the one who picked the gun up off the table and shot your daddy dead. Aunt Alma's words streaked across her mind. It hadn't occurred to Cady to doubt that. She hadn't sought the file in search of absolution. But neither had the contents shed much light on the event.

She turned to the last inserts in the file. They weren't from the night of the shooting, she noted immediately. And they hadn't originated from the sheriff's office.

They were copies of USMS reports.

Their inclusion rocked Cady. Perhaps they shouldn't have. The federal agency had likely been alerted by law enforcement whenever Lonny Maddix had been sighted. First was a copy of her father's sheet, surprisingly long for spending only one brief stint in prison previously. Then she took more time reading the summary of the bank robbery that had led to her father's federal warrant. There had been three men involved rather than the two she'd heard about. Stan Caster had driven the getaway vehicle. Paul Trimbull had partnered with Lonny in the actual robbery of the Community Savings Bank in Black Mountain and had been fatally shot by the security guard.

She skimmed the details about how Lonny and Stan had evaded law enforcement, but she focused on the steps the marshals had taken to track the two of them. Family. Girlfriends. It was a gut punch to read the list of women's names that had been associated with her father. He'd successfully avoided capture for more than a year before his death. Stan Caster had been captured within weeks.

Aware of the passing time, Cady began to read more quickly. Another report detailed a near miss the marshals had had when they'd had Cady's family's house surrounded six months before that fateful night.

> Subject ignored numerous opportunities to surrender and exchanged gunfire with marshals. The gunfire was followed by a standstill, in which an extraction plan was discussed. Before that could commence, the front door opened and Hannah Maddix emerged, pleading for an end to the shooting. She reported that the subject was inside, using their three-year-old daughter, Cady, as a shield from the gunfire. Minutes later, Lonny Maddix exited the rear entrance with the child draped over his back and fled on foot, shooting at team members. No shots were returned for fear of striking the child. Members attempted to follow on foot but were kept at bay by gunfire. Lonny Maddix escaped with the toddler, who was recovered unharmed six hours later in Maggie Valley, where it is believed the target stole a car to aid in his escape.

Cady stared at the text until the letters swam under her gaze. Her thoughts were stampeding like a thundering herd through her skull, impossible to corral. But one thing remained clear in the onslaught of accompanying emotion: her life had been identified by a single act. Guilt was her constant companion for killing her father when she was four. A father who had cared so little for her that he'd intentionally put her life at risk.

She forced herself to shuffle back through the pages of the incident report for the night her father was killed. Noted the time. The call to the sheriff's department had gone in at 11:30 p.m. Long after a four-year-old would be in bed. Based upon what she'd just read, the late hour wasn't because her father demanded to see her. It was all too obvious that he'd cared nothing for her. She'd likely been wakened by the turmoil and gone searching for her mom, igniting a series of events that would always haunt her.

Cady reached blindly for the bottle in front of her while she worked her way through the file again. Noted the number of welfare checks the office had made on Hannah Maddix and her daughter. They hadn't been enough to ward off the inevitable.

Finally, she lifted her gaze. Ryder was watching her, his expression grim. She knew in that moment he'd already read the file. Her hand trembled just a little as she closed the folder.

"Thank you. I'm not sure it changes anything, but I . . . Thank you." It was all she could manage. She was awash in a tangle of emotions. Cady didn't try to identify them. Couldn't. "Did you find it in a file drawer, finally?" He was drumming one index finger on the counter, a rhythmic tapping. Again she was struck by his unusual nervous energy.

"I found all those files in a secret compartment in the ceiling of my dad's garage."

Stunned, she could only stare at him. A moment later, her gaze fell to the other folders. "Are these—"

"They're unconnected to your case. At least I can't find a link. I talked to my chief investigative deputy. He thought maybe they'd been hidden because there was something in them an opponent could use in an election. But he couldn't come up with a reason why they wouldn't have been in the system."

A mental image formed. Of the man in the sheriff's uniform sitting on a chair in their kitchen with Cady's mom on his lap. One hand inside her shirt, cupping her breast.

She looked away, vowing again to keep the information from Ryder. It took effort to manage a steady tone. "So these aren't all homicide files?"

"Cady." His hand snaked across the bar to take hers. "They labeled yours an accident, not a homicide."

"I know." She was more shaken by the last hour than she wanted to admit. "I mean, the rest aren't all similar crimes?"

"Not at all. A call about a property dispute. Domestic assault. Petty theft." Ryder lifted a shoulder. "Like I said, no link that I can find. Also nothing that would cause my dad to hide them. To keep them off the microfilm he used for old records at the time."

And now she understood his odd manner. The not knowing was eating at him. Likely he was imagining the worst. "That is strange," she admitted. But she privately wondered if the subjects in the other files were also women.

And if Butch Talbot had had a relationship with all of them.

Chapter 35

Hero pawed at the plastic cone encasing his head. Looked at Cady beseechingly. "I know, right? It's humiliating." The vet had encased his left rear paw in a thick cotton sock and taped it tightly to prevent scratching. An old T-shirt was secured around his body, protecting the wound. Cady stroked him, a ball of relief filling her at having him home. Well, not *their* home. But the animal seemed more comfortable at Ryder's than she did. His bed was next to Sadie's in the kitchen. Their bowls were lined against the cupboards. His discomfort had nothing to do with his location and everything to do with the wound that had him walking stiffly and the protective guard around his neck.

"Here. You have no idea how much this pains me." She handed him the clown, and he immediately took it in his mouth. Shook it gently.

"Take that as a sign of great devotion, buddy," Ryder put in.

The vet had opened early for them. Ryder had helped Cady bring Hero home, because the dog clocked in at 160. She never would have been able to carry him. The animal had surprised them both by being able to walk. He limped badly. But he'd seemed to be in a hurry to leave the vet office behind.

The front door opened. "Hey, Mom." Ryder rose and strode toward his mother. Cady followed more slowly. "Thanks for coming so early."

"You know darn well I've been up for hours."

"Mom, meet Cady Maddix. Cady, Laura is a notorious early riser. It's a disease."

Ill at ease, Cady aimed a smile at the petite woman who swatted her son lightly. "It's so good of you to agree to do this. I know it's an imposition."

"Not at all. I have plenty of free time, and I'm just across town." Laura smiled sunnily as she approached. "I also have experience with dogs, although I no longer have one at home. I dog-sit for Sadie from time to time." The woman crouched down before Hero and extended a hand for him to sniff. "Oh my, you're handsome. Look at you, you brave boy. Is that your toy? Is that your favorite?"

"He's developed an obsessive attachment to it," Cady replied, watching the dog nose the woman's hand. "I can't get him to give it up. It's like watching a creepy puppet show or a Chucky movie playing in real time."

Laura gave a deep-throated laugh and rose gracefully. "If it gives him comfort while he heals, that's a good thing. Tell me everything I need to know. Oh, and better give me your phone number on the off chance I need to call you."

Cady showed her the list of instructions the vet had given and went over each step before reeling off her phone number. "It's really more about checking on him and making sure he hasn't somehow gotten the bandage off. If he licks or scratches at it, he could tear out the stitches."

An alert on her cell sounded, interrupting her. Adrenaline licked up her spine when she read the new email. Running toward the closet for her jacket, she shrugged into it as she pulled open the front door. "We've got a location."

Laura Talbot looked at her son when the door closed behind Cady. "Well. She left abruptly."

"There's been a break in her investigation," Ryder explained. He tried not to think about the fact that she might soon be running directly toward the man who may have been the shooter.

"You know, when you mentioned a law enforcement officer was staying with you, I figured it was a man. You didn't say differently."

"Didn't I?" He walked to the bedroom and came back with his weapon, strapping it on before fetching a coat.

"What office did you say she works for?"

He smiled down at her, familiar with her gentle probing. "I didn't."

Laura made a moue of disappointment. "You don't say much, that's for certain. For some reason, her last name is familiar. I can't quite recall why."

Ryder's muscles went tense at that, but his mom was on to another subject. "I almost keeled over with shock seeing a woman here, but any hopes I harbored were dashed pretty quickly."

"Really."

"Not that she isn't attractive, but she's very fierce, isn't she?" Sadie came over and dropped a pull toy at Laura's feet. She obligingly picked it up to play tug with the animal.

Fierce. Ryder considered the word as it applied to Cady. It wasn't totally off the mark. "I think you're responding to her vest and weapon."

"Anyway." The dog won the contest and bounded away with the toy. "Seconds later, I realized she wasn't your type, so my fledgling hopes were shattered once more."

"What's my type again?"

"Oh . . ." His mom cocked her head. "Someone like that cute little Lisa O'Reilly you dated for a while."

Ryder thought of the woman without a twinge of nostalgia. "While her physical attributes were . . . ah . . . impressive, they were unmatched by intellectual capability."

His mom laughed. "You're so bad. So no, I wouldn't wish that on you. Perhaps someone more like Molly Embry at the library. Have you met her?"

"I don't spend much time in the stacks these days." He walked over to drop a light kiss on his mom's head before turning toward the door. "Thank you again. Call if you need anything."

"I need more grandchildren," she called after him.

"Anything but that," he amended before closing the door.

Chapter 36

"I got pings on one of Forrester's phones for the first time earlier this morning." Cady was updating Miguel and Allen in the supervisor's office. "It's the cell he used to answer Fielding's recent call. Maybe he just keeps it off when it's not in use."

"But every time he powered it on or off, it would leave a trace," Miguel murmured.

She nodded. "Based on the records, I suspect he disposes of the cells after a period of time. He's careful. Doesn't use text messaging. And the data dump from the provider only goes back eighteen months. We have his calls to Fielding. The only other ones listed were to Mexico."

"Mexico." Allen drummed his fingers on the desk. "Think he's scouting a place to go when he leaves North Carolina?"

"He'd be smarter to go to a country without extradition treaties," Miguel said.

Allen's speculation could be true. But Cady found herself wondering if the call had been made to a drug contact. Because she had zero proof for the thought, she kept it to herself. "We can't be sure. But . . ." It was difficult to quell the excitement pulsing through her veins. "The cell he used to call Fielding prior to this one? Twice call records pinpointed his location to Ayden. I checked, and the dates correspond to the time Tina Bandy's family was living there."

"Chad Bahlman?" Allen asked.

"Two days before he was killed," Cady confirmed. It wasn't proof, but it was damn coincidental. "He appears to limit his use of the phones and likely turns them off most of the time. But the available location data place him mostly within the state and occasionally just over the border into neighboring ones." *He could have gone anywhere,* she reflected. And she couldn't help believing that his failure to do so had something to do with Dylan Castle.

She pointed to a spread-out map in front of her. "This morning's ping places him somewhere in the space outlined in red."

Allen studied the map. "That's at least ten square miles."

"It's a place to start. We know it's a prepaid cell." A little more difficult to locate than a smartphone but not nearly as secure as criminals would like to think.

Miguel leaned forward to peruse the map. "So he could be within this area in any one of these four counties. Watauga, Avery, Caldwell, Wilkes." His mouth was a grim line when he flicked a glance at Cady. "Close enough to get at you."

The thought had already occurred. Her home in Waynesville was in Haywood County, less than three hours away. "It means he was fairly near as of this morning," she agreed evenly. But there was nothing in the records to indicate Forrester's location on Tuesday, when the shooting took place.

She pushed aside a thread of frustration. Forrester may have other phones he still used that they didn't know about. They could be missing a wide swath of historical location data. But they had today's.

"So where do you want to start?" Allen asked.

"Tillis indicated that Forrester had an affinity for prostitutes. Maybe we talk to some of those women in the area. Show them pictures of Forrester. Loomer too," she added after a moment. "We don't know they're together, but we can't be sure they aren't."

"All right. Remember to wear vests. And, Cady, we got a replacement vehicle for you." Allen reached into his desk drawer and withdrew a set of keys. "Try to treat it nicer than you did the Jeep."

She caught the keys he tossed to her. "This better not be a van." The vehicles used by the marshals on the job were acquired by way of forfeiture laws. They were chosen for their ability to blend in, not for their appeal.

"I bet it's the PT Cruiser in the lot." Miguel grinned at her. "That'd be totally your style."

"Oh hell no."

"I'll let you be surprised," Allen said dryly. "Keep me posted of your whereabouts."

Miguel walked to the door, but Cady lingered. "Ah . . . I have one more thing." When the other marshal paused, she waved him away.

Allen straightened. Eyed her shrewdly. "If you need more time off, that isn't a problem. You went through a lot this week."

Vaguely insulted, she wanted to ask if he'd offer the same to a male marshal. Then swallowed the words because she knew he would. He was a good guy. Not an office bureaucrat but a deputy marshal who helped out on their warrants when needed. "It's not that. You know my mom's condition." Of course he would. It was the reason stated for her desired transfer from Saint Louis.

"Is she getting worse?"

Her shrug was nonchalant. The churn of emotions elicited by the question was anything but. "She has concerning episodes. It's too soon to tell if they point to a decline. But I can't discuss traumatic events from the past with her. I just learned recently that she was approached six years ago by my dad's partner in a bank robbery. Stan Caster." Allen's expression hardened.

"The money from the bank robbery was never recovered. She reported the encounter, and he landed back in prison."

He reached for a pen and scribbled a note. "I'll find out his where-abouts. If he's still inside, we're going to make damn sure you're notified the next time his release date nears."

Cady couldn't be sure whether or not Hannah had received such an alert. And she wouldn't ask her. But if the man tried to contact her mom again, he'd answer to her.

Allen put the pen down and looked up. "Anything else I can do for you?"

"No, I'm good. Thanks."

"Then go make Rodriguez jealous." A hint of a smile played around the man's mouth. "I don't envy you having to listen to his bitching for the rest of the day."

"If only I'd known the key to getting a new vehicle was having my office-issued pickup used as target practice."

Cady mentally tabulated the remark as the dozenth Miguel had made about the black 2018 Jeep Wrangler she'd been assigned. "Look at it this way. Sometimes you'll get to ride in it."

Their boots crunched on the graveled lot as they approached the strip club called the Lumberyard. Given its isolated location—miles outside the town of Sawmills—the lot was surprisingly full at that hour.

"Not the same. You know what this is? This is a pity vehicle. Allen must have done a whole lot of begging to get it for you." He deserved the elbow jab to the gut. "Not that you don't deserve it," he hastily added.

"Glad you agree." They stepped aside for a portly man in his mid-forties who almost fell out of the door as it opened. Cady watched him try to maneuver his way to his vehicle. "It is way too early in the day to be that drunk."

"Focus," he advised as they stepped inside the darkened club. They didn't get more than a few steps in before a bouncer accosted them. He boasted biceps that looked like he bench-pressed Volkswagens in his spare time. "You members? Otherwise the membership fee is twenty bucks. Gets you five dollars off the cover charge for each visit."

Cady showed him her star. Their visits didn't require discretion. "We're interested in talking to some of your female employees about a warrant we're working."

"They can't help you."

She leveled a look at him. "You don't know what questions we have, do you?"

Reluctantly, he stepped aside, and they walked into the club. It bore more than a passing resemblance to the others they'd visited already that day. They were hitting all the places local law enforcement had noted with the most instances of illegal sexual activity. They also had a list of repeat offenders for solicitation and their last known addresses. It was too early for activity at some of the spots. But many of the "gentlemen's clubs" opened in the afternoon.

Inside, she and Miguel split up to work the room. He usually got more information from women than she did. No surprise there. With a visage to make Raphael weep and a running faucet of charm he rarely wasted on Cady, females tended to open up to him.

Still, she tried with the waitstaff, showing pictures of Loomer and Forrester and getting nothing for her time. She moved on to the females lounging in filmy lingerie at the bar or at tables. Just finished up or waiting for their time onstage, Cady figured. The one at the bar said, "Honey, if they ain't regulars and real good tippers, I don't really see 'em, y'know?" She didn't get much more from the first woman at the nearby table, who boasted a pair of boobs she could set a tray on. But her companion studied the pictures intently before handing them back with a shake of her head.

"What'd they do?"

"They're wanted for questioning."

The stripper gave Cady a look. "No, I mean for what? Because whatever it is might make a difference whether they'd come to a place like this."

Intrigued, Cady tapped Forrester's picture. "Kidnapping. Wanted for questioning in three homicides." She moved on to Loomer. "He may be with him."

The woman reached up a finger, twirled a lock of her long black hair. The gesture was oddly schoolgirlish. But she was probably younger than she looked in all the makeup. "So a guy like the kidnapper isn't going to hang out in a place like this. I don't think so anyway."

Cady tucked the photos away. "Why's that?"

She shrugged, and the slinky robe bared a shoulder. She didn't seem to notice. Or care. "He wouldn't want to be noticed, would he? Clubs like ours attract cops. Then there's the money. I mean, every bar in the state will require him to pay a membership fee. But here he's also going to get hit with cover charges sometimes and parking fees when we're busy. The full-nude places—which this ain't—can't sell alcohol, but people can bring it in. But then the club owners make them buy it back to drink there, which is bullshit." She waved in the general direction of the bar. "Our drinks are expensive compared to what you'd get at a regular private club with no adult entertainment. He might not have the cash to pay the additional costs at a club like ours."

She had a point. Several of them, in fact. "What's your name?"

The woman smiled. "Janice. Just Janice. That's not my stage name, of course."

"Janice watches too much *Law & Order: SVU*." The other stripper tittered.

"So where would a man like the one you're describing go for sex? Anonymous. Rough."

Sobering, Janice shared a look with her friend. "Guys like that are everywhere, you know? No backroom activity here," she hastened to put in, as if Cady couldn't see the curtained booths. "But prostitutes would be most likely. Someone in a club gets beat on, you got the bouncer, the manager looking out for the girl. Hookers got no one, 'less they work with a pimp. And sometimes it's the pimp tuning them up in the first place."

"Where are the busiest places for prostitutes to frequent around here?"

Another shrug. The robe lowered another few inches. Cady resisted an urge to reach out and move it back into place. "Any shitty motel, I'd guess. Some work truck stops exclusively. Lots of people around in case they get in trouble, and they can get regulars, you know? Guys who drive the same route."

The woman had given her food for thought. Cady dug in her pocket for a twenty. Janice snatched it away and had it folded and out of sight in an instant. "You want my opinion on politics, now that's free."

Declining politely, Cady moved away, scanning the area for Rodriguez. She found him crowded into a corner with a partially nude woman in a raunchy nurse outfit blocking his exit. He sent Cady a beseeching gaze. She grinned. The man's social life might have a revolving door, but he was a choirboy at heart. Taking pity on him, she made her way over to rescue him.

"Honey? Is this scary lady bothering you?"

The woman looked at her over her shoulder. "That your wife? She's too skinny, baby. You need some curves you can grab on to." Miguel extricated his hand when she would have placed it on one of the curves in question.

"Excuse us." Cady grabbed Miguel's arm and pulled him away. "He's already had all his shots. Christ," she added in an undertone as they strode toward the door. "I really can't take you anywhere."

"I thought she pulled me aside because she had info, but she just wanted to get me cornered."

"Literally. I think she wanted to examine you. That place she put her stethoscope was a ways from your heart."

"Funny."

They strode out the door and headed toward the vehicle. Cady reached for the fob and unlocked it.

"There's no reason to share that episode at the office."

She placed her hand on her heart in feigned shock. "I would never tell anyone that I found you between a doc and a hard place."

"Here we go," he muttered.

"I only saved you because nobody puts baby in the corner."

Heaving a theatrical sigh, he opened his door and slid inside the vehicle. "You're a verbal sadist, know that? Are you done?"

Smirking, Cady got in and buckled her seat belt. "For now."

Clearly anxious to change the subject, he said, "No one inside recognized either photo. This was a bust."

"Not totally." She told him about Janice's theory. He was silent while she consulted the GPS on her phone before pulling out of the lot.

"She made some valid points," he allowed finally. "So are we shifting our priorities here?"

"I agree with Janice. There's a lower probability of Forrester being recognized in clubs than by prostitutes working alone. Plus, they're most vulnerable. Let's go talk to some working girls."

Chapter 37

Ryder wasn't totally surprised to get a message from Cady saying she'd be late. And that she had nothing to report for the day's efforts. A triangulation of ten square miles was almost useless.

He'd been busy at work, but the scene last night was never far from his mind. Cady was as self-contained as anyone he'd ever seen. But poring over that file of the night thirty years earlier had to have been an exercise in misery. Especially the new information about her father putting her life at risk.

Some men were a waste of oxygen, and Lonny Maddix fit that description, Ryder thought grimly. He had no regrets about the man's death. Except when it came to the burden Cady bore because of it.

The file hadn't shed new light on the night Lonny was shot. The thought had gnawed at him all day until an idea had occurred. He'd take advantage of being alone this evening to put it into action.

It had taken only the most innocent of questions to some of his staff to elicit the information Ryder needed. He stepped inside Country

Meadows Nursing Home at 6:15. The woman who'd answered the phone when he'd called earlier had assured him that mealtime would be over. She'd also given him Harvey Klatt's room number.

Ryder made his way down the appropriate hall and paused in the doorway of Haywood County's former chief investigative deputy. There was only one bed and dresser inside. The elderly man was dozing in the recliner in front of a TV.

He knocked loudly on the opened door. "Mr. Klatt?"

With a start, Klatt straightened. Looked his way. "Don't just stand there," he said querulously. "Come in."

Ryder approached him and stuck out his hand. "Ryder Talbot, sir. I believe you knew my father."

"Damned if I didn't." Klatt's grip was surprisingly strong. "Met you a time or two as well. You weren't very old. Seven or so. Go ahead and pull up that other chair. Gotta say, it's a pleasure just to see the uniform again."

Ryder did as he was told and settled into the seat. "I've noticed your name on old files. You were chief investigative deputy before your retirement."

Klatt nodded, reaching up to fix the thick glasses more precisely on his nose. His white hair was sparse, and the cane beside the chair told its own story. But the man looked fit otherwise. Ryder hoped his memory was in good shape as well.

"For twenty years or so." He shook his head. "I was first hired in the late fifties. Things were different then. You didn't have to deal with all the PC bullshit thrown at law enforcement officers these days. The sheriff was still king of the county. Way it should still be, you ask me."

Ryder smiled. "It's different now, that's a fact."

"Why, I remember once, early sixties it was . . ." And the man was off. One story melded into another, and Ryder listened intently to each. There was little doubt that whatever else had brought Harvey Klatt to the care center, his mind, at least, was intact.

After twenty minutes, the elderly man paused. "Bring that water pitcher over here, would you? Way you let me drone on, I'm parched."

Ryder got up and fetched the pitcher and a cup. Took them to Harvey, who poured himself a glass. "Want one? Got another cup somewhere."

"No thanks." Ryder waited for the man to drink and lower the glass.

"Your daddy was a good cop too. Tough but fair. He did his best by this county, and that's what got him reelected over and over again. I knew him well enough to know how pleased he'd be that you followed in his footsteps."

Suppressing a wince, Ryder said, "Thank you, sir. You had some big cases when the two of you worked together, didn't you?"

"God, yes. Never a dull moment in our line of work, am I right?"

"That's a fact. But the reason I came to speak to you isn't very exciting, I'm afraid. I wanted to ask you about some files I found in my dad's house. Half a dozen of them and they look like they've been there awhile."

"Official files?" The man frowned, pulled at his chin. "How old?"

Ryder told him the range of dates. "I can't find any connection among them. Just wondered why my dad would keep them out of the system. One of them is the Lonny Maddix file."

"Maddix." Klatt made a sound of disgust. "What a piece of shit that prick was. Your dad and I spent way too much time on that son of a bitch. Got what was coming to him in the end, though. Saved the taxpayers a fortune to just bury the asshole instead of putting him away."

A chill worked over Ryder's skin. "Pretty random way to die. His little girl shooting him like that."

Klatt smiled, revealing snowy-white dentures. "Sometimes the trash takes itself out, son. Other times, you have to give it a push."

Although Ryder probed further, the elderly man reversed his earlier loquaciousness. They traded small talk for several more minutes before Ryder took his leave. As he strode to his vehicle, silent alarms were shrilling through him—because Ryder couldn't be completely sure that Harvey Klatt hadn't just admitted that he and Butch Talbot had somehow been involved in the way Lonny Maddix had died.

Chapter 38

Bruce blared his horn at a dumb-ass in a slow-moving truck. Throwing a glance in the review mirror, he changed lanes and sped by the driver. Another boring day staking out a grocery store had frustration churning inside him. He'd thought his luck had finally changed when he'd watched the kids coming out of school. Had even followed a guy and girl for several blocks. But in the end, he hadn't been able to ID the teenage boy. Damn kids all wore hoodies and hats, making it nearly impossible to tell one from the other. He'd swing by the storage shed he rented and find the binoculars he kept there to use tomorrow.

Thirty minutes later, he pulled to a stop in front of the unit. It was twenty minutes from the place he and Eric lived. The other man didn't know about it, and that's the way Bruce was going to keep it. He retrieved the flashlight from the glove compartment and found the key on his key ring. He switched on the light and got out to unlock the padlock. He raised the overhead door and stepped inside, sliding it down behind him.

He walked to a pile of boxes in the corner and rummaged around in the top one until he found the binoculars. Setting them aside, he unstacked the cartons until he could access the bottom one. Lifted out a lockbox. With the aid of the beam, he dialed the combination and lifted the lid. Two more sets of fake identification sat on top. He reached beneath them and removed one of the stacks of cash. Shoving it in his coat pocket, he locked it up and replaced the boxes.

Because he was there, he walked over to the pile of blankets in the opposite corner and unwrapped them for a quick check. The extra stash of weapons was accounted for.

Satisfied, he recovered them and picked up the flashlight, then crossed to the door. There were rules to being prepared. One was to have everything in order in case he needed to move fast.

The other was to leave no witnesses behind.

Chapter 39

"How you like them mashed potatoes?" Teeter scooped up another helping and dumped it on Dylan's paper plate without waiting for an answer. "Always think they taste better with cheese added to them."

The man was right. Dylan brought a spoonful to his mouth. He couldn't remember the last time he'd had a home-cooked meal. Mom was rarely here, and when she was, they usually had pizza or some other frozen stuff.

"Where'd you learn to cook like this?" The hamburgers his uncle had made weren't as good as those from the restaurant the marshal had taken him to, but they weren't bad.

"Worked in a diner for a while. Now, that's a pain-in-the-ass job. When it's busy, it's hard to keep up. Everyone always yelling at you. Better equipment, though. Your mom don't have shit in the kitchen for pans. She left some money, so I went to the store and got some and more food. All you got here is junk." T took a big bite from his second hamburger. Chewed. "That how you usually eat?"

Dylan lifted a shoulder. "Mom works a lot. And she isn't always around on her days off, either."

T snapped his fingers, his mouth full. After a moment, he swallowed and said, "That reminds me. Your mom won't be back after work tonight. Said she had to meet a friend for a couple of days." He winked at Dylan. "Betting the friend is a guy, am I right? Your mama always did have at least one man on the string."

Appetite suddenly gone, Dylan pushed away his plate. So this was going to be the way it was now? His mom not even bothering to tell him herself what she was doing?

"C'mon." T gave him a playful punch to the shoulder. "Ain't that bad. A woman's got needs, right? Your mama works hard; she plays hard too. When you're growed, you'll probably do the same."

He didn't want to talk about his mom's "needs." "I guess." Dylan got up and folded the plate over the rest of the meal. Stuffed it in the trash.

"What the fuck you doing, boy?" Moments later, Dylan was grabbed by the back of his shirt. Shaken violently. "What's wrong with you, throwing away good food like that?" He was released and then shoved with enough force to knock over the trash can, landing in a heap in the corner next to it.

Scrambling to his feet, he shrank away when he saw T standing over him, fists clenched, his face a mask of rage.

At first, Dylan's mind went blank. He'd had nothing left on the plate but some potatoes and a couple of bites of a hamburger. But whatever the reason, he knew when he was about to get his ass kicked. "I'm sorry. You're right. I'll pick it up. Put it in the fridge and save it for tomorrow."

"Damn right you will." Teeter towered over him as he retrieved his plate and the other garbage that had been strewn in the altercation. Dylan rose warily and got a second paper plate to put over the one in Teeter's hand. Shoved them in the refrigerator.

"Get me a beer while you're in there, would you?"

Dylan obeyed, setting it on the table next to Teeter.

"You help me clean up the kitchen, and then I'll whup you in *Call of Duty*." T winked at him. "Betcha don't know your old uncle T has been playing video games since before you was born."

"Okay." Like he wouldn't agree to anything at that point. But the man's temper seemed to have faded as quickly as it'd flared. He was back to ol' easygoing Uncle T. Leaving Dylan to wonder what the hell had just happened.

Dylan didn't know what time it was, but he guessed nearly midnight. The snores from the next bed could drown out a jackhammer. This was bullshit. His mom's bed was empty for a couple of nights, and there was no reason he needed to suffer in here.

Quietly, he got out of bed and moved stealthily from the room. The cat shot out from beneath his bed and took a swipe at his ankle, claws extended. *Shit. Fuck.* He hopped out of the room, jaw clenched on the curse words blazing through his mind. He'd seen a bandage on T's wrist, and he said it was from the animal scratching the hell out of him. The damn cat was as schizophrenic as Teeter.

Easing the door shut behind him, he flipped on the light in his mom's room and limped to the side of the bed, where he assessed the damage. There were three red scratches above his foot. Like this night could get any more bizarre.

Gingerly, he settled himself in the bed and pulled up the covers. The hours he'd spent playing video games with Teeter would have been halfway fun if Dylan hadn't been waiting for him to go off again. Dylan had mostly let him win—damn straight he had. It was worth it to keep the man in a good mood.

Not for the first time, he wondered how long it had been since his mom had seen Uncle T. Dylan didn't remember enough about him to say for sure, but if Tina had known how crazy T was, he was pretty sure she never would have invited him to stay here.

He turned to his side. Punched the pillow into a more comfortable shape. Dylan let his mind wander to far more pleasant things. Like the time he'd spent after school with Grace.

His body went hot. T had agreed to pick him up after school, and Dylan had figured they'd work in the library there. But Grace had had other plans. She'd started talking in history class about doing their work at Johnny's, a nearby teen hangout. The suggestion had been as tantalizing as a desert mirage to a thirsty man. And completely out of the question. Just thinking about it had him in a cold sweat all day. He'd spent hours trying to figure out how to tell her no.

But in the end, what came out of his mouth had been yes.

Even after everything that had gone down in the past, with a killer still after him, he'd taken clear leave of his senses. And damn if the risk hadn't been worth it.

He smiled, recalling how excited she'd been, practically skipping the two and a half blocks to the place. She'd teased him about insisting on walking on the outside of the sidewalk. Called him gallant, whatever that meant. But really, he'd just wanted a good view of the street and the vehicles on it. His heart had been thumping so hard on the way there, he'd been certain she could hear it. But once inside the diner, he'd relaxed. And it'd been fun, watching the craziness of the waitstaff. He'd saved the bulk of the money his mom had given him so he could pay for their order. And he didn't think it was an ice-cream high that had him figuring he'd been right earlier about one thing. Grace liked him.

He'd watched some of the other kids at the tables scattered around. It was easy to tell which were friends and which were more than that. The way she touched his arm when they were talking about the paper . . . the way she tossed her hair over her shoulder and smiled at him real slow . . . that meant something. He might not have been quick on the uptake, but when he'd been walking to shop class, he'd passed another guy from history who'd said, "So, you and Grace, huh?"

Dylan had mumbled something about being project partners, and the kid had laughed. "Blind man can see the vibes she's putting out. Better catch some of that before she moves on."

Then the kid had walked away, leaving Dylan stunned.

So it wasn't just his imagination. And after hearing that, there was no way he wasn't going to do exactly what Grace wanted. Even though his palms were pools of slippery sweat and a loud muffler on a car had him practically diving behind something to take cover.

"You're jumpy," Grace had teased. But then she'd slipped her arm through his as they walked, and his focus had shattered. The kid at school was right. Dylan was pretty sure he had a chance with Grace.

And he wasn't going to do a damn thing to screw it up.

Chapter 40

Cady made regular stops at drive-throughs because she knew the key to keeping Miguel's mood stable. The hours were spent in mind-numbing tedium. Many of the addresses for the working girls didn't pan out. And when they found one that did, oftentimes the women were less than cooperative. But they had gotten a few who recognized the photo of Forrester she'd shown them.

The real shock had come when two of the ladies had recognized the picture of Loomer.

"If we learn nothing else tonight, just getting closer to verifying Loomer and Forrester are together will have been worth it." Cady pulled into a trailer park and cruised down the rows, looking for the next address on their list.

"That might be overstating things."

When she saw she'd gone too far, she checked the in-dash backup camera and reversed. Her personal car had the same feature, but her previous USMS vehicle had not. She waited for Miguel's sarcastic comment, but he just looked past her when she stopped.

"Someone's home. There's a light on inside."

She parked, and the two of them approached the steps to the home. The door rattled under Cady's knock. When it was answered, a woman in a figure-hugging bodysuit and thigh-high boots answered. "Angela Stryker?"

She looked from one of them to the other. "You look like cops. And I ain't done nothing." The door started to close.

Cady spoke quickly. "Deputy US marshals, and we're not here because of anything you did." The door paused an inch from shutting completely. "We're looking for someone. Maybe you've seen him."

The crack of the door widened enough to show the woman's face. It was devoid of makeup, and her hair was pinned close to her head. They'd obviously interrupted her getting ready for the evening.

"I doubt it."

Cady took the two photos from her pocket and handed them to her. "Do either of these men look familiar? We have reason to believe this one"—she tapped Forrester's photo—"was in this general area as recently as last night."

The woman's face went pale. "He was? Where? Fuck, if he's close by I ain't going out tonight. Ain't worth it."

"You know him?"

The door came wide open again. And the woman framed in it had lost the edge with which she'd greeted them. Now she looked genuinely frightened.

"We only have an approximate idea of where he was." Miguel's voice was soothing. "We can't pinpoint it exactly. Maybe you can help us with that."

Angela was already shaking her head. "Nope, I can't, because wherever he is, I make sure I'm not. If I see him, I head the other way."

"Tell us how you know him."

"Just a minute. I need a smoke." She disappeared from sight for a moment but returned with a lit cigarette. "So it was three years ago first time I was with him. No, four years. I made the mistake of sitting down next to him at a bar." Her hand trembled as she brought the cigarette to her lips. Inhaled deeply. "We got to talking, and he wanted all night.

That don't happen very often. And he seemed good for it, too, 'cuz he showed me the money up front. Said half before and half after. It took me a while to agree, but the idea of that much cash . . ." The rest of her sentence trailed off. The implication was clear. Angela wasn't exactly living in the lap of luxury.

"He wanted me to go to his place. Said we'd have to drive awhile to get there. I wasn't born yesterday, so I said no way. It was a sticking point with him. He argued awhile but finally agreed to meet me at a motel I use."

Cady's skin prickled at the retelling. "He tied me up. Gagged me. At first I thought he was just into kink, but he was like a possessed animal. He got off on my pain, and there was plenty of it. If I fought, he'd beat me. And before the night was over, he'd choked me so hard, I passed out. Then I'd come to, and he'd do it again. I never expected to live to see morning—that's the honest-to-God truth. When he was finished, he dressed and walked out. Never paid the rest of the money like he said, but I didn't even care. I was *alive*."

"I'm sorry that happened to you." Cady's throat was tight. Erotic asphyxiation, Michael Simmons had said. *He liked to watch*. She was certain Angela was right. The woman had been lucky to walk away alive the next day.

"I couldn't work for a week. Even then, I had bruises for a month. *That's* good for business."

"Did he give you his name?" When the woman shook her head, Cady pressed on. "Was this other man with him? Maybe in the bar that night?"

Angela exhaled a thin stream of smoke and leaned forward to take another look at the picture of Loomer. "If he was, I didn't notice him."

"Did you see the man who hurt you again after that?"

She nodded. "A few times."

Miguel pulled out a notebook. "Can you remember where?" The woman reeled off four locations, and he jotted them down.

"I warned the girls about him. This line of work, we gotta watch out for ourselves. But it didn't do no good." She looked away for a long minute. Her throat worked. "'Bout a year later, a friend of mine went with him. Twice. And after the second time, I never saw her again."

Women in Angela's line of work were often transient. But even knowing that didn't dampen Cady's interest. "What's your friend's name?"

"Marcy Linton. She was from somewhere in the northeast. Don't know how she landed down here. First time she was with him was about two and a half years ago. She didn't have no problems. Said he wanted to take her to his place next time. Somewhere in the mountains."

"Where'd she meet him?"

"There's a travel stop north of here. Moe's. Not one of them chain places. Gets a lot of semi traffic." The cigarette had been smoked down to the stub. She disappeared for a moment and came back with a second one.

"How much later was it when your friend met with him again?"

"I'm not sure," Angela responded. "'Bout a month went by when I thought, hey, I haven't seen Marce for a while. I started asking around. One of the girls saw her getting into a car with him."

"Did you see his vehicle when you went with him?"

The woman shook her head in response to Cady's question. "We agreed to meet at the motel. I went to the cops in town here." Her face darkened. "They didn't take her disappearance serious. 'Cuz she's got a sheet and a habit and she's moved around some."

But whatever the police's opinion of Angela's concern, her statement would have started a paper trail. Cady made a mental note to follow up on it.

"So you guys are feds. Guess you want this guy bad." Angela's expression turned assessing. "What's he done?"

"Kidnapping." The woman paled at Miguel's answer. "And he's wanted for questioning in three homicides."

"I knew it. I fucking knew it." She took short, quick draws on the cigarette. "Maybe I can help you out. But only if you do something for me."

Cady already knew where this was going. "You mean look into your friend's disappearance."

Angela gave a slow nod. "You promise me that, and I'll talk to everyone I know in this business. I'll have 'em call me if they see him around. I know lots of gals, and not just this county, either. Someone contacts me about him, I'll let you know right away." She opened the door wider and tossed the still-burning butt of the cigarette onto the tufts of frosted grass. "I've been fucked over by cops more times than I can count. You different?"

"I'll follow up and get back to you," Cady promised.

Staring hard at her, Angela finally gave a decisive nod. "Then give me your number."

Chapter 41

Ryder woke to the smell of coffee. He opened one eye. When he discovered the cup was wielded by a green-eyed strawberry blonde, he opened both. Sat up and yawned.

"Apology coffee," Cady said as she handed him the cup. "For waking you when I got home last night."

He took the cup and sipped, his eyes closing appreciatively. "Technically, Sadie owes me the apology, since she started the bark fest when you got here."

"She wanted to make the coffee, but with no opposable thumbs and all, we had to team up."

His mouth quirked. "I don't know what time it is, but it has to be too early for humor."

"Too bad. Then I won't tell you about Rodriguez getting molested by a stripper wearing a raunchy nurse outfit."

Wide-awake now, he straightened in bed. Took another sip while running an appreciative eye over her. Black jeans. Black cami, which he already knew would soon be covered with a button-up shirt before she put on her vest and shoulder harness. "On second thought, that sounds like a don't-miss story."

She stole the cup from him and took a gulp before returning it and giving him all the details of the scene. He chuckled. Damned if he couldn't picture the whole thing. "How come you never take me to places like that?"

"Believe me, I'm doing you a favor. I had to shower when I got back last night. And I left my jacket to air out on the deck. Some of the women we talked to were smokers. I may have to burn it."

He leaned farther back into the pillows. "What got you up so early? After last night, you've got comp time coming."

She shook her head. Stole his cup again and drank. "I've fed the dogs and taken them out. Changed Hero's bandage. Your mom shouldn't have to do it today unless he tears something loose. There's a task-force meeting this morning at the courthouse. We got enough information last night to narrow our parameters. Maybe enough to start putting search teams together. And something else came up I need to check into before things get started."

He took the mug from her. "If you go in just a little later, something could come up here."

"Sorry."

But she didn't look sorry, he reflected regretfully. Not even a little.

"What'd you do last night?"

His stomach clenched on cue. "Not much. Hung out. Watched a game I'd recorded." Which he had. After he'd returned from the nursing home.

"I was wondering whether there was anyone in your office who was around when my father died."

Ryder kept his gaze steady on hers, his jaw clenched. Omission or not, this still felt like lying. And he didn't want to lie to her. Not when it'd taken so long to get her to trust him, just a little. "Jerry Garza was. But when I asked yesterday, he didn't have any information to share. He wasn't on the response team."

"What about the deputies who were? The chief investigative officer. Are they still in the area?"

God, he hated this. "What do you think they could tell you that wasn't in the report?" he hedged.

She gave a frustrated shake of her head. "That's the question, isn't it? Maybe this whole thing is a waste of time. It's probably a mistake to give too much credence to something my mom said when she was in a confused state."

"Maybe." His chest hollowed out when he noted the misery in her eyes. She wouldn't thank him for keeping this from her. But until he had verifiable facts, that's exactly what he was going to do.

Chapter 42

"I had fun yesterday."

Dylan glanced around the classroom to be sure Lawson wasn't near before he smiled back at Grace. "So did I. That place was crazy." He'd enjoyed it more than he should have. He'd woken out of a dead sleep last night, twin nightmare visions of Matthis and Bahlman dancing in his mind, their heads blown clear off. He'd taken a helluva chance going out in broad daylight like he had.

But when Grace looked at him like that, his regrets faded.

"We didn't get as much work done as we would have staying here. But we're way ahead of anyone else in class."

"Because one of us is a slave driver," Dylan said, straight-faced, and then grinned when she punched him.

"You'll be thankful in another few days when everybody else is scrambling to finish and we're already polishing our presentation. Oh, and I brought you something." She turned to dig in her backpack hanging from the back of her chair.

He checked on Lawson's proximity before studying Grace when she couldn't catch him at it. Today she was wearing tights, different boots, and a long shirt-type thing. Her hair was up in back, showing off all those earrings marching up her ear. Dylan didn't think they were weird anymore. Kinda cool, really.

She turned, hand extended, and he slowly reached out to take the item from her. A cell. Nothing fancy, a flip phone that looked a lot like the ones his mom had.

"What's this for?"

"I like your idea of switching paragraphs six through eight, Dylan. I think the paper would flow better."

Dylan could almost feel Lawson looming over them. He palmed the cell and moved his hand under the desk as he leaned over to look at the sections she was pointing to on her laptop. Damn, the guy moved fast. He'd been across the room a minute ago.

"Keep up the good work, you two." Dylan watched the man move on.

"Damn, you're sneaky," he breathed. He unclasped his fingers to look at the cell, torn. "I can't take this."

"I have an iPhone, but my parents wouldn't let me take it when I went on the class trip to Peru last summer. They bought me that, with, like, two hundred prepaid international minutes on it." Grace was talking fast, the words practically tumbling from her. "I used about thirty minutes of it. We could text each other. Or call." She lifted a shoulder, her gaze fixed on the screen of her computer. "But if you don't want to . . ."

Shit. Dylan snuck a quick glance at her. Had he hurt her feelings? It felt strange taking something from a girl, and his mom would go ballistic if she ever found out he had a phone. She hadn't said he couldn't have one, but she always put him off. She was never going to get one for him. He knew that's why they didn't have internet, either. If Tina could make sure he never talked to anyone—ever—she would. He knew how careful they needed to be. But it wasn't like he was going to let anything slip with Grace. Just the thought of her finding out about his past had sweat slicking down his spine.

"It's all right, really. It doesn't matter. You're probably okay with not having a phone. Forget about it."

"No one in this century is okay not having a phone."

She finally looked at him. "My mom has forgotten all about that cell. And if she found it, she'd probably take it to the church or something. They're always collecting stuff for the missions. I'd rather you have it than some stranger."

Now he felt even worse about it. Like it was charity or something.

"If you're going to be all weird about accepting it, I suppose I should pay my share for the food at Johnny's yesterday."

"What?" He frowned. "No. Why?"

She just cocked her head, brows raised. Comprehension dawned. The girl was too damn smart for her own good. It was like she could see right into his head and form an argument for thoughts he hadn't even had yet. "No, it's okay." He shoved the phone in his pocket. "Thanks. Things are pretty lame at my house. It'll be cool to be able to text nights and weekends."

Grace smiled. "I think so too. I already put my number in it for you. But you can add all your other friends if you want."

His smile froze. Maybe if they had more than one class together, Grace would have realized that he didn't have any other friends. And Dylan needed to think long and hard about whether being friends with her—or more—could possibly put her in danger.

Chapter 43

"Cady? You got a few minutes?"

She looked up, startled to see Allen standing in the doorway. She'd gotten to work early and had been busy gathering details for the task-force meeting, which was due to start—she glanced at the clock—in fifteen minutes.

"Sure." She got up and followed him to his office, her gut clenching on cue. She could guess the reason for the meeting.

He crossed to his desk and picked up a sheet to hand to her. "Stan Caster is still a guest at Butner. Harassing your mom was deemed a parole violation, and he'll have completed his entire sentence this June."

Her chest eased. At least he wasn't out yet. "Well, it's better to know that than be taken by surprise if he appears again." Cady glanced up from the sheet.

Allen's expression was sober. "The warden made a note to specifically warn him against that prior to release. You'll get notified before they let him out. At least you'll be prepared."

"Thanks, Allen." Cady would make damn sure Alma was apprised as well. If Caster showed up again, he'd discover Hannah was no longer vulnerable. She had protectors now.

Not like thirty years ago.

The task force was already assembled when Cady walked into the conference room. SBI agent Rebedeau spoke first. "I hope you're going to tell us there's been another ping."

"No, but we do have a new development," she answered. "Before I get into it, does anyone else have an update to share?" The law enforcement task-force members had been selected for their investigative and tactical skills. Or, in the case of the feds, for their areas of expertise.

ATF agent Gabe Pearson cleared his throat. "I've been following up on the eTrace of the weapon found next to Cady's property after the shooting. A gun range outside Fayetteville initially bought it nine years ago. The range has since changed hands, and current owners claim there were no records kept of customers using the range. The weapon disappeared from the supply more than five years ago during the first owner's tenure. The subsequent report to the sheriff's office didn't take place until the sale was going through. They didn't sell firearms, so they either allowed a customer or an employee to walk off with one of the weapons."

Rebedeau's muttered curse had Cady's gaze flying to the normally good-natured agent. Gabe smiled thinly. "Exactly. But I'm hounding Fred Hannity—the ex-owner—hard. He's trying to come up with a complete list of his employees during the time he had the place. I'm reaching out to each of them to see if I can get more information. People's memories fade after a few years. The names he's given me so far have been added to the digital file."

Cady turned to Curtis Weddig. "Was your cyber agent able to come up with anything linking Forrester to an online drug ring?" She could read his answer in his expression.

"Sorry, no. Law enforcement shut down The Silk Road, the largest black-market deep website for illegal drugs, a few years back. Busting the replacement sites that have popped up in its absence is an ongoing task. Anything high profile would be on our radar. Smaller sites, not so much. And without a name or URL . . ." He lifted his shoulders.

She accepted the news with equanimity. "What's the update on Suzanne Fielding's cell?"

Rebedeau answered. "Obviously, Forrester didn't call the cell while it was at the lab, but they're done with it. You'll probably want to give it back to her."

Cady nodded. "I'll have it run over to Madison County. A deputy is monitoring Fielding in her home twenty-four seven."

"What about having her generating the contact?" Pearson asked.

"She says she rarely does that. If she doesn't have new information for him, I'm afraid a call might spook him into dumping the phone altogether." She looked around the table. "Any other updates?" When no one else spoke, Cady continued. "Yesterday, Miguel and I interviewed two prostitutes who identified Eric Loomer and one who ID'd Bruce Forrester from pictures." She waited for the murmur that rose to quiet. "The woman who ID'd Forrester was physically abused by him during a sexual encounter. She lives in Boone, and he said his home was about thirty minutes away. Another of her friends said he told her it was in the mountains. We used that information to redefine the search area." Miguel passed out copies of the new map.

"The red borders show the original parameters set from the triangulation on Forrester's cell. The yellow dots reflect where Forrester has been reportedly seen in the last few years within the original parameter. So the new boundaries have been outlined in black."

"Still looks to be about seven square miles," Buncombe County deputy sheriff investigator Andy Garrett muttered. He was studying the map through dark-framed readers.

"It is. So we'll check the more isolated areas first. Unincorporated townships. Mountain homes. If we forgo cities and towns for now, that would narrow the search to the spots outlined in green, which are about four-point-two square miles. I suggest multiple teams, each covering one of these areas. I think we'll discover that Loomer and Forrester are together." It was too much of a coincidence that both men had been sighted in the same area. "Since Loomer's uncle had his property booby-trapped and admitted teaching similar skills to his nephew, we should take the precaution of adding explosive detection dogs." Cady's gaze settled on Watauga County deputy Jack Rossi. "I'm hoping your county's K-9 is available." Before the meeting she'd called the Waynesville PD and enlisted similar assistance.

"I'll make the contact." His voice was a low rumble.

Cady went on. "We'll check with the sheriff offices within the parameters and ask whether they've had complaints about explosions or loud noises coming from any of the areas we're going to search. If Loomer booby-trapped the property, something or someone has probably triggered a trip wire at some point." She was impatient with herself for not thinking of it before.

She also needed to take a new look at the reports she'd pulled for missing females in North Carolina and the surrounding states. She hadn't found a pattern to explain Cassie Zook's abduction. But Angela's information about her friend's disappearance had Cady wondering if Forrester had started with women who wouldn't be missed. For some reason, he'd changed that behavior with Zook. And given his paraphilia, there was no reason to believe he wouldn't continue to escalate.

Until Cady stopped him.

Chapter 44

The burly man running a mop over the floor in Captain's Tap in Blowing Rock turned around and gave Cady and Miguel a quick once-over as they came through the door. "We ain't open yet."

"We're not looking for drinks." Cady surveyed the heavily bearded guy as they approached. She'd noted the bulge beneath his T-shirt in back. Knew he was armed. "Deputy US Marshals Maddix and Rodriguez." She stopped a few feet away from him, just shy of the wet area. "Are you the owner?"

"Who the hell else would clean this place?" When Cady just looked at him, the man finally replied, "Yeah. What's the problem?"

Miguel pulled out photos of Forrester and Loomer. "We understand these two have been seen in here before." Angela had mentioned only Forrester, but Cady didn't quibble with the phrasing.

"So?"

Impatience surged. "Look at the pictures," Cady ordered. "Do you recognize the men?"

The man glanced at the images and shrugged. "I'm only here nights on the weekends when it's busy. And then I ain't noticing faces. I'm making sure the staff are doing their jobs and keeping their hands out of the register."

"Show these prints to your staff," Miguel instructed him. They'd made plenty of copies of the pictures before leaving the office after the task-force meeting. "If anyone sees either of these men, call the local police department immediately."

The man took the photos unenthusiastically. Cady had a feeling the pictures would be in the garbage before they hit the sidewalk out front. They'd already spoken to the Boone and Blowing Rock police chiefs and the Watauga and Caldwell sheriff offices. There'd be law enforcement patrols of the bars in their areas until both Forrester and Loomer were apprehended. She figured she'd let that be an unpleasant surprise for the owner.

The thought lightened her mood. "Enjoy your day."

Miguel remained silent until they were outside. "Why did I get the idea you were channeling *Dirty Harry* back there?"

"Given his attitude, thinking of all the walk-throughs the PD is going to be doing over the next day or two is really making *my* day."

He grunted. "Let's hope they're a little more cooperative in the next establishment." They strolled down a block and across the street to the next place. The blonde behind the bar at Maxi's took one look at them and disappeared into the back room. She returned with a tall, thin man with long sideburns and dark slicked-back hair wearing aviator sunglasses.

"Now we know what happened to Elvis," Miguel murmured as the man waved them to the back of the bar.

Cady stifled a smile as they joined the man. He seated himself in a corner booth. "Michael Cordon," he said. "Sit down. I don't conduct my business in front of the customers."

They remained standing. "We're fine." Cady performed introductions and ran through the information they'd given at the last place. On cue, Miguel produced the photos of Forrester and Loomer. Cordon glanced at them and handed them back. "Don't know them."

"If one of these men comes in, have your staff call the police immediately," Miguel said. "There will be uniforms doing regular checks."

"Now, why you want to do that?" Cordon's tone was almost a whine. "We're a quiet place. We don't need trouble, and having a badge show up is the quickest way to lose customers."

Unsympathetically, Cady said, "Call over your bartender."

Heaving a sigh, Cordon bellowed, "Tess!"

It was a few minutes before the woman joined them, looking from Cady to Miguel suspiciously. "What's this about?"

Miguel handed her a set of pictures. "Do you remember either of these men coming in here?"

Tess looked at them and then glanced at her boss. "Uh . . . no. Can't say I recall seeing them."

"That's interesting." Cady caught her eye. Held it. "Because we have a witness who claims she's seen this man"—she tapped the image of Forrester—"here on more than one occasion. What hours do you usually work?" She took a couple of steps, positioning her body between the woman and her boss.

"Different shifts."

The woman was a master prevaricator. "How many hours a week? How many nights are you here?"

"Most of them," she finally admitted.

"If you see one of these individuals, contact the police. This man," she said, plucking Forrester's picture to hold up, "is wanted for kidnapping and for questioning in multiple homicides." The woman's eyes widened. "Not someone you want hanging around this place, is it?"

"No need to browbeat the help." Cordon's smile didn't resemble the King at all. "That's my job."

"We'll leave you to it. Just remember, the sooner we catch up to the men in the photos, the sooner the police will decrease their presence in your place."

Cady's cell sounded as they walked toward the entrance. Checking it, she told Miguel, "The K-9 units are on their way. The rest of the task force will join us in an hour. We still have one more stop here, and then we need to speak to law enforcement in Avery and Wilkes Counties."

"We'll do that. They can show the pictures around at the bars in their areas. Gives us time to get something to eat."

Silently, she agreed. And not just because she knew how important it was to keep Rodriguez fed. They'd left Asheville more than four hours ago. She was ready to get the house-to-house search started. A building urgency was rapping at the base of her skull. And it wouldn't be suppressed until Bruce Forrester and Eric Loomer were both behind bars.

Chapter 45

"We must be the lamest kids in the building," Dylan said, only half-jokingly. The library was deserted after school. Not surprising since it was a Friday. Even the librarian had rushed out at 3:30 after checking on them in case they needed anything.

Grace looked stricken. "Did you have something to do this afternoon? I didn't even ask. I didn't mean to guilt you into this."

It took more courage than it should have to reach over for her hand and squeeze it. He felt the thrill in his gut. "If I didn't want to be here with you, I wouldn't be. Got it?"

Her expression cleared. And God, when she looked at him like that, all doe-eyed and trusting, there wasn't a damn thing he wouldn't do for her. Maybe that should have scared him. But mostly it made him feel ten feet tall.

"Got it."

She was so self-confident most of the time that when she got sweet and shy, something inside him sprang to the rescue, like a damn knight or something. It made him brave enough to lean in, pretend to be looking at her computer screen.

But instead of facing the screen, she turned toward him and pressed her lips against his. Dylan froze. Her eyes were shut, so he closed his, too, and the pressure of her mouth on his made him a little crazy. He let go of her hand and slipped his arm around her to draw her nearer, because Jesus God, he didn't want this to end. Like, ever.

The kiss stretched out. Moments stringing together like stepping-stones across a still pond. And then Grace pulled away a little and said huskily, "I guess you know I like you, Dylan Castle."

His heart was thudding in his chest like a wild thing trying to escape. He smiled and said, "Guess you know I like you back."

Grace and her mom had left the parking lot before Teeter pulled up in his crap car. Which was fine with Dylan. He felt light as air when he jogged out to meet him. As days went, this one ranked up there with the best in his life.

"Bet you're glad to be free of that place for the weekend."

Dylan had barely gotten his seat belt fastened before T took off. "Yeah. I guess."

"You guess?" The man eyed him.

T really oughta be paying attention to where he was going. "Watch out for that planter." They had concrete tubs scattered in the lot to help direct traffic flow. Kids hit them all the time. "I mean, sure. But it's not like there's much to look forward to sitting at home, either."

"I get it." The man's head bobbed up and down. "Kid your age oughta be playing sports. Hanging with friends and chasing tail. Your mom knows it too. That's why she's had me looking out for you."

"You mean why she asked you to come and stay?"

"That too."

Dylan wasn't sure what the hell the man was talking about, but all of a sudden, the thought of spending the weekend locked up in that damn house with no one but T for company deflated his earlier mood. He still had the phone, though. Grace had given him the charger for the cell after school. He turned his face toward the window. It was second nature for him to obsessively watch the vehicles on the road. To scan the traffic for an old green pickup.

But he'd have to wait until T was asleep to text Grace. Maybe he could do it from the bathroom, but his uncle would notice if he stayed in there too long. If he'd been feeling a mile high when he'd left school, he was crashing down to earth now. Having Teeter there was much worse than being alone all the time. What little freedom Dylan had once had was melting away. It was time to start thinking about how he was going to convince his mom to get rid of him.

He searched for a reason Tina would accept. She'd seemed convinced Dylan needed more protection while Forrester was on the loose. Just thinking of the criminal finding them again had dread snaking down Dylan's back. But maybe the marshal—Maddix—was close to capturing the guy. It'd been a week since they'd talked. He grasped on to the thought like a life preserver. If this thing were over soon, Teeter could go home. His mom would back off. Dylan could move freely around town, like a normal kid.

He could walk down the street with Grace without worrying that any minute a bullet might end him. Might even miss him and hit her.

His throat went tight as a mental vision of the scene played across his mind. His earlier mood was completely shattered. That was a dream. This was reality. *His* reality.

T took a sharp turn into their drive, but it didn't jolt Dylan from his morose thoughts. Fucking SBI agents didn't tell them jack even when they checked in. Maybe Maddix was different. He hoped so. Because now that he had the thought, he couldn't shake it loose. He was going to call the marshal. And hope like hell she would give him some positive news.

Chapter 46

Bruce came out of the bedroom, duffel bag over his shoulder, and closed the door behind him. Turning, he saw Eric in the hallway, beer in his hand. The drinking had been steadily increasing, he noted. The case of beer he'd bought a couple of days ago was nearly gone. It was a problem, and Bruce was going to have to deal with it soon. Drunks were sloppy. Made poor decisions. And he couldn't afford any mistakes.

"Where the hell you going now?"

"Out. Might be gone a day or two. No more."

Eric frowned. "Another delivery?"

"No."

He drained the beer and lowered the bottle. Belched. "You taking the whore in your bedroom with you?"

Bruce's fingers curled. "Don't worry about her." She was bound, but she could hop to the bucket in the corner of the room. "I'll feed her again when I get back. You get to FedEx today?"

The other man turned his back to walk to the kitchen. After another beer, no doubt. "You don't see any packages sitting around, do you?"

Tamping down his surging irritation, he followed him. Eric was asking for an ass kicking, but Bruce needed him calm. Responsible.

That was the problem with having to rely on someone else. They often turned out to be an asshole.

The binoculars today had been worthless. Bruce still hadn't been able to pick the kid out of the mob leaving the school. He'd driven back to one of the Food Mart parking lots, knowing he needed a new plan. And when one finally formed, it was almost perfect in its simplicity.

Bruce knew the type of bars Tina Bandy used to hang out in. Had seen her in them more than once in Hope Mills. He could make the rounds, ask about her. Places like those, no one would give a shit.

He'd drive back to Asheville tonight and start. He could always sleep in his car and try scoping out another store tomorrow, then repeat the bar scene tomorrow night. He'd have the woman before the weekend was over.

And with Bandy, he'd have the kid. Heat suffused him. His five-year search would finally be over.

"We've got more orders that need to be packaged and ready to mail out Monday. You can work on that." He had Eric vary the locations of the FedEx offices and post offices he used to avoid drawing attention. Their online business was picking up, and with the increased volume came more exposure.

Eric grabbed what had to be one of the last bottles from the refrigerator and turned back to Bruce. Stared at him. "What's that bandage on your wrist? Your new bitch do that when you grabbed her, or did a whore leave her mark on you last week?" He tittered, then twisted off the top of the beer to take a swig from it.

Bruce stared hard at him, gratified when the other man looked away. "Just . . . ain't seen it before," Eric mumbled.

Bruce pushed down the long sleeves of his T-shirt. "Focus. I have to take care of some loose ends. I'll be back tomorrow, next day at the latest. Stay here. No going to town, no whores. We've got a lot of product left, and I don't want it unguarded."

Ignoring the mutinous look on the other man's face, he walked across the kitchen to the entrance of the garage, his thoughts drifting to the Fed Fielding had called him about. Maddix. One of the loose ends he needed to deal with.

He opened the driver's door and threw his duffel bag over the seat before sliding behind the wheel. After dealing with Bandy and her kid, he looked forward to discovering firsthand if there was any grit behind Maddix's star. He'd never met a cop yet who wasn't a pussy hiding behind the badge. He could discover what she'd learned about him before they settled down to business.

And when he was finished with her, he'd have the pleasure of watching the life ebb out of her eyes. Up close and personal.

Chapter 47

Once the task force had reassembled along with the K-9 units and their handlers, Cady split them into three groups. The one without a canine took the unincorporated areas. Cady led a team going door-to-door in the homes scattered in the Blue Ridge Mountains rising above Boone like a sleeping giant. They were armed with lists of property owners and their addresses, but that didn't help with the numerous rental properties popular in tourist areas like this one.

They were four to a squad. It was already nearing dusk, which limited their time this evening. They'd quickly settled on the most efficient way to proceed. The handler and dog would clear the property before the other three members approached the house.

Many of the homeowners weren't home. Maybe some were still at work, but a good number of the nicer residences were likely summer places and would be empty. Sometimes a house had a view of the next one, but others were separated by miles. As Cady walked back to the Jeep from another unanswered door, she turned to look up at the ridgeline of mountains. If the men were using trip wires to protect their property, they'd want a place that was isolated.

Cady had texted Ryder on the way here to let him know that she'd be late again. A sliver of guilt pricked her. Others were spending more time tending to Hero than she was. But there were never any recriminations from Ryder about the times work kept her away. He'd responded with questions about their hunt and the familiar admonition to "stay safe." A benefit, she supposed, of being involved with a cop. He understood when the job took precedence.

Involved. She waited for the familiar apprehension to rise at the thought. But although the emotion was there, it was more muted than usual. Like something inside her was coming to terms with the relationship faster than her head was.

"K-9's heading back," Miguel noted. Cady nodded, pulled a hat and gloves from her coat pocket, and donned them before opening the door of the Jeep. Rounding the hood, she met Miguel and Rebedeau and headed for the drive. The K-9 officer gave them a thumbs-up and moved toward the back of the vehicle to let the dog inside it. Lights winked on in the A-frame they were heading for. Someone was home.

Cady was closest to the door, so she did the talking when an older woman opened it in response to her knock. "Deputy US Marshals Maddix and Rodriguez and SBI agent Rebedeau, ma'am. We're wondering if you've seen either of these two men." She took the pictures from her pocket of Forrester and Loomer and handed them to the woman.

"Let me get my glasses," the lady said querulously. "Can't see a damn thing up close without them." She turned and moved slowly out of sight.

"Why doesn't she keep them on a chain around her neck like everyone else?" Miguel muttered. Cady elbowed him as the woman shuffled back into view. She perched the reading glasses on her nose and opened the door to take the pictures. Studied them intently.

"No, I don't think so," she finally said, and handed the pictures back to Cady. "What'd they do, get themselves lost?"

"We are trying to locate them," Cady said diplomatically. "Do you live here alone?"

"No, my husband's in the garage. Spends half his life in there and never has a blessed thing to show for it. Just bang on the door. I'll tell him you're coming." The door shut abruptly in their faces.

Miguel said, "I think I can guess what takes her husband out of the house frequently."

Cady smirked. The garage had an entry in addition to the double garage door, and she pounded on it, hunching further into her coat.

The man who answered the door was stooped and looked older than his wife. "Go on inside, Doris; I got this," he called over his shoulder before he turned to look at them through thick bifocals. "You're cops, Doris said."

Cady didn't correct him. "We're wondering if you could take a look at these pictures and tell us if you've seen either of these men before."

The man took his time studying the photos. Finally, he said, "This one I'm sure I've seen." He held up the image of Eric Loomer. "More than once too. He's come into the hardware store where I help out sometimes. We've got a FedEx station there. That's where he always goes. He's a jewelry maker."

Taken aback, Cady said, "What makes you think that?"

"Asked him once." He reached up to settle his glasses more firmly on his nose. "Just making conversation. He said he takes orders from all across the country. He makes one-of-a-kind keepsakes."

Interest flickering, she asked, "Online orders?" If Loomer and Forrester were operating an internet business, she could be certain it had nothing to do with jewelry. Bruce Forrester had gone to prison for selling drugs. And from what Suzanne Fielding and Jeff Benson had said, he'd resumed the practice upon his release and continued a drug operation in Hope Mills. People returned to what they knew. And maybe he'd used Byrd's information to expand his operation online.

"I guess they'd have to be, wouldn't they? Never gave it a thought." The old man tapped Forrester's picture. "This one I'm not so sure about. But"—he sent a furtive look behind him—"I might have seen him in a bar I go to once in a while. Retirement was never meant for two people to spend every blessed second together."

"Where's the hardware store and bar, sir?" There was a thrum of excitement in Cady's veins. The more sightings they accrued, the more quickly they could shrink the parameters until they had Forrester's location pinned down.

"In Boone." The man jerked his chin in the direction of the town below them. "I work a few days a week. Maybe I stop on occasion at the Thirsty Moose on Thursdays. The store's open late that night."

Recognition flickered at the name of the tavern. It was one of the establishments mentioned by Angela, Cady recalled.

"Do you remember the last time you may have seen either man?" Rebedeau asked.

The man handed back the photos, then pulled at his lip. "Don't exactly know. The one in the hardware store . . . maybe last fall. Before Christmas anyway. But like I say, he comes in sometimes. The mean-looking fella, last month or so. If it's the same guy I'm thinking of. Always chatting up the ladies of the evening, if you get my drift."

"Have you ever heard gunfire around this area? Or anything sounding like explosions?" Cady asked.

"Not this time of year. Hunting season's over. And I don't know what kind of explosions you're talking about, but sound travels 'round here. From a distance, it might be difficult to tell the two apart."

"Thank you, sir. You've been very helpful."

"Sure you don't need me to ride with you?" the elderly man asked hopefully. "I could take you to town. Show you the places I'm talking about."

"We'll be back if we need assistance," Cady promised. The three turned and made their way back to the Jeep.

"Almost feel bad for leaving him behind," Miguel said, shoving his hands deep into his pockets. "And it's making me rethink any wistful thoughts of my eventual retirement."

"Since that's about two decades and at least one wife in the future, I wouldn't waste time worrying about it." Reaching the Jeep, Cady got in and turned on the ignition. "I could leave it running the next time," she said over her shoulder to Officer Turner, the K-9 handler. "It's getting colder."

"It's okay. Felix has a thick coat, and so do I."

Sue Rebedeau slid in next to Turner and pulled out her phone. "I'll text the other teams and update them." Cady took a moment to check her own cell. She'd silenced it before beginning the door-to-door. Now she found one missed call from a number identified as SBI. There was also a voice mail.

She tapped the key to listen to it. Was shocked to hear a familiar voice.

"Hi. Um. This is Dylan. Dylan Castle." His tone was hushed. Cady had to strain to hear him. "We had lunch together last week. And I was wondering . . . This might be stupid. But . . . um. We haven't been updated about how the search for Forrester is going for a while. I know you've only been on the team for a week or so. But maybe if you get a minute, you could give me a call. Okay, thanks. Bye." The last words were spoken in a rush.

"Did you decide to quit here, Cady, or are we going to continue the search?" At Miguel's question, she slipped the phone into her pocket and put the Jeep into gear. Consulting the map on the console next to her, she pulled onto the road. But it was the teen's message that occupied her thoughts. She'd worried after spending an hour with him last week that he was depressed. Now his mood seemed tinged with desperation.

She should return his call at some point. Offer him some reassurance. But she didn't want him to get careless. They'd had multiple sightings of Forrester in this area, which was less than two hours from Asheville. That was much too close to the Bandy family for comfort.

She slowed to a stop in front of the next home, a soaring structure of glass and rough-hewn beams. It'd likely cost hundreds of thousands of dollars more than the simple A-frame they'd just left. Something told her that the owners didn't spend their spare time in the Thirsty Moose.

When the handler and dog got out to check the property, Cady exited the Jeep as well. Shutting her door, she leaned against it as she took the phone from her pocket and placed a call to Dylan. Half-relieved when it went to voice mail, she said, "Dylan, this is Marshal Maddix. I can tell you we are progressing in our search for Forrester. But I don't want you to let down your guard, either. Stay vigilant. I hope we have good news for you and your family soon."

Disconnecting, she turned to follow the beam of the flashlight wielded by Turner as they walked the property. She was already second-guessing her call, her wording. Impatiently, she shrugged away the doubts.

Dylan's plight had struck a chord in her from the first. There was nothing wrong with giving him a reason to hope that soon his nightmare might be over.

Chapter 48

"This is nice, just the two of us."

Ryder looked at his mom across the counter bar. "Thanks for bringing dinner over. But I've got to say, a steady diet of your meals would have me spending twice as much time at the gym." The pork chops, mashed potatoes with gravy, and pie she'd brought were all of Ryder's favorites. His mom liked to cook. He felt a pang thinking of what it was like for her, learning to make dinner for one.

Remnants of the meal had long since been cleared away, along with the mountain of leftovers. Those she'd insisted he keep. It'd take him and Cady a week to finish them off, and that was if she ever started keeping regular hours again.

"Where's Cady this evening?" Laura picked up the cup of her decaf coffee and sipped.

"She's working a warrant."

His mom shook her head a little as she set the cup down on the granite counter. "I'm not sure what that means."

"Marshals chase federal fugitives." He'd forgone the coffee for a beer. Toyed with the bottle as he spoke. "She's on the trail of one now." Although Ryder hadn't been updated since the one text earlier that day, he knew that likely meant the task force was still searching. And he respected her enough to at least try to squelch the concern that wanted to rise. It welled from a deeply personal place, not a professional one. One she wouldn't welcome if he put voice to it.

Hero let out a soft yelp in his sleep, and the two of them glanced at the dozing dogs. The animal had the clown Cady hated so much trapped in his front paws. With the cone around his neck, he looked like he'd been trapped in a lampshade after a particularly wild canine party. Sadie's eyes had come open at the sound he made and looked over as if to make sure her friend was all right.

"I finally recalled why her last name is so familiar." Laura eyed Ryder over the rim of her cup as she drank. "Maddix, I mean. There was a big case your dad worked in the county a long time ago. I assume she must be the daughter of that bank robber."

He gave a slow nod, unwilling to go into details, even with his mom. It was Cady's story. One she'd had to live with for most of her life. Thoughts of what she'd discovered in the file he'd finally found still had his chest going tight. She'd been dealt a devil's hand in life. Her cards weren't getting any better.

"Was it one of the files you were looking for at my house a while back?"

"It was. They turned up, though." And not for the life of him was he going to reveal exactly where he'd found them. He'd been protecting his mom from discovering her husband's secrets since he was a teenager. The behavior was ingrained. Butch Talbot's one admirable trait had been the love he'd shown his wife. The choices he'd hidden from her, however, told a completely different story. And those choices would forever color Ryder's memory of his dad.

"Well, I'm glad to hear it." Laura lifted the cup to her lips and sipped. "I got to thinking that maybe I'd lost them. I'm certain that was one of the files your dad had at home for—oh, weeks, it seems like. You know how crabby he was about anyone touching his desk. But even after that, I noticed a pile of official folders in the bottom drawer a couple of different times. When I asked about them, he said he was following up a link among all the cases."

Everything in Ryder stilled. If a link existed among them, it had nothing to do with the cases per se. After the conversation with Klatt, Ryder was half-convinced that the files all represented some sort of official misbehavior on his dad's part. He met his mom's gaze and managed a tight smile. Even five years after Butch Talbot's death, Ryder was still keeping the man's secrets.

Chapter 49

Dylan got up and made a production of stretching and yawning. It wasn't totally an act. He could feel a headache coming on. He'd emptied the only Tylenol bottle he could find, but it hadn't helped much. "I'm going to turn in early."

"What the hell?" Teeter glowered at him. "Sit your ass down. You've been running to the bathroom all night, and now you're going to sleep when it's barely ten o'clock on a Friday night? What's the matter with you, boy?"

He'd been in the bathroom sending quick texts to Grace. And calling the marshal. He'd kept his hoodie on, because the pockets allowed him to smuggle both phones in and out of the room. But Dylan had feared the man would grab him and discover them. The SBI cell could be easily explained away. The one Grace had given him couldn't.

"I've been really cold all day. And my head hurts." That wasn't a lie. There was a fog crowding into his skull, like when he used to get migraines.

"Is it just your head or your stomach too? I don't want to catch the flu. You've been to the bathroom three times. You got the trots, that the problem?"

Mortified, Dylan just lifted a shoulder. Only a few short days ago, he'd been down because of all the time he spent by himself. Now it took a major effort just to get a few minutes alone.

"Better that you sleep in your mom's bed." T had settled on an explanation without Dylan needing to answer. "I sure as hell don't want whatever you got." The man shut off the game consoles. "Go ahead. I can spend the night reading."

Dylan stared. He couldn't help it. And of course, T noticed.

"What, you don't think I can read?" He stood, and Dylan inched away in case he was going to go off on him again.

"Everyone can read," Dylan mumbled.

"Yeah, not everyone likes to, but I got used to passing the time when I was in the army. Most people don't know how much downtime you have when you ain't training or fighting."

It was the first Dylan had heard that T had been in the military. He wondered if that was why Teeter was so weird now. Maybe he had PTSD or something.

T moved to the couch and picked up a dog-eared paperback Dylan hadn't noticed before. "This yours?" He held it up. "Found it in your room."

Dylan recognized it. *To Kill a Mockingbird.* "Yeah. I had to read it last year for English."

"It's pretty good. So go on, now." Book in hand, Teeter headed toward the refrigerator. By Dylan's count, he was on his eighth beer since they'd gotten home. "And if you puke, you're cleaning it up yourself."

"Yeah. I will." Dylan made his escape. When he got inside his mom's room, he closed the door behind him and sagged against it in relief. It was like he was tethered to Teeter, and these close quarters didn't make the proximity any easier to take.

He pulled out one cell. Flipped it open. The wrong phone, he immediately realized. It was the one SBI had given him. But he had a message from the marshal. Mindful of T in the other room, he pulled up his hood before listening to it. Afterward, he walked over to the bed, sank down on the edge, and replayed it again. Then he listened a third time, his mind racing.

She'd all but said this would be over soon. Close enough anyway. Something unfurled in his chest. Something he hadn't felt in a long while. Hope. He'd had it dashed lots of times before. Whenever they'd moved, he'd thought they'd finally be safe. He'd always been proven wrong.

Maybe this time would be different. Maybe finally the killing would be over.

He shoved the phone back in his pocket. Took out the one Grace had given him. She'd sent three texts since he'd last messaged her. Dylan stretched out on the bed and arranged the pillow so it shielded the screen.

He read the first one. I'm so bored! Mom dragged me to the dumbest movie ever. Only good thing about it was the popcorn.

The next read, Figure your uncle is close so you can't text often. OMG how do u stand it? KHYF. Bad enough with my ps wanting 'quality family time' evry nite.

Random but u think Lawson is married? I saw someone who looked like him walking from theater with someone super young. Pedo?????

That one was a head-scratcher. Mr. Lawson? Naw, Dylan texted back. Maybe he's got a young wife. He's not that old, u no.

He smothered a laugh when her response swiftly followed. A gif of an old guy with a long white beard. Dylan was going to have to play with the phone some. Figure out how to use the emojis and gifs. Although he didn't think this cell ran to anything fancy.

Hey know what else? Ps talking about going to Charlotte 2 visit SIS 2MORO. Told them I can't go. HW due next week.

Man, he was lame at this. Ps was parents. HW . . . homework. He'd have to look up the lingo when he got to school Monday. Yeah heard something bout that, he typed back. HW I mean.

Ha, yep! BBQ at Kevin Randall's. If ps go I mite live dangerously. Emoji of a key and a car followed.

Dylan stared at the message for a long minute. Grace was his age. Well, three months older. They'd talked about it. He knew she had a permit too. He'd never even brought up getting one with his mom because the answer was a no-brainer. Nothing to drive and nowhere to go.

I could pick u up. Start BBQ at six but anytime ok. Lock uncle in closet???

Shit, that's exactly what he'd have to do. There was no way in hell Teeter would ever give him permission. His mom would freak. And truthfully, the idea made Dylan's chest go tight. He'd nearly had a heart attack just walking down the street with Grace to Johnny's. Sneaking out at night to go to a party . . . his whole body tensed at the thought. Even though it'd be dark. Who the hell could see him?

But there was no way to get rid of T. And it was the first time Dylan was relieved to have him here, at least as an excuse.

His skull felt like someone was hammering spikes into it. The glare from the screen of the cell made his eyes burn. He closed them, just for a moment. Pictures exploded across his mind, one after the other. The three guys killed because of Dylan. He'd never seen any of them in death, but there they were, Ethan and Chad bloody and unrecognizable. Trev, eyes wide and staring in his watery grave.

He clutched his head and rolled to his side, but the mental reel continued. *You control your thoughts; they don't control you.* The doc's long-ago words swam over him. Dylan scrabbled for the comfort of the image of Trevor, swinging on that rope swing. In his fantasy, the woods were full of light. The trees crowding the banks of the creek opened up, as if in welcome, as Trevor swung higher and higher. A ray of sunlight painted his body as the sound of his laughter echoed and reechoed.

But the vision melded into another one. Trev and him in that hollowed-out log they always went to. Trev opening his hands to show Dylan . . . what? The throbbing in his head squashed the image.

He reached for the comfort of the rope-swing vision again, but it refused to form. Instead, a billow of black smoke blew through his mind, carrying images of Trev and him running, the backpack swinging from his friend's hand. The remote-controlled boat dancing on the swollen creek, its light winking as it bounced off one rock to the other.

Panic crowded into his chest again, and Dylan pulled the pillow over his head to shut it all out. Grace. He clung to the thought of her like a talisman and fell into an uneasy sleep, fingers curled around the cell.

Chapter 50

The task-force groups operated in tandem, efficiently working the houses on the road and going back to recheck the ones where the owners had been absent earlier. They'd covered the county blacktops perpendicular to each end of the road and then made their way a mile up the mountain to start anew on the next street. The team below them had cleared two unincorporated areas in the time since they'd all started.

Cady headed back toward the Jeep with Miguel just behind her. She shoved her gloved hands deep in her pockets. The air seemed clearer at this elevation, crisper. The night sky was a velvet blanket pricked with diamonds, some of which seemed to have scattered across the hills below, accentuating the houses there. If she had time to admire views, she thought as she opened the driver's door, there'd be far worse things than falling to sleep with one like this.

Instead she'd be heading home, with nothing to show for their efforts today. She shook off the morose thought and started the Jeep as the others piled into the vehicle. The process would take time. And they were getting closer. She could feel it.

Reaching for the in-dash radio, she contacted the rest of the team. "Let's call it a night. We'll start again in the morning. Those who want to stay in the area should be able to find accommodations in town.

County sheriff units will be stationed on the bordering roads." She replaced the radio and eased onto the blacktop.

"Hate the thought that he might still be up there. Maybe notice the activity down here and get scared off." Miguel sounded as disappointed as she felt as he fastened his seat belt in the front passenger seat.

"The deputies will be stopping passing cars to ID the passengers." The law enforcement net was as tight as they could manage. But it wasn't foolproof. Miguel's words were a reminder of that.

Cady stopped at the end of the road and spoke to the deputies positioned there before pulling away. She gave one long glance in the rearview mirror at the homes hidden by the night and altitude. And tried to believe their security efforts were enough.

Chapter 51

Bruce Forrester tipped the beer bottle up to his lips, his gaze fixed on the entrance as the door pushed open. Hanging out in the type of dive bars Tina Bandy had once frequented was a helluva lot more pleasant than spending hours every day in a Food Mart parking lot. He carefully watched a dark-haired man with a couple of days' growth of beard stumbling through the door. Bruce had gotten nowhere with the bartender or the other people he'd approached. He'd try once more before moving on to the next place.

He waited for the bartender to approach the guy with his order before moving down a couple of barstools and holding up a bill. "I got this."

The stranger took the beer and looked over the rim at Bruce. "Thanks."

"I was wondering if I could ask you a question. I was supposed to meet this woman about buying her car for my nephew, but she never showed up. Tina Bandy. You know her?"

"I know a Tina comes in here sometimes." The man drank, then lowered the bottle to wipe his mouth on the sleeve of his denim jacket. "Fun gal, you get my drift." He smirked, drank again. "You wouldn't want her piece-of-shit car, though. One of them foreign jobs and rusted to boot."

A glimmer of excitement worked through him. Bruce lifted the bottle to his lips before answering casually, "Well, she ain't askin' much, and the kid will probably wreck his first vehicle anyway. I don't remember what make she said it was, but it's black, right?"

"Brown." The man belched loudly. "One of them Japanese cars. It won't be worth much. No more than a couple of thousand, probably."

"You know where I can find her? I'd like to get a look at the car, but her cell is going straight to voice mail."

The stranger shook his head. "Sorry."

Bruce finished his beer and got up to leave, adrenaline pulsing through him. Finally, a lead. All he had to do was troll the parking lots of bars and the grocery stores until he found a matching vehicle and then follow that bitch home, where he'd have the whole family in one place.

Sometimes, he thought as he made his way out the door and across the parking lot, *it's almost too easy.*

Chapter 52

Fuck this shit. Eric Loomer surged from his seat at the kitchen table and paced across the room. Back. He was out of beer and patience. Why the hell should Bruce get to set all the rules? Pretty convenient that *loose ends* just happened to take him away on a Friday night.

Maybe he was planning to grab another woman. Eric stopped and considered the thought. But the one in his bedroom wasn't dead. Not yet anyway. And it'd be unusual for Forrester to bring another so quickly. Usually he was satisfied using the whores in the nearby towns.

Thinking of the female Bruce had left behind, Eric strode to the man's bedroom door. He'd made it clear she was for his use only, but Bruce wasn't here. And it wasn't like the woman was going to say anything. Eric unlocked the door and snapped on the light. Her wrists were tied in front of her, and her ankles were bound. The sight had warmth pooling in his groin. But closer inspection doused the sensation. Her eyes were vacant, like she wasn't all there anymore. And the bruises around her neck, on her body . . . *Jesus.* Snapping off the light, he backed out of the room and locked the door from the outside. Forrester could be a madman.

He pulled out his cell and checked the time. Bars were still open. Decision made, he grabbed his coat off the back of a chair, picked up the drugs he'd packaged, and carried them out to the garage and stored them behind the workbench with the rest of the product. He'd had plenty to drink today, so he'd be extra careful. He got behind the wheel of his car. He'd take gravel all the way to town and back.

No way Forrester would ever know.

"Blue Moon draft." The female bartender shuffled away to fill Eric's order. He let his gaze wander the nearly empty bar. It was well after midnight. The whores had already found their marks and led them out to their cars or to a cheap motel. He could wait and see if any came back in. Or maybe he'd cruise by the truck stop and see if he could find some action.

The lady set the beer glass in front of him and snatched up the bill he'd laid out. Bitch wouldn't bring back change, either. That's the kind of place this was.

But his irritation faded quickly. Coming to town felt like a big fuck-you to Bruce, and that was enough to keep Eric in a good mood. Bruce had his secrets. He knew that. The man told him only enough to keep their operation running. He took a long drink from the glass in front of him and lifted his gaze to a basketball game highlight showing on the TV above the bar. They were supposed to be partners, sharing in the responsibilities and profits fifty-fifty. Eric had long suspected Bruce liberally skimmed off the top of the cash take. He'd done it before in Hope Mills. If they hadn't had to leave the area so suddenly, Forrester might have gotten himself killed by the supplier.

But Eric had his secrets too. He'd been the one to teach Bruce how to turn their online Bitcoin profits into cash. How to navigate offshore bank accounts and transfer the money often enough to blur the trail. He smiled, raised the glass to his lips to drink. He also knew how to trace Bruce's history on the computer they shared. He'd diverted part of every deposit Bruce had ever made into his own account. Screw or be screwed. That was life's number one lesson.

He lifted his gaze again, catching the bartender's eyes on him. Something in Eric stilled. She wouldn't meet his gaze, grabbing the rag and scrubbing the bar, moving farther away. She fetched a shot for another customer, but then she ducked away from the bar and was lost from sight.

Eric tried to shrug away the paranoia filling him. The woman was gone less than a minute. But when she came back, nothing about her manner calmed his nerves. Especially the way she avoided his gaze.

He couldn't say where the surge of suspicion came from, but obeying it, he gulped down the rest of his beer and slid off the barstool. Walked swiftly to the door. After his years with Forrester, he had plenty to be paranoid about. Eric pulled a ball cap out of his pocket after he left the bar and put it on, pulling the brim low. He walked quickly to the car he'd parked around the corner, got in, did a U-turn, and headed out of town. He'd take the same gravel roads home, even though they took him out of his way, higher into the mountains and down again to their place.

Eric never saw the police cruiser that pulled up to the bar he'd vacated. Or the two cops who walked inside.

Chapter 53

The snuffling sound was getting closer. Something solid hit her hand, followed by a wet sensation. It wasn't until a furry paw batted at her fingers that Cady opened her eyes. Then squeezed them shut again. "You look like a furry lamp," she muttered. Hero put both paws on the edge of the mattress. Batted at her again.

Cady propped herself on one elbow and reached out to pet the animal. She could tell from the sliver visible around the border of the shades that the sky outside had lightened. She needed to be up. Swinging her legs over the bed, she grabbed a T-shirt from the floor and slipped it on. Picking up her cell from the bedside table, she checked it for messages and then tried to shake off the remnants of sleep as she padded to the kitchen, the dog at her heels.

Bacon. Cady stopped in her tracks and inhaled deeply. The aroma was even more heavenly than coffee. Hero trotted over to pick up the clown he'd left for a few seconds. His gait was smoother. He was moving a bit easier. She almost didn't even mind the clown anymore as long as he continued to improve.

Well, she amended, seating herself at the counter bar. She wouldn't mind until he was fully healed. Much.

A bare-chested Ryder was tending two skillets, one with bacon and the other with eggs. He flinched when the meat fizzled and snapped.

"Didn't your mother ever teach you not to cook bacon partially nude?"

He put down the fork he'd been wielding and approached her. "I don't think the topic ever came up. But now that you mention it, that's my shirt you're wearing." He bent to press a lingering kiss on her lips, his finger curled in the neckline of the tee. "I need it back."

"Funny guy. Finders keepers. Tell me there's coffee."

He poured a fresh cup and set it in front of her before grabbing the spatula to flip the eggs. "I don't think I'm cut out to be a short-order cook."

She sipped the coffee, her eyelids closing in pleasure. "You'll need to put in for combat pay."

"You got in late, but you must not have found Forrester last night." Her eyes popped open again at his words. "Surveillance car is still there. And here you are, up at the butt crack of dawn again this morning."

"A charming description. Absolutely poetic."

He grinned at her over his shoulder, and tendrils of heat unfurled in her stomach. Ryder Talbot really was a fine-looking specimen of manhood. And the sentiment was only partially due to the fact he was about to feed her.

Between sips of coffee, she described the events of last night, ending with, "We had to quit the door-to-door around nine thirty. But I got a message about one a.m. from Boone PD. Loomer was sighted at one of the bars there." He paused in the act of lifting a piece of toast to his lips. She shook her head. "He was gone by the time the cops arrived, and there was no vehicle description."

A hard fist of frustration clenched in her stomach. If he'd been scared off by the bartender's behavior, he could have alerted Forrester. They both could have fled. And Cady would be no closer to finding Cassie Zook or putting both men behind bars.

She glanced at the clock on the microwave. It was just after six. Although she'd gotten only a few hours' sleep, Cady felt refreshed. Or would after a shower. "We left county cars stationed at the ends of all the roads where we'd been. Every vehicle going by would be checked. I'm not familiar enough with the area to know how he could have evaded them. Maybe we don't have the right parameters."

Ryder turned off the heat for the burners and expertly transferred the food to plates. "And maybe he never saw the cops. Has no idea he was ID'd." Setting them on either side of the counter, he fetched forks and sat down, sliding one to her.

A Pollyanna attitude, she thought, but she found herself clutching at the possibility. She crunched on a piece of bacon before digging in to her eggs. She couldn't remember when she'd last eaten. Reaching for the milk, she said, "We'll find out. We continue the search for the cabin today." And hoped like hell they found it, with Cassie Zook still alive.

Hero came to her side and sat politely, one paw on her bare knee. She looked from him to Ryder. He was firm about not feeding Sadie human food. But still . . . the dog looked so pathetic. And he really had tried to save her life. With a deft sleight of hand, she transferred a piece of bacon from her plate to the animal.

Sadie barked once, then stared hard at Ryder, as if using powers of doggie hypnosis. "See what you did?" He broke off a bit for the other dog and tossed it to her.

"I can't help it. He's been through so much."

Ryder's lips curved. "I never would have figured you for a softy."

She wasn't. At least she never had been. But then, she'd never had a pet before, either.

The image of the dog's gunshot wound and her gut-wrenching fear for his survival would take a while to fade from her memory.

"Figure I'll tag along today. In an unofficial capacity." Ryder was working through the food on his plate in record time. "I'll call my mom. See if she can watch the dogs again."

"I'm not going to turn down extra help."

Hero gave a polite woof. It took more effort than it should have to ignore him.

"Okay." Ryder got up and rinsed his empty plate and put it in the dishwasher. "I knew there was a reason I couldn't sleep in today."

Cady shoveled in the last few bites of eggs before getting up to clean her plate as well.

"First I need a shower, and I have to stop by and see my mom before we leave town." She felt a familiar tug of guilt. She wouldn't be able to spend time with her today, as was their custom. Alma would be perfectly happy about that, but Cady was achingly aware that opportunities for her and her mom's outings were dwindling.

"Will she be up?"

Cady straightened. "She will be by the time we get there."

"Okay. I'll drive."

She headed for the guest bathroom so Ryder could use the master one. The words on her father's USMS report danced across her mind. Deliberately, she tried to shove them aside. She grabbed a towel from the cupboard and stripped, wondering again what her mother's reaction had been when her husband had used her toddler daughter as a human shield.

And how she'd ever let the man back in her life after that incident.

Chapter 54

"Not a bad breakfast for a first timer." Uncle Teeter shoved the last bite of toast into his mouth. His scraggly hair was still uncombed, but he always woke up with an appetite no matter how much he'd drunk the night before.

Dylan was pretty impressed as well. The sausage links hadn't been difficult, and he already knew how to run a toaster. But T had shown him how to fry the eggs just right. And he'd broken the yolk on only one of them.

"Tomorrow I'll teach you to make perfect pancakes."

Although he was full, the idea sparked interest. "That'd be cool." He could use all this cooking stuff. Once Teeter was gone and things went back to normal, he could make himself some hot meals when his mom was gone. Ones that didn't come from a microwave.

"Are you cleaning up, since I made breakfast?"

T's chair scraped the worn linoleum when he pushed it back. "Hell no, I was instructing you the whole way. When you do it on your own, then I'll wash up. I'm going to take a shower."

When he left the room, Dylan swiftly cleared the table and threw away the paper plates. He waited until he heard the sound of the water running before he dug the cell Grace had given him out of the pocket of his hoodie and checked it.

Ps woke me up early w/ great news! They're leaving for Charleston til 2MORO nite!

A hard knot formed in Dylan's stomach. There was no way he was going to be able to slip away from T. He stayed up later than Dylan did. And Grace was going to think he was lame. Another week and this project was over. Then there'd be no reason for them to stay after school together. How long before she got sick of being with someone who could never fucking go anywhere?

Her next message read, I no u cant shake uncle. But if u figure a way I'll pick u up!

The shower had turned off. Casting a quick look over his shoulder, Dylan texted back, Cool! Maybe I could drug him or something.

LOL

Hearing the bathroom door open, Dylan shoved the cell back in his pocket and hurriedly started scrubbing the skillets.

"Hey. You guys got any Tylenol? I couldn't find any in the bathroom."

Dylan turned his head and immediately wished he hadn't. He didn't need the sight of T wearing only a skimpy towel around his waist seared into his retinas. He'd emptied the bottle last night, but he wasn't going to tell T that. "Let me see if I can find something." He went by Teeter, giving him as wide a berth as he could. Going into his mom's room, Dylan crossed to her closet and went through her purses again. He remembered some bottles in a couple of them from the time he was looking for the gun.

But all he found was a container of Midol. He took it back to Teeter, averting his eyes as he held it out. "Found this."

"Hell, boy, I ain't having a period!"

Dylan flushed. "It says it has a pain reliever in the ingredients."

Teeter turned the bottle so he could read it. "Huh. Well, I'll try it. But after I get dressed, I'm going to town to get the real stuff."

He probably had a hangover, Dylan figured. But when Tina had one, she sure didn't chow down as much as T did. She didn't eat at all. He finished scrubbing the pans and put them away. T returned a few minutes later, dressed, as he was wiping off the table, stove, and counters.

"Gotta get cat food too. And beer."

The refrigerator had been full of beer when his mom had left, Dylan recalled. Sacks of empties sat next to the trash can.

"You want anything?"

"Naw. Thanks," he added hastily.

"When you was little, you always wanted a treat from the store, I remember." T grinned at him. "You want me to bring you a treat, kid?"

Dylan sort of remembered that. "I'm okay."

"Suit yourself." The man went for his coat and then headed to the side door. "Lock up after me."

As if he needed the reminder. Dylan secured the door after T left and took out the cell again. Checked for new texts. There weren't any.

Because Grace was leaving it up to him. Nothing more to say unless he figured out a way to get . . .

A crash in the next room had him jumping a foot. *What the . . . ?* Dylan rounded the corner into the living room in time to see the cat tearing out of his bedroom like its tail was on fire. He went in to check it out and groaned aloud.

The piggy bank he'd often talked himself out of smashing was lying in pieces on the floor. The cat must have knocked it off the dresser. Dylan went to the kitchen and dug a couple of plastic bags out of the trash and went back to clean up the mess, cussing the animal the whole way.

He put the pieces in one sack and the change in the other. He'd have to vacuum the smallest bits. Dylan tried to scoop up fistfuls of the coins, but there were tiny pieces of plaster among them, and soon his hands were nicked and bleeding. He wiped them on his jeans and then stopped when he spied something. Reaching out with one finger, he stirred through the mound of change. There was a half of a metal file. He'd broken a nail file off in the opening once when he was trying to pry out enough coins to buy ice cream when he went to town with Trev and his mom.

There was something else there, mixed with the coins. He fished out a gold key.

What the heck . . . ? A greasy tangle of fear knotted in his stomach. Dylan dropped it into the money bag as if it had burned his fingers. He didn't remember what it might have gone to. But something flickered in his memory, there and gone too quickly for him to grasp it.

Suddenly in a hurry, he picked up the rest of the coins and tied the top of the bag in a knot. He looked around for a place to stuff it where his mom wouldn't notice when she cleaned. Finally, he stuck it in a corner on the top shelf of the closet, hoping she wouldn't see it. If she learned the bank was broken, he already knew she'd blame him.

Before he vacuumed, he went to the bathroom and opened the cabinet to look for some Band-Aids. When he didn't find any, his gaze was drawn to the half-empty prescription bottles inside it. An antibiotic for his last sinus infection. An even older one with Colton's name on it. Dylan took out a third bottle. Tina Bandy. He didn't recognize the name of the medication, but the only time his mom had been sick that he remembered was when she strained her back at work a couple of years ago and had muscle spasms. She'd been off two weeks.

Muscle relaxants. A thrum of excitement lit Dylan's veins. That's what she'd taken then. They'd knocked her out. She'd slept most of the day.

Mind racing, Dylan wondered how many pills it would take to put T to sleep.

Chapter 55

"Cady!" Hannah Maddix looked up from her breakfast with a smile. "What a nice surprise."

"I can't stay." She squeezed her mom's hand. "I just wanted to come by and tell you myself."

Alma didn't share Hannah's delight at the early visit. She'd said nothing after answering the door, just turned and stalked back to the kitchen. She could hold a mammoth-size grudge. Cady had to figure that she'd put Bo up to the call. And that he'd reported back when Cady hadn't shown up to see him in jail.

She did a quick visual survey. Hannah looked lovely in a pale-blue blouse that they'd bought a few weeks ago on one of their shopping trips.

"Work again?" Hannah's brows drew together. "You're too dedicated, Cady. I hope you get compensated for that."

"It's fine, Mom. And I'll make it up to you. I promise." Hannah walked her to the door. "If I'm free tomorrow, I'll stop by again." Cady ignored the glare her aunt threw her as they went by her chair. "Take you out to Della's or something."

Hannah smiled. "I do like ice cream, no matter the temperatures outside."

One hand on the doorknob, Cady kissed her cheek. "I'm well aware."

The sound of her mom's laughter lightened a weight she'd been carrying since last weekend. Hearing it was a bittersweet reminder to treasure the good times still ahead, rather than dwell on signs that those times were limited.

She opened the door, and her mom walked out on the porch with her. Then she frowned. "Where's your vehicle?"

"I'm riding with a friend today."

Hannah descended the steps slowly, staring hard at Ryder's county SUV. "Why is there a sheriff's car here?"

Foreboding curled in Cady's gut. "Mom, let's go back into the house."

But she shook off the hand Cady placed on her arm and went farther down the drive, still staring at the vehicle. "What's he doing here? Why are you with him?" Her voice was filled with confusion. And a rising edge of hysteria.

Ryder opened the door and stepped out of the vehicle at their approach. Then stilled when Cady waved him back.

"Get out of here!" shouted Hannah shrilly, running toward him. "Stay away from my daughter. Haven't you hurt her enough?"

Cady caught up and positioned herself between the two of them, trying to distract her mom. "You have your socks on outside. Look at your feet. You're going to get cold. What's Alma going to say?"

But Hannah ducked around her and made a beeline for Ryder. Reaching him, she slugged him in the chest. Once. And again. "I never should have listened to you! Never! Why should a little girl do what you and all the other cops couldn't? I'll never forgive you for that. Not ever!"

She rained blows upon him until Ryder's hands came up to cover hers, holding them firm but still. "My name is Ryder, Hannah. Look at me. You don't know me. Look at me."

"You said it was just a precaution." Hannah was weeping now, the fight streaming out of her like steam from a teakettle. She leaned heavily against Ryder. "I never should have agreed. She was just a little girl. And we turned her into a killer."

We turned her into a killer. We turned her into a killer.

Hannah's words pounded a constant tattoo in Cady's head, each etching a brand there. They'd lingered the entire time she'd calmed her mom, helped her back into the house. During the tongue-lashing she'd gotten from Alma for causing another upset, Cady had accepted the responsibility silently. Had walked back outside and gotten into Ryder's vehicle and they'd pulled out of the drive. Drove several miles without exchanging a word.

Her chest ached from the tangle of emotion lodged there. Sometimes the truth didn't set one free at all. Sometimes it was an anvil drawing one inexorably into an abyss of despair.

"I need to tell you something," Ryder said quietly.

Cady didn't react. Just continued to stare out the passenger window.

"I tracked down my dad's former chief investigative deputy. The one before Jerry Garza. He said something similar to what your mom just did. It sounded an awful lot like he was intimating that my dad had something to do with setting the scene for that night."

That night. So many details were missing from her memory. And she'd never been certain if her recollections were gleaned from what she'd been told or if they were her own. She could see herself standing in the kitchen. Her father leaning against the back door, laughing at Hannah on the floor. Blood dripped down her mom's face, staining her pretty nightgown. She couldn't recall what the weapon on the table looked like, but Cady had a vivid recollection of the weight of it in her hand. The sound it made when she'd fired it.

"He was always one step ahead of the marshals." Her voice was thready. The two-page USMS report in the sheriff investigative file verified her statement. How different things might have been if Lonny Maddix had been captured earlier.

Her thoughts were ping-ponging inside her. It took every ounce of strength she had to corral them so logic could take over. "Even if that final scene was orchestrated, it sounded very much like my mom went along with it."

"The power dynamic wasn't equal between the sheriff's office and her. She was likely pressured. Coerced." The tightness in Ryder's voice pierced Cady's misery. This revelation was as debilitating for him as it was for her.

She shook her head, self-recrimination filling her. "I should have known that seeing your vehicle could set her off. I knew she had a history with your dad." Hearing her own words shook her from her inner turmoil for a moment. A hot flood of remorse filled her as she faced him. "I'm sorry. I never meant to tell you that." His expression had frozen. His grip on the steering wheel looked unnaturally tight.

"You only confirmed what I've been thinking for a while now. My dad was a serial cheater. I've known that since I was a teen."

But she'd substantiated it. Regret gnawed at her.

"You recognized that picture of him," he continued, slowing to take an exit. "The first time you came to my office, when it was still hanging on the wall, and then last time, when we were searching for the files in the basement. I could tell from your reaction."

She'd fully planned to keep those details from him out of an unfamiliar sense of protectiveness, even knowing he wouldn't thank her for it. "I was six, maybe. I'd gotten up hours after my bedtime. Gone looking for my mom. I found her and your dad in the kitchen."

"In a compromising situation."

His tone was still flat. His face expressionless. And she knew he was keeping the pent-up emotion walled away, much as she was. "Yes."

"I was seventeen the first time I realized my dad was cheating on my mom." His tone was too even. Too expressionless. "I was coming home from a pep rally at school. It was maybe seven o'clock or so. I dropped off the last of my friends and headed to my house. But I saw my dad's personal car ahead of me in this residential neighborhood. I recognized the license plate. I was just getting ready to call him when he turned into a driveway. The garage door opened, and he drove inside it. Then it closed. When I got home, my mom said he was working late again. And I knew then what was going on. It wasn't the only time, either. I'm starting to think he had a relationship with all the women in the files I found. Maybe something had gotten out about his behavior, and he hid them away so no one could dig them up as ammunition during a campaign. I just need to check the addresses again. I'm guessing one of them will be the house I saw him at when I was a teenager."

How did both of us become ensnarled in the same web of deceit? Cady wondered dully. It defied description.

"Your aunt didn't seem particularly reasonable."

She gave a short laugh. The understatement of the century. "She's not, but this time she was right. The last two times I've seen my mom, she's had an episode. I'm the common factor here."

"Cady." The sympathy in his voice had her eyes burning. "The mitigating factor is her disease. The deterioration of her memory. The past is more vivid than the present for her. You said she'd calmed down once you got her indoors."

And that lightning switch between fury and the slightly befuddled state had been even more heartbreaking. "If she continues to have issues today, there's a sedative Alma can give her." But Cady hated to think of her mom spending her remaining time drugged. Dazed.

He changed lanes. Belatedly, she saw the flashing strobe bar of a trooper who'd pulled a car over. "When I talked to Dr. Baker on Monday, he said negative emotional memories have more lasting power. If there was something traumatic in her past, it'd make sense that she'd relive it over and over, especially with something to spark an association." Something like a new nightdress. A sheriff's car. Or the presence of her daughter? Her fingers curled into her palm, the nails pressing deep.

"We can't change the past." Ryder slid her a glance. "We both have to face the possibility that our parents may have colluded all those years ago. And my father was likely the one who gave your mom the idea of what to do the next time Lonny Maddix showed up at her door."

He said nothing else, but he didn't have to. Cady's mind had already gone there, picking at the fresh wound like a crow on carrion. Whether Butch Talbot had wielded unprofessional influence or not, her mom had gone along with the plan. And neither of them had considered the lasting effects on the child after using Cady to rid them of their Lonny Maddix problem.

Chapter 56

Eric opened his eyes and looked around the bedroom. Then rose, swinging his legs over the side of the bed. He'd been in a cold sweat the entire drive back to their rental. The nerves hammering in his pulse had made him so flustered, he'd gotten turned around on the gravel roads. It'd taken twice as long to get home as it should have. He'd pulled into the garage with a rush of relief that had had him sagging against the steering wheel.

Jesus, he'd gotten himself into a state. He snagged a pair of jeans from the floor and pulled them on before going out to the kitchen. Finding it empty, he continued on to the garage entry and stuck his head out the door. Bruce hadn't come home. Shutting the door again, he leaned against it.

He'd almost—almost—called Forrester last night and told him his fears. Embarrassment mingled with relief, because he'd talked himself out of it. Bruce would have told him he was being a dumb-ass, and it was bad enough that it was true, without the other man knowing it too.

He set about making some breakfast. With a sideways look at Bruce's closed bedroom door, Eric set a couple of pieces of dry toast on a paper plate and walked to the door. Unlocked it.

The woman hadn't changed positions since he was in here last night. Her eyes were wide and staring. For a moment, Eric was afraid she was dead. And he'd have to deal with that mess too. But as he approached, he saw her blink. Setting the plate on the bed next to her, he ordered, "Eat." Then he retraced his steps and relocked the door.

Crossing to the table, he sat down, his stomach reminding him he hadn't eaten last night. He scooped up some eggs and shoved them into his mouth. Bruce hadn't planned to even feed the woman until he came back. Sometimes, Eric thought as he chugged out of the orange juice carton, he was convinced the man was little more than an animal.

Chapter 57

Cady got out of the Jeep and waited with Ryder, Miguel, and SBI agent Rebedeau while Officer Colin Turner walked toward the drive with the sleek Belgian Malinois at his side. Through the overgrown brush partially shrouding the property from view, she could see slivers of the house. Denuded trees crowded the structure, branches nearly sweeping the roof of the building. While many of the homes they'd cleared on the search were ostentatious displays of wealth, with banks of gleaming windows and decks to take in the view, this one was smaller. Unkempt. Heavy wooden shutters blocked the windows. Maybe it belonged to a long-absent owner or, more likely, a landlord more interested in collecting the rent than maintenance.

"How many owners have recognized the pictures of Loomer and Forrester?" Ryder asked, pulling a pair of gloves out of his coat pocket. Although Waynesville was supposed to be a balmy fifty degrees today, temperatures at this altitude were midthirties. Cady had forgotten to warn him about that, but apparently he'd come prepared.

"A couple yesterday and just the one today." All had indicated sightings of the men in Blowing Rock or Boone, which made Cady even more certain they had to be close to the fugitives' hideout, despite their lack of success finding it so far. And Cady didn't kid herself—if the men were up here, they wouldn't surrender quietly.

She turned and squinted up the mountainside. Another team was working the houses on the road above them. Surely the homes didn't ascend much higher. They'd already cleared houses along two more roads so far today and revisited those that had been empty last night.

Miguel unfolded a map. Studied it. "The higher we go, the more isolated the homes get. This one is two miles from our last stop. The next one is about that far too. Like you said, they'd want that seclusion." When he was finished with the map, he refolded it, tucked it inside his coat.

Her radio crackled then. "Green Fork Road, clear. Heading to Broadstone Lane." Cady had the radio in hand, ready to answer, when she caught sight of Turner waving at them. The dog was sitting. It'd alerted to explosives on the property.

Chapter 58

"Everyone and their sister musta been grocery shopping today. Help me with the beer, will you?"

Dylan took the twelve-packs T handed him and carried them to the refrigerator. He hadn't heard the car come up the drive. When Teeter had pounded on the kitchen door, Dylan had jumped a foot. Maybe from a guilty conscience. In the man's absence, he'd ground four muscle-relaxant pills into tiny particles. It'd been more difficult that he'd thought. He'd finally used a hammer. Then he'd emptied one of the containers of antibiotics and carefully poured the powder into the bottle. After hiding it under the bed in his mom's room, he'd played video games, nerves frayed, waiting for T to return.

"Here." The man handed him a sack, then took off his shoes and relocked the door. "Gotcha something anyway. You used to like them when you was a kid. They're the ones with the double frosting."

Mystified, Dylan dug into the bag. Grinned when he drew out a package of Double Stuf Oreos. "Hey, I love these things."

"See?" Shrugging out of his coat, T tapped his temple. "I remember all that shit. Never had kids of my own. You and Colton was the closest I ever got."

"Thanks." But Dylan's earlier pleasure dissipated. Now he felt like a complete douche. He'd spent the morning planning how to drug the guy, and T trots out a memory like that? Dylan put away the stuff from the store, leaving the Tylenol on the counter. Good thing he hadn't texted Grace his plans for tonight. He couldn't go through with it. He'd be a complete asshole if he did.

When he walked into the living room, T was already settled on the couch, the controller in his hand.

"I should have had you pick up a new game when you were in—"

"What the fuck!" T interrupted him, his face a mask of rage. His glare would melt steel. "Did you mess with my game?"

"No." The whiplash transformation in the man had Dylan instantly wary. "I mean, I started a different one. It shouldn't have done anything to the one you paused."

"Well, you fucking erased it! Goddamn it, you fucking moron." Teeter sprang up and stalked toward him. "How many times I gotta tell you not to touch my shit?" He grabbed Dylan by the shoulders and slammed him against the wall. Once. Twice. Three times.

Dylan shoved him hard in the chest. "Get your hands off me!" The guy was crazy! As schizoid as the damn cat he'd brought with him.

"You want to try something, little man?" Gone was the easygoing Uncle Teeter. The guy shoving his face close to Dylan's was a stranger. One who'd gone from joking to enraged in one second flat. "Better grow another six inches if you wanna take me on." He gave Dylan a final push and went back to the game.

Holy shit. Dylan stood stunned for a minute before tearing down the hallway to his mom's bedroom. He shut the door and turned to slide down it. Anger fogged his mind. His fists clenched into tight balls. His chest pounded with pent-up fury and something else. Shame. And that pissed him off even more.

What the hell just happened? It was like someone flipped a switch in T. Just like the time he'd freaked because Dylan had tossed away some uneaten scraps. There was something seriously wrong with the guy. His mom probably didn't even know about it. How long had it been since she'd seen him? Maybe he'd had a breakdown or something.

That was probably it, Dylan decided. He felt the cell buzz in his pocket, but he didn't reach for it. Anger was churning through him, and he was in no mood to talk to Grace. If the marshal called to let him know Forrester was in custody, he'd leave until his mom came back. He didn't care where he went. Anywhere.

The thought had some of the emotion streaming out of him. After Maddix's message, he'd hoped it'd be over soon. And he didn't know how much more he could take. Because if he wasn't freaking out about getting shot from Forrester driving by in a green pickup, he had to worry about what would happen the next time T went off. The man was crazy as a betsey bug. And he was armed. Not a great combination.

He leaned his head against the door, suddenly feeling defeated. Jesus, it just never ended. Maybe he'd have been better off all around if he hadn't spent so much time trying to hide from Forrester. If Dylan had just walked up to the truck the first time he'd spotted it and let the man blow him away, he could have saved Ethan's life. Saved that Bahlman kid too.

A familiar vise of guilt squeezed him. Even when this was done, his responsibility for three deaths lingered. There was no running away from that. No happy ending. Tears stung Dylan's eyes. He blinked them away.

Soon. That's what the marshal had said. But damn, times like this, he didn't know if getting out of this alive was even worth it.

He stayed in the bedroom for a long time. Heard the sound effects of T's game in the background. The cell in his pocket buzzed a couple more times. Several minutes passed before his hand crept into the pocket of his hoodie. Drew out the cell and read Grace's messages.

Got idea for project. You as Thomas Jefferson?

Not a chance. He went to the next one.

Or no costumes. PPP with founding fathers. Click to different ones when we reference their quote.

It took him a moment to decipher "PPP." PowerPoint presentation. Definitely better than costumes. Some of the tension seeped out of him. I'd be down w/ PPP, he typed back.

Or Jeopardy game class can play with us. Turn paper into quiz.

Where did she come up with these ideas? Ok 2, he texted.

U texting in bathroom again? Followed by an emoji with the tongue hanging out.

Bedroom. So don't strangle uncle. It was stupid how just texting with Grace could make him feel better. She made the world fade away a bit. Had him thinking of just him and her.

Sorry. Sucks.

Yeah. Dylan wasn't even aware of what he was going to say until his fingers typed the next message. I figured out a way to get away 2nite tho.

NK?????

He paused, a sliver of trepidation darting through him. If T figured out Dylan had put something in his beer, the scene earlier would be nothing compared to the man's rage. But lingering resentment punched through the foreboding. Fuck him—he deserved it. So he slept for a while. Big deal. And it wasn't like Dylan got a chance like this every day. Deliberately, he texted, I'll let u no a time later.

T pounded on the door at Dylan's back as Grace's response appeared.

Cant wait!!!

"You gonna pout in there like a girl all day or you coming out and playing?"

Resolve hardening, he stood up. Opened the door. He'd play, all right. But T didn't know the rules to Dylan's new game.

Chapter 59

Cady held the team meeting a mile away, on a gravel road that hopefully would get little traffic. The collection of vehicles was sure to draw attention from any passersby.

"It's a trip-wire explosive," Turner told the group once the teams were all assembled. "It's set up about ten yards from the front of the house and seems to run the perimeter. It's visible when you get closer."

"That's similar to what Loomer's uncle had," she said, sliding a glance at Miguel. "A deer set it off as we were leaving."

"That'd mean it was victim initiated rather than command initiated," Turner responded.

"Any sign that the structure was wired?"

The officer hesitated. "I didn't go around the entire property. The dogs can sometimes detonate the wires. I'd need to double-check."

Cady thought for a moment. "Seems to me, we have two options. The two fugitives may still have a victim inside. A surprise entry is the best solution, but it's out of the question unless we can ensure the entrances aren't wired. Once they know we're out here, it can easily turn into a hostage negotiation, which could go south in a hurry."

"We could summon a bomb squad mobile unit," Miguel said. "It'd take a couple of hours to get one here. Is the victim in imminent danger?"

Cady's jaw went tight as she considered what she'd learned about Forrester's relationships with women. She didn't know if Cassie Zook was still alive. But if she was, every minute she spent with the fugitives ratcheted up her risk. "She's been in danger since he abducted her," she replied. She thought for a moment, then looked back at the handler. "You walked up the drive okay."

Looking mystified, Turner responded, "Sure. The drive and concrete walk to the front door are free of wires; otherwise there's a chance your bandits would trigger them themselves."

She nodded. "Maybe there's a third option. But we need to move fast."

Chapter 60

Cady peered into the Jeep's side mirror at the house behind her. The single-story structure still looked deserted. The shutters over the front window would block a view to the front. The door looked solid. Which meant no one was going to look out and see them. *Hearing* them, though. That was the risk.

At her signal, the team members in the vehicle spilled out, all of them, like her, in tactical gear. Cady backed the Jeep up slowly and stopped as close to the attached garage as she could. Officer Turner, Miguel, and Ryder approached swiftly. She got out and watched the men lift Felix, the K-9, to the top of the Jeep. Turner scrabbled up after her. She watched, with bated breath, as the dog examined the edge of the garage roof within her range. Finally, Turner looked over his shoulder and gave a nod. Cady opened the right back passenger door and climbed onto the seat, bracing her hands on the roof of the vehicle.

Heaving herself up was made more difficult by the gear she wore, but once there, Cady ran to the rear of the Jeep and jumped to grab the garage roof. Struggled onto it. She was panting by the time she stood. Miguel handed her the equipment. Then Turner joined her, the other team members on the roof of her Jeep lifting the dog to join her handler. There was no way of knowing if the noise they made would be detected. She needed to assume that it would be and act quickly.

She got on her hands and knees and crawled rapidly. If there was a back entrance and the dog cleared it of explosives, they'd do a simultaneous entry. Members would join her in the rear yard, with others spread outside the perimeter on both sides and an entry team through the garage. But they'd planned for several scenarios.

She flattened herself against the roof while Turner—with a hand on the dog's collar—carefully led the animal over the peak, bracing his feet as he went down to keep his balance. Adrenaline was doing a hard knock in her chest as she watched the dog work along the lower edge of the roof. When she got the signal from Turner, Cady took the radio from her belt and spoke into it in a low voice. "Option A is a go. Positions."

Chapter 61

Eric Loomer flipped the light on in the garage and headed to the work-bench. He may as well get the rest of the packaging ready for mailing on Monday. Then he wouldn't have to do a blessed thing tomorrow except lie on the couch and watch TV. Bruce should be back by then. And that son of a bitch would open up about what he'd been doing all week, unless he wanted to get himself a new partner.

Something caught his attention. There was noise on the roof, like branches hitting it, over and over. But they didn't have a tree that close to the garage. What the hell?

He listened for a few more minutes, then rushed into the house. Headed to the front door. Cracked it open. The drive was empty, but he caught glimpses of unfamiliar vehicles down the road, through the bared brush. *Shit, shit, shit!* He hadn't been paranoid last night after all. Someone had followed him back here.

Panic surged through his veins. He shut the door and grabbed his coat before dashing to his bedroom for his Glock. He paused a second, then backtracked to Bruce's bedroom. Shoving open the door, he strode to the bed and pulled the woman to her feet. His arm snaked around her neck, and he dragged her after him as he ran to the back door. He opened it a sliver. The backyard was empty.

He pressed the muzzle of the gun against her temple. "You make a sound and I blow you away. Got it?"

She nodded. Maybe she wasn't as out of it as he'd thought. He stuck the toe of his boot into the open crack in the door and tightened his grip on the woman as he pulled her out onto the deck. Down the three steps to the yard.

"Eric Loomer." His head craned one way and then the other. Where the hell? "United States Marshals Service. You are surrounded. Step away from the woman and set down your weapon. Put your hands behind your head and get down on your knees."

"The fuck . . ." Above. The words were coming from above him. He looked up. Stared. Four black-clad figures were on the roof of the garage and the house. Helmeted. Anonymous. Each held a rifle pointed at him.

"Step away from the female and set down your weapon. Now! Right now!"

The woman was deadweight in his grip. He shoved the gun against her face again. "Stay back," he yelled. They wouldn't shoot him as long as he had her, would they? "Stay back, or I blow her head off." The line of rifles never wavered. The barrels followed him as he hauled her across the yard. No fucking way was he going down for this. No. Fucking. Way. "Stay back," he shouted again. The only exit was the thick hedge of bared brush bordering three sides of the yard. But he could make it. He . . .

The woman in his arms came to life. She drove an elbow into his gut, twisting and fighting wildly, forcing him to readjust his grip on her. "Goddamn it, stay still." He raised the weapon to bring it down on her head, but she'd leaned forward, sinking her teeth into the arm he had around her neck. He screamed in pain. She went limp, and he had to release her to avoid being pulled to the ground. Without her as cover, he was exposed. He turned and crashed through the brambles, the branches tearing at his clothes. Clawing at his face.

He heard the voice again as he burst out of the brush. "Cassie Zook, roll away from the bushes. This way! This way! Move! Perimeter team, suspect on the run, northwest corner of the lot."

Eric sprinted toward freedom, becoming belatedly aware of two things. More rifle-armed shooters were waiting for him. And the wire. The fucking wire . . . It rushed up too fast. He leaped, trying to clear it.

When he caught it with the toe of his boot, the sound of the blast ripped through the air, and his body exploded in agony.

Chapter 62

"I feel like a badass." Grace shot Dylan a wicked smile as she put the car into gear and pulled slowly away from the side of the road.

"Bonnie and Clyde," he joked. He put on his seat belt—he might need it; he had no idea what kind of driver she'd be—and leaned against the seat, his heart galloping. And that was only partly because he'd run the mile and a half to the house where he'd had her mom drop him last time. Most of the seething emotion in his gut was because of the way he'd gotten free.

It'd taken a little doing getting the powder into Teeter's beer. He'd finally decided to wait until the man had already had a few. Dylan had pushed him on that end. "Want another beer, Uncle T?" A little powder had gone into each. He'd encouraged an early supper, although he'd worried that food would counteract the alcohol and muscle relaxants. While Dylan was cleaning up afterward, he'd twisted off the top of a beer and taken the medicine bottle out of his pocket, pouring the rest of the powder into it. Then he'd tightened the cap again and taken it out to his uncle, who was watching TV in the other room.

"Did you really drug your uncle?"

"Muscle relaxants. He'll be fine." Dylan spoke with more authority than he felt. There was a tangle of guilt in his chest, but the man had

had it coming. And for a while this afternoon, he'd thought nothing was going to happen. T had just done a lot of yawning. But an hour after that last beer, he was snoring like a chain saw, stretched out on the couch, the remote still in his hand.

"I'm impressed."

Because she really sounded like she was, he shrugged away the lingering anxiety. "I was desperate. If I hadn't gotten out of that house soon, I'd have offed myself."

She braked for the stop sign at the end of the road. Made a perfect turn toward town. "My biggest fear is that some nosy neighbor saw this car leave our garage. Hopefully my parents didn't have time to talk to anyone about their plans. They were sort of last-minute."

"My biggest fear is that he'll wake up before I can crawl back in the bedroom window." They grinned at each other like seasoned coconspirators. Getting the damn screen off after raising the window in his mom's room had been a chore by itself. He'd left it unsecured, just setting it back in place after he'd gotten through it. He hoped he could pull it up after him when he returned, so he could lock it again. Dylan leaned forward and turned the radio to a station he liked.

"I've had driver's ed, and I have a permit. I'm still on stage one, though, so hopefully if a cop sees us, they'll think you're an adult."

Driver's ed and a permit weren't even on the horizon for Dylan. But he knew the rules. She wouldn't be able to drive without an adult until being on stage one for six months. "Is this going to be your car when you can drive alone?"

"I'm working on my dad to buy me something new." She made a face. "My mom probably won't let him, though. She says all kids wreck their first car."

"Not always." Colton hadn't had an accident yet. At least not that Dylan knew of.

"I know. But she's like helicopter mom personified. This is her car. She'll probably get a new one."

He couldn't even imagine living in a family where you assumed your parents would buy you a car. Or had parents who could. It was a big deal at his house when his mom brought home groceries. Once again, he wondered if Grace would be interested in him if she really understood how different their lives were.

Or if she knew he was responsible for three kids' deaths. The thought was accompanied by a dark snake of dread.

One of her hands left the wheel and snuck over to take his. And just like that, Dylan's doubts faded away. She took her eyes off the road for just a moment to look at him. And smile that smile that had his stomach doing flips. "I'm really glad you came tonight."

His fingers curled around hers. "Yeah. Me too."

Chapter 63

Cady called up to surgery, but Eric Loomer was still in recovery. She walked down the hallway and pushed open Cassie Zook's door. The woman watched her entrance with expressionless eyes. "Your sister is on her way." Cady's voice was quiet. The woman's Asheville hospital room had muted lighting. Soft music playing. None of it seemed to have much effect on the patient. Cassie Zook's stare was as blank as it'd been when she'd been rescued from the mountain home.

"Do you remember me from this afternoon? I'm Cady, with the Marshals Service. The man who abducted you. Do you know where he is?"

Cassie's fingers worried the edge of the sheet covering her. It was the second time Cady had tried speaking with the woman. First at the scene, while the medics had been checking her over. That time had been met with a similar lack of success.

"Did you overhear the two men talking?" She tried another tack. "Did they argue?"

Her fingers stilled. But she remained silent.

"Was your abductor in charge? Did he tell the other man what to do?"

There was the tiniest of movements. A slight nod of her head. Encouraged, Cady went on. "How long has the other man been absent?"

The other woman turned her head on the pillow to face the wall. But after a long moment, she said, "Last night. After dark."

Where had Forrester gone? The question throbbed through her like an open wound. Angela had told them about the time he paid for an entire night with her. But if he'd hired a prostitute last night, he'd have returned home by the time of the rescue.

"Did he tell the other man where he was going?"

"I was kept . . . in his bedroom. I didn't hear much."

Cady glanced again at the woman's throat. She'd survived a nightmare. But her trauma would linger long after the bruises healed. "Had he ever left you this long before?"

"No. But this week, he came and went."

Her mind raced. What was special about this week? What other interests did Forrester have? Tina Bandy's family? Apprehension twisted in her gut. She made a mental note to check on them.

"The man who abducted you is Bruce Forrester. The one injured at the scene is Eric Loomer. Do you know what they were doing in that house? Did they ever have visitors?"

The woman was silent for so long that Cady thought she was finished answering. But finally she whispered, "I don't know. I don't think so. Sometimes they'd go out together at night. Yesterday . . . he left for most of the day. Came back for a couple of hours." She shuddered violently. "Then he packed a bag. I didn't see him again."

Left for most of the day, Cady mused. Came home and took off again. It didn't narrow down Forrester's destination much. There were places in Tennessee he could get to and back in that time frame. Any number of places in North Carolina.

Including Asheville.

The hospital door opened with a quiet swoosh, and Cady rose when she saw the nurse enter. "Visitors are limited to five minutes."

She motioned Cady out of the room as she rounded the bed and spoke to Cassie in a low, soothing voice.

Cady rejoined Miguel and Ryder at the end of the hallway. Both were holding steaming cups of coffee. She shook her head when Ryder offered her his. She'd had enough caffeine to float.

"Did you have better luck this time?" Miguel asked.

She relayed the conversation, ending with, "I'm going to put in a call to the Buncombe County Sheriff's office. It wouldn't hurt for someone to check on the Bandy household."

"I'll do it," Ryder volunteered. She sent him a grateful look as he turned and took a few steps away, pulling out his cell.

"You missed Rebedeau." Miguel took a swig from his Styrofoam cup. "She went up to the surgical floor to check on Loomer's progress."

The surgeon had suggested more operations would be needed, given the trauma Loomer's body had sustained. She was anxious to interview him. He, better than anyone, would have a read on Forrester's whereabouts.

"Is it possible we missed Forrester? That he spotted us and took off?"

She followed Miguel's question seamlessly. "I don't think so. Cassie said he's been coming and going all week. Yesterday he was gone all day, came back, and then packed a bag and left."

"To go where?"

She lifted a shoulder. "Hopefully, Loomer can tell us." The lack of answers was frustrating. She focused on what she knew about Bruce Forrester. He was motivated by his fetish, greed, and revenge. The first two qualities would keep him close to the house. Revenge . . . If he'd learned Dylan Castle was there, that might take him to Asheville. "We'll know more when we get forensics on the computers found in the home." The search warrant she'd acquired had given them wide access to the house's contents. They'd discovered the drugs in the garage, along with false IDs for both men, but the missing answers might be hidden on the computer.

When Ryder rejoined them, Cady said, "Let's see if we can speak with Loomer." They turned as one and headed to the elevator.

"How serious is Zook's condition?" Ryder asked.

"She'll recover from her physical wounds, according to the nurse." Cady stabbed at the button that would take them to the surgical floor. "Emotionally, though . . ." The woman had been missing for nearly two months. Cady could only imagine the brutality she'd endured. Psychological scars lingered long after physical injuries healed.

A snippet of memory surfaced, as if summoned by the thought. *You don't like bad guys, do you, Cady?*

From long practice, she shoved it aside. Discovering its origin hadn't made it easier to handle, she reflected grimly. Not in the least.

They stepped into the elevator and rode up two floors. As the elevator doors opened and they stepped into the hallway, the cell in her pocket buzzed. She stepped away from the others to answer it. "Maddix."

"Cady, it's Cumberland County deputy investigator Blake Patten. I read the update on the digital file. Congratulations on catching one of those assholes."

Smiling at the man's description, she walked toward the waiting room. "No lead on Forrester yet. But we'll get him."

"Don't doubt it," he replied in his distinctive drawl. "Want to give you the news on our end. We dredged Cutter's Swamp. Damned if we didn't find a decomposing garbage bag with a few bones inside. Found several more loose bones in the water. Now it's up to forensics to say whether they all belonged to the same person and to harvest the DNA. But seems like your informant gave you a solid tip."

"He'll be happy to hear that," she said dryly. True to her word, she'd make a call to Tillis's warden to tell him as much. "Didn't happen to find the chain saw used to kill the guy, did you?"

"'Fraid not. Did find some little metal beads in the bottom of the bag, though. You know the kind used to spell out names on a bracelet or necklace? Letters were worn away, but we dipped them in fingerprint powder and we could make them out. Got an A, I, N, T. Anything else will wait on lab testing."

Which could take weeks, she knew. The case was separate from the warrants on Loomer and Forrester, so they'd wait their turn in the crime lab. Thanking the man for the update, she hung up. Then stopped in the doorway of the waiting room, a thought piercing her. There may have been other letters still resting on the bottom of the pond. But by themselves A, I, N, T could be rearranged to spell Tina.

Surely it was a coincidence that Tina Bandy had lived in Hope Mills, just miles away from Cutter's Swamp when Brady Boss went missing.

Chapter 64

"Might try the guy over there with the man bun." The bartender's voice dripped derision. "To hear him tell it, he knows Tina better than most."

Bruce Forrester followed the direction of the man's gaze as the bartender moved away. His lips twisted. Never could figure how a self-respecting man could wear his hair like a damn woman. But he grabbed his beer and ambled over to the scruffy-looking stranger, pulling out a chair to the table where he sat alone. "The bartender said you might know a gal by the name of Tina Bandy," he said when the guy looked up from his glass, startled. He went through the same song and dance he'd been using in these places about the car for sale and wanting to buy it for his nephew.

"Yeah, I know her. I mean, I *know* her." The man belched around the words. "Don't give me the time of day no more, though. Not that I give a shit. She was a lousy lay."

Bruce tipped his bottle, as if in toast. "No loss, then, right? You have her number?"

The guy shook his head. "Deleted it after she started blocking my calls. I mean, who the hell she think she is?"

"You don't need that shit."

"Damn right." The stranger tossed back the rest of his drink and waved over a waitress. Bruce laid a ten on the table. Nudged it toward him.

"Next one's on me."

"Thanks." As the woman approached the table, the man dug in the pocket of his jacket and pulled out a pen. "I can do better than a phone number, though." He grabbed a napkin from the dispenser on the table. "Don't remember her address, but I was there a few times. I can draw a map to her house."

Bruce grinned broadly. "That works for me."

Chapter 65

Tina grabbed her cell from beneath her pillow and answered it before its ring woke the man sleeping beside her.

"Tina?"

"Yeah." She shrugged out of Emmett's sleepy embrace and sat up in bed.

"It's Sheila."

"Says so on the screen." Dumb bitch. Sheila No-idea-of-her-last-name worked at the Food Mart with her. They exchanged hours sometimes, so the two of them were semifriendly.

"I work at Yay-hoos at night. Working right now."

"So?"

Emmett whispered something dirty in Tina's ear, and she gave him a quick kiss. The guy had stamina *and* an imagination. The combination was rare.

"I just saw Cory Bartelson draw a map to your place for some stranger who was asking around about you."

A cold blade of fear stabbed through her. "What's the guy look like?"

"Forties, maybe, reddish-brown hair with two days of scruff on his face. Mean eyes."

Her bowels went to ice. *Forrester? Fuck fuck fuck fuck!*

"Thanks. I owe you." She couldn't keep the shake from her voice. Emmett heard it, too, and went still.

"Damn straight you do. You're gonna trade hours with me three times, no excuses when I ask, got it?"

Tina hung up without responding.

"What's wrong?"

"Trouble at home. Gotta make some calls." She slipped from bed, grabbing her T-shirt from the floor and struggling into it as she walked into the next room. With fear sprinting up her spine, she swiftly made plans. First call would be to T. Get him and Dylan out of the house and somewhere safe and then contact the cops.

Because she knew exactly what Bruce Forrester wanted, aside from all of them dead. And she knew what he'd do to get it.

Chapter 66

"I had fun." Grace looked across the front seat to smile at Dylan. "I mean, the party was sort of lame."

They were parked in front of the drive at the house her mom had let him out at before. "I don't know. When that kid started dancing with the trash can your friend just puked in, that was pretty funny."

She laughed. "It was hysterical. I don't know what Tiffany was drinking tonight, but she'd obviously had plenty."

A lot of kids had had plenty. Dylan had stuck with the one beer someone had shoved in his hand when they'd walked in. Had taken a large swig and nearly gagged. How could T drink that stuff? It tasted like swamp water.

"Someone said they put Everclear in the punch. It's probably best Tiffany puked it up."

"And it was smart to get out of there before one of the neighbors called the cops."

"No kidding. I'd be grounded until the end of the year if my parents ever found out." The darkness of the car's interior cocooned them. Made it easier to pretend the rest of the world didn't exist.

"We wouldn't want that." He slid across the seat toward her. Put his arm around her shoulders. "Where would Clyde be without Bonnie?"

Was it his imagination or did she inch closer to him? Grace's voice sounded breathless when she answered, "Partners in crime both need to be free."

He lowered his face to hers. Whispered against her lips, "I like having you for a partner. For everything." Their kiss had his temperature spiking. Her mouth moved under his in a way that made him a little bit crazy. Everything he'd gone through tonight, every damn thing, was worth it just for the taste of her.

Dylan didn't know how long they made out. A lifetime that still didn't seem long enough. Finally, Grace broke away.

"I better go."

He looked at the dash clock. It was after ten. And there was no telling how long Teeter would sleep. "Yeah. Me too."

"I'll take back roads as much as I can, but I'm more likely to get caught when I'm driving alone."

"Text me as soon as you get home, okay?"

She nodded. "You too. I hope your uncle is still knocked out."

Dylan hoped so too. He snatched another kiss and then slid toward the passenger door. "You're a good driver. Just drive the way you have been all night and everything will be fine."

"You think so?" She smiled at him. Blew him a kiss. "Talk to you soon."

"Yeah." He got out of the car, shutting the door, and stood there until she pulled away. He started up the drive in case she was watching him in the rearview mirror, but there were lights on in the house ahead, so he didn't want to get too close to it. He stopped and waited about ten minutes, shivering in his hoodie. Then he took off diagonally across the lawn so he could cut through the field toward his place.

He started to jog, although he was in no particular hurry to get home. Tonight had felt so damn *normal*. Even when he'd been paranoid and half-worried he was going to get caught.

For a minute, he could feel Grace in his arms again, taste her lips against his. And Dylan knew the night had been worth the risk.

It'd been the best damn night of his life.

◆ ◆ ◆

Getting in the window proved to be a whole lot trickier than getting out of it. When he was finally inside, it occurred to him that there was no way he could pull the screen up behind him and relock it. He'd have to leave it where it was against the house. Reset it from the outside sometime T wasn't looking. Giving a mental shrug, he pulled down the window, locked it and drew the shade. Then he turned. And fell back against the window again when a long, lean shadow filled the open doorway.

"Where the fuck have you been?"

Busted. There was no reason to lie. "I went to a party."

"Party!" Teeter's voice went so high, it almost squeaked. But it wasn't funny. Nothing about getting caught by a psycho was in the least bit amusing. "What the fuck is wrong with you?" He lunged toward him, and Dylan balled his fists. He wasn't going to take the man's shit anymore. If he wanted to whale on him, Dylan was fighting back.

"You picked a great time to go AWOL, boy. The shit has hit the fan. Grab your things. We gotta get out of here for a while."

"What?" he said. T grabbed him by the arm and pulled him toward the doorway. "What are you talking about? I'm not going anywhere."

"You should have thought about that a few hours ago. Cops have been here, and what did I find when I went to get you out of bed? Damn pillows stuffed under the covers to look like a body. What do you think they're thinking now that they didn't find you or your mom at home?"

Dylan felt a twinge of fear. "Cops. SBI?"

"Sheriff. Get in your room." The man shoved him toward the doorway. "Grab some stuff. Pack a bag. We have to leave for a day or two."

"Leave? You're crazy. I need to talk to my mom." Maybe the muscle relaxants Dylan had snuck the man had finally sent him around the bend. T was making zero sense.

"Listen to me." T stood in the doorway of Dylan's bedroom. Dylan could see now that the man's things, which had been piled on top of Colton's old dresser, were in a garbage bag on his bed. "I talked to your mom. Forrester knows where you live, got that? We need to make ourselves scarce."

His knees went weak. Forrester. The monster who had haunted his nights for near as long as he could remember. The man who'd killed three people already. That they knew of. "What about Mom? We need to contact the SBI. The marshal."

"She's safe. And she's calling the cops. We need to get somewhere safe too. Now, move your ass."

This time, Dylan didn't argue. Fear was a powerful motivator.

Chapter 67

"*One* of you can talk to Mr. Loomer." The nurse's voice was firm. "Five minutes, tops. The doctor was clear on that. He should be back in his room now: 506."

Cady nodded, glancing at the clock on the wall. It was a quarter to eleven. Exhaustion was apparent on the visages of Rossi, Rebedeau, Miguel, and Ryder. She knew if she looked in the mirror, she'd see a similar mask of weariness. Cady headed toward the room, already formulating the most pressing questions for Loomer.

She nodded toward the officer stationed outside his room and went through the doorway. Loomer's bare torso was heavily bandaged, as were his hands and arms. From what the doctor had said, his legs had taken the worst of the blast. Cady stood next to the man's bed. "Eric Loomer." She waited for him to open his eyes. Turn his head toward her. "I'm Deputy US Marshal Cady Maddix."

"You. On the roof." His voice was hoarse. But the accusation in it was unmistakable.

She nodded. "Where is Bruce Forrester?"

"Fuck if I know."

A fist of frustration clenched in her belly. "If we don't find him, you take the fall for everything. The drugs. The woman."

"It was all him. He set up the drug operation. I just packaged and mailed them. I don't even know anything about the business outside of that. And I never kidnapped no one. He's the one who'd bring women home sometimes."

Women. Tension settled in her shoulders. "How many were there?"

He closed his eyes. "Half a dozen maybe. He'd go all over. Different states and towns. Mostly whores. He said they'd never be missed."

Half a dozen. The number staggered Cady. Spreading out his hunting grounds had done exactly what Forrester had hoped. Made patterns difficult to establish. And picking mostly transient victims, like Marcy Linton, had also worked to his advantage.

"The women—that was all him. I never laid a hand on them. You ask that one from the house—she'll tell you the same."

"Has he disappeared before? Does he have another place to go?"

"If he does, he's never talked about it. Mostly if he's gone all night, he's with a whore." He stopped, seemed to think for a moment. "I was a victim, too, you know. I wasn't free to come and go. I was like a prisoner."

Her mouth twisted. "All those people who ID'd you walking around freely in Boone and Blowing Rock must have missed your leash and collar."

"I was scared," he insisted. "Scared for my life."

"Uh-huh." By tomorrow, it would occur to him to call an attorney, and once he did, that story would probably become their bible. Another thought occurred then. He'd undoubtedly assisted in disposing of the bodies of the other women. And his help leading law enforcement to the dump sites would carve a significant amount of time off his eventual sentence.

The realization burned, but it wasn't her main concern at the moment. "You've worked with Forrester for a long time. Helped him with his drug operation in Hope Mills. Don't bother lying about that," she added when he opened his mouth to object. "We have eyewitnesses who put you, Forrester, Weber, and Tillis in Hanson Woods at the end of Farley Road the night of August 2, 2013. There was a woman present as well." At least, according to Tillis. She watched Loomer carefully. Saw the verification she was looking for in his expression. "Who was she?"

He shrugged, then winced at the action. "I don't know; I didn't see. Forrester had her in the tent. Talked about teaching her a lesson. I swear, I never saw her face. He marched her down there with a bag over her head and put her in a tent while we was . . ."

"Making meth."

"Then them kids came by and spooked us. Forrester chased 'em off, and when he came back, he said we had to leave."

"Why was he in such a hurry?" Cady asked.

"Maybe he figured the kids would tell their parents about seeing us and they'd call the cops. I don't know."

Or maybe, Cady thought, *he'd guessed the surviving boy would do exactly that.* But Dylan had been too traumatized to do more than hide.

Loomer was still talking. "After he came back from chasing them kids, he figured out the woman had run off while he was gone. He was super pissed at us, and things got heated. We all went our separate ways. He called me the next day and said how we needed to lie low for a while. Said he had another idea how just him and me could make some money . . ." He stopped abruptly.

Her lips curved. The man had just admitted going with Forrester freely.

As if realizing it, Loomer abruptly shifted focus. "You know, I fed those women sometimes. Gave them water. Forrester usually forgot."

"You didn't help them escape, though, did you?"

"Like I said, I was as much a captive as them. Forrester does this mind-control thing."

When forensics got done with the computer they'd seized from the house the men had rented, Cady was certain they'd discover financials that would show Loomer had been well paid for his "captivity."

Her cell vibrated, and she pulled it from her pocket. Seeing the local sheriff's office on the screen, she went to the hallway to answer it. "Maddix."

"Marshal Maddix, it's Buncombe County deputy Brent Haskell." The deputy was talking fast. "I went out to Tina Bandy's place a half an hour ago and found no one home."

Concern flickered. "Maybe they were asleep?"

"That's what I thought. I had to respond to another call, but I was going to make a return trip and see if I could rouse someone. But Bandy just called. Says she sent Dylan somewhere safe because she heard Forrester was in town asking about them."

She went still. "Was he ID'd?"

"A waitress at Yay-hoos described him well enough to convince her. Someone apparently gave him her address. I'm on my way back to the house to meet Tina there. She wants to get some things before she takes off."

"Safest place for her and the family is at your office while we check this out."

"I'll try to convince her of that. But sounds like the boy is already gone. She won't say where."

Cady swore mentally. The hardest people to protect were those who refused to follow directions. "Do what you can. If she insists on leaving, make sure you have a number and address for them. How long ago was the sighting?"

"Couple of hours, maybe."

"We'll check it out. Keep me posted."

Hanging up, she went to join the others. "Dylan's gone." Cady summarized the deputy's message for Agent Rebedeau.

"What?" The agent rose from her seat. "Where is he?"

"Tina Bandy seems to be the only one who knows, and it sounds like she's preparing to run." Cady shifted her gaze to encompass the others. "Bandy's spooked. Forrester has been sighted here in Asheville."

Urgency churned through her as they turned as one and headed for the exit. After all these years, it seemed as though the man might have finally caught up with his quarry.

Chapter 68

Dammit all to hell, the place was empty.

Bruce Forrester stormed back to the kitchen, a hot flare of temper burning through him. Maybe the idiot in the bar had sent him to the wrong house. He considered that for a minute. But there were female belongings in one of the bedrooms and two beds in the other with clothes that could belong to male teens. Which didn't help, because they were still *gone*.

He drew in a deep breath. Ordered himself to think. Maybe Bandy had just taken the kids somewhere. They could be coming back. And until they did, he could search the dump for the property stolen from him five years ago.

Just another reason they'd all die a slow, painful death.

He retraced his steps to her bedroom. Most logical place to start. He began pulling out the nightstand drawers, rifling through them. Checking the back, sides, and bottom for something taped there. After he was done, the dresser got the same treatment. Then he turned his attention to the bed. Got down on his knees to check under the mattress.

He froze when a glare of light flashed around the edges of the front window's shade. Bruce got up and crossed to it, hooking the shade with a finger to peer out. A broad smile crossed his face as he watched the car approach the house. His smile vanished in the next moment when a sheriff's SUV pulled in after the vehicle.

Fuck! He looked around quickly. His entrance into the house had been made simple enough when he'd found the screen missing from the side window in here. Just a matter of finding a rock behind the garage where he'd parked his car. He'd smashed the glass, reached inside the hole, and unlocked it. Simple.

You'd think Tina would be a bit more careful about her security.

The sound of the key in the kitchen door lock galvanized him into action. He ran silently to the window he'd accessed and raised it again. Then he climbed out of it and crouched on the outdoor sill, bracing himself with his hands on either side of the frame. The shade settled back into place.

Moments later, he heard a voice. "Thanks for the walk-through. You can wait outside. I just need to gather up a few things."

There were some words Bruce couldn't make out. Then, "I said wait outside! I gotta pack some woman products, and I don't need you watching, okay?"

He waited until he heard a car door slam. Hopefully it was the deputy. Then, carefully, he slipped back inside the room. A light was on in the second bedroom. He went to the doorway and allowed the satisfaction of the moment to wash over him before saying, "Hello, Tina."

Chapter 69

"Where are we going? A motel?" Dylan's voice was hopeful. There was no need to go far if they were just going to lie low for a little while. And Mom could meet them there.

"Think I got money for that?" Teeter answered. "Most of the cash your mom left is gone already."

Dylan watched the man carefully. He was jittery but not out of control like he'd been twice before when he'd manhandled Dylan. Maybe this was the effect of the muscle relaxants.

The pills he'd fed the man could cause him to fall asleep at the wheel, so Dylan was keeping his eyes open. Not that it was hard, with the news about Forrester finding them. Panic skittered inside his chest. *Welcome back to the real world,* he thought bitterly. But if his mom had called in the SBI, they should be on Forrester fast. The thought did little to calm him.

Dylan had tried to bring his backpack, with his laptop and SBI cell in it. Teeter had made him leave it. All he had was a toothbrush and a change of clothes. Hopefully that meant they wouldn't be gone long.

A thought struck him then, and he went still. Grace. She'd have texted if she got home safely, but he hadn't messaged back the way he said he would. And he didn't dare let T know he had a phone with him, because he had a feeling it would take very little to push the man completely over the edge.

"What about the cat?" he asked. Not that he gave a shit, but the ride was giving him plenty of time for doubts to crowd in. How did he know his mom had actually called T? What she'd really told him?

"It's got plenty of food and water for a couple of days," T answered. "It'll be fine."

"Is Mom going to meet us where we go?"

"I don't know. Probably. She'll call when she's on her way."

He didn't find the news as comforting as he should. He wished they were all together now, going to the same place. And what about Colton? Had his mom warned him too? Every one of them was in danger. And all because of Dylan.

All of a sudden, the best night of his life seemed like a distant memory.

Chapter 70

"Where's the key?"

Forrester stalked toward Tina, and it was all she could do to not piss herself. She inched backward until she was pressed against Dylan's bedroom wall. Her gun was in her purse in the kitchen. Her only chance was to race by him and into the other room. An instant later, he was in front of her, wrapping one hand around her neck. Squeezing.

"Where. Is. The. Key?"

Her fingers came up to claw at his hand. One of her knees shot upward and nearly caught him in the jewels. He let her go, and she sagged against the wall. His backhanded slap snapped her head to the side. "Try that again and you die right here. I've waited five fucking years. Where is it?"

"I don't know." Seeing his fist curl, she hurried on. "It was in a piggy bank sitting right on that dresser last time I was home. Now the bank is gone. I don't know who took it."

"Probably one of your kids. Where are they?"

In a distant part of her brain, she realized he didn't know Colton didn't live with her anymore. At least he was safe for now. "I don't know. The law was out here earlier tonight, checking on Dylan. They called me when they found him gone." She was lying for all she was worth now.

"I was looking around to see what's missing. He might have just snuck out to see friends or something."

"Does he have a phone?"

"Yeah." She was safe as long as Forrester thought she could get in touch with her son. Tina was going on instinct, just like she had been by keeping that damn key all these years. She didn't have a plan except to stay alive. She knew what this man was capable of.

She was marked for death, unless she could get that gun from the kitchen.

"Then let's go before the cop out there comes back." He grabbed her by the nape and marched her out of the bedroom, snapping off the light behind them. "Here's what we're going to do. You're going to grab some garbage bags from the kitchen. Fill them with whatever shit you can find, and then you're going out, opening the trunk and throwing them in. And then . . ." The fingers tightened on her neck painfully. "You'll back the car around the corner of the house like you need to make a three-point turn to drive out again. I'll leave through the kitchen window and get in the back. You'll be in my sight the entire time. If I shoot, I won't miss." His hand dropped from her nape, and a moment later a gun barrel pressed there. "You alert the cop out there, and you'll be dead. Understand?"

Sweat rolled down her face, and she nodded rapidly. She'd cheated death before. She could do it again. But she had to stay alive long enough to make a plan.

He shut off the kitchen light and let go of her. Her legs wobbly, she fetched the trash bags and filled them with stuff in the cupboards. When she turned around, an anguished cry nearly escaped her.

Forrester had her purse tucked under one arm.

"Let's go."

Tina's brain shut down. She moved like an automaton. She went out the kitchen door, acutely aware of the weapon trained on her. Tina threw the bags into the trunk and drove around the corner of the house.

For one crazy moment, she thought about revving the engine and running him over when he appeared. But he was already there somehow. The back car door opened and closed. "Let's go. Just remember I have a gun pointed at your spine. And the car seat ain't gonna stop a bullet."

She drove down the lane toward the deputy's vehicle, raising a shoulder to wipe her face on her jacket. Her whole body was trembling like she had palsy. She buzzed the window down when the deputy got out of his vehicle and approached her. "I already called Agent Rebedeau. She told me where to go. I'm gonna collect Dylan and wait where she said."

"I'll escort you."

She could almost hear the trigger being cocked in the back seat. "The fuck you will! The location is on a need-to-know basis, Rebedeau said. If she wants to give you that information, she'll tell you. Now back up. I don't want to be here if Forrester comes 'round."

"Wait here while I call Davis."

Her fingers clenched on the wheel as the deputy turned away.

"Move!" The voice came from the back seat.

"He's blocking the drive!" she hissed.

"Go around him, fuckhead!"

Tina cranked the steering wheel and stomped on the accelerator. The car shot forward, bumping over the grass until she'd cleared the SUV before swerving back to the lane.

"Turn left out of the drive."

She did as Forrester told her. And tried not to think that with every instruction she followed, she was one step closer to her death.

Chapter 71

The bartender at Yay-hoos identified Forrester from a picture and so did a very intoxicated Cory Bartelson. But it was the information from Sheila Vickers, the waitress, that Cady was most interested in.

"I was close enough to hear him talking about Tina Bandy, and her and me work together. So my ears perked up, y'know?"

"What did you hear?" she asked.

"That dumb-ass"—she jerked a thumb at Bartelson, who was being questioned by Miguel—"telling the guy he could draw him a map to her house. A stranger," she said with disgust. "Do you arrest people for general stupidity?"

"There aren't enough jail cells in the country."

Sheila flashed a smile at Cady's answer. "Anyway, I called Tina to let her know. Because I'd want to know if a dumb-ass gave out my personal information."

"You did the right thing. Is there anything else you noticed?"

"Damn right. When he left, I walked to the door, like I was stepping out to get some air for a minute? I saw him get into his car. A black Malibu. Recognized the make because my boyfriend has the same."

Excitement flickering, Cady thanked her and headed to where the agents waited at the entrance with Ryder. Her cell rang on the way. She took it out of her pocket. Reading it was the Buncombe County sheriff's office, she answered, "Deputy Haskell?"

"Tina Bandy just left the property like a bat out of hell. And I can't be certain Forrester wasn't in the car with her."

Her stomach nose-dived. "Tell me everything." She listened as he described the woman's suspicious behavior. How he went back through the house and found the kitchen window open. The glass smashed out of a window in Tina's bedroom. Because she heard the self-castigation in his voice, she kept her tone expressionless. "Any chance you could have missed the kitchen window when you were in there with her?"

"Not a chance. Just some frilly curtains in front of it. The bedroom . . . that one was covered with a shade, and I didn't check behind it. He could have gone back out of it and reentered when I left the house."

"But you think Forrester was in the car with Bandy when she left?" The rest of the team stilled when they heard her words.

"I think it's a possibility."

"Okay. She was driving her car?"

"Yes. A brown Toyota Corolla. Not sure of the year but an older one."

"Put a BOLO out on it. Statewide. Get the plate number from DMV."

"I'm on it."

Disconnecting, she gestured toward the door, and the team members followed her out of the bar.

"We can call the Watauga County sheriff's office." Rebedeau took off her glasses. Rubbed her eyes. "Have them put a surveillance team on the house outside Boone just in case."

If Forrester did have Tina Bandy, Cady doubted he'd head home. But they should cover all their bases. "Do that." Cady pulled out her phone again and scrolled through her emails. "No pings on any of the three numbers we have for Forrester. If he uses one of those cells to communicate with Loomer, he didn't check in with him today." Loomer's cell had been confiscated at the scene, but it would be days before the forensics analysis was done.

"Forrester may not know about the bust at their rental," Ryder said. "He'd think it was safe to take her there if so."

"If he discovers Dylan's location, he'll go after the boy," Cady said with certainty.

"Forrester isn't above torturing Bandy to get that information," Miguel put in.

And he'd enjoy it, Cady thought. He liked to watch. The terror and agony and, yes, the life ebbing from his victim. The family had escaped him for five long years. His thirst for revenge would be paramount. "I'll summon a state patrol aerial assist unit and have them look for Tina's car. They can focus on roads east of here, since we'll have a Watauga County unit on the rental near Boone."

"What do we do in the meantime?" Miguel asked. He was prowling the area in quick strides, tension apparent in every step.

"We wait."

Chapter 72

Dylan lay on the couch, kept awake by the man's snoring on the mattress across the room. *The only one in the place,* T had told him when they arrived. They'd dragged it from a bedroom to the middle of the living room. Because he didn't trust Dylan not to go out another window, he'd sniped.

Where the hell would I go? he'd wanted to ask. He'd never been to Marion before. They'd driven almost forty-five minutes to get to what he could tell—even in the dark—was a shitty house with an equally shabby attached garage that practically leaned against the home. It'd belonged to T's dad, he'd said. He'd died a few months ago.

Dylan thought that maybe this was where T had been living, but once they got inside, he realized his mistake. The place was caked with dust and cobwebs. When he'd tried to snap on a light, T said the utilities and water had been shut off. Discovering that actually made Dylan feel better. Like they wouldn't be staying long. How the hell could they, without heat or working toilets?

He didn't know how T could sleep when he hadn't heard from Dylan's mom again. He'd caught him making a call in the kitchen. One that must have gone unanswered. But when he asked, T just kept repeating that she'd get there when she got there.

Swinging his legs over the edge of the couch, he sat up. Not for the first time, a hard edge of resentment formed inside him. He didn't even know his mom's freaking cell number. He couldn't call her himself and ask her what was going on. If she was all right.

She had to be. Dylan told himself that and tried to believe it. She was the one who'd found out about Forrester being around. She'd said she was calling the SBI, so she was probably helping them find him. Maybe the agents wouldn't let her leave their custody.

But the nerves jittering in his gut made it hard to believe.

He dug in his pocket for the cell Grace had given him. Sure enough, there were half a dozen messages from her.

Hey, I'm home. How bout u?

Everything ok?

Dylan, text me!

Now I'm worried. Let me know what's going on.

Ok ur probly asleep. But I'm sorta freaking here.

And then a voice mail, saying pretty much the same thing.
Sorry, he texted back. Fell asleep. All ok.

But it wasn't okay. The paranoia he'd lived with for years was back, stronger than ever. Forrester had found them again. And there was no way Dylan could sleep while wondering who'd be the next to die.

Chapter 73

Unconsciousness approached and receded like a ragged wave. Tina tried to rise and rapped her head on something above her. Groaning, she fell back. She was rocking side to side, jolting over bumps. She was in a car.

The trunk. Memory glimmered. Forrester in her house. In her car. She bit back a cry when she recalled the way he'd made her pull over on that gravel road. Emptied the trunk and forced her to her knees with the barrel of his gun against her temple.

Where's the kid? Dammit, bitch, where is your kid?

When she hadn't told him, he'd pistol-whipped her. Beaten her within an inch of her life. Even if she could get free, Tina didn't think she'd get more than a few feet before keeling over.

Her head was foggy. She couldn't think clearly. But she'd gotten Dylan to safety. She hadn't told Forrester where he was, even with the beating.

They hit a rut that had her body bouncing. Tina didn't know where he was taking her. But she knew what awaited her when the car stopped. She could almost feel the rope cutting into her neck.

She just hoped she died before giving up her son's whereabouts.

Chapter 74

Although Cady had suggested the others go home while they awaited word on Forrester's whereabouts, they'd all accompanied her back to the hospital to linger in a shadowy waiting room. Her cell sounded, and seeing the Buncombe County sheriff's office on the screen, she answered quickly. "Maddix."

"It's Haskell. I checked the DMV for Bandy's plate number like you said. That Corolla she was driving tonight isn't registered to her. Only car in her name is a blue 2006 Impala."

She frowned, shooting a look across the waiting room at Agent Rebedeau. She had her head tipped back against the wall, her mouth slightly open as she slept. "And it wasn't Forrester's vehicle, because you followed her driving it to her house." *What the hell?* Her mind raced. Maybe the Corolla belonged to a friend.

"That's not all." A note of excitement entered the deputy's voice. "I checked Bandy's garage to see if the Impala was in there. It wasn't. But I found a vehicle parked behind it. A black Malibu."

"Forrester's car." The waitress at Yay-hoos had ID'd it.

"It's registered to a Ted Akins of Wilmington. Address is bogus."

Of course it is, she thought grimly and scrubbed a hand over her face. "We found a couple of fake IDs in Forrester's things. That's probably another one." It would explain why they'd had no luck running the names on the IDs they'd found. He hadn't been using them. "Okay. Get me a list of the owners in the state of older-model brown Toyota Corollas."

"Way ahead of you. I'm sending the list to your email."

Everyone was awake now, eyeing her impatiently. "Thanks, Brett." She disconnected the call and updated the others as she opened the email the deputy had sent. Scanned the names on it. There were fewer than a dozen, unsurprising given the age of the car. None was in Asheville or the surrounding area.

Cady took another look at the list the deputy had sent. There was something niggling at the back of her mind. Something familiar, but she couldn't quite lay her finger on it. Lack of sleep was making her brain fuzzy. She stood. She'd go out to the car and get her computer. Look through the additions to the digital file.

Silently, Ryder fell into step beside her as she left the room. As they headed to the elevator, Cady wondered where Dylan was hiding. How far away Forrester had gotten.

Picturing grains of sand sifting through an hourglass, she had the sensation of time running out.

Chapter 75

Apparently, only one of them was going to sleep tonight. Dylan couldn't turn his mind off. The longer the hours stretched, the more worried he got for his mom. She wasn't great at communication. He kept reminding himself of that. She might've thought, since Dylan and T were safe, she could focus on . . . what? There, he always drew a blank. She should be with SBI by now. And it'd be safe to call T.

If she was able to.

Driven to move, he rose and walked quietly through the house. There wasn't much to it. It was even smaller than the one he lived in. Dylan went to the kitchen and looked around for a basement door and didn't find one. Again, just like their rental.

Moving to the front door, he looked out the window. Moonlight slanted through the scraggly yard showing patchy weeds at least a foot high. They'd parked in the graveled drive, which was weird because there was a crappy garage attached to the house. Why hadn't they parked inside it? He retraced his steps to the kitchen and found a door. He tried to peer out the grimy window but could see nothing in the shadows. He unlocked it and quietly inched his way down the two steps to the cracked concrete floor. It was dark as pitch in here. Dylan pulled out Grace's cell and pressed "On" so he could see with the lit screen.

There was a hulking shape in the center of the building. Something covered with a patchy tan tarp. He went toward it, tapping the phone again when the screen dimmed. Hooking one edge of the tarp in his fingers, he pulled it up and back. Uncovered a wheel.

He sent a cautious gaze over his shoulder. If T woke up and discovered him gone, he'd freak, and it was in Dylan's best interests to keep the man calm.

But he still had the muscle relaxants in his system. They couldn't be all the way worn off. Dylan pulled harder on the tarp, removing it so he could see what was beneath. It was a vehicle of some sort. Probably in as bad a shape as the rest of the property. He held up the lit screen to get a closer look. Then stumbled back in shock, a wall of panic flooding through him.

An old green pickup with a rusted-out wheel well. One he'd seen before. At least twice.

Holy shit. With shaking hands, he held up the cell and stared in horror at the truck. The same pickup he'd seen in town before Ethan was murdered. The same one Dylan had reported sighting before Bahlman was killed. Forrester had been at the wheel both times. He'd *seen* him. Had T brought him here to deliver him to the man? Were they working together?

"I'm really sorry you had to see that, boy."

Dylan jumped and spun around at T's voice. Could barely make out his shadow in the doorway.

"You'da been a whole lot better off if you hadn't gone snooping around."

Chapter 76

Sometimes his temper got the better of him. Bruce Forrester squatted next to the Corolla's open trunk and slapped Tina Bandy's cheek un-gently. She'd been out for a long time, and he didn't think she was faking it. He picked up her limp arm and twisted it hard. She groaned, but her eyes never opened.

Well, shit. He saw headlights a moment before a vehicle flew by on the gravel, leaving a plume of dust in its wake. But he'd parked on a secluded farm drive out of sight of the road and the darkened house beyond them. He wasn't concerned about being seen. He was worried about the woman waking up.

He'd dumped Bandy's purse, and her gun was in his pocket. She'd had a small bottle of water in the bag and a little makeup case. Bruce had both with him now. He unscrewed the cap and dumped the water in her face, grabbing her chin when she would have moved away from the stream. "Wake the hell up. I ain't got all night."

Her eyelids fluttered. She was coming around. He dumped some more water in her face and reached for the makeup case. Took out the nail clippers and thumbed the nail file to point forward. A person could inflict a lot of pain with a metal file, regardless of its size.

Tina Bandy was about to find that out.

Chapter 77

"You don't have to keep me tied up." Dylan's voice was almost steady. "I don't know where you think I'm going to go."

"You fucking sneak away every chance you get." T stopped his pacing to come over to the couch where Dylan sat and gave it a vicious kick. Then another. "You're a huge pain in the ass, you know that?"

And what are you? The words almost burst from Dylan. But he wasn't sure he could handle the answer. Imagining it was bad enough. The SBI had said that his description of the pickup he'd seen prior to the shootings matched one Forrester used to have. The one sitting outside in the garage. So how else had T ended up with the truck if he wasn't working with Forrester?

The thoughts spun around and around in his head like a whirlpool. T stormed off into another room, but Dylan saw the glow of his cell. He was making another call. And maybe it wasn't to Tina, like he kept saying. Maybe he'd been calling Forrester all those times since they got here. The man might already be on his way over.

Despite the chill in the house, his skin went clammy. His heart began to gallop. Dylan fought against the bonds on his wrists and ankles, but the twine held strong. He forced himself to think. He had only T's word that Mom had told him to get him out of town. What if he'd been colluding with Forrester the whole time? Keeping tabs on where their family went, then letting the other man know? It made an awful sort of sense.

T came back into the room. And Dylan could tell just from his stride that he was still hyped up. "I know things look bad, but it's gonna be okay. You just need to keep calm."

Straining against the bonds on his wrists, Dylan said, "Maybe you should tell me what's going on."

"You're a kid," the other man snapped. "That's the problem. Kids don't see things adults do. You can't understand. Like that night in Hope Mills. You. Don't. Get. It."

"What?" But the man was already turning away. "What don't I get?"

"I need to buy some beer." And T was gone, leaving Dylan alone in the darkened home.

Alcohol probably wasn't going to make the man less volatile, but that was the least of Dylan's worries at the moment. What had T been talking about? He hadn't been in the woods that night. What did he know?

What might Forrester have told him?

He went still, for once trying to summon the scene from that night instead of dodging it. Him and Trev sneaking up to peer into the clearing. The excitement in his friend's voice when he spied that rope swing. The men looking up and over to their hiding place. Getting chased. The old panic crept into his chest, sending his pulse into overdrive. Images, like movie clips flashing across his mind. Trev and him in that hollowed-out log, hiding. It was their go-to spot. They rarely went to the creek without first crawling into it. He could see Trev there with him, plain as day, both of them scared and shaking. But they hadn't gone to the creek that night. Had they?

His temples started to throb. Soon the fog would crowd into his mind, making it hard to think. Hard to remember. But he needed to. What didn't he have right about that night?

Trev running beside him. A backpack swinging from his hand. Trev pressing something into Dylan's palm. Something small with sharp edges. A key?

But even as he reached for them, the memories receded, like a tide rolling out. Instead he saw the pictures his imagination had supplied. Of Ethan and Bahlman bloody and motionless. Of Trev, eyes wide and staring in the creek bed. And the light of the remote-controlled boat flitting back and forth like a firefly as the boat bounced off rocks in the water.

Nausea surged as the pounding in his head intensified. Dylan squeezed his eyes shut. Scrabbled for that positive association the doctor had talked about. The vision he'd manufactured of him and Trev, swinging out over the creek, both of them at once this time clinging to the rope swing.

But the picture refused to form. He just kept seeing that boat, hidden in the darkness save for the light. Bumping and careening down the creek until it was lost from sight.

Chapter 78

"You're quiet." Ryder bumped Cady's shoulder companionably as they walked out of the hospital cafeteria. "You need to eat something, even if the fare in the vending machines leaves a lot to be desired." He'd redirected her there after she'd retrieved her laptop from the Jeep. He'd bought enough sandwiches and chips to feed a small village, stuffing them into bags he snagged from behind the cafeteria's counter by the cash register.

The thought of food made Cady's stomach churn. "My mom called several hours ago. With everything going on, I let it go to voice mail." She could feel his eyes on her, but she didn't look at him. Couldn't.

"Did you listen to it?"

Cady shook her head. "Later." Later, when her mind stopped avoiding the details Hannah had revealed yesterday morning. The wounds were too fresh, too raw, to examine right now. The thoughts and emotions clawing for release wouldn't be put off indefinitely. She knew from experience that they'd wait till she slept to spill across her consciousness, forming a nightmarish new montage to torment her.

She wasn't a coward. Cady realized she had to confront her truth or risk being devoured by it. That, too, she'd learned from experience.

"Do you want to discuss it?"

She didn't even pretend not to know what Ryder was alluding to. "It's been a lot to process. I need to sort it out on my own."

He set the bags on the floor in the empty hallway, and then his arms encircled her, his chin coming to rest lightly upon her hair. "Okay. I'll be here when you do."

She steadied her chin before it could tremble. Even a week ago, she would have maintained that sympathy made a person weak. Pity made them pathetic.

Cady let herself lean a bit against his chest. Waited for an inner alarm that didn't sound. Because she knew he *would* be there, with an understanding no one else could share. She'd never let anyone close enough to do so. It was a measure of her state of mind that the admission didn't scare the hell out of her.

Cady brought up the digital file and scrolled through the most recent updates while the others devoured the food Ryder had laid out. When she got to ATF Gabe Pearson's information, she slowed. Read more closely. "John Teeter."

Miguel looked up. "Who's that?"

She picked up her phone and double-checked the email Haskell had sent listing owners of older brown Corollas in the state. There. Cady stared at the name, then lifted her gaze. "Gabe has been talking to all the former employees of the gun range where the weapon was stolen from. The rifle used to shoot at me. He's tried to contact Teeter but can't find him at home in Fayetteville."

"And?" Miguel asked around a mouthful of sandwich.

"And John Teeter also has a 2008 brown Toyota Corolla registered in his name." She had everyone's attention now. "The same make and model Tina Bandy was driving when she left her home and the deputy behind."

Chapter 79

When T returned with the beer, Dylan pretended he had to take a leak so the man would have to untie his ankles and retie his hands in front of him. After the quick trip outside, though, T had bound his feet again and pushed him down on the couch. But at least now he could reach the pocket of his hoodie. Could use the phone, maybe. *And dial who?* an inner voice jeered. He still didn't know what part of T's account was truth and how much was lies. If Tina had really asked him to get Dylan away, he didn't want to screw something up for her.

But if T was working with Forrester, the faster Dylan could get cops here, the better.

His temples still throbbed, and for the first time, he was glad there was no electricity in the place. He knew from experience that lights would make his head explode.

"I grew up in this place, believe that? My dad and whoever he was living with at the time had the bedroom. Kids slept out here. On the furniture or floor, whatever there was. You think you have it so fucking tough now. You don't got a clue what tough is."

Dylan could barely make out the man's shape in the recliner across the room. Which meant that T couldn't see Dylan well, either. His hands crept toward his pocket. Toward the cell. "That must have been crazy, all those people in this house."

"Damn straight. And no one gave a shit about us, either. Long as we stayed out of their way, we could have danced naked down the street, and they wouldn't have batted an eye. You got lucky with your mom. She took care of you boys. Far better than what she got from her ma or me from my dad."

"I know." He had Grace's cell in one hand but now what? Call 911? It wasn't like he could talk. His heart was a wild thing in his chest. His palms so wet, the cell was slippery in his hand. "She's a hard worker too."

"Always has been."

Dylan searched his memory but couldn't recall the number for SBI. He'd seen the marshal's far more recently. She'd left him that message. He'd noted it again then. Fighting back the cold spike of fear that threatened to drive through him, he tried to visualize the number.

"I've been thinkin'. You're still a kid, but you've had to grow up fast. Maybe you're old enough to understand some complicated stuff."

He nearly laughed at that. The man wanted to talk complicated? Dylan had lived with complications ever since he'd made that ill-fated decision to talk Trevor into going to the creek that night. He'd touched off a domino effect of human tragedy, an explosive chain reaction he'd been helpless to stop. Dylan searched for the keys on the phone. He thought he recalled the numbers, but keying them in correctly when he wasn't looking at the cell was tricky. "I'm going to be sixteen," he said. He got the sequence pressed in. But he had no idea if it was the correct one. And he couldn't check to be sure. At least the sound was off. He always kept it that way so no one would hear Grace texting or calling.

"That's right. Nowhere near an adult, but sometimes you have to handle adult shit anyway."

There was a glow coming from his pocket. Dylan shoved the cell farther inside it so T wouldn't notice.

"I get that." Keep the man talking and hope like hell he had dialed correctly. And that the marshal would pick up. His stomach sank. No one answered calls from unfamiliar numbers. Especially not cops. Defeat swept through him. Maybe the cell wasn't going to do him any good after all. But he had to give it a shot. T went silent, and Dylan searched for a way to keep him talking. "Were you named after your dad? Was he John Teeter too?"

"Yep, I'm a Junior, so they just called me T."

"How old were you when you got out of here? When you left Marion?"

"Couldn't leave fast enough," the man said. "Joined the army on my eighteenth birthday. That's when I learned however bad a place is, there's always someplace worse, you know what I mean?"

Dylan looked at his pocket. He couldn't see the glow from the cell. Had no idea if he'd even made a connection. His mind kept returning to the green pickup in the garage. There was no good explanation for it being in T's possession. Sweat slicked down his spine, considering it. The not knowing was a special kind of hell.

"You remember that book I found in your room? The *Mockingbird* one?"

"Yeah."

"Well, I'm your Boo Radley, son. I've been protecting you right along. You just didn't know it."

Protecting him by helping Forrester find him? A flare of fury fired through Dylan. "I don't know what that's supposed to mean."

"It means you guys was in deep shit when you left Hope Mills. Your mom shoulda come away with me then, but instead she went to Tami." He gave a disgusted laugh. "What's that bitch gonna do, pray the trouble away? But moving didn't help nothing. And one thing we both knew, things wasn't gonna get better until that bastard was caught. I had to think of something. Some way to keep your family safe. That's why I gave your mom an extra phone. So her and me could talk without SBI finding out if they got nosy."

"I saw Forrester driving that pickup out there, Teeter." The words burst out of him. "I *saw* him. Someone had to tell him where we were." And he was pretty damn sure that someone was sitting in the chair across from him.

"You thought you seen him. Because I made myself look as much like him as I could."

Everything inside Dylan froze. Organs. Blood. Brain. *No.* He recoiled from the man's words. There was no way it could be . . .

"You guys wasn't gonna be safe while Forrester was on the loose. Them cops weren't doing a thing to catch him. What they needed was for someone to light a fire under 'em. Get them sparked up enough for a real manhunt. I took his truck. I stole a gun he'd used at the range. And I came up with a plan to save you all."

Chapter 80

"Gabe." Cady took a quick guilty look at the clock on the wall. "It's Cady. Sorry about the hour."

"What time is it?" the man asked sleepily.

"John Teeter." She spoke quickly. "He worked at the gun range where the weapon went missing. You checked his house in Fayetteville."

"Yeah." The agent sounded more alert now. "I've also had deputies going by daily to see if he's around. So far nothing."

"Any other properties in his name?"

"No." Her heart plummeted as their possible lead shattered. It rebounded when the man went on. "His dad had a place, though. He died last summer. I had the local PD check his home. It was deserted."

"Where was it located?"

"Uh . . . let me get up and check my notes."

Her phone buzzed with an incoming call. She didn't recognize the number so was prepared to ignore it. Until she recalled that Suzanne Fielding had given Forrester Cady's number. It was a long shot but . . . She answered the call but didn't speak. There was a murmur of voices, but she couldn't make out the words. Cady nearly hung up until she could make out a voice she recognized.

"I saw Forrester driving that pickup out there, Teeter. I *saw* him. Someone had to tell him where we were."

Her blood iced. Cady switched the call to speakerphone. "Dylan?" she said, feeling Ryder's surprised gaze. But a moment later, she fell silent again. The conversation taking place on the other end didn't include her.

At Ryder's murmured, "Dylan Castle?" Miguel and Rebedeau went still.

"You thought you seen him. Because I made myself look as much like him as I could."

Two realizations occurred simultaneously. Dylan had dialed her on purpose. And given what Teeter had admitted, the boy could be in immediate danger.

Gabe was ringing back in. She switched over to answer the call. "Where is John Teeter's father's property?" she asked urgently.

"Just outside the Marion city limits. Why?"

She switched back to Dylan's call in time to hear him say, "You killed those kids just to get the cops' attention?"

Rebedeau surged to her feet, color riding high in her cheeks, both her fists curled. Cady seconded the reaction. Everything inside her was fixated on the answer.

"See, that's where it's hard for you to understand, being a teenager and all. But it was the only way, Dylan. I was protecting you. You and your family."

"Fuck that fucker," Ryder muttered savagely.

"They're in Marion," Cady said, hurrying to the hospital exit. The team followed closely behind her. The call was still open, but the phone had gone silent for the moment. As they ran down the quiet hallway, she couldn't shake the thought that a man who'd just confessed to two murders might figure he couldn't afford to allow the boy to live to tell anyone.

Chapter 81

Cady had Ryder drive her Jeep with dash strobes flashing, with Miguel in the back and the other team members on their tail. But the call from Dylan went dead before they'd been on the road five minutes. Worry for the boy uppermost in her mind, she contacted the McDowell County sheriff's office via the VIPER law enforcement channel on the radio and asked for a deputy to surveil the Teeter house. She'd no more disconnected than the pilot updated her over the radio that he was stopping to refuel.

The miles whipped by, shadows racing outside her window. Soft snores were coming from the back seat. Miguel had fallen asleep minutes after they'd pulled out of the hospital parking lot. He had a unique knack for catnaps that she sometimes envied. But sleep was the furthest thing from her mind right now. Her brain was a racetrack, with thoughts whizzing around it.

Dylan. Teeter. Forrester. Tina Bandy.

The scene with her mom Saturday.

She had managed to shunt her mom's revelation aside as she dealt with the developments in the case. It was front and center in her mind now, however. Demanding answers. Eliciting more questions.

At four years old, she'd been coached in how to fire a weapon. The certainty throbbed in her brain. She knew her mother well enough to realize she could never have shot her husband. Lonny Maddix had had a hold on her. Still did, in a way. Butch Talbot would have recognized that. And—with her mother's tacit approval—had constructed a fail-safe. If Hannah couldn't defend them from Lonny, with the right instruction, maybe Cady could.

The thought was traumatic. But far better than believing that using Cady had been calculated. Self-defense could be a messy claim without witnesses. But no one would blame a child. That was a tragic accident.

Squeeze the trigger nice and slow. Only point it at bad guys. You don't like bad guys, do you, Cady?

Bad guys who hurt her mom. Made her cry, made her bleed. The callous manipulation of a child still cut deep. She knew it always would.

Cady wondered at the mind's power of self-preservation that had shielded her all these years. Draped her earliest memories from all but the most cryptic snippets that had slithered out around the edges. Until her mom's outburst had shredded that shroud and provided context for those random scraps. And her life would never be quite the same.

"McDowell County deputy Lance Walls here, Marshal." The voice came from the radio. Cady picked up the transmitter. "I'm in front of the old Teeter place in Marion right now. Place is dark. But there is a car in the drive. Looks like a light-colored Impala from here. You want me to go up to the door?"

"Wait for us. We're only fifteen minutes out. Make sure your car remains out of sight from anyone inside looking out."

"You planning an entry?"

"That's SBI's call at the moment." Her warrants were limited to Loomer and Forrester. Disconnecting, she radioed Rebedeau and relayed the information.

"I've got a judge on standby," the agent said. "We'll finish the paperwork and send it in. Should have a warrant by the time we get there."

"We good to go?" Ryder asked when she hung up. Cady was aware of Miguel leaning forward to catch her response.

"Sounds like it." She just hoped that the house stayed dark and quiet until they got there. Her hope was dashed ten minutes later when the deputy outside the Teeter home radioed back. "We've got movement."

Cady and Ryder exchanged a glance. "Are they leaving?"

"No. Another car just pulled into the drive. No headlights. Can't be certain of make and model except it's a dark-colored compact sedan."

Ice bumped in Cady's veins. That description would fit a brown Toyota Corolla.

Chapter 82

The man could sleep through a zombie attack.

Dylan listened to Teeter snore. He didn't know if it was the beer, lack of sleep, or muscle relaxants still in the man's system. There was no way he could follow suit, so he focused on loosening the bonds the man had tied around his wrists and ankles. If he could get free, he'd get the hell out of here. He'd be safer with the cops than with this batshit-crazy loon. That's what he should have done before, but then he'd seen that truck and . . . His mind blanked on the thought. He couldn't think about what the man had revealed. Not if he wanted to escape.

He'd disconnected the call he'd made to the marshal. There was no way to tell if he'd even dialed the right number. Dylan couldn't depend on the law to save him. The cavalry probably wasn't coming. He was going to have to escape on his own. Get away from the killer sleeping like a baby across the room from him.

He worked his wrists repeatedly, flexing and relaxing them over and over. One piece of twine had snapped, but he still hadn't been able to free himself from the other bonds. *Tying people up must be the one thing Teeter is actually good at,* Dylan thought bitterly. But he could finally feel the twine on his wrists slackening. He redoubled his efforts. A moment later, he loosened it enough to work one wrist out.

Shit. He rubbed at it with his other hand. Dylan could feel the indentation where the damn rope had been. Quickly, he went to work getting the twine off his other wrist and turning his attention to the bonds at his ankles. It wasn't easy in the dark, but his fingers finally found the knot the man had made and started untying it.

After several minutes, he stopped, his eyes on the darkened windows. There were curtains there, but slivers of light shone around the edges. Shadows flashed by those slivers, back and forth. The familiar itch started at the back of his neck, but Dylan squelched the paranoia that wanted to rear. He didn't have time to be scared. He needed to get the hell away.

Finally, he got the bonds unwrapped from his ankles, keeping his gaze on T the entire time. The keys to the car would be in the man's jeans pocket. No way to get to them without waking him up.

No way to get at the gun that was probably still lying on his lap.

Dylan stood silently and crept toward the kitchen door. This time he'd focus on finding the exit in the garage. And then getting through it. He eased the door open and tiptoed onto the top step. Searched for the next one with his foot before descending. He stumbled a little when he reached the floor. There wasn't even a splinter of light inside the structure. He reached into his pocket. He used the lit cell phone screen as he picked his way to the front. His heart plummeted. The only exit was the garage's wooden double doors. A long two-by-four needed to be removed before he could open them.

But first he paused next to the hulk of the pickup. Maybe T had left the keys in it. He'd never driven before, but unless it was a stick, he could handle it. He'd find help a lot faster driving than he could on foot. He opened the driver's door and leaned in, checking the ignition for the keys. When he didn't find them, he searched under the seat. Closing the door, he rounded the truck bed and went to the other side to check the glove box. Nothing.

Dylan stifled a surge of disappointment and went to the old garage doors. The bar lifted out of the metal holder easily enough, but it was long and unwieldy. It took a few minutes to extract it and set it aside in one corner. Then he pressed a palm against the seam in the center. The doors creaked open a foot. He heard a slight sound and threw a panicked look over his shoulder. Had T wakened and come after him? But in the next moment, the noise was repeated, and Dylan realized it was coming from the driveway. He peered out but could see nothing in the darkness. Long moments stretched as he waited, scarcely daring to breathe. When he heard nothing else, he turned sidewise to sidle through the opening in the doors. Before he was halfway through, he saw a shape in the drive. A car? In the next instant, a shadow loomed over him. Close. Threatening. He was crowded back through the opening, and something slammed against his temple. He fell to the dirt floor, his head spinning.

"Been a long time, kid." Rough hands yanked him by the sweatshirt to pull him to his feet. "We've got a lot to talk about."

Chapter 83

Cady and the team donned tactical gear as McDowell County deputy Lance Walls updated the group. "I saw a figure, a man I think, get out of the car and head toward the house. He went through the garage."

"How long ago?" she asked.

"A few minutes before you arrived."

"You only saw one person? Not two?" At the deputy's affirmation, she took a moment to wonder about Tina Bandy. She must have given up Dylan's location. If Forrester had no other use for her, she may already be dead.

"She could still be in the car," Ryder said beside her as he fastened his vest and put his coat back on.

"We'll bring a crowbar." If the woman wasn't inside the vehicle, they'd try the trunk. Miguel rejoined the group, holding up something in his hand. The Range-R device. Cady nodded to him, and he jogged away from the staging area toward the house. To the others, Cady said, "Miguel will determine the number of people inside and their location.

We'll fire flashbangs into the home, followed by an entry team." She looked at Walls. "No sound of gunfire?"

"No."

Given how dangerous Forrester was with his bare hands, Cady thought grimly, the answer did nothing to relieve her tension.

Chapter 84

Dylan was shoved back inside the house and across the room. From there, the man pushed him to the floor. Not just any man, he thought dimly, trying to still the spinning in his head. Forrester. It might be dark, but he'd recognize the voice anywhere. A paralyzing terror gripped him.

"The fuck . . ." Teeter roused and grabbed at the weapon in his lap.

Forrester jammed the barrel of his weapon against Dylan's temple. "I've got a gun at the boy's head. Raise that weapon and I blow it off."

T stilled. "You okay, Dylan?"

But Dylan was unable to answer. His worst nightmare had sprung to life. The specter that had haunted him for years. And he didn't see any escape.

"You've got three seconds."

There was a moment's pause before something clattered to the floor. Forrester took two quick steps and scooped up the gun. "Now, on your knees. Hands behind your head." When the man obeyed, Forrester struck him across the face with the weapon. "Let's see who we have here. Because from the sound of your voice, you aren't the old-maid aunt Tina said she left her kid with."

The man's words pierced Dylan's horror. His mom said that? That meant—*oh, Jesus, no.* Forrester had his mom. A vise in his chest squeezed his heart so tightly, Dylan could barely breathe. Was his mom still alive? Or had Forrester killed her after she told him where they were?

A small light shone as Forrester held up his phone. "The fuck— Teeter? What the hell are you doing here? Let me guess." Dylan shuddered when the man's voice went menacing. "That looks like my truck in the garage, isn't it?" He pulled his leg back and kicked the man viciously. Once. Twice. Again. "Thieving bastard."

"You went off and left it." Teeter curled up in a ball to protect himself, his voice little more than a whimper. "It wasn't doing no good to no one just sitting there."

"Like that's an excuse." The man stilled. "Bet you're the one who killed them kids that got blamed on me too. Son of a bitch." He raised his foot again, but this time Teeter grabbed it.

Dylan acted on instinct then, rising to his knees and throwing his body against Forrester, driving him off-balance. He landed with a crash, and both Dylan and Teeter dove toward the man's weapon. Then stilled an instant later when Forrester broke free of them and aimed the gun at Teeter.

"I'd have killed you anyway, but this . . . this will be a pleasure." The sound of the shot was deafening in the small home. Forrester pulled Dylan off the floor and pushed him toward the man. "Get his keys. Hurry."

Dylan's fingers fumbled as he obeyed. "T," he whispered as he drew the key ring from his pocket. The wet gurgles coming from the man nearly made him weep. Had Forrester killed him? "Hang on, you hear?"

Forrester grabbed his hood and yanked him to his feet, snatching the keys out of his hands. "Pick up that twine on the floor." The light on his phone lit up the pieces Dylan had discarded. "Bring it with you."

He gathered it up, then was grabbed again and hauled toward the door. "Now that I have my truck back, we'll drive that. Just have to back up and grab my cargo out of the car's trunk." The ugly laugh he gave sent fear streaking down Dylan's back. They went to the garage, and Forrester opened the door to the truck. "Climb in and over. Pull anything and I'll put a bullet in your spine."

Dylan scrambled into the truck, terror making it impossible to think. Forrester followed him in and started the vehicle. Put it into reverse. He was going to nudge the doors the rest of the way open with the vehicle, Dylan realized. He grabbed his seat belt to fasten it.

But before the pickup had moved more than a few inches, one of the garage doors opened wider. Dylan's heart leaped. A black-clad person sidled inside. Was it the marshal? His fingers were already scrabbling to release the seat belt. This might be his one chance to get away. If he could open the passenger door and roll out . . .

But Forrester had seen the figure too. He ducked, rolled down the window, and stuck his gun through it. The stranger dove out the door. Forrester fired, the sound of the shot echoing and reechoing in the small building. Dylan froze, straining to see the stranger in the darkness.

"Fuck, fuck, fuck!" The man beside him cursed. Shifted gears.

Through the rearview mirror, Dylan could see more people running toward the garage. It was the cops. It had to be. A desperate spear of hope had him reaching for the handle to his door just as Forrester stomped on the accelerator. The truck lurched forward, bursting through the back of the run-down garage and jolting over the yard beyond. When they came to a road, Forrester yanked the wheel, and they sailed over the curb onto the blacktop.

Dylan gave one last look in the window behind him, hope dying a quick and brutal death. He'd barely had a chance to register that a rescue had been in progress before they were speeding away from it.

Away from any possibility of getting out of this alive.

Chapter 85

"Medics are on the scene," Deputy Walls reported via the radio. "We found a woman in the trunk, unconscious and badly beaten. The man inside the home is alive but has already lost a lot of blood. They're both being taken to the hospital in Morganton."

Cady lowered the radio transmitter long enough to throw another concerned glance toward Miguel in the darkened back seat. Ryder was burning up the blacktop, strobe flashing, with the rest of the task force following closely. She'd given the aerial assist pilot their location, and the chopper was on its way. "I still think you should have waited for the medics."

"I'm fine." Miguel's terse answer had her facing forward again. Cady knew from experience what the other man was going through. The bullet had gone through the garage door before it'd hit him, and the vest had provided protection. But even so, the impact was significant. He had no broken ribs, but at the very least, he was going to have a helluva bruise.

Guilt niggled. She was the one who'd sent him through the garage to see if the entrance to the house was open. If it were, the flashbang would have been fired through it rather than through the front window, where it could have hit any of the people inside.

Because the emotion was useless, she pushed it aside. He wouldn't thank her for it. And they all knew what the job entailed.

"For an old truck, it can really move." Ryder's gaze was trained on the vehicle's rear lights that winked in the distance.

"Forrester's a mechanic. He probably worked on it. I'm not familiar with this area. Where do you think he's headed?"

"We're on 80 now, which will turn into the Blue Ridge Parkway if he doesn't turn off."

"That runs clear up to Mount Mitchell State Park." Miguel was heard from the back seat.

Cady reached for the radio again to alert the Yancey County sheriff's office. She couldn't predict Forrester's actions. But she was guessing he was hoping to lose them in the heavily wooded area of Mount Mitchell State Park. It was time to summon the rest of the task force.

Adrenaline rapped hard in her chest. It'd do no good to wonder what was going on between Forrester and Dylan right now. As long as the truck was moving, the boy was probably safe.

It was when it stopped that they needed to worry.

Chapter 86

Dylan ducked, but Forrester's backhanded fist grazed his jaw. Rattled his teeth.

"I'm gonna ask once more before I start shooting pieces off you. Where's the fucking key? The one you took out of the backpack when you little fuckers grabbed it in the woods that night. Your mom didn't have it. Said it used to be in a bank in your bedroom. But the bank's gone."

Dylan wiggled his jaw, his thoughts racing like frantic little ants as an image flashed across his mind. Trev handing him something in the log. He hadn't been sure if it was a memory or his imagination. But there had been a key in the bank. He would have sworn he'd never seen it before the cat broke the bank into pieces.

The man's fist raised again, and Dylan hugged the door. "It's in a plastic bag. In my closet." He flinched when the man swore violently.

"You're going to pay for every minute you kept me from my money."

Dylan risked a glance outside. The scenery was still speeding by. The road had gotten twisty, and they were moving much too fast. He'd thought more than once about opening the door and leaping out. Figured he'd kill himself at this speed. Could that be worse than what Forrester had planned for him? He wasn't sure.

His mind went to his mom. To Uncle T. Dylan had had it all wrong. T was a killer. He still couldn't wrap his head around it. But the man hadn't been working for Forrester. And right now T might be lying dead in that house. "Where's my mom?" he asked. His voice was shakier than he would have liked. "You better not have hurt her."

"With any luck, she'll die from the beatdown I gave her. I'm just sad that I didn't get to see it."

The breath strangled in Dylan's lungs. She couldn't be dead. Couldn't. After all this time of avoiding Forrester, living on the run, only to have the man do his worst anyway? A dark cloud threatened to form in his mind, blocking rational thought as emotion took over. He punched through it. The only way to discover if Tina was alive was to survive this thing.

He risked a glance over his shoulder. There were headlights in the distance that seemed to keep pace with them. They'd dip away behind hills or around curves but always returned. Maybe it was the cops. The thought didn't summon as much anticipation as it should have.

He was hoping with everything he had that Forrester hadn't killed his mom.

Chapter 87

He couldn't shake the fucking headlights on his tail. Bruce looked in the rearview mirror again. Just when he thought he'd lost the cops, a car would come over the rise of a hill behind him. Its speed told him exactly who was back there.

He pounded the steering wheel with a fist, his mind racing as rapidly as the truck's engine. Getting back to Asheville and grabbing the key was his priority. With it, he could finally access the hundred grand he'd stashed away in a lockbox in a Charlotte bank. He didn't dare go back to his storage shed. Or call Loomer. He'd get the cash, go to Atlanta, and take the first flight out of the country.

Were those headlights behind him getting closer? Bruce pressed harder on the accelerator. Having a hostage suddenly seemed more of a liability than a solution out of this mess. He slanted a glance at the kid. Caught him staring at him. He dropped his eyes pretty damn fast, though. He'd already learned exactly what Bruce was capable of.

He could get rid of the boy now, leave his body in the snow on the side of the road, but he might be lying to him about the location of the key. His family was made up of born liars. Better to keep him until he had the key in hand.

He saw the signs for Mount Mitchell State Park flashing by him. It was like he'd driven here on instinct. They'd camped in the park several times when he was a kid, when his dad had kicked the drugs for a time. Bruce had loved the shadows of the forest. He'd known the trails well. Better, maybe, than anyone in the cars chasing him.

Bruce slowed enough to watch for one of the motorcycle roads that wound in and out of the woods. There. He waited until no lights showed in his rearview mirror. Then he jerked the wheel so hard, the boy bounced in his seat high enough to rap his head against the ceiling. He slowed to a stop. Hopefully, he didn't have to go too far in to be hidden from the passing cars. But there was no way to be certain one of the cops wouldn't spot the pickup. So he'd have to misdirect them.

"Give me that twine."

The kid slowly bent to the truck floor and then came up fast, swinging his clasped fists at Bruce's face. They hit him square in the jaw, and by the time Bruce's head had cleared, the teen was almost out of the truck. Bruce leaped across the seat and caught him by the hood of his sweatshirt, yanking him off-balance until he fell back into the vehicle. He grabbed his gun and pressed it against the boy's cheek. "I don't need you anymore. Don't push me to kill you now."

"Like you killed Trev?" The kid's eyes were wild. Full of hate. Bruce yanked at the boy until he scrambled awkwardly into the truck. Leaned across him to grab the twine.

"Who the fuck is Trev?" He made short work of tying the kid's wrists together and then took great pleasure in looping the twine around the boy's neck. Twice.

"My friend. In the woods that night. You killed him. Because you're a fucking animal!"

Bruce got out of the car. Sank into several inches of snow. Cursing, he rounded the hood and went to the teen's open door. He tied the free end of the twine to the metal loop on the doorjamb and then slammed the door again. The weapons were heavy in his pockets. He had the one he'd taken off Teeter—the son of a bitch—and Tina's, as well as his own. He went back to his door and snapped, "Turn your face to the window." Waited for the boy to obey before slipping one of the weapons onto the floor of the back seat. "I never killed no one in the woods that night, although I sure as hell wanted to. Wishing now I'd killed the both of you when I saw you, though." He smiled nastily. "Your mom was there that night. Bet you didn't know that, did you? Maybe she killed your little friend." He slammed the door and ran back to the road. He jogged up it until the first set of headlights picked him up in its beam. Then he crossed through the ditch and burst into the thick trees. By the time the cops got organized and went to follow him, he'd have doubled back to the truck and headed out again.

He wondered if the marshal was back there in one of those cars. The way things were going, he wouldn't be able to get to enact any of the half-formed plans she starred in. Survival was his ultimate goal.

But if someone were going to die tonight, it wouldn't be him.

Chapter 88

Ryder pulled to a stop on the road. Backed up. "Look up that slope there."

Following the direction he was pointing, Cady saw the tracks he indicated. Ryder left the vehicle running, and they all got out of the Jeep to inspect them in the glow of the headlights. "They look fresh. But where'd he leave the truck?"

"There are lots of little roads that twist in and out of the trees up and down the mountain." Miguel came to stand beside her. "Some of them would be closed in winter, but not all."

A car eased to a stop behind the Jeep. Two more of the task-force members got out to join them, bringing their number to seven. Cady left Ryder to update them and stepped away to radio their location to the pilot before rejoining the others. They were donning tactical gear when a couple of sheriff cars pulled up behind them. Cady approached the deputies emerging from the vehicles. "Deputy US Marshal Maddix."

"Yancey County deputies Everett, Hayes, Jones, and Miller." The speaker was highlighted in the still strobing light bars. "We've brought the winter gear you requested for your crew. You'll need it. There're eight inches of snow on the ground, more in some places. Temps in the midteens."

"I appreciate it. I need two of you to guard the perimeter. The others try to find the pickup the fugitive drove in. Older, dark green. He had a teenage boy with him." Dylan was still alive. She had to believe that.

After a few moments standing in the stiff winds whipping over the mountain, she felt her teeth begin to chatter. She had a hat and gloves but was more than eager to don some of the winter garb the deputies had brought, even if the boots and coat were two sizes too big.

The rest of the group got dressed, then selected tac lights and weapons from the back of the Jeep.

"Rugged territory," Miguel observed, pulling on a stocking hat. "There are lots of trails on the mountain. I've been up here a few times, but I wouldn't want to try them at night."

"He'd have to be familiar with the area to head to even the easier ones," Deputy Everett said.

"Trails or no, I'm guessing there are plenty of places to hide up here." Shifting her focus, Cady said, "The aerial assist pilot is fifteen minutes out."

She throttled back the urgency building inside her. The overriding impulse would be to plunge into the wooded area after Forrester. She was indelibly aware of every minute head start he had on them. And what that time could potentially cost them. But the need for strategy outweighed impulsiveness. She'd establish a search grid before they got started.

And when they did, they'd make good time following the fugitive's footprints in the snow. But knowing that did nothing to diminish the sense of foreboding spreading in her gut.

Chapter 89

Bruce grabbed a denuded bush to pull himself up the incline. He'd never been here in winter and hadn't expected this much snow. The work boots he wore weren't waterproof. The Carhartt jacket was warm enough, and he'd pulled up the hood. Tied it. Good thing he had gloves in the pocket, because he needed them.

The snow would give away his path, but the spruce-fir forest he was walking through provided cover. He'd continue on for a while and then double back, messing up the trail leading to him. That'd gain him some time.

And while the fuckers were trying to figure it out, he'd head back to the pickup. Get rid of the cops they'd surely stationed near the road. Sneak into Asheville and get the key from Bandy's house. The fake ID he had was the same one with which he'd opened the account in Charlotte. Once he had the key to the safe-deposit box there, he could empty it before driving to Atlanta and hopping a plane.

Formulating the plan kept his mind off the chill creeping through his body.

His foot tripped over something hidden in the snow, and his arms wheeled in an attempt to regain his balance. Gravity won. He fell heavily on one shoulder, sliding halfway down the slope he'd just climbed.

He fought to haul in a breath, the cold air slicing at his lungs like a razor. Moments passed before he could struggle to his feet again. He checked to make sure he hadn't lost the weapon he had tucked into the back of his pants and brushed himself off before attempting the ascent again. The sooner he got back to the road, the better. He wasn't on a path. He couldn't even fucking see a path. A guy could break his neck out here in the dark.

His only consolation was that the cops wouldn't fare any better than him.

Chapter 90

The truck was freezing. Dylan concentrated on loosening his bonds for the second time that night. It distracted his mind, which wanted to poke along the hem of darkness that Forrester's final words had summoned.

Don't think. Just get free. The twine around his throat was tight enough to be uncomfortable. It got even tighter as he struggled with the bonds on his wrists. He scooted closer to his door to put some slack in it. And tried not to consider that he could freeze before Forrester came back. Or before anyone else found him.

He'd seen the headlights flashing by through the side mirror. Counted at least four sets. It was the cops. Had to be. He hoped there were a lot of them. Forrester wouldn't be taken down easily.

Dylan had faced the window when the man had ordered him to, but he was pretty sure Forrester had put something in the back. Dylan wondered if it was a gun. He'd seen Forrester take T's. If it was a weapon, and if Dylan could get free, he'd have some protection if the man came back.

His wrists were sore and raw. He gritted his teeth as he continued to work them against the twine. Forrester had tied them tight, but the rope was stretched from the last time Dylan had been bound. He thought he felt some give in it.

I never killed no one in the woods that night, although I sure as hell wanted to.

Dylan stilled. The man was a liar. A killer. But he hadn't killed Ethan Matthis and Chad Bahlman. T had done that. A shudder worked through his body. Didn't mean Forrester was telling the truth about Trevor, though.

Your mom was there that night. Maybe she killed your little friend.

"Liar." Dylan whispered the word. Forrester had tried to mess with his head, but nothing he said could be believed. There were only men in that clearing. Dylan had seen them.

He redoubled his efforts on the bonds at his wrists, uncaring when his struggles dug the twine deeper into his skin. He'd gotten free before. He would again.

There was a bit of slackness now. Flex and relax. Flex and relax. He focused on the movements in an effort to keep the slivers of images from darting through. Failed.

What didn't he remember about that night in the woods? A lot, he knew. He had no memory of the night they said he'd spent in that tree. A sharp pain pierced his temples. The familiar images flashed through his mind. There was Trev and him in the log. Trev dead in the creek. The boat's light bouncing and dancing. Dylan winced at the pain. It didn't make sense. He'd thought they'd both run to climb the tree. Was he wrong? Had they hid in the log? He knew they'd never gotten to play with the boat.

But so much was still blacked out, as if an inky curtain had been drawn over the memories. And somehow Dylan knew that the darkness Forrester had disappeared into was no less dangerous than the shadows in his mind hiding his recollections of that night.

Chapter 91

Sulky clouds traced sooty fingers across the pale watery moon and smudged over the stars. Cady's flashlight beam was a moving beacon punctuating the darkness. The only sounds were the squish of her boots plowing through the snow and the whistle of the wind cutting through the trees. The branches of the firs were heavily laden with snow. When she'd brushed too close to one, it'd dumped its load down her back.

In the daylight, she'd appreciate the beauty of the changing landscape they passed through. But the thick stands of firs were a potential ambush spot for their target. The rocky slopes with their bare deciduous trees hid countless obstacles beneath the snow. Each time she saw one of the other beams waver wildly, it was a reminder of the treacherous ground they traveled.

And the potential targets they presented by wielding the flashlights.

Forrester's trail had been easy to keep in sight but not necessarily simple to follow. The task-force members were spread over regular intervals on either side of it. But they moved more slowly than she'd have expected.

A narrow cluster of rocks was ahead to the right of her. The shape stimulated her imagination. A kid wearing a backpack. A hunched goblin.

A man bent with the weight of a small child on his back to prevent a volley of gunfire . . .

The voice from the radio on her belt snapped her out of her reverie. "Air to ground. We're five minutes out."

The parallel string of lights continued moving forward, the beams crossing each other as they arced side to side in a silent synchronized dance. The lights caught the frost slicked on the bark of the trees they passed, painting them silver. Slowly, inexorably, the line marched forward. Until Cady stopped. Stared at the jumbled mess of footprints before her. She reached for her radio.

"We've got a problem with the trail. Everyone stop while we figure this out."

Chapter 92

Bruce peered around the side of the outcropping of rock he was crouched behind and considered his options. He'd known he'd have multiple cops to deal with. Even from here, he could count the dim glow of several flashlights in the distance. They no longer seemed to be moving. Which could only mean they'd found where he'd fucked up the trail. The ploy gave him the extra few minutes he needed to lose them for good.

Bruce crawled away from his cover, his whole body shaking from the cold. He'd yanked off a spruce branch and held it in one hand. He'd head diagonally, deeper into the firs, but in the direction of the truck. Try to sweep the branch over his footprints to blur them. Crouching down, he hurried as much as he was able, tripping once over something hidden beneath the snow. Picking himself up, he dusted off and headed forward again, throwing a look over his shoulder to see whether the lights had started moving again.

But it wasn't the dim beams that caught his attention. It was the unmistakable rumbling of a motor fast approaching overhead. In the next moment, he heard the rapid *whop-whop-whop* of chopper blades.

A helicopter. Bruce turned and ran back toward the jagged rock formation he'd recently abandoned. For the first time this evening, he felt genuine fear.

Chapter 93

Shivering, Dylan felt the bonds on his wrists give way. He wrestled out of them and then unwound the twine from his throat. Rubbed the tender skin there. He scanned the surrounding area carefully. Forrester could come back. Dylan had to get out of here before he did.

He crawled into the driver's seat and tried to reach behind it, searching for whatever the man might have left there. He found nothing. Taking a breath, he opened the door, and frigid air rushed in. Dylan wouldn't have considered the interior of the truck warm, but the temperature was far colder outside it. He got out of the vehicle and sank into several inches of snow. Swore. Blindly, he stuck his hand into the back. Searched the seat. Then the floor. His fingers closed around something metal. A gun. Grabbing it, he carefully scrambled back into the pickup. Slammed the door. Setting the weapon on the dash, he blew on his hands. Rubbed them together. Because his feet were now freezing, he tucked them under his body to warm them up. And decided what to do next.

Even armed, he didn't want to be here when Forrester got back. Dylan craned his neck to look out the back window. There was the faintest beam of light painting the pavement. Unmoving. Did that mean one of the cop cars was out there? Maybe searching for the truck?

No one else would be up here in the middle of the night. He'd give it another few minutes. See if it came closer.

His body was shaking with cold. Wrapping his arms around his middle, he pressed as close as he could to the truck's ripped seat back. He knew from science class that he needed to create a seal of warmth.

Trev and me pressed together in the hollowed-out log, trembling with fear.

No, that wasn't right. He shook his head violently. They'd run to the tree. They'd run. Dylan had looked over his shoulder, but Trev wasn't there. Forrester had gotten him.

I never killed no one in the woods that night, although I sure as hell wanted to.

Liar. Nothing Forrester said could be trusted.

Trev grabbing the backpack before we'd run away. Dylan folded both arms over his head to stop the clanging that had started there. Maybe, maybe he almost remembered that. Pressing something in his hand in the hollow log. But that could have been any time they'd been in the woods. It could have been a stone. A stick. Once they'd found an arrowhead.

But it hadn't been an arrowhead in his bank.

Them men are long gone. Don't be such a pussy. Look how far we've come. Put it in here.

The voice rang through his memory like a long-ago echo. Dylan's head was hammering. His gut heaving. *Go back to the house if you're so scared. But I'm playing with it.*

He began to rock, attempting to suppress the nausea in his stomach. Dylan tried to picture the rope swing. He and Trev swinging out over the creek.

But only Trev's picture would form. Lying there in the creek, his eyes wide and staring as the dark water whispered around him.

Chapter 94

"The pilot will start from where we picked up the trail again." Cady had to raise her voice to be heard above the sound of the helicopter as she spoke through the radio. "Once Forrester is spotted, we'll triangulate the area and converge on him from all sides, if possible. Remember he'll be armed."

She could have added that a man like Bruce Forrester was unlikely to surrender. He'd relish taking as many down with him as he could. But it wasn't necessary. Every task-force member here knew what they were up against. And none of them was leaving until the man was in cuffs or dead.

Everyone adjusted their night-vision goggles into place. They'd need them to see the thermal imaging laser pointer the pilot would use when the FLIR pinpointed Forrester's position. The lasers on their rifles would pick up their target. And seal Forrester's fate.

The chopper moved away slowly. Sometimes it rose, and other times it lowered close enough to the ground that she could feel the rush of wind from the rotors. If Forrester was still around—and Cady didn't know how the man could have made it back to the road yet—the pilot would find him.

The search team moved again in tandem, more swiftly now that they didn't have to search every possible hiding place along the way.

The pilot spoke over the radio. "Air to ground. FLIR can't see through trees. You'll have to check out the stands of spruce yourselves. Thirty degrees to the left of team member one." Cady looked at Miguel on her right. He was already moving toward her. From the bob and weave of flashlight beams, she knew the line of searchers was reforming. She slipped the rifle off her shoulder as she kept her beam pointed at her feet. One by one, the lights switched off as the members closed in around the trees. If Forrester was hiding there, no use providing him with targets.

Cady approached silently, crouching behind a spruce, trying to see between the snow-capped branches. Forrester could be behind any of the trees. Beneath one. Crouching under it.

She looked for tracks. Not seeing any, she turned sideways to sidle between two of the firs, nearly jumping when her movement caused one icy branch to sweep across her neck. Crouching down, Cady flicked on her flashlight again, sweeping the beam from one tree to another beneath the lower branches. Yellow eyes peered out at her. In one smooth movement, she had her weapon up and trained.

Deer. Cady released a breath, only then aware of the racing of her heart. Reaching for the radio, she murmured into it, "A family of deer beneath one of the spruces."

"Yeah, I see it." Miguel.

A few minutes later, having searched more thoroughly, the team moved away from the firs and reformed their grid line search formation. As they trudged forward, she saw the tracks of something besides the man they followed. A big cat. Mountain lion maybe. Perhaps it'd find Forrester before they did.

Light snow began to fall, the flakes dancing on the breeze. Cady was long past the point of being able to appreciate the view. Her fingers were beginning to stiffen even inside the gloves. Every so often, she'd raise one gloved hand to warm her nose. If it began to snow in earnest—and if the wind picked up—they'd lose Forrester's trail. And likely their aerial support. She was acutely aware that their window of opportunity was limited by the chopper's fuel tank.

"Air to ground. We have a target." Urgency sprinted up Cady's spine at the pilot's voice. "The rock formation thirty degrees to the left of position one. Target is actively hiding in the brush pile on a ledge behind it. Watch your step. There's a helluva drop three feet farther back."

Once again, the line of team members turned as one. As they got nearer, Cady could see the unmistakable laser pointer visible with her goggles. She looked for cover for their approach. She wanted to get as close to the rock formation as she could manage. A single spruce stood near it, but only some boulders and scrub brush would shield them on their way to the fir.

The chopper slowly orbited to gain a different vantage point.

"Positions one and two to the right of the formation," she said quietly into the radio. "Three and four to the left. Five, six, seven take the perimeter." Silently, the members moved toward their positions.

"Air to ground. Target is moving. Pushing aside the brush. Holding a handgun."

The ground beneath the snow grew rockier. Cady and Miguel ran to crouch behind one boulder. Then another. She held out a hand. Counted down from three. They ran in tandem to the spruce. Belly-crawled beneath it. It provided good cover. But to get a visual of Forrester, they'd have to get parallel to him.

Cady looked at Miguel. Motioned. He nodded, and they began moving toward a boulder twenty feet from the rock formation, mindful of the cliff the pilot had mentioned.

Her cell vibrated in her pocket. She dug it out, her gloved fingers fumbling a little. Saw a number she didn't recognize on the screen. Not the one Dylan had called from. She almost ignored it. But recognition flickered. It was one of Forrester's numbers. And Fielding had admitted sharing Cady's phone number with him.

She connected, holding the cell to her ear but saying nothing. There was breathing on the other side. Maybe a sound that could have been teeth chattering. Then a voice she didn't recognize, shouting over the sound of the helicopter. "Marshal fucking Maddix."

One hand crept to the radio on her belt. Turned down the volume. "Bruce Forrester?"

"You out there?"

She waved to get Miguel's attention. Pointed to the phone she held, then the rocks to the left of them. He needed no other hints. His hand went to the radio on his belt.

"You know I am. There are a lot of us here. You're surrounded. Throw out your weapon. Come out with your hands behind your head." She crouched behind a mound of rocks. Peered around it. She still didn't have a view of behind the formation.

"That's not my only option."

"It's your best option. You can survive this thing." The falling snow was heavier now. If Forrester was on the ledge, his footing would be even more precarious. "Who wouldn't choose life?"

"Maybe you're smarter than the average cop. But that's not saying much."

"Air to ground. Target is holding something in each hand." The pilot's voice came over the radio. "Weapon. And something smaller. A phone, maybe."

Cady gave a tight smile. She looked at Miguel, pointed to the edge of the formation. Made a motion to indicate for them to draw closer. He shook his head violently.

"I didn't kill them kids, you know."

"My warrants are for drug charges. Abduction. We can talk about the rest. I want to hear your side of things."

"You don't lie any better than your cop friends."

"You're going to freeze out here." The chopper was low. She had to raise her voice to be heard over its noise. "You likely won't last the night." She didn't know how he was dressed, but he wouldn't have had time to prepare for an escape.

"I tell you what, Marshal. Why don't you come back here and bring me out? If I see you—only you—I'll come in quietly."

"Show good faith first. Throw out your weapon. East or west, your choice." Miguel belly-crawled over to her. Indicated for her to put the man on speakerphone. Cady did so.

"Lost my gun when I took a fall down a hill a while back. I've got nothing to show you."

Liar. The pilot had already sighted it. "Then put your arms behind your head and walk slowly toward me."

"I had plans for you, you know." There was something dark in the man's tone. A wet, syrupy evil. "I really needed to watch the life leave your eyes."

Ice skated over her skin. "I'm going to have to disappoint you on that. Come out now, Bruce. No one has to die tonight."

"Someone always has to die, Marshal. Tell your friends I'm coming out. I'm not armed. Don't let one of these bastards shoot me."

Miguel quietly relayed the information to the team, except for the lie about being unarmed. She watched him point to the left. Understood that Rossi was in position. He stabbed a finger to his chest and then gestured toward the right. She nodded, and he crawled over to get in position to cover her.

She shifted the cell to her left hand. "Slow and easy, Bruce. The rocks are slippery." She shifted her rifle. Aimed for the spot where he'd emerge from the formation.

"Air to ground. Target is moving toward the east. Still armed."

A moment after the pilot's warning, a bullet pinged off the rock Cady's head was resting against. In quick succession, she heard one hit near where Miguel was stationed. She returned fire. There was a steady exchange of gunfire for a couple of minutes. Then it stopped as suddenly as it had begun. In the silence that followed, Cady wiped the snowflakes from her face and peered around the rock. If she could get parallel to him, she'd have a shot. But only if the position didn't threaten Rossi on his other side.

Almost in tandem with that thought came the pilot's voice. "Air to ground. Target is descending the side of the cliff."

He certainly wasn't climbing down one-handed. Cady stuck the phone in her pocket as she rose and stepped cautiously to the edge of the bluff.

"No farther!" She trained her weapon on the fugitive as she shouted above the noise of the chopper. Out of the corner of her eye, she saw Miguel, Ryder, and Rossi as they all took stations along the edge. As if in slow motion, she saw Forrester reach one arm behind him. Then bring it around, holding a weapon. She crouched, her rifle still trained on him. His body jolted as he lost his grip. Limbs scrabbling for purchase, he flailed wildly before he squeezed off a shot in midair. Then his body did a slow plummet to the gorge below.

Cady stared, stunned. But even the light flurry made it impossible to see more than ten feet down. The chopper dipped and lowered. She shouldered her weapon as she and Miguel rounded the front of the rock formation to meet up with the rest of the team.

"How the hell did he even think he had a chance climbing down in the dark and in this weather?" Rebedeau was shaking her head, still staring at the darkness below the edge.

Cady followed her gaze. *Someone always has to die.* Forrester's words rang in her head. She still wasn't sure whether he'd taken a chance or made a choice.

But the end result was the same.

Chapter 95

"We've got a situation." Deputy Miller met Cady at the road when they returned. Her thoughts immediately rushed to Dylan. He hadn't been in the truck? Or was he . . . Her mind danced away from the thought. "What?"

"I'll take you to Everett and Jones. Let them explain it." She and Agent Rebedeau followed the man to the county SUV, and they turned to drive a quarter mile down the road, pulling up beside another sheriff's car. Recognizing Deputy Everett, she walked over to him.

"Marshal," he said in greeting. "Get your fugitive?"

"He's dead," she said shortly. "The pickup?"

He raised a finger and pointed to a narrow road twisting through the trees ahead of them. Cady would have missed it if it weren't for the tire tracks. "Took us a while to find it. Finally picked up a glint off the fender with my flashlight."

"And the boy?" She had to force out the words.

"He's alive." Tension streamed out of her. "We called medics. They're a mile out. But he wouldn't leave the truck, Marshal. He's armed, and he wasn't giving up the weapon willingly. He's asking to talk to you."

"He's traumatized," SBI agent Rebedeau said quietly from her stance beside Cady. "Probably doesn't realize he no longer has to protect himself from Forrester."

The boy's last five and a half years had been one endless trauma, Cady agreed silently. "Take me to him." She fell in step beside the deputy as they waded through the snow to where the pickup was parked.

"I gave him blankets. He wrapped up in those, at least. He didn't threaten us with the weapon. I just . . ." When the man hesitated, Cady looked at him. "I'm worried he's a threat to himself. Something is off about him."

Cady kept her tac light low as she opened the passenger door. Climbed into the truck. She shifted the beam enough to see Dylan's face. He was huddled in blankets, but both hands were in front of him, the gun clutched in one. "It's over, Dylan," she said gently. God knew what kind of abuse he'd gone through during his time with Forrester. On top of the other events of the evening, the boy might have had a breakdown. "Forrester is dead. He can't hurt you or your family anymore. Give me the gun. Let's go home."

"Forrester said he didn't kill Trev that night." The teen's voice was choked. "He said he wished he'd killed us both but he never killed anyone."

He'd said as much to her. "I'm not sure we can believe him." She glanced away from his face to the weapon again. The boy gripped it tightly. "We'll figure out the truth, Dylan. And I promise I'll tell you everything we discover. You have my word." She inched closer as she spoke.

The teen moved away from her, pressing against the door.

"You were clever." She kept her voice low. Intimate. "The way you got Teeter to tell you everything after you called me. His admissions were damning. He'll pay for what he did. Neither he nor Forrester will be a threat to anyone ever again."

"That doesn't bring those kids back, does it?"

"No." She couldn't sugarcoat it. He knew the truth as well as she did. "It doesn't help them. But it's justice. That's all we've got."

"Justice," he whispered. "Then I should die too." He brought up the weapon, tucked it snugly beneath his chin. "Because this all started with me. It's my fault."

Cady's fear for the boy surged. "Put the weapon down. Right now, Dylan. Put it away. I understand how you feel. Better than you could know. But no matter our history, we have two choices in this world, and we alone are in charge of making them. We can wallow in our past actions or we can move beyond them. Make that move now. Hand me the weapon."

Time crept to a stop. Cady found herself holding her breath until the boy finally lowered the gun. Held it loosely. She reached out and removed it from his unresisting grip, never taking her eyes from him. There was more here. More even than the cloak of guilt and responsibility he'd worn the first time she met him.

"You still don't get it." She had to strain to hear him. When he lifted his head, she could see the tears staining his cheeks. The misery in his expression. "I was the one who convinced Trev to go to the creek that night. I was the one who persuaded him to stay even after Forrester chased us."

A chill of dread was working through her body. "*After* he chased you?"

"I still can't remember more than bits and pieces . . . but . . . I recall the boat's light in the creek." His voice was so choked, she had trouble making out the words. "I made him go back after we hid. We were tussling over the boat. I remember a splash." He was sobbing in earnest now. "I can see him sometimes, his eyes open in the water. I must have pushed him. He could have hit his head on a rock when he fell. All this time I blamed Forrester. But it's. All. My. Fault."

Chapter 96

She slept only a few hours, but Cady woke refreshed. Ryder had already left the bed. Probably to deal with the dogs. She pulled on a robe, grabbed her phone, and checked her messages on the way to the kitchen, intent on making coffee. A lot of it. Instead, she found Ryder at the breakfast counter, sipping from a mug. With one glance in her direction, he got up and fetched another cup, filled it, and brought it over to her.

She clasped her hands around its warmth gratefully. "You are a prince among men."

"My only claim to royalty." He waited for her to take several gulps before saying, "The surveillance car is gone."

She frowned. "Forrester's dead, but they haven't tied that weapon to him." The rifle found after the shooting at her place was still with the lab. Or . . . She narrowed her eyes. "What haven't you told me?"

"I should have checked my email Friday." He took another sip. "Damn careless of me, really. If I had, I would have known that the lab results on the rifle came back. There was a mess of latents on the weapon. Two of them belonged to Forrester."

It took a moment, but then a slow smile curved her lips. "That *was* careless of you." Had Allen learned of the results Friday, she'd have been pulled from the warrant on Forrester.

"Has the search and rescue team brought up the body yet?"

She winced a little. "Half an hour ago. It had been mauled pretty badly. Maybe by that mountain lion we saw evidence of during our search."

"Karma." He raised his mug to her.

Maybe, she thought as she sipped from her cup. But Forrester had evaded the punishment he deserved in the most final way possible. It didn't seem quite fair. The dogs were yapping at the back door, so Cady got up and let them in.

Hero walked in carefully and pressed against her. She ran her hand along his back. "Only another few days before those stitches are out," she told him.

"He'll probably need to wear the cone awhile longer, to keep him from licking the wound," Ryder said.

Still, it'd represent one step closer to recovery. And she'd celebrate that right along with the dog.

"What's on for today?" he asked.

"I need to head to Asheville. John Teeter and Tina Bandy were stabilized at Morganton, then airlifted to Asheville Memorial." Dylan, according to the text she'd received from Agent Rebedeau, was in a juvenile psych ward in Morganton under suicide watch. Her chest hurt thinking about the boy. "And I want to check on Cassie Zook." She wondered if the woman's emotional state had stabilized. Emotionally, at least, she had a long road to recovery. "Then I have to return the rental car I parked at the courthouse after the shooting."

"I assume Eric Loomer has lawyered up."

She nodded, draining her mug. Setting it down, she added, "It was just a matter of time." Now the dance would begin, trying to mitigate Loomer's responsibility for his actions the last several years. She couldn't even summon her usual irritation at the situation. She was too worried about a teenage boy. Alone in a strange place, burdened with guilt, worried about his mom.

Forrester got off easy, she thought as she walked to the shower. The boy would carry his guilt for the rest of his life.

◆　◆　◆

They were on their way to Asheville when she got a video from Special Agent Rebedeau. Cady opened it and let it play so they both could hear it.

SBI agent Davis was speaking. "Can you state your full name for the record, please?"

"John Teeter."

"Mr. Teeter, please explain the nature of your relationship with Tina Bandy."

The man hung his head, wiping his eyes with the back of one hand. "Tina and me was like brother and sister. Ever since her mama came to live with my daddy. Even after they split up, we was still tight."

Agent Rebedeau said, "You were living in Fayetteville when she lived in Hope Mills?"

"Yeah, that's right." He sniffled and lifted his head. "Wasn't easy for her raising those kids by herself. Their daddy had run off by then, left her alone. I helped out when I could."

"Were you trying to help her by stealing that weapon from the Fayetteville gun range?"

At Davis's words, Teeter looked wary, glancing between the two agents. "They saying I did that?"

"The ATF investigation points that way, yes."

He was silent for a moment. "So here's the deal. Tina needed extra cash, so she helped Forrester run the drugs some. But he got pissed off at her. Now, I don't want you to think she did this willingly. But he

forced her and Tillis to get rid of a body. Someone he killed. And . . .
her necklace broke. Had them beads spelling out her name? And Tillis
must have told Forrester, 'cuz he was going to kill her for it. That night
in the woods, Forrester had one of her friends call him when they was
out with Tina. He grabbed her when she was outside one of the bars
having a smoke. He had it all planned. They was gonna do some meth,
then hang her. Make people think it was suicide. They had the rope
already tied around a branch when she got there."

"Who's 'they'?"

"Forrester and Loomer, Tillis and Weber. Then later, Tina heard
a ruckus. She didn't know then Forrester had heard the boys and run
'em off. When the guys were all distracted, she snuck out of the tent
and took off. They'd tied her hands but not her feet. She got home,
and Colton untied her. Then they jumped in the car and headed to
my place."

"Without Dylan."

Teeter scratched his head. "You gotta understand, she didn't know
the boys were down at the creek. Didn't know Forrester had chased 'em.
Yeah, she saw his bed was empty but figured he was at Boster's and she
needed to leave, pronto."

"Mother of the year," Cady muttered. The more Teeter tried to
cover for the woman, the worse he painted her.

"When did she discover Dylan gone?" asked Davis.

"The next morning, real early, Mrs. Boster called and asked if Trevor
was at Tina's place. We came back and looked around. Then she called
the cops when we didn't find 'em."

"Weber and Tillis never mentioned she was there," Agent Davis
said.

Teeter's shoulder bobbed in a shrug. "They was gonna help kill her.
Think they're gonna tell the cops that?"

"How do you have Forrester's truck in your possession?"

Teeter twisted his fingers together on the scarred table. "Someone had to help them. The cops weren't gonna get the job done. I knew that right away. I stole the truck. Took the weapon he'd used at the gun range a couple of days earlier. Just in case he went after the family. Which he did. The kids must have taken a key out of Forrester's backpack. Like maybe to a lockbox or something. Tina'd heard he'd been skimming from the boss. We thought maybe she could use that as leverage against him."

Cady rubbed her forehead. The woman had all but painted bull's-eyes on the backs of herself and her family. And it was hard not to consider how the choices of parents could have outsize negative impacts on children.

Teeter untwined his fingers. Pressed his palms on the table. "I quit my job. Went hunting for Forrester. But the guy was a ghost. I never could get a line on him, even though I figured he was in the state. Because things would be fine for Tina for a while, but then she'd hear from folks that someone was asking 'round about her. It was just a matter of time until he caught up with her. Since I couldn't find the guy, I needed to motivate you all to get the job done. If you locked him up, Tina would be home clear. And so would Dylan."

"You thought killing those boys would light a fire under us? Make us hunt down Forrester faster?" At Davis's hard tone, the other man hunched his shoulders. Studied the table. "Whose idea was it to try to kill Deputy US Marshal Maddix?"

"Tina called and said the marshal had been there talking to the boy. I decided shooting at her might get the cops' attention even more than killing them kids. They'd never rest if they thought a cop was in danger. So I bought one of them GPS thingies. Tina said how she was gonna call to get the marshal to the house to talk. So I drove up there the night before. Stayed at a hotel until the marshal was on her way, then parked behind Tina's garage. While she was there, I put the GPS on her vehicle. I tracked the marshal on my phone and grabbed it off her vehicle while

I waited at her place." He stopped for a moment before hastily adding, "Tina didn't know nothing about it."

A chill chased down Cady's spine at the obvious lie. Someone had to alert him when Cady was on her way to meet Tina. It was unsettling to hear the man report every step he'd taken "to protect" the family. To hear the earnestness with which he defended his choices. Regardless of his motivation, Teeter was no better than Forrester.

Then another realization slammed into her. When Tina Bandy recovered, she'd be going to prison. Even if the courts were merciful to Dylan Castle, he'd have no family to return to.

It was as if the teen had been born under a dark star.

"Someone's getting entirely too rambunctious for still having stitches," Cady commented as she and Ryder finally rounded up the dogs that evening and got them back into the house. The animals had spent the better part of fifteen minutes chasing each other around the backyard after dinner. It was good to see Hero moving better. But she still dropped to her knees to check his wound after he trotted back inside.

"Can't say I blame him." Ryder headed back toward the recliner where he'd been watching yet another basketball game. "Your phone sounded when you went out to the deck. Maybe it's your aunt calling you back."

Cady had called twice and texted as many times on the way home from Asheville to check on her mom's progress. Other than a terse message assuring her that Hannah was okay, there'd been silence from Alma. Crossing to where she'd left her cell on the breakfast bar, she picked it up. Listened to the message. It wasn't from her aunt, which was unsurprising. It was from her landlady, Dorothy Blong. After listening to it, she went to prop her hip against the side of Ryder's chair. His arm came out, and somehow she ended up on his lap. The man was sneaky. With his free hand, he picked up the remote beside him and shut off the TV.

"We packed a lot into the last week or so," he murmured into her ear. "I have a few ideas for de-stressing."

"You are full of ideas," she agreed. She took a moment, unsure how to broach the news. "That was my landlady. She's thinking of not stopping at repairs on the rental but doing a full remodel and then putting it up for sale. If I'm interested, she'll let me dictate how I want things done."

He went still. "Are you in the market for a new place?"

There was something in his tone. Something that set her instincts humming. "I sold my home in Saint Louis, so I have the cash."

"Which you could save, if you lived here."

She waited for the familiar rush of panic. For the inner alarm bells to shrill. They were there but more muted than usual. And that brought another source of tension. "Another few weeks and you'll be pushing me out the door." Her attempt at humor fell flat.

His hand stroked up her spine. Down again. "I think we both know that isn't true."

"We've only known each other for three months." It was difficult to tell who she was trying to convince. But harder still to consider the enormity of what he was suggesting.

"And you've been building your defenses for decades. They're force-field strength, for damn good reason." That amiable tone of his was guileful. "Think I don't know what I'm asking?"

He doesn't, she thought shakily. He couldn't. Any other man—every other man—would be shown the door the minute they pushed. The instant they expected more than she wanted to give. The hell of it was, for some reason, she'd already allowed Ryder closer than anyone before him. And while she wasn't doing her usual frantic backpedal, she was at a full stop. "This is too fast for me."

"Now, why am I convinced glacier speed would be 'too fast'?" But a tinge of humor was back in his voice. The sound of it eased a measure of her tension.

"Whatever decision I make, this is me, not running." And he had no idea what that cost her. Or, more frighteningly, maybe he did.

"I was a left tackle in football."

The non sequitur had her smiling. "Why am I not surprised?"

"What I'm saying is, it's my nature to knock over obstacles in my way."

"I've appreciated your restraint. Although if you tackle me, you'll wind up with a black eye."

"Not you." He pulled her closer. "The roadblocks you erect."

"I'm not throwing up roadblocks. I'm saying that whatever I decide to do about the acreage, it won't impact us." And just offering that reassurance had her palms going slippery.

"Okay." His body relaxed against hers. "As long as you understand I'm not done persuading."

A slow smile curved her lips. "I'd expect nothing less."

Chapter 97

Three weeks later

They'd arrived too early on purpose. Cady and Ryder sat on a bench outside the courtroom in the Buncombe County courthouse while Laura Talbot excused herself to use the restroom. Cady had her phone in her hand, going through emails. But nerves played havoc with her focus. In a few minutes, a judge was going to make a decision that would affect the rest of Dylan Castle's life. And if the outcome wasn't what they hoped for, they had no recourse. It was enough to send Cady's imagination into overdrive.

She'd made a point of seeing the boy a couple of times a week. He was in a group foster home here in Asheville, and Cady thought he was doing as well as could be expected. He'd been anxious about a phone charger he'd left at home, so she'd fetched it for him. Only later had she learned he used the cell to communicate with a girlfriend. She was okay with that. With all that had happened and with his mother facing accessory-after-the-fact charges for the disposal of Brady Boss's body, the boy needed as much normal as he could get.

She took a grim sort of satisfaction that Stephen Tillis wouldn't be granted early release anytime soon. Cumberland County deputy Blake

Patten had found another witness verifying Tina Bandy's testimony that the man had helped with the disposal.

"Did Dr. Baker get back to you?" Ryder asked.

"His nurse did. I still haven't made up my mind about the new medication he's suggesting for my mom. Lots of side effects." Or maybe she was reacting to the fact that the man had advised switching from a med for mild to moderate Alzheimer's to one to treat moderate to severe symptoms. It was a tangible sign that the disease was progressing. Making decisions based on logic when the issue was rooted in emotion was always challenging.

He reached over and took her hand. "Choosing for others is always harder than making choices for yourself." Ryder muttered a curse. "I didn't mean . . . I wasn't talking about . . ."

"It's okay." She squeezed his hand. "I know what you meant. But I've come to the conclusion that the choice your dad and my mom made thirty years ago wasn't easy for them, either." And it'd been far more difficult to reach that conclusion than it should have been. "For a while, all I could focus on was what they'd done to me." The sense of betrayal could still stab deep if she let it. "I don't have a child. But I know if I did, I'd do everything I could to protect them. I can imagine how desperate she was after watching Lonny Maddix use me as a human shield. I get that she'd do anything to make sure he could never hurt me again."

"You're more forgiving than I am."

"I don't know about that. I'm just trying to understand." And she wasn't there yet. But Cady wasn't going to let the past taint the time she still had with Hannah, either.

Ryder glanced at the clock on his cell and then looked up. "Here comes Mom. Court's ready to start." They rose and waited for Laura to join them before walking into the courtroom.

Dylan Castle sat next to his guardian ad litem and public defender at a table in front. Cady and Ryder were seated behind him. Next to Ryder sat Laura Talbot. Juvenile court judge Sarah Ellis studied some documents for several minutes before looking at Dylan over her reading glasses. "Please rise, young man."

He stood, his stance ill at ease.

"I understand your mother is in police custody."

"Yes, Your Honor." The boy's voice was miserable.

"And your brother is nineteen. Unable to care for you."

"Yes."

"The court has taken some time to study your history and to determine if charges should be filed against you. Involuntary manslaughter. Obstruction."

Dylan flinched a little at the last two words.

The judge pinned the boy with a penetrating stare. "The medical opinions about your mental state at the time of the incident and these last five and a half years qualify as mitigating factors. Therefore, the court accepts counsel's recommendation for diversion. Do you understand what that means?"

Dylan shook his head. Cady could almost see the guilt eating away at him. His voice was barely a whisper. "No, ma'am."

"There will be conditions you need to abide by. Professional counseling. Regular attendance at school. Staying out of trouble." She took the glasses off her nose and studied him, her gaze stern. "You've had a tough road. But lots of people are dealt bad hands, young man. They shouldn't determine the rest of your life.

"Next, the court will decide on a foster guardian for you until your parent is able to care for you. The facility you're in now has a very good reputation."

Dylan remained silent, but his shoulders slumped a little.

The judge continued, "But you have some pretty impressive people in your corner—do you realize that?"

"I . . . Ma'am?"

"I have letters from Deputy US Marshal Cady Maddix. Two from State Bureau of Investigation agents Davis and Rebedeau, all requesting the same placement for you."

Seeming confused, Dylan looked at his attorney, who laid a hand lightly on his arm.

"These people seem to think that a solid foster home and mentoring might serve your interests better than a group home. And I'm inclined to agree."

"You mean I'd move?"

"You would. Your new foster mother would be Laura Talbot. Her son is sheriff of Haywood County, and I have every reason to believe you'd be well cared for and your physical and emotional needs met. So I'm ruling that in one week's time, you'll be released to foster parent Laura Talbot. The best of luck to you, Dylan."

"Thank you, Your Honor."

After the judge left the courtroom, Dylan's social worker turned him around and introduced him to Laura and Ryder. Cady hung back, content to survey the expressions on the boy's face. Where his voice earlier had held a hint of the despair he'd shared with her after Forrester's death, now it was alight with confusion. And maybe a flicker of hope.

She watched him converse with the others for several minutes. But was unprepared when Dylan whispered something to his social worker and then made his way over to her. "You did this, right?"

Discomfited, she said, "We all had a part. You have a lot of people pulling for you, Dylan."

He looked away, his throat working. "We both know I don't deserve it."

"The judge thought you did. I agree with her." His eyes sheened, and Cady felt an answering pang of sympathy. "Tragic accidents can happen, but they're still accidents. One act in your childhood doesn't have to define the rest of your life." Maybe her past could be useful for once, if she could use the experience to help him move beyond his guilt. "It can tear you down, hold you back, or you can choose to fight through it. It's your choice."

"I . . ." He shuffled his feet. Met her gaze again. "I guess I choose to fight. But I'm not quite sure how."

She gave him a half smile. "You're going to get a lot of help with that."

ACKNOWLEDGMENTS

A writer's hive mind is a scary place. It seems like every book takes a village, but this one required an army! With deep appreciation to Deputy US Marshal Robert S. for answering endless questions about USMS procedures and operations. I've appreciated your help!

Thank you to Dr. Gary Keller for last-minute brainstorming on mental and emotional states caused by trauma. Your insight is invaluable.

The Policewriters group is a great resource when I get stuck on a plot point. I want to thank Mike Black especially for your ready answers and for putting me in touch with other experts as needed.

Rick McMahan, (retired) senior special agent ATF, was a fountain of information about explosive detection K-9s, explosives, and tracing a weapon's ownership, which was very helpful.

I'm indebted to A. L. "Buddy" Collins for answers to legal questions about criminal law in North Carolina and to Jason Bahnsen for pretty much every other legal question that pops into my head. Couldn't have done it without you two!

Many thanks to Liz Flaherty and her geologist son, Chris Flaherty. Chris, your answers about various North Carolina mountains were fascinating. I'm just sorry edits changed where my bad guy had to die, LOL.

I'm also grateful to M. A. "Mat" Tribula, unit commander / chief pilot, NC State Highway Patrol-Aircraft Operations for the extensive insight into aerial assistance. I'm so envious of your very cool job!

Lieutenant John M. Weinstein helped me narrow down the type of weapon used in the story and explained proper terminology, which was tremendously helpful.

Jim Swauger, digital forensics investigator, is always there for my cell phone data retrieval questions, which are apparently never-ending. Many thanks, Jim.

Maxine and Harold Beckner provided necessary veterinary information for my character's poor wounded dog. Thanks for saving him.

A huge thank-you to Sue Rebedeau, high bidder for the Lucky Stiff auction item. Your donation to NIVC Services Inc. entitled you to naming rights to one of the characters in *Down the Darkest Road*. Hope you enjoy her!

Deep appreciation to my agent, Danielle Egan-Miller—may that day be the one and only time you have to talk me off a cliff.

I'm deeply grateful to my fabulous editors, Jessica Tribble and Charlotte Herscher, who wielded the scalpel so delicately, LOL. It only hurt a little!

For Johnnie B., who had to suffer through an extra-long bout of deadline dementia this time around. I'll make it up to you. Promise!

ABOUT THE AUTHOR

Kylie Brant is the author of more than forty novels, including *Cold Dark Places* in the Cady Maddix series, the Circle of Evil Trilogy, and the stand-alone novels *Pretty Girls Dancing* and *Deep as the Dead*. A three-time RITA Award nominee, five-time RT Award finalist, and two-time Daphne du Maurier Award winner, Brant is a member of the Romance Writers of America, including its Kiss of Death mystery and suspense chapter; Novelists, Inc.; and the International Thriller Writers. Her books have been published in thirty-four countries and have been translated into eighteen languages. Visit her online at www.kyliebrant.com.